MAIL ORDER BRIDE SERIES

NO.8
1872
USA

AL & JOANNA LACY

# A MEASURE OF GRACE

OTHER BOOKS BY AL LACY

**Angel of Mercy series:**
  *A Promise for Breanna* (Book One)
  *Faithful Heart* (Book Two)
  *Captive Set Free* (Book Three)
  *A Dream Fulfilled* (Book Four)
  *Suffer the Little Children* (Book Five)
  *Whither Thou Goest* (Book Six)
  *Final Justice* (Book Seven)
  *Not by Might* (Book Eight)
  *Things Not Seen* (Book Nine)
  *Far Above Rubies* (Book Ten)

**Journeys of the Stranger series:**
  *Legacy* (Book One)
  *Silent Abduction* (Book Two)
  *Blizzard* (Book Three)
  *Tears of the Sun* (Book Four)
  *Circle of Fire* (Book Five)
  *Quiet Thunder* (Book Six)
  *Snow Ghost* (Book Seven)

**Battles of Destiny (Civil War series):**
  *Beloved Enemy* (Battle of First Bull Run)
  *A Heart Divided* (Battle of Mobile Bay)
  *A Promise Unbroken* (Battle of Rich Mountain)
  *Shadowed Memories* (Battle of Shiloh)
  *Joy from Ashes* (Battle of Fredericksburg)
  *Season of Valor* (Battle of Gettysburg)
  *Wings of the Wind* (Battle of Antietam)
  *Turn of Glory* (Battle of Chancellorsville)

**Hannah of Fort Bridger series (coauthored with JoAnna Lacy):**
  *Under the Distant Sky* (Book One)
  *Consider the Lilies* (Book Two)
  *No Place for Fear* (Book Three)
  *Pillow of Stone* (Book Four)
  *The Perfect Gift* (Book Five)
  *Touch of Compassion* (Book Six)
  *Beyond the Valley* (Book Seven)
  *Damascus Journey* (Book Eight)

**Mail Order Bride series (coauthored with JoAnna Lacy):**
  *Secrets of the Heart* (Book One)
  *A Time to Love* (Book Two)
  *Tender Flame* (Book Three)
  *Blessed Are the Merciful* (Book Four)
  *Ransom of Love* (Book Five)
  *Until the Daybreak* (Book Six)
  *Sincerely Yours* (Book Seven)

# A Measure of Grace

## MAIL ORDER 8

## AL & JOANNA LACY

Multnomah® Publishers *Sisters, Oregon*

*Special Acknowledgment*
*Congratulations to Brittney Ann Hinson of Ashford, Alabama,*
*for submitting the winning entries in the Mail Order Bride contest.*
*These letters and newspaper ad are found in this book as if written by the*
*hopeful groom and his potential mail order bride.*

—ᴍ—        —ᴍ—        —ᴍ—

A MEASURE OF GRACE
published by Multnomah Publishers, Inc.

© 2001 by ALJO Productions

International Standard Book Number: 1-57673-808-6

Cover illustration by Vittorio Dangelico
Design by Uttley DouPonce DesignWorks

Scripture quotations are from:
*The Holy Bible,* King James Version

*Multnomah* is a trademark of Multnomah Publishers, Inc.,
and is registered in the U.S. Patent and Trademark Office.
The colophon is a trademark of Multnomah Publishers, Inc.

Printed in the United States of America

For information:
MULTNOMAH PUBLISHERS, INC.•POST OFFICE BOX 1720•SISTERS, OREGON 97759

Library of Congress Catalogining-in-Publication Data
Lacy, Al.  A measure of grace / by Al and JoAnna Lacy.  p.cm.
(Mail order bride series ; bk. 8)  ISBN 1-57673-808-6 (pbk)
1. Mail order brides–Fiction. 2. Women pioneers–Fiction. 3. Idaho–Fiction.
I. Lacy, JoAnna.  II. Title.
PS3562.A256 M43 2001    813'.54–dc21    2001003825

01 02 03 04 05—10 9 8 7 6 5 4 3 2 1 0

*With great pleasure, we affectionately dedicate this book
to our author representative
Chad Hicks.*

*You are one of the reasons we find so much joy in writing
for Multnomah Publishers!*

*We love you, Chad.
Al and JoAnna*

1 THESSALONIANS 5:28

MAIL ORDER BRIDE SERIES · NO. 8 · 1872 · USA · AL & JOANNA LACY

# Prologue

THE *ENCYCLOPEDIA BRITANNICA* REPORTS that the mail order business, also called direct mail marketing, "is a method of merchandising in which the seller's offer is made through mass mailing of a circular or catalog, or advertisement placed in a newspaper or magazine, in which the buyer places his order by mail."

*Britannica* goes on to say that "mail order operations have been known in the United States in one form or another since colonial days but not until the latter half of the nineteenth century did they assume a significant role in domestic trade."

Thus the mail order market was known when the big gold rush took place in this country in the 1840s and 1850s. At that time prospectors, merchants, and adventurers raced from the east to the newly discovered goldfields in the west. One of the most famous was the California Gold Rush in 1848-49, when discovery of gold at Sutter's Mill, near Sacramento, brought more than 40,000 men to California. Though few struck it rich, their presence stimulated economic growth, the lure of which brought even more men to the west.

The married men who had come to seek their fortunes sent for their wives and children, desiring to stay and make their home there. Most of the gold rush men were single and also desired to stay in the west, but there were about two hundred men for every single woman. Being familiar with the mail order concept, they began advertising in eastern newspapers for women to come west and marry them. Thus was born the "mail order bride."

Women by the hundreds began answering the ads. Often when

men and their prospective brides corresponded, they agreed to send no photographs; they would accept each other by the spirit of the letters rather than on a physical basis. Others, of course, did exchange photographs.

The mail order bride movement accelerated after the Civil War ended in April 1865, when men went west by the thousands to make their fortunes on the frontier. Many of the marriages turned out well, while others were disappointing and ended in desertion by one or the other of the mates, or by divorce.

In the Mail Order Bride fiction series, we tell stories intended to grip the heart of the reader, bring some smiles, and maybe wring out a few tears. As always, we weave in the gospel of Jesus Christ and run threads of Bible truth that apply to our lives today.

MAIL ORDER BRIDE SERIES

NO. 8
187
USA

AL & JOANNA LACY

DARK THUNDERHEADS WERE PROWLING like beasts of prey over the jagged Sawtooth Mountains of central Idaho, driven southward by a stiff wind on a late spring morning in 1864.

Residents of the small town called Elkton—which was located just two miles from the southern Sawtooth foothills—were moving about the town, keeping their wary eyes on the approaching storm.

Lydia Carpenter stepped out the door of her modest white clapboard house, noting the unmistakable smell of rain in the air. When she felt a blast of wind buffet her, she realized it was blowing harder than she had thought. Pausing on the front porch, Lydia reached up, grasped the ribbons of her straw hat, and secured it more tightly under her chin.

Taking a deep breath of the moist air, she stepped off the porch, bent her head into the wind, and headed for Main Street. In less than five minutes, Lydia reached Main, turned right, and headed toward the center of Elkton's business district, which was four blocks in length.

On the northeast corner of Main and Second Streets stood the Elkton General Store, which Lydia and her husband, Art, had owned for just over ten years.

Lydia always enjoyed her walk to the store, and though she found herself wishing the wind was not quite so strong, she was fond of rainy days and springtime. She wore a contented smile as she moved briskly along the boardwalk, greeting people as she went.

Upon entering the store, she found Art was busy behind the counter, taking care of customers.

"Uh-oh!" said Art Carpenter, chuckling. "Here's the boss. I'd better get busy!"

The customers laughed, and one man said, "She's liable to fire you, Art, if you don't work faster!"

Art laughed. "No need to worry about getting fired. Slave labor doesn't get fired. They just feel the lash of the whip!"

"And don't you forget it, Arthur!" Lydia said as she moved behind the counter and removed the straw hat.

Smiling at the first customer behind the one Art was waiting on, Lydia said, "Bessie, may I help you?"

A portly Bessie Higgins laid her groceries on the counter, smiled, and said, "Thank you, Lydia."

As she began totaling the purchase, Lydia said, "Looks like we're going to get a good rain. Those clouds are pretty dark."

"Yes," said Bessie. "I wish it hadn't come today. My son, Harold, is one of the ranch hands who's making the Bar-S cattle drive to Ketcham this morning."

Lydia frowned. "Oh, that could be dangerous if lightning strikes while the cattle are being driven over there. Can't Mr. Shaw wait and drive his cattle to Ketcham tomorrow or the next day?"

"Not from what Harold told me last night," said Bessie. "Mr. Shaw has already promised those eastern beef buyers he would have a hundred and fifty head of cattle delivered to the Chicago stockyards on the hoof next Tuesday. In order to keep his promise, he has to put them on that train today."

"Well," said Lydia, "at least it's only a seven-mile drive from the Bar-S to Ketcham. Maybe they can get them there before the worst part of the storm hits."

"I sure hope so," Bessie said, worry evident in her eyes.


At the 10,000-acre Bar-S Ranch some five miles west of Elkton, foreman Buck Colburn was standing on the front porch of the small log house which was home to him, his wife Annie, and their sixteen-year-old son, Knight. His son stood beside him as they watched some of the cowhands near the corral, separating steers to be driven to the railhead from the rest of the huge herd. The bawl of the cattle and the clatter of their sharp-pointed horns as they jostled one another could be heard above the wind's howl and the shouting of the cowhands.

Knight Colburn, who like his father was tall and lanky, said, "Dad, it wouldn't hurt for me to miss school today so I could go with you on the drive. As you well know, my grades are good and it wouldn't be too hard for me to catch up on a day's schoolwork."

"I'm glad your grades are good, son," said Buck, "but there's really no need for you to go on the drive and miss school. We're only taking a hundred and fifty head. I'm taking seven men with me, and Mr. Shaw is coming, too. Nine men is all that's needed to do the job."

Knight glanced at his father with a puzzled look in his eyes. "Isn't Jordan going?"

Buck shook his head. "Not this time."

Jordan Shaw was Knight's best friend. Knight knew that the ranch owner had often let his son miss school to go on cattle drives—some which took as much as a week.

"How come Jordan isn't going, Dad?" asked Knight.

"The boss is still very upset at Jordan for losing his temper last week and throwing that rock through the hardware store window. He told Jordan there was no call for him to throw a temper tantrum just because Ben Slayton wouldn't sell him that new revolver without his father's permission. Jordan may think he's twenty-one, but he's only sixteen."

Knight nodded slowly. "Jordan has admitted to me several times that he has trouble controlling his temper, Dad. I've told him over and over, if he would open his heart to Jesus like I did, not only would the Lord save his lost soul, but He would give him the power to get that temper under control."

Buck watched his cowhands as they worked to separate out the full number of steers for the drive. Shaking his head, he said, "You and your ol' dad both had temper control problems before we got saved, son. And mine was much worse than yours. But thank the Lord, we're both doing a whole lot better."

"Yeah," said Knight, chuckling. "And Mom's plenty glad of that."

"Oh! Speaking of Mom…here she comes."

At that moment, Annie Colburn, the ranch cook, was crossing the yard toward the Colburn house from the bunkhouse, where she had just fed the last of the ranch hands a hearty breakfast. As she drew near the porch, she took a long look at the approaching storm, then stepped up on the porch and brushed some wind-blown hair from her eyes. "Buck, I wish you didn't have to make the drive today. I don't like the looks of those clouds."

"I don't either, honey," said Buck, "but we have to get the steers to the railhead today."

"I know," she sighed, then looked at her son. "Have you managed to talk your father into letting you skip school and go along on the drive?"

Knight shook his head. "I tried, Mom, but it didn't work."

"Good," she said. "You need to be in school. And you'll be safe there. I don't like to see any cowhands driving cattle on a stormy day."

At that moment, Harold Higgins turned around in his saddle and waved at the foreman. "We're ready, Buck!" Higgins had Buck's horse saddled and ready for him.

Buck waved back, then folded Annie in his arms. Kissing her on the forehead, then the cheek, he said, "Now, sweetheart, don't you fret. We'll be fine. I'll see you this afternoon." He said to Knight, "Have a good day at school, son."

Knight nodded, forced a smile, and put an arm around his mother.

Since Annie Colburn had come to know the Lord Jesus Christ some three months ago, she had been a happy, cheerful person, always looking on the bright side of life. But on this particular morning, as she watched her husband swing into the saddle, she was feeling a sense of dread deep inside. Over the years, Buck had often run into storms while driving cattle. Why was she feeling a strange fear this time?

Buck waved at his wife and son, and they waved back as he rode away with the herd and the other riders.

Looking heavenward toward the dark, wind-driven clouds, Annie said in her heart, *Dear Lord, I can only commit Buck to You. Please take care of him.*

The riders and their herd swung southward, putting the ranch house and the other buildings between them and the foreman's cabin as they headed into the woods. Annie caught a glimpse of Buck's back as he passed from view and said, "Go with God, darling."

Hearing his mother's words, Knight leaned down, kissed her temple, and gave her a tight squeeze.

Mentally shaking off her feeling of gloom, she looked up at her son, who towered over her, and found a smile for him. "You're so much the picture of your father in so many ways, Knight," she said, placing her small, work-roughened hand on his arm.

The youth gave her a lopsided grin. "That's always music to my ears, Mom. The more I can look and be like Dad, the happier I am. He's my number two hero."

Annie's smile broadened. "I know. Your number one Hero is the one who suffered, bled, and died for you on Calvary's cross."

"Yes, ma'am. He sure is. The Lord Jesus will always be my number one Hero."

"Well, son," said Annie, hugging his arm to herself, "it's time for you to head for school."

Studying her eyes, and not seeing the usual sparkle there, Knight asked, "Mom, are you all right?"

Pressing another smile on her lips, she said, "Of course I am, honey. It's just that I miss your dad already, and he's hardly off the place."

Even as Annie was speaking, Jordan Shaw came out the back door of the big ranch house—which was positioned some sixty yards in front of the foreman's cabin. Jordan, who stood five inches shorter than Knight, was carrying his slicker and book pack. He motioned for Knight to meet him at the corral, and headed that direction.

Knight stepped into the log house, grabbed his slicker and book pack, and kissed his mother's temple one more time. "I'll see you this afternoon, Mom."

Annie flashed him a sunny smile. "Have a nice day at school."

On the cattle drive, the Bar-S men kept a close watch on the dark, heavy clouds rolling in behind them over the Sawtooth Mountains, pulling their hats down tight to keep the ever-increasing wind from snatching them away.

Foreman Buck Colburn was riding on the right side of the herd with ranch hands Ace Decker and Keith Nolan. William Shaw was at the rear, with two other men, and the other three drovers were on the left side of the nervous, bawling herd.

They were pulling out of the woods where they would cross the rolling open fields all the way to Ketcham, and rain began to fall lightly, becoming a fine spray as the wind currents close to the earth hit it. The riders were slipping into their slickers as horses and cattle kept moving.

Soon the entire sky was a black, swirling mass. The rain came down harder, the wind grew stronger, and the cattle became more restless. The trail ahead of them lay locked in the grip of the storm. The edges of the valley that surrounded them were blotted out as the clouds dropped low and touched the earth. The timberline on the mountains behind them was lost in the driving mists.

The wind, booming across the valley, gusted huge sprays of rainwater against the drovers and their bawling herd like high waves smashing across a stormy sea.

They were almost halfway to Ketcham when lightning cracked high overhead, but the flash of light and the ensuing clap of thunder were enough to startle two steers who broke from the herd on the right side and ran hard.

Quickly, Buck Colburn jerked the reins and galloped after them with Ace Decker and Keith Nolan looking on as they wiped rain from their eyes. Ramrod William Shaw focused on the scene, wishing the storm would move on.

Colburn was some one hundred fifty yards away when he finally got ahead of the two steers and sharply reined his mount to turn them back toward the herd. As the gelding wheeled about, he stumbled and fell on the slick grass, sending Buck out of the saddle and rolling on the rain-sodden ground.

Lightning split the ebony sky again, this time coming closer to the earth. As Buck was slipping and sliding in an attempt to gain his feet, his horse got up and galloped away in the opposite direction from the herd.

Gasping for breath, and holding his rib cage which was shooting pain, Buck shouted for his horse to come back, but the frightened animal kept going.

At the same time, five steers split from the mass of cattle on the right side, heading straight toward Buck Colburn. Decker and Nolan spurred their horses quickly to go after them.

Buck stiffened at the sight of the racing steers and prepared to remove himself from their path as they drew closer.

Seconds later, a bolt of lightning shot like a dagger of white fire out of the thunderheads, striking the ground less than thirty yards from the left side of the herd, frightening them. The herd was already turning to the right, and when the deafening thunder boomed like a thousand cannons all around them, they bolted.

Decker and Nolan drew rein as the five steers they were chasing scattered every direction, and wheeled their mounts. They saw the herd stampeding toward them.

With the five steers scattering, Buck Colburn ran toward the herd and his men, but when the frightened cattle turned and charged in his direction, he skidded to a halt and froze in place. He looked to the right, then to the left, but knew it would be impossible to get to safety on foot before the spreading, charging herd reached him.

From where he was sitting on his horse, William Shaw stood up in the stirrups, waved his hat at Decker and Nolan, and pointed at the foreman, who was in the direct path of the charging cattle. "Buck! Buck! Go after Buck!"

Decker and Nolan could not hear their boss's voice, but they saw him waving his hat and pointing at Buck Colburn.

Nolan looked at Decker. "It's Buck! He's trapped! The boss wants us to go after him."

Buck was now frantically waving his hat at them, shouting for help.

He had judged the distance between himself and the two riders, and knew if one of them rode to him at a gallop, he could pick him up with time enough to get them out of the path of danger.

"What shall we do?" Nolan shouted to Decker. "Shaw is waving at us furiously!"

Shaking his head while both their horses danced about fearfully, Decker said, "I ain't takin' no chance on gettin' killed just to save Buck!"

"Me, neither!" shouted Nolan. "It ain't worth it!"

"Right! Let's get outta here!"

William Shaw and his other men looked on, seeing that there was time to save Buck from certain death if Decker and Nolan acted quickly. Their stomachs wrenched when they saw the two cowhands spur their mounts, gallop away from the charging herd, and head for safety in the dense forest to their left.

"Dirty cowards!" cried Harold Higgins, and rode his horse up beside William Shaw. "Boss, I gotta do something! I can't let Buck—"

"It's too late, Harold," Shaw said with a quiver in his voice. "You'd never make it from this far away."

"But, boss, he—"

Another bolt of lightning lashed out of the sky.

"It's too late," said the owner of the Bar-S. "It's too late."

Thunder boomed, vibrating the earth.

Out in the open field in the path of the stampeding herd, Buck Colburn's rain-pelted face was taut, stricken. His breathing was shallow, fast, his chest rising in sharp movements. Though he knew he could never get out of the path of the stampede, he ran to his left, slipping and sliding on the wet grass. All the time, he was keeping his line of sight on the solid wall of wild-eyed cattle as they bore down on him.

William Shaw and his other men looked on in breathless horror.

Buck stumbled and fell, rolling on the rain-soaked earth. Still watching the charging cattle, he jumped to his feet, gasping for air. Terror and panic were stabbing his heart as the front line of steers were drawing so close he could see the whites of their bulging eyes.

He fell again, but this time, he would not make it to his feet.

His last thoughts were of Annie and Knight.

2

BY ONE O'CLOCK IN THE AFTERNOON, the storm had blown out of the valley, and the sun was shining down from an azure blue sky.

Annie Colburn was in the bunkhouse kitchen washing dishes, pots, and pans after having fed a hearty lunch to the half-dozen ranch hands who had stayed to tend to duties on the Bar-S. From time to time, she glanced out the window above the counter where she worked and let her eyes take in the welcome sunlight that brightened the huge yard that surrounded the ranch buildings.

All morning long, as Annie had done her own housework then prepared lunch in the bunkhouse kitchen for the ranch hands, she had not been able to completely dispel the feeling of dread that seemed to pick at her mind like a carnivorous bird. A prayer for the safety of Buck and the other men on the trail had been continuously on her heart.

When at last the storm was over and the sun was sparkling off the raindrops still clinging to the leaves of the trees outside, she breathed a little easier.

As Annie dipped a pan into the rinse water, her attention was drawn to two riders coming in on lathered horses. It took only a second to recognize Ace Decker and Keith Nolan. Leaning close to the window, she looked behind them to see if the rest of the drovers were coming in, but there were no other riders in sight. She wondered why Ace and Keith would be coming in ahead of the rest of them. Shrugging, she went back to her task.

Almost half an hour passed.

Pausing for a moment while dipping the final dishes in the

17

rinse water, Annie dried her hands on her apron and pressed stiff fingers against a sore spot in her back. While leaning against the counter, trying to get relief from the pain, she glanced out the window, taking in the pleasant sight of the green grass and the spring flowers that had recently poked their heads up through the softening soil. She smiled and said, "It was such a long winter. Thank You, Lord, for the springtime."

Her eyes searched for the rest of the drovers, and again she wondered why Ace and Keith would return to the ranch so far ahead of the others.

She dipped a skillet into the rinse water, and at that moment, she saw William Shaw come out the back door of the big ranch house and make a hurried beeline for the bunkhouse. The door that led to the large room where the men slept was out of her view. She had only caught a glimpse of Shaw's face, but he appeared to be angry.

Then Annie saw the group of riders trotting in and heading for the barn. Before she could pick out Buck in the bunch, her attention was drawn to Sylvia Shaw, who was stepping off the back porch of the ranch house, and heading directly toward the door of the bunkhouse kitchen and mess hall, which was separate from the sleeping quarters.

Drying her hands on the apron again, Annie moved to the door and opened it. As Sylvia drew near, Annie knew by the ashen look on her face that something was awry. She waited till the boss's wife moved through the door, and as she shut it, she said, "Sylvia, what's wrong?"

Sylvia Shaw, who was only a year older than Annie, wrung her hands as tears misted her eyes. She took hold of Annie's hands, swallowed hard, and said with quivering lips, "Lightning caused the herd to stampede, honey. It's—it's Buck…"


Two days later, at the cemetery on the outskirts of Elkton, Pastor John Steele was conducting the graveside service. The sealed coffin sat on the ground next to the yawning grave. The pastor stood at the head of the grave, Bible in hand.

Standing near the coffin was Buck Colburn's widow, with her tall son at her side. Next to Knight was his best friend, Jordan Shaw. Jordan made sure his shoulder was touching Knight's arm. Knight had his other arm around his mother.

Standing a step behind them were William and Sylvia Shaw, with their nineteen-year-old daughter, Lorene, and her fiancé, Mark Hedren.

Neighboring ranchers and their families were there, as well as the majority of Elkton's citizens, including every able-bodied member of the Elkton church. The ranch hands from the Bar-S were there, also, but two of them were conspicuously absent. Ace Decker and Keith Nolan.

As the pastor was making some opening remarks, Knight glanced at Jordan from the corner of his eye and thought about the streak of wildness that ran through his best friend. Since they were young boys, periodically Knight had covered for Jordan to keep him out of trouble. By Jordan's shoulder brushing his arm, Knight knew he was trying to show his affection in this moment of sorrow.

Pastor Steele, who had a head of thick salt-and-pepper hair, opened his Bible. "I want to read to you what the Lord Jesus said about sinners like you and me needing the new birth in order to go to heaven. In the third chapter of the gospel of John, it opens up giving us a conversation between the Son of God and a ruler in Israel whose name was Nicodemus. This man was deeply religious and known to be moral and upright. In verse 2, Nicodemus says he knows that Jesus came from God, for no man could do the miracles Jesus had done except God be with Him.

"Verse 3: 'Jesus answered and said unto him, Verily, verily, I say unto thee, Except a man be born again, he cannot see the kingdom of God.' The kingdom of God in this context is heaven. Jesus makes it plain that no one can even see the kingdom of God, much less enter it, unless he has been born again. He goes on in verse 6 to show that there is a fleshly birth, which all of us have had, or we wouldn't exist, then says there is also a spiritual birth. This is the second birth, which makes us children of God. The first birth puts us into the family of our earthly parents. The second birth puts us into the family of God."

Pastor John Steele went on. "I want to make it clear that the second birth takes place in only one way: by receiving Jesus Christ into our hearts in repentance of sin by calling upon Him as stated in Scripture. In John 1:12, Scripture says of Jesus, 'As many as received him, to them gave he power to become the sons of God, even to them that believe on his name.' In repentance of sin, Christ must be received into our hearts, and this comes by our calling on Him, acknowledging that we are sinners in need of salvation and forgiveness. Romans 10:9–10 and 13 make it very clear: 'That if thou shalt confess with thy mouth the Lord Jesus, and shalt believe in thine heart that God hath raised him from the dead, thou shalt be saved. For with the heart man believeth unto righteousness; and with the mouth confession is made unto salvation. For whosoever shall call upon the name of the Lord shall be saved.'"

Closing his Bible, the pastor ran his gaze over the faces of the crowd and said, "One day just three months ago, I met Buck and Annie on Main Street in town. I was new here then, having become pastor of the church in late February. We introduced ourselves, and as we talked, I learned that Buck and Annie were not Christians. They needed to move on, so I explained to them in brief about their need to be saved, and invited them to church. That very next Sunday morning they came, and brought Knight with them.

"I could see at the close of the sermon that the gospel light had shined into their spiritual darkness. It was evident on all three of their faces. But they did not move at invitation time. However, they came back the next Sunday, and when the invitation was given, all three of them walked the aisle and received the Lord Jesus Christ as their own personal Saviour."

Knight tightened his grip on his mother as both of them choked up, recalling that moment.

The preacher again ran his gaze over the faces of the crowd. Smiling, he said, "Based on the fact that Buck Colburn received the Lord into his heart that day and was born again, I can tell you that he is in heaven at this very moment in the presence of his Saviour."

The smile faded, and was replaced by a grim look as Steele said,

"Many of you standing here have never been born again. You have never put your faith in the Lord Jesus Christ to save your soul and wash your sins away in His precious blood. If it was your funeral I was preaching today, I would not be able to say that you were in heaven. I plead with you. Don't put it off. Your own day of death lies somewhere ahead of you, and you don't know when it might happen."

Steele's eyes were now shimmering with tears as he looked at the widow and her son. "Annie, Knight, I know you miss Buck terribly. You both feel like part of your heart has been cut out. But don't wish him back. He has been in heaven two days. He is looking at this moment into the bright face of the Son of God. This world would be a dark place to him now. Just look forward to that glorious day when you will meet him in heaven, never to be separated again."

Knight put both arms around his mother. In turn, she clung to him, and they wept as they held each other. Jordan Shaw laid a hand on Knight's shoulder.

Pastor John Steele closed the service in prayer. He stepped to the widow and her son, spoke some soft words of comfort, then stepped aside to allow others to approach them.

Among the people who passed by Annie and Knight was pretty Nellie Freeman, who had dated both Knight and Jordan for better than a year. However, since Knight had become a Christian, Nellie felt more attracted to Jordan. He hadn't become a religious fanatic like Knight did.

When the last of the crowd had come by, Annie looked up at Knight. "Son, I...I want to kneel beside the coffin before we go."

"Sure, Mom," he said, and holding her hand, helped her to drop to her knees beside the wooden box that held the earthly remains of his father.

Jordan still stood next to Knight as they waited silently for Annie to have the time she needed.

As she knelt beside the coffin, Annie looked into the yawning rectangular hole in the ground, then patted the coffin lovingly. Tears streamed down her ivory cheeks and fell unbidden on its lid. "Buck," she said in a low whisper, "I miss you so much. But...you're in the bright presence of Jesus now, and I can't wish you back. God let you be my best friend since childhood, then blessed me even more when we became husband and wife. Then he blessed me even more than that when He saved us both that wonderful day three months ago. And now, we have His promise that we will have all eternity together in heaven."

Annie sniffed, dabbed at her tear-streaked face with an embroidered handkerchief, then closed her eyes and said in the same low whisper, "Dear heavenly Father, what am I to do now? I still have a child to support, as well as myself. You know I am willing to work hard and do whatever is necessary to make us a living. Please guide Your heartsick servant and open a way for me."

As the tears continued to fall, the blessed Comforter brought Jesus' words to her mind: "I will never leave thee, nor forsake thee." The gentle fingers of peace twined their way into her heart. "Thank You, precious Lord," she said, dabbing at her tears again.

She looked up at Knight, and found his tender eyes on her. "I'm ready to go."

Knight grasped both of her hands in his and helped her to her feet. He then folded her in his young, strong arms and held her tight. "I don't want you to worry, Mom," he said softly, his eyes filled with concern. "I'll take care of you just like Dad would want me to."

Annie reached up and patted his cheek, which was just beginning to show the first signs of a downy beard. "We'll both be just fine, son. The Lord will provide. Let's go home."

Knight turned to his best friend. "Thank you for staying by me, Jordan. I appreciate it more than I can ever tell you."

Jordan grinned. "You've stayed by me through thick and thin over the years, Knight. I owe you the same."

"You don't owe me anything, but there's just one thing I want for you."

Jordan nodded and pulled his lips into a thin line. "I know. You want me to be saved."

"More than anything in the whole world."

"I'm just not ready to do that, yet."

Knight's face was grim as he looked his friend in the eye. "None of us knows how long we have in this world. Dad was ready to go, Jordan, but you're not."

All Jordan could do was force a thin smile.

Turning to his mother, Knight took her hand and said, "Let's go, Mom." Then to Jordan: "See you at the ranch."

Jordan hurried to his horse, mounted, and rode away.

Holding hands, mother and son headed toward the waiting buggy. Knight helped her in, climbed in beside her, and snapped the reins.

Together they began the journey into a future without a husband and father, but with a loving heavenly Father to lead them.


While the funeral was going on at Elkton's cemetery, Ace Decker and Keith Nolan were lying on their bunks in the Bar-S bunkhouse.

Hands clasped behind his head, Nolan said, "Ace, I think we're gonna be in real trouble with the boss for not showin' up at the funeral."

Decker scratched his left ear. "Well, if he's mad at us when he gets home, he'll just have to get over it. After the tongue-lashin' he gave us two days ago, blamin' us for not savin' Buck from the stampede, I'm not happy with him, either. Word has spread about it, I'm sure. I just couldn't withstand the eyes of everyone at the funeral who'd be blamin' us for Buck's death."

"Yeah, me neither. Ain't no way I could've gone to the funeral. It's bad enough havin' the rest of the cowhands on this place snubbin' us. But it'd be even worse havin' to face all the other ranchers, plus the people of the town."

Both men grew quiet and soon were dozing.

Some two hours had passed when Ace Decker awakened at the sound of horses blowing and men talking. He opened his eyes and looked at his friend on the next bunk. Keith Nolan had also just awakened and was cocking an ear toward the sounds.

"They're back," said Decker.

"Yeah. And we're in for it. I can feel it in my bones."

The words had barely left Nolan's mouth when the bunkhouse

door swung open. Both turned to see William Shaw's husky form silhouetted against the brilliant sunshine. Shaw spotted them lying on their bunks, stepped in, and slammed the door.

Both men sat up as Shaw stomped toward them, an angry flush darkening his cheeks, and his jaw squared. His fiery eyes measured the two cowhands. "Why weren't you two at the funeral?"

Decker and Nolan looked each other, then Decker raised his eyes to meet the boss's glare. "We couldn't face the crowd, knowin' that everyone in and around Elkton has been told it was our fault Buck got himself trampled to death."

"It was your fault!" boomed Shaw. "When I waved at you and got your attention, there was plenty of time for one of you to gallop your horse to Buck, pick him up, and ride out of the way of the charging herd. But both of you took the coward's way out, got yourselves to safety, and let Buck die."

Decker jumped off the cot, face bloated with anger, and snapped, "That's the way you saw it, boss, but it ain't the way it was! There absolutely was not time for one of us to safely get to Buck. Don't be hangin' his death on us! We ain't cowards, but we ain't fools, neither. There was a chance we couldn't have made it to him in time."

"That's right!" said Nolan, rising to stand beside his friend. "It's like we told you day before yesterday when you chewed us out, boss: we'd have been gamblin' with our lives to attempt it. You can't blame us for Buck dyin'! We didn't start the stampede."

Shaw's eyes were suddenly cold. His icy stare remained a fixed and calculating pressure against both men as he hissed through his teeth, "There was time to save Buck, and you know it. You are cowards! And you're both fired."

Sudden shock flashed across both faces, draining them of color.

"N-now, boss," said Decker, "y-you don't mean it! We've been with you for almost f-five years. We've done you a good job."

"Yeah," said Nolan. "We've worked hard here. Please don't fire us! We ain't cowards."

"Hah!" blared Shaw. "You proved you were cowards when you didn't show up at the funeral. You couldn't face the crowd because you let Buck die in order to safely preserve your own rotten hides."

"It ain't fair for you to fire us!" said Decker. "Like Keith said, we didn't start the stampede."

"I'm not arguing with you anymore about it," said Shaw. "Pack up your gear and get off the ranch."

Nolan scrubbed a palm over his eyes. "But—"

"I said get off the ranch!" roared Shaw. "Or I'll call for some of the men to throw you off."

Decker and Nolan eyed each other, then quietly took what few personal items they had in the drawers of the nightstand between their bunks and headed for the door.

William Shaw followed them, and when they stepped outside, a group of ranch hands were collected on the porch, having heard what was going on inside. To the group, Shaw said, "You boys keep an eye on these two. I just fired them. They're going to the barn to saddle up and get off the ranch. If they don't move fast, give them reason to do so."

To a man, they nodded.

Decker and Nolan could feel the eyes of the men on their backs as they hastened to the barn. When they led their horses out of the corral a few minutes later, there were more ranch hands on the bunkhouse porch eyeing them warily.

They swung into their saddles and put the horses to a gallop. When they were off the ranch, they slowed the horses to a walk, and looked at each other.

"Are you thinkin' what I'm thinkin'?" asked Decker.

A wicked sneer twisted Nolan's features. "If you're thinkin' that we need to find a way to get even with Mr. William Shaw for firin' us, I am."

"Exactly," growled Decker. "He's gonna suffer. I don't know how, yet, but he's gonna suffer."


On the day after the funeral, William Shaw walked up to his son, who was harnessing a team of horses to one of the ranch wagons at the huge Bar-S barn. "Pick up a dozen sacks of oats and a dozen sacks of barley, Jordan. Just have George put it on my bill."

"Will do, Papa," said Jordan. "Anything else?"

"No. That'll do it."

"All right. See you later."

There was a stiff wind blowing from the north off the snow-capped peaks of the Sawtooth Mountains, and it was cold enough to make Jordan wear his denim jacket.

Half an hour later, Jordan pulled the wagon up in front of Crum's Feed and Grain in Elkton and slid down from the seat. He met up with a rancher he knew as he was crossing the boardwalk. They greeted each other, then Jordan entered the store.

George Crum, who was about William Shaw's age, was behind the counter, scribbling notes on a sheet of paper. Looking up, he said, "Oh. Hello, Jordan. What can I do for you?"

"Papa sent me to pick up twelve sacks of oats and twelve sacks of barley, Mr. Crum. He said to put them on his bill."

George nodded. "Lester's in the feed barn out back. Just drive your wagon back there. He'll help you load up."

Jordan felt his stomach muscles tighten. He had been hoping that Lester Crum wouldn't be working at the store today. Lester was a schoolmate of his and Knight's, and he didn't like either one of them.

Jordan didn't like Lester, either.

Moving outside, Jordan climbed in the wagon, guided the team around to the side of the building, then headed them toward the rear of the property where the feed barn stood. He noted that a crew of men were digging a ditch on the adjacent property, and had dirt and rocks piled alongside it.

When he moved into the barn, Lester was up on a flatbed hay wagon, pitching straw into a pile on the dirt floor. When he saw Jordan, he gave him a sullen look. "Whattaya need?"

"A dozen sacks each, oats and barley," Jordan replied in a friendly tone, trying to keep things civil between them. "Your pa has already put it on our bill."

Lester pointed to a far corner of the barn. "You know where both are kept. You'll have to load 'em yourself. I ain't about to help you."

Frowning, Jordan stepped up to the side of the wagon. "Your pa said you'd help me load up."

"Well, I ain't goin' to."

"Lester, why do you insist on being so hard to get along with?"

The blond sixteen-year-old laid down his pitchfork, hopped off the wagon, and met Jordan eye to eye. "I don't. Except to you and that no-good friend of yours."

"And why is that?" asked Jordan, moving even closer to him.

"I haven't been able to stand Knight since he became a stupid religious fanatic. That's why. And I can't stand you because you're his friend."

"So what has Knight done to you since he became a Christian?"

"He's made me sick to my stomach with all his talk about Jesus, and heaven and hell, and all that gibberish. I don't like him tryin' to ram it down my throat."

"Come on, Lester," Jordan said with a sigh. "Knight isn't like that. He talks to me about becoming a Christian, but he doesn't try to ram it down my throat. He's simply sold on what's happened to him and wants to share it with others. He has the right to believe what he wishes. Don't tell me he tries to shove it on you."

"I don't want to hear any of it, and he's stupid for believin' it! Somebody oughtta pound his face for bein' so stupid."

Jordan felt his blood heat up. "Knight isn't stupid, Lester! And if you don't take it back right now, it's your face that's going to get pounded!"

Lester bristled. "Oh, yeah? And just who's gonna pound it?"

"I am!" Jordan made a fist and drew it back.

"Hold it right there!" came the booming voice of George Crum as he hastened from the door toward the boys. "Don't you hit him, Jordan!"

Fist still clenched, Jordan looked at Crum with fire in his eyes. "He insulted Knight Colburn, and I don't like it!"

"Now just calm down," said George, drawing up. "What do you mean he insulted Knight?"

"Lester said Knight was stupid for being a Christian, and that somebody ought to pound his face for being so stupid."

George glanced at his son. "Lester is entitled to his opinion."

"Yeah? Then tell him to keep it to himself! I'm not going to stand here and listen to him insult my friend."

"Well, don't stand there," said George. "Load up your sacks of grain and take 'em home. They're already on your father's bill."

Jordan's impulse was to pound George's face, but he resisted the temptation. Turning away, he went to a small cart and wheeled it to the spot where the grain sacks were piled. Father and son stood and watched while he piled a dozen sacks of oats on the cart, then wheeled it outside and loaded them into the wagon.

Jordan was still struggling to maintain control of his temper when he returned with the cart to pick up the second load. While he was putting the sacks on the cart, he could hear George speaking in a low voice to Lester, and what words he could pick up were like fiery darts, for George was telling Lester he agreed that Knight Colburn was a fool for being one of those "born-again" types. George added that Knight's parents were also fools, and a lot of good his religion did Buck when he was facing the stampede.

Jordan's breathing was erratic with fury as he wheeled the cart out the door and loaded the sacks onto the wagon. When he was climbing into the seat, father and son appeared at the door, and George said, "You shouldn't treat Lester like you did today, boy. Don't you ever threaten to hit him again."

Jordan's eyes turned to the color of slate. He spoke from his built-up anger in a knifelike tone. "If you don't want him to get punched, then tell him to keep his mouth shut about Knight!"

George's eyes widened and his face flushed. Shaking a fist at Jordan, he rasped, "Get outta here! Go on! Get outta my sight!"

Jordan snapped the reins and turned the wagon around. When he looked back at the spot where George and Lester had stood, they were gone. He put the team in motion again, and as he headed toward the street, red-hot fury was welling up in him. It showed in the lines of his mouth and the flush of his face.

Suddenly Jordan's attention was drawn to the pile of dirt and rocks that ran parallel to the ditch that was being dug on the adjacent property. At the moment, the ditch diggers were absent. Pulling rein, he jumped out of the wagon, hurried to the dirt pile and picked up a fist-sized rock.

Returning to the wagon seat, he guided the team back onto the street, then angled the wagon toward the front of the feed and grain store. As he hoisted the rock to throw it, he was aware that there were people on the street who could see him, and he had a flash of memory about the trouble he had gotten into when he had thrown the rock through Ben Slayton's window. But he was so angry, he didn't care.

Teeth clenched, the sixteen-year-old hurled the rock into the window, shattering it.

When Jordan Shaw arrived back at the Bar-S, he was still fuming over the incident at the feed store. He pulled the wagon inside the barn and began unloading the sacks and piling them next to the feed bin. He was almost finished when he heard two male voices outside. One of them was his father, but he wasn't sure who the other man was.

As he lifted the last sack onto the pile, he turned to see his father entering the barn along with Elkton's town marshal, Mike Woodard.

His heart leaped in his chest.

There was anger on William Shaw's face, but he held it and let the marshal speak.

"Jordan," said Woodard in a tight voice, "I'm arresting you for breaking the window in George Crum's store."

Jordan swallowed hard. Keeping his voice calm, he said, "Marshal, Mr. Crum prodded me into it. Lester started the trouble by saying insulting things about Knight Colburn. Knight is my best friend. Mr. Crum made it worse by also insulting Knight's widowed mother and dead father. I was just—"

"That was no cause to break his window," said Woodard.

Jordan looked to his father. "Papa, you can't let him arrest me. I couldn't just stand there and let those two talk that way. I had to—"

"Jordan," William said levelly, "this is the second time you have done something like this in two weeks. I paid Ben Slayton for the hardware store window, and I made bail for you so you wouldn't have to do time in jail. But this time you're going to pay George Crum for the window out of your own money, and you're going to do your time in jail. Maybe it'll help you learn to control that flinty temper of yours. You shouldn't have let what Lester and George said about the Colburns cause you to throw a rock through their window."

Jordan's countenance fell.

"I'm going to keep you behind bars for fourteen days, Jordan," said the marshal. "I hope it'll teach you how wrong you were to destroy Mr. Crum's property."

Tears misted Jordan's eyes. "Papa, please. Please reason with him. I don't want to go to jail. Please, help me."

William's features were stony. "I warned you last time not to ever do anything like that again. Since you didn't listen, it'll do you good to spend two weeks behind bars." A scowl creased his face. "You're a shame to this family!"

Jordan looked away from his father's blazing eyes.

Woodard took hold of the boy's arm. "Let's go, Jordan."

William was still glaring heatedly at his son as the marshal took him out of the barn. When they drew up to the marshal's horse, Woodard said, "Climb up in the saddle. I'll sit behind you."

Feeling sick inside, Jordan obeyed, and the marshal swung up, reached around him, took the reins, and put the horse to a trot.

As they rode away, Jordan looked back to see his father standing with arms folded across his chest, still glaring at him.

# 3

JORDAN SHAW HAD BEEN IN HIS CELL for less than an hour when he heard the office door that led to the cell block open, followed by footsteps coming down the narrow hallway. He was sitting on the canvas cot, looking at Willie Beemer in the cell next to him. Willie, who was the infamous town drunk, was known to spend a great deal of time in Elkton's jail for trouble he caused when he had spent too much time at one of the saloons. He was sleeping soundly. The other four cells were unoccupied.

When the door opened, Jordan's attention was drawn that direction. He stood up when he saw who it was. Moving to the bars, he managed a weak smile. "Knight! It's good to see you."

Drawing up to the cell door, Knight said, "Since there isn't any school today because the teachers are having that special meeting, Mom sent me into town to buy some things at the general store. I ran into Bessie Higgins there, and she told me she saw Marshal Woodard bringing you into town on his horse, and that he took you into the office."

Jordan's brow furrowed. "You didn't hear about it on the ranch?"

"No. Anyway, as soon as Bessie told me you were here, I came over. I'll have to get Mom's groceries later. Marshal Woodard told me about you breaking George Crum's window and why. He said I could come back and see you. Jordan, I appreciate your standing by me when Lester spoke against me, but you shouldn't have let it make you so mad that you tossed that rock through the window."

Jordan shrugged. "You're my best friend. I didn't appreciate him

31

making fun of you for being a Christian. He said you were stupid, and called you a fool for being one of those born-agains. His dad agreed, saying your parents were also fools, then he made me really mad when he said, 'A lot of good Buck's religion did him when he was facing the stampede.'"

Knight's eyes misted. "Marshal Woodard didn't tell me about that."

"He doesn't know about it. I told him that George Crum had insulted your widowed mother and your dead father, but I didn't go any further with it." Jordan paused, then said, "Did the marshal tell you he took me to the feed store and made me apologize to George Crum for breaking the window?"

"Yes. He also told me that your dad said you have to pay for it."

"Mm-hmm. I know I lost control of my temper, and I shouldn't have thrown the rock through the window, but I just couldn't stand the way they spoke about you and your family. I know I have a problem with my temper and I've tried to do better with it, but I can't seem to keep a level head when I get mad."

"Well, again, I really appreciate your loyalty, Jordan," said Knight, "but I don't like to see you behind bars because you lost your temper. As you well know, I used to have a real problem with my temper, too, but when I got saved and learned to let Jesus take control in my life, I found that things got a whole lot better. I'd really love to see you open your heart to Him. First, because you need to be saved so you can go to heaven when you die, and second, because the Lord can change you down inside and make things a whole lot better in your life while you're here on earth."

Jordan lowered his head and looked at the floor. "Like I've told you, Knight—I'm just not ready to do that, yet."

"Well, just what's it going to take to make you ready? God warns in His Word not to put off salvation, Jordan. If you—"

Knight's words were interrupted by the sound of footsteps in the hallway that led from the office. Jordan's head came up, and when the door opened, Knight looked around. Marshal Woodard stepped into the cell block with Sylvia and Lorene Shaw on his heels.

"Someone else here to see you, Jordan," said Woodard.

Both women rushed to the cell and embraced Jordan through the bars. Sylvia had tears in her eyes as she said, "Thank you for coming to see him, Knight."

"He's in here sort of because of me, ma'am. It's the least I could do. I'll be going, now," he said to Jordan. "But you can look for me every day while you're in here."

Tears were in Jordan's eyes. "You're a real, true friend, Knight. Thanks for coming. See you tomorrow."

As Knight headed through the door, the marshal picked up two straight-backed wooden chairs from the corner of the cell block and placed them in front of Jordan's cell. "Here, ladies. Sit down."

Sylvia and Lorene thanked him. Both wiped tears from their cheeks and the strain of the situation showed in their eyes. As they sat on the chairs, Woodard unlocked Willie Beemer's cell. Beemer had been sitting on his cot, silently looking on. "All right, Willie," he said, "you've done your time for the latest trouble you've gotten into. Let's go."

When the marshal and Beemer were gone, Sylvia and Lorene scooted their chairs closer to the bars. Tears were spilling down Jordan's face. "Mama, Lorene," he said, sniffling, "I'm sorry for bringing this grief on you. I'm sorry for bringing it on the whole family. Please forgive me."

Mother and sister both reached through the bars.

"I forgive you, son," said Sylvia. "I wish you'd learn to control that temper. I know you were defending Knight and his parents, and what George and Lester did was wrong, but throwing the rock through the window was wrong, too. But, as I said, I forgive you."

"I forgive you, too," said Lorene.

"Thank you, sis. And thank you, Mama. I couldn't stand it if you didn't forgive me. Mama..."

"Yes, son?"

"Would—would you tell Papa I want to see him so I can ask his forgiveness, too?"

"I'll tell him. I'm not sure what he'll say, but I'll tell him."

Sylvia and Lorene stayed for better than half an hour, then left, saying they would see him the next morning.

The next morning, when Sylvia and Lorene were ushered into the cell block by Marshal Woodard, they embraced Jordan through the bars, then sat down once again on the chairs. Woodard returned to the office.

Concern was evident in Jordan's eyes as he said, "So Papa didn't come with you."

"No," Sylvia said softly. "We told him you wanted to see him so you could ask his forgiveness, but he won't be coming. He said you need to sit here alone in your cell and think about what you did."

Jordan's features pinched. "So he doesn't want you and Lorene to be here, either?"

"Not really, but he said he wouldn't stop us if we wanted to come back."

Lorene's features were pinched. She drew a shuddering breath and said, "Mama, I hope Papa will get over this soon. Mark and I are getting married in just over a month. If this issue isn't settled, it will hurt the spirit of the wedding."

Sylvia patted her arm. "Don't worry, honey. It will be all right. Papa will cool down by then."

"I'm so sorry, sis," said Jordan. "This whole thing is my fault."

"I can't argue that it is," said Lorene, "but Papa doesn't need to be so stubborn. You've apologized to George Crum for breaking his window, and you are going to pay for the new one. You sent a message to Papa through Mama and me that you want to apologize to him. What else does he want?"

"He'll get over it once Jordan's home and they can talk, honey," said Sylvia. "Everything's going to be fine."

Jordan did not let on, but he doubted that everything was going to be fine. By William Shaw's actions, it was clear he didn't want his son around anymore. He wasn't welcome at home. And no matter how hard his mother tried, everything was not going to be fine.

That afternoon when school let out, Knight hurried to the jail to see Jordan. When he walked into the cell block and approached the cell, Jordan was sitting on the cot with his head bent down and his face in his hands. When he looked up, Knight knew something was wrong.

Slowly Jordan rose from the cot and moved to the bars. "Hello, Knight," he said, "it's good to see you again."

Reaching through the bars, Knight laid a hand on his friend's shoulder. "Hey, pal. What's got you looking so despondent?"

"It's my father."

"What about him?"

"Yesterday after you left, I asked Mama and Lorene to tell Papa I wanted to see him so I could ask his forgiveness for bringing this shame on the family. When they came to see me this morning, they told me Papa said he isn't coming. He just wants me to sit here in the cell and think about what I've done." He took a shaky breath. "And now Lorene is afraid Papa's attitude is going to ruin her wedding."

Knight shook his head. "No, no. Your father isn't going to let anything hurt the wedding. He'll get over this thing in a few days. You've got a good father, Jordan. Let me tell you what he did last night."

"What?"

"He called Mom over to the house and talked to her in his den. He wants her to stay on as ranch cook. He's going to raise her wages so we can make it, and he said Mom and I could still live in the ranch foreman's house. He hired Lloyd Jensen as foreman, and since Lloyd is single, he's going to keep living in the bunkhouse. Lloyd volunteered, so Mom and I would have a place to live. Your father is paying Lloyd even more because of this."

Jordan let a slight smile curve his lips. "Well, I'm glad for both you and your mother, and I'm glad Papa is treating you so well. But he sure doesn't think much of me."

"Sure he does. Like I said, he'll get over it in a few days. He'll still want to set you up with your own ranch when you're of age."

"I'm not sure he will," said Jordan, "but one way or another, I'm still going to have my own ranch someday. I'm going to get married, have a family, and be a cattle rancher for the rest of my life. It's all I want."

"You think you'll marry Nellie Freeman?"

Jordan's eyebrows arched. "Well, that sort of depends on whether you are going to want her, doesn't it?"

"It did till I got saved. Now I know Nellie isn't for me. Somewhere in this world, God has a Christian girl all picked out for me, and in His own time and His own way, He will bring us together."

"Oh. Well, I guess that does shed a new light on the Nellie situation. Have I been seeing right? Has she been a little distant to you since you got saved?"

"Yes. But that's all right. Like I said, God's got the right girl all picked out for me."

"We haven't talked about the future for a long time, Knight. Are you still settled on journalism as your life's career?"

"Sure am. I definitely know that my main talent is with words."

Knight went on to say that Claude Hayward, owner of the *Elkton Sentinel*, was teaching him how to write newspaper articles, and every week he would give him an assignment for a particular article to write as if it was actually going in the paper. He also said that two weeks ago, Mr. Hayward had printed the article he had written about Idaho's wildlife, surprising him.

"And that was a good article," said Jordan. "I really liked it."

"Thanks," said Knight. "Having it actually printed was a real encouragement. My parents, Pastor and Mrs. Steele, and many of the townspeople told me how well they liked it. Mr. Hayward says I definitely should pursue writing as my career. I really love journalism. I hope someday I can own a newspaper, myself."

"That would be great," said Jordan. "I hope you can, too." He sighed. "I wish your father was alive to see you become a success. My father doesn't care what happens to me, just so he doesn't have to look at me. If he really cared, he'd have been here to see me by now. All I wanted was for him to come so I could ask his forgiveness. But he's so ashamed of me, he isn't about to forgive me for what I did."

Knight decided there was nothing else he could say on the subject that would make his friend feel any better. He would have a talk with Mr. Shaw when he got back to the ranch.

Lorene Shaw answered Knight's knock on the back door of the big ranch house. "Hello, Knight. What can I do for you?"

"I just came from town, Lorene," said Knight. "I spent some time with Jordan, and he's very despondent because your father won't come see him. Could I talk to your father, please?"

At that moment, Sylvia drew up, having heard Knight's words. "Of course you can," she said. "He's in his den. Come in. I'll take you."

Lorene stayed at the door and watched her mother lead Knight down the hall.

The den door was open. William looked up from his desk where he was working on some important looking papers.

"Knight just came from visiting Jordan in the jail," said Sylvia, pausing at the door. "He asked to see you."

"Of course," said William. "Come in, Knight. What's this about?"

Sylvia moved into the room, pausing a few steps from the desk.

Standing in front of the desk, Knight said, "First of all, sir, I want to express my appreciation for what you've done to help Mom and me. It was very generous of you."

"Glad I could do it," said William, laying down the pencil he was holding. He let his edgy glance dart momentarily to Sylvia. "And what about Jordan?"

Knight could sense that a tense atmosphere hung over the Shaw household. He, too, flicked a glance to Sylvia, then looking down at the Bar-S owner, said, "Sir, I'm concerned about Jordan. He—well, he's very despondent because you won't come and see him. He wants to tell you how sorry he is for what he did, and to ask you to forgive him. Would you go see him, sir? Please?"

William shook his head doggedly. "No, I will not. Jordan has shamed the family name in this community, and he needs to stew in his own juices while he sits in that cell and thinks about getting that temper under control. I assume you'll be seeing him tomorrow."

"Yes, I will, sir."

William's face was like granite. "Well, you tell him for me that

I'm not walking into that jail for people in the town to gawk at me. And that's final. He can just sit there and consider what he's done to this family. Anything else?"

"No, sir," said Knight, his tone showing the disappointment he was feeling.

"I'll walk you out, Knight," said Sylvia.

Affording her a thin smile, he said, "That won't be necessary, ma'am. Thank you for bringing me in so I could talk to Mr. Shaw."

Sylvia nodded, her face a bit pale.

Knight walked to the door, stopped, and looked back. "Thank you again, Mr. Shaw, for what you did for my mother and me."

William's face softened. "Like I said, glad I could do it."

Knight moved into the hall and disappeared. Sylvia set harried eyes on her husband. In her heart, she was fighting a battle. One that mothers the world over have fought from time immemorial: having to stand as a mediator between a stubborn husband and a wayward child.

Sylvia felt that William was being too hard on Jordan, and that his wounded pride was causing him to be too stubborn to give a little in the situation.

Sylvia said in a soft tone, "Dear, I think you've gone too far in shunning your own son."

William shook his head, jutting his jaw. "No. I've been much too lenient with the boy for far too long. The only way our son is going to learn the lesson he needs to learn is to show him what he has done to this family, and that he must suffer the consequences for his behavior. In life, you can't just go about doing as you please regardless of who it hurts. Jordan needs to learn that no man is an island, and whatever you do affects other people around you… especially those closest to you. What he did in this situation is bad, and I'm trying to teach him to be responsible. Always getting him out of scrapes will not help him to learn his lesson."

"But all he's asking—"

"Sylvia, don't you know it hurts me to see my son behind bars? I would much rather have paid bail for him again, brought him home, and saved all of us the shame we've had to bear. But I can't do that this time. I must be strong about it in order to help him learn a valuable lesson."

Tears surfaced in Sylvia's tender eyes. "I'm not asking you to bail him out. I'm asking you to go and let him confess his wrong and ask your forgiveness."

William left his chair and folded Sylvia in his arms. Holding her close, he said, "Please try to understand, honey. Please back me in this."

She eased back in his arms so she could look into his eyes. "William, I'll back you in letting him stew while sitting in that cell, but while he's stewing, can't you at least go to him and let him ask your forgiveness?"

"No. He won't stew properly if I go to him. I must do it my way, Sylvia. Please try to understand."

Sylvia rose on her tiptoes and kissed her husband's cheek. "I'll try," she said, then turned and slowly left the room, her heart still very heavy.


The next day, when Jordan was eating the lunch Woodard had brought him, he heard footsteps in the hall and looked up to see his friend enter the cell block.

"Knight! I didn't expect to see you till after school."

Moving up to the cell, Knight said, "I passed up lunch so I'd have time to come see you. Has your mother been here today?"

"No. I expect her and Lorene to come soon."

Knight nodded. "Well, you wanted me to talk to your father and ask him to come see you. I did. But he said he won't be coming. I'm sorry."

Jordan's face sagged. "Thanks for trying."

"Sure. Wish I could have convinced him, but his mind is made up. But listen, Jordan, don't give up on him. I'm sure it will be all right when you get out of here and go home."

Jordan moved his head slowly back and forth. "No, it won't. Papa doesn't want me to come home."

"Oh, sure he does," Knight insisted. "He's just upset and hurt over what you did. He'll get over it."

"I wish you were right, but he won't get over it. He's washed his hands of me."

Knight couldn't think of anything else to say on the subject. "Well, I wanted to let you know as soon as I could that I had talked to him. See you later."

"Thanks for trying, pal," said Jordan. "See you later."

Knight had been gone only a few minutes when Marshal Woodard once again ushered Sylvia and Lorene into the cell block and placed the chairs in front of the cell so they could sit down. He picked up the food tray Jordan had slid under the cell door and left. Sylvia and Lorene hugged Jordan through the bars.

As they sat down, Sylvia said, "Knight came to the house yesterday afternoon right after he had been here to see you. He talked to your father, and—"

"I know, Mama," cut in Jordan. "He was here about fifteen minutes ago. Passed up lunch at school to come and tell me what Papa said."

"Your father loves you, son," said Sylvia. "He's just trying to teach you a lesson. He doesn't want anything like this to ever happen again."

"I've learned my lesson, Mama," said Jordan. "I won't ever do anything like that again. But all I want is to know my father is willing to forgive me."

"I know, son. But it will just have to wait till you finish your sentence and come home."

Looking at his mother with steady eyes, Jordan said, "Papa doesn't want me to come home. Ever."

"Oh, of course he does," she said, reaching through the bars to grasp his hand. "Of course he does."

"It'll all be different when you get home, Jordan," said Lorene. "You'll see."

Looking past her son to the denim jacket that lay across the foot of his cot, Sylvia said, "Would you like me to take your jacket home, son? It's getting warmer every day. By the time you get out, you won't need it."

"No, that's all right, Mama. Thanks, but I'll just keep it with me."

Sylvia nodded. "All right."

Sylvia and Lorene stayed a while longer, then embraced Jordan another time through the bars and left.

Ace Decker and Keith Nolan now had jobs at Fletcher's Sawmill several miles northwest of Ketcham, near a dense forest, and had rented a small cabin in the foothills of the Sawtooth Mountains. They were still fuming at the treatment they were given by William Shaw and talked about their desire to get even with him. They would do so when they could come up with just the right plan.

Knight Colburn continued to visit his best friend every day, but was not able to convince him that things would work out between him and his father. Sylvia and Lorene also came every day, and sometimes Mark Hedren was with them. They, too, were unable to persuade Jordan that his father would ever forgive him.

Early on the morning of Jordan's thirteenth day in jail, Marshal Woodard entered the cell block, carrying the usual breakfast tray. On some days, there had been other prisoners, but once again Jordan was alone.

Instead of sliding the tray under the cell door, Woodard balanced it in one hand, took the keys off his belt, and unlocked the door. Handing the tray to Jordan, he said, "I've been thinking… how would you like to get out a day early?"

Jordan widened his eyes. "A day early?"

"Mm-hmm. You've been a model prisoner. I think you should be rewarded. As soon as you've eaten your breakfast, you're free to go. I just need you to stop in the office and sign a paper, saying I let you out a day early. That way, if there's ever any question about it, I can show that it was by mutual agreement."

A broad smile spread over Jordan's face. "Sure! I'll be in the office in a few minutes! Thanks, Marshal."

While Jordan ate his breakfast, he pondered the situation. He was more convinced than ever that his father did not want him to come home. He had not planned to go home, but would go into the Sawtooth Mountains and stay in an old abandoned cabin he

41

had come across a few months earlier while hunting big game alone. The cabin was situated in dense timber at about eight thousand feet above sea level. He had found packaged beef jerky and dried fruit in the cupboard and had eaten some. He hoped it was still there, because he was going to the cabin. This was already settled in his mind when his mother had offered to take his denim jacket home. Even in late spring, the morning air was cold in the mountains, and he would need it.

When he had finished his breakfast, Jordan donned his denim jacket, and carried the tray to the office. Marshal Woodard was alone, sitting at his desk.

Placing the tray on the desk, Jordan said, "Thanks, Marshal, for shortening my sentence by a day. I appreciate it."

"I appreciate the good behavior, son. Now no more rocks through anybody's windows, all right?"

"Yes, sir. I've learned my lesson."

"Good. See you around."

Jordan stepped out on the boardwalk and looked up and down the street. It was still early, and the shops and stores were not yet open. Only a few people were moving about. Taking advantage of it, Jordan made a dash to the corner of the building and hurried to the alley. Trying not to be seen, he made his way through alleys all the way to the edge of town, then headed toward the mountains using a little-known trail into the high country.

During lunch hour, Knight hurried to the jail, wanting to be all the comfort he could to his friend, and was surprised when Marshal Woodard told him he had released Jordan a day early for good behavior.

Excited for Jordan, Knight decided to be late getting back to school. He ran to the small barn behind the school where he and other ranch and farm students kept their horses, mounted quickly, and galloped full speed for the Bar-S.

As he rode up to the big ranch house, Knight saw his mother walking from the kitchen of the bunkhouse toward their little log cabin, but she didn't see him.

Rushing up on the porch, he found the door open and knocked. "Hello! It's Knight!"

Lorene appeared from the parlor, and Sylvia was coming up the hall from the kitchen.

"Hello, Knight," said Lorene. "What are you doing home at this time of day?"

"I found out about Jordan getting out a day early and just wanted to see him for a few minutes. Is it all right?"

Looking perplexed, Lorene said, "I...I don't understand. Are you saying my brother is out of jail?"

"Yes, he—you mean he's not here?"

"No."

Sylvia drew up. "What's this? Did I hear you say Jordan is out of jail?"

"Yes, ma'am," said Knight. "I went to see him at lunchtime, and Marshal Woodard said he had let him out just after he fed him breakfast this morning. He released him a day early for good behavior."

Sylvia's brow puckered. "Then...then he's gone somewhere else. He's not coming home."

"I'd better tell Papa," said Lorene, and hurried toward the den.

Sylvia's hands trembled. "Oh, my. Oh, my. Knight, if he was released early this morning, he could be a long way from Elkton by now."

"Yes, ma'am. He—"

"What's this?" came William's voice as he ran up the hall with Lorene on his heels. "Knight!" he said, drawing up. "Lorene tells me Marshal Woodard let Jordan out of jail a day early. And you're here because you thought he would be home."

"Yes, sir," said Knight, "but I guess I shouldn't be surprised. He kept saying day after day that you didn't want him to come home. He's gone somewhere else, for sure."

Sylvia's face was ashen. Jordan's words he had spoken that day at the jail echoed through her mind. *Papa doesn't want me to come home. Ever.*

"Oh no!" she gasped, putting her hands to her cheeks. "Oh no!"

WITH HER HANDS STILL PRESSED TO HER CHEEKS, Sylvia Shaw looked at her husband. Tears filled her eyes. She was having a struggle within herself to keep from saying, "William, I told you this would happen! You've gone too far in shunning your own son!"

Though she said nothing aloud, William met her accusing gaze and was well aware of the message in her eyes. Swallowing hard and lowering his head to hide the excess moisture in his own eyes, he looked toward the floor. "Honey, I—I'm sorry. I was only trying to teach him that he must learn to be responsible for his own actions."

Immediately, Sylvia's heart went out to her husband as he raised his head and looked at her. Quickly covering the few steps that separated them, she put her arms around his neck.

Making a soft, wordless sound, he closed her in his embrace. "I'm sorry, Sylvia, dear. I should have listened to your reasoning. I have been too hard and too calloused. Now look what I've done."

Gripping his upper arms, Sylvia looked up into his ravaged face. "It's all right, sweetheart. We'll find our boy. You did only what you thought was best. We can only hope he has, indeed, learned his lesson. He knows we love him."

Lorene moved to her parents and embraced them both. "Yes," she said softly, "we'll find him."

As the three of them clung to each other, Knight asked hesitantly, "Do...do you have any idea where Jordan might have gone?"

The trio let go of each other and turned toward him. William wiped a hand across his eyes. "It's hard to say, Knight. As you know, he's got friends on ranches and in town."

Sylvia dabbed at her reddened eyes with a lace-edged handkerchief. "Knowing Jordan, he might have gone somewhere to be by himself, but we sure need to explore all the possibilities."

"I'll saddle up and ride to every one of the ranches where he has friends," said William. "And if I don't find him on one of those, I'll go into town and check there."

"I'll go with you, Mr. Shaw," said Knight.

William smiled. "You're welcome to come along, son, but shouldn't you get back to school?"

"It won't hurt to miss a little school, sir. While you're saddling your horse, I'll run back to the house and tell Mom what's happened, and that I'm going with you."

"All right. Meet you at the barn."


The sun's last red glow was fading in the western sky as William Shaw and Knight Colburn rode onto the Bar-S and headed for the ranch house.

As they drew up to the front porch and glanced northward while dismounting, they could see out over the Sawtooth foothills where twilight was settling gray on the crests, dark in the hollows. High up on the jagged snowcapped peaks, the final vestige of the sun's light glowed weakly on rocky crags.

Two ranch hands were moving past the house in the direction of the barn. When they saw their boss and Jordan's best friend dismounting, they hurried toward them.

"Here come Shorty and Vic," said Knight.

"Good," said William, turning to observe as the two men drew near. "I'll have them unsaddle our horses and put them in the corral."

"Boss," said Shorty, "Mrs. Shaw told all of us about Jordan. Since he's not with you, I assume you didn't find him."

"No, we didn't," said William. "But we'll pick up the search again in the morning."

"Sure hope he's all right," said Vic.

"He has to be," said William. "Would you boys mind unsaddling our horses and putting them in the corral for us?"

"Be glad to, boss," said Shorty.

William and Knight thanked them, and as the horses were being led away, William sighed. "Well, I wish we had good news to carry in there."

"Me too," said Knight.

As they started across the porch, the door swung open, and three female faces appeared.

Looking past them into the fading light of day, Sylvia said, "Y-you didn't find him?"

"No," William said heavily. "We checked on every ranch where Jordan has friends, and at every friend's house in town, but no one has seen him."

Sylvia burst into tears.

Annie Colburn wrapped her arms around her. "Now, honey, don't despair. Jordan's a loner in some ways. He's probably holed up somewhere by himself."

"Right, Mama," said Lorene, taking hold of her mother's hand. Then she said to her father and Knight: "We've got supper cooking. Get washed up, and we'll be ready to eat in a few minutes."

Whenever Annie and Knight ate with the Shaws, William always asked Knight to pray over the food. Though the Shaws were not Christians, Annie and her son appreciated the respect they gave them.

After Knight had prayed, and the food was being passed around, Sylvia said, "William, do you suppose Jordan has gone into the mountains? He really loves it up there."

"I was about to tell you, Knight and I were talking about that very thing while riding back from town. Remember last winter— what was it?—November or December, when Jordan went hunting alone and told us about finding an old abandoned cabin up there? Said he stayed in it a couple of nights."

"I remember that, Papa," said Lorene. "Did he say where it was?"

"Only that it was south of Castle Peak and west of the east fork of the Salmon River."

"That takes in a lot of territory," said Sylvia.

"Yes, but it also narrows it down a great deal, when you consider the entire Sawtooth range," said William.

Sylvia nodded.

Looking at Annie, Knight said, "Mr. Shaw is going into the mountains to look for the cabin tomorrow, Mom. He said I could go with him if you gave me permission. May I go?"

Annie smiled. "Your grades are excellent, and I know how much you want to go, Knight. I'm sure you can catch up on your schoolwork. Yes, you may go with him."

"Thank you," said the sixteen-year-old with a smile. "I want to be with him when he finds Jordan."


Being afoot, travel was slow for Jordan Shaw, but by noon, he had made his way through the thick forest of the foothills, and by the time the sun was setting, he was in the high country with the granite mountains towering over him on all sides. Just north of him stood majestic Castle Peak, with the brilliant, golden light of sunset adorning its summit.

Jordan was following a familiar ridge of blue granite as the air cooled with the elevation, and he spotted the old abandoned cabin in the deep shade of the surrounding pines.

His heart quickened pace as he drew near the cabin. "Nobody here," he told himself aloud. "Sure hope that jerky and dried fruit are still in the cupboard."

Eyeing the stack of uncut logs at the side of the house, he was glad to see that its supply had not been diminished.

The rusty latch resisted his thumb pressure but gave way after a few seconds, and the hinges complained loudly as he opened the door. Looking around by what little light was left, the interior of the cabin appeared exactly as it had when he last saw it. Hurrying to the cupboard, he smiled when he found the packages of beef jerky and dried fruit intact. He was also glad to find the box of matches untouched.

"Yes!" he said with elation. "Nobody's been in this old cabin at all since I stayed here!"

At the fireplace, Jordan found enough wood to do him for the night. The old ax he had used before still leaned against the wall. Knowing that even in the spring the nights were cold at that altitude, he told himself he would cut more wood for the fireplace in the morning.

The morning sun sent its rosy and golden shafts over the eastern elevations to tip the pines around their cabin in the foothills while Ace Decker and Keith Nolan saddled their horses and put a bridle on their pack mule.

When they were ready to go, Nolan picked up his rifle and slid it in the saddleboot. "Well, Ace, ol' pal, it feels good to get a day off and have some time for huntin' deer."

"Sure does," said Decker, putting his foot in the stirrup and swinging into the saddle. "I can taste that venison already. Let's go."

Some two hours later, they topped a pine-covered ridge and Decker said, "Well, we're at about seven thousand feet now. Best to go on foot from here."

Dismounting, they tied the horses and mule to spruce trees and proceeded toward higher ground, rifles in hand.

A thousand feet higher up, Jordan Shaw left the old cabin just before nine o'clock and climbed up through the dense forest, carrying the battered bucket he had used when staying in the cabin before. The air was quite chilly, and Jordan was glad he had worn his denim jacket.

Soon he came to the broad, shallow stream he remembered and dipped the bucket in the ice-cold water. He took a long drink, filled the bucket to the brim, and headed back to the cabin. Breakfast would only be jerky and dried fruit, but at least he was in a place where he felt welcome. He missed his family, and wished his mother and sister had not been subjected to grief because of his deeds, but since his father didn't want him there anymore, he would never go home again.

By ten o'clock, Jordan had devoured his breakfast and stepped out of the cabin, ax in hand. Going to the side of the cabin, he rolled a log off the stack and began chopping pieces small enough to fit in the fireplace. A fallen tree lay close by. Soon the warmth of the sun and the exertion of chopping made him warm.

He took off the denim jacket, draped it over the fallen tree, and resumed his work.

Ace Decker and Keith Nolan steadily made their way up the steep, tree-laden slope, talking in low tones, eyes running back and forth for any sign of deer.

At one spot, they stopped to catch their breath, and Decker touched his friend's arm. "Listen! What's that?"

"What?" whispered Nolan. "I didn't hear anything. Are you talkin' animal or—"

"Shh! There it is again!"

This time it came sharp and clear, from somewhere higher up.

"Oh," said Decker. "Somebody's choppin' wood up there."

Suddenly there was movement among the trees about fifty yards up the slope.

"Hey!" said Nolan in a subdued voice as he shouldered his rifle.

Decker spotted the small buck deer, and was bringing his rifle to bear when Nolan took quick aim and fired.

The bullet struck the buck in the hind quarters. He leaped out of sight into the dense forest, and the hunters were in quick pursuit.

Beside the old cabin, Jordan Shaw was about to finish cutting wood when he saw movement in his peripheral vision. Turning to see what it was, he focused on a small buck deer stumbling his direction through the trees, its coat dripping blood. He had thought he heard a shot a few minutes ago while chopping wood, but wasn't sure. Now he knew it was someone shooting the deer.

As the buck came closer, it was evident to Jordan that he was in extreme pain, and his bulging eyes didn't even notice the human who stood at the woodpile beside the cabin.

Jordan dropped the ax and ducked down behind the woodpile so as not to startle the wounded animal if it did happen to see him.

The buck was grinding his teeth in agony as he staggered blindly up to where Jordan had stood seconds before, then suddenly collapsed, falling on the dead tree where Jordan's jacket lay. Jordan knew the deer was dying as his blood soaked the jacket. His eyes had rolled back in his head, and his sides were heaving as he sucked hard for breath.

Unable to allow the dying deer to suffer any longer, Jordan decided to end its life by striking it on the head with the ax. Hurrying to the spot, he picked up the ax, and raised it over his head. But before he brought it down, the buck let out his last breath.

He was lowering the ax when suddenly he heard a male voice shout, "Jordan Shaw! What are you doing here?"

Turning, Jordan saw Ace Decker and Keith Nolan running toward him amid the trees.

While they ran, Ace spoke in a low voice from the side of his mouth. "I have an idea how to get back at William Shaw for what he did to us if Jordan is alone. If I give you the nod, put your gun on him."

Nolan grinned. "Will do."

Though his father had fired the two men, Jordan decided to be friendly. Still gripping the ax, he smiled. "I heard the shot a while ago, then the deer showed up. He fell and died where you see him."

"All right," said Nolan. "We'll go down, get our horses and pack mule, and haul him home."

Running his gaze to the cabin, Decker asked, "Who's with you, Jordan?"

"Nobody. I'm here by myself."

Decker's eyebrows arched. "By yourself? You're stayin' here in the cabin by yourself?"

"Yes."

Decker flicked a glance at Nolan and nodded.

Suddenly Nolan worked the lever of his rifle and from the hip, pointed it at Jordan's midsection. In a cold voice, he said, "Drop the ax, kid."

Jordan frowned, shock showing in his eyes. "What's going on?"

"Why are you stayin' here by yourself?" asked Decker.

Jordan looked at the ominous black muzzle, then at Decker. "Why is he holding the gun on me?"

"You'll find out in a minute," said Decker. "Now, answer my question. But do as Keith told you first. Drop the ax."

Letting the ax slip from his fingers and fall to the ground, Jordan said, "All right. I'll tell you."

While the two former Bar-S cowhands listened intently, Jordan explained about his breaking the window at George Crum's feed store, and being arrested and sentenced to fourteen days in jail by the marshal. He told them how he was released from jail a day early yesterday, and wanted to get away from everything and everybody for a few days, so he came to the old cabin, where he had stayed before.

"So when you plannin' to go home?" asked Nolan.

Figuring it was none of their business about the problem between his father and himself, Jordan said, "I don't know, yet. I'll go home when I'm ready. Why are you pointing that gun at me, Keith?"

"Because we just found a way to get back at your father for firin' us over Buck Colburn's death," Nolan said evenly.

Jordan's face blanched. "Y-you're going to kill me?"

Ace Decker laughed. "Naw, we ain't gonna kill you, kid. We ain't murderers. But we're gonna get back at your pa by makin' him think you're dead. We're gonna take you to the cabin where we live in the foothills. You'll be our prisoner. When you don't show up at home in a few days, your ol' pa will be lookin' for you. When he doesn't find you in a month or so, he'll think you're dead. This will cause him great sorrow, which will give us our revenge."

Jordan's features were white. "But you can't hold me like that. It's not right. You'll just get yourself into trouble with the law, and—"

"No, we won't," said Decker. "Keith and I are plannin' on leavin' Idaho in a couple of months. Before we go, we'll leave you tied up in a secluded cave we know about. It's about two thousand feet higher than where we stand, right up there close to Castle Peak. By the time you work yourself free, we'll be long gone. Ain't nobody gonna find us. But it'll sure feel good knowin' we made your pa hurt inside, thinkin' you were dead."

"Please," said Jordan. "Don't do this. It'll make my mother and sister suffer, too."

"Can't help that," said Decker.

"Please. Don't put them through this," begged Jordan.

"It's gonna happen, kid," said Nolan, "so you might as well shut your mouth about it."

Jordan saw it was of no use to beg them. They felt no compassion toward anyone in his family. He remained mute while Decker and Nolan bound his hands behind his back, and tied him to a tree. Leaving him there, they took over two hours to go down to where they left the horses and the mule. He watched while they hefted the dead deer onto the mule's back, then they hoisted him into Decker's saddle. Decker swung up behind him, Nolan mounted his own horse, and with William Shaw's son their captive, they rode down the trail.

An hour later, near the old abandoned cabin, a young but huge cinnamon-colored grizzly wandered out of the forest, moving silently in spite of his great size. Sniffing the air, he followed the scent that had first met his nostrils some distance higher up, carried by the cool breeze.

When he saw the cabin—with which he was familiar—he knew the source of the scent lay in that direction. When he was within a few yards of the cabin, another scent seemed to mingle with the first one, and he stopped. The second scent was unpleasant.

He rose up on his hind legs, lifting his eight hundred pounds to his full nine-foot height, and studied the area. The second scent was the foul smell of man. He shook his head and snorted to clear his nostrils of it.

Dropping down on all fours again, he moved closer. When the

first scent became stronger, he spotted its source. The red fluid shed by some mountain animal; red fluid that he had tasted and enjoyed many times since growing into maturity from his cub days.

Moving in closer, he spotted the blood-soaked denim jacket that lay draped over the fallen tree. Hurrying to the spot, the massive bear lowered his head, salivating, and sniffed the jacket. Suddenly the smell of man was so strong, it weakened the blood scent and infuriated him. In a frenzy, he ejected a wild roar, clawed at the jacket, ripping it some, then picked it up with his teeth and headed into the forest toward higher elevation, leaving his fresh tracks in the soft earth.

The grizzly had gone some twenty yards when he found the man scent too obnoxious and let the jacket fall from his mouth. Leaving it behind, he kept on climbing.

Late that afternoon, William Shaw and Knight Colburn guided their horses up the steep slope through the forest, searching for the old cabin west of the east fork of the Salmon River and south of Castle Peak. They had come upon other cabins, but none were abandoned.

Suddenly William spotted a cabin through the trees and pointed with his chin. "I wonder if that's it, Knight."

"Could be," said Knight, peering at it.

They soon drew up to the front of the old cabin and dismounted. They entered the cabin and found evidence that someone had been staying in it quite recently. The ashes in the fireplace were still warm and there was beef jerky in the cupboard, along with dried fruit. The battered bucket that sat on the counter had fresh water in it.

As they moved back outside, William said, "I think this is it, Knight. All the dust in there tells me it hasn't been used for a long time, yet the fresh food and water and the warm ashes say it has been used quite recently."

"Well, if you're right, sir," said Knight, "Jordan has to be around here somewhere."

Suddenly William's attention was drawn to the freshly cut

wood on the north side of the cabin. "Let's look over here." He stepped off the porch, hurrying that direction.

Knight was quickly beside him.

When they reached the spot, they saw the ax lying on the ground and the fresh blood on the fallen tree. They noticed the hoof prints, and the boot prints in the soft earth.

Suddenly Knight gasped and said, "Look! Bear tracks!"

Both men knelt down and Knight indicated the outline of the twelve-inch-wide indentations in the soft earth. "I wrote about grizzly paws in my newspaper article that Claude Hayward printed, Mr. Shaw. I did a study about grizzlies and other bears for the article. These are grizzly paws."

"I read the article," said William, swallowing hard as he looked back at the blood on the tree. "The grizzly made its kill right here, then apparently took whatever animal it had killed to eat it elsewhere."

They studied the other marks in the ground, and both were puzzled about the unmistakable evidence that men and horses had been on the spot recently, but it was impossible to tell whether it was before or after the grizzly made its kill.

Choking on his words, Knight said, "M-Mr. Shaw…someone—someone was cutting wood right here. The…the ax is still lying on the ground. I…I hate to say this, but the victim may not have been an animal. It could have been whoever was chopping wood."

William looked at the blood on the fallen tree in morbid horror. His face lost color. "Oh, it can't be—it just can't be! No! Not Jordan! It can't be!"

Pointing up the slope toward the northwest, Knight said, "The grizzly's tracks lead that way."

"Let's follow it," said William.

Taking their rifles from the saddleboots and leaving their horses tied to trees, William and Knight headed up the slope toward higher country, following the bear's tracks.

Only minutes later, Knight pointed ahead. "Look! It's something bloody lying on the ground."

They hurried together, and when William saw that it was a shredded, bloody denim jacket, he cried, "No-o-o-o! It can't be Jordan's jacket! It just can't be!"

With trembling hand, Knight picked it up, pinching it by the collar between his fingers. "I...I'm afraid it is Jordan's, sir."

William Shaw recognized the jacket and knew it belonged to his son. Guilt overwhelmed him as he touched the tattered jacket. "What have I done? I've been a stubborn fool. I wouldn't listen to Sylvia, and now my son is dead!"

Not knowing exactly what to do, Knight put an arm around the brokenhearted man and patted him on the back. "Mr. Shaw," he said, "you only did what you thought was best for Jordan. We all understand that."

William looked into the compassionate eyes of Knight Colburn and said, "Thank you. Thank you. Knight, I've got to find Jordan's body. I have to."

"I understand, sir," said Knight. He pointed up the trail. "The grizzly apparently took the body to his lair somewhere higher up."

With heavy hearts, William and Knight followed the grizzly's tracks, but were stopped short only minutes later when they topped a rise and found themselves at a stream bank less than a hundred yards from where they had found the jacket. The stream was wide but shallow. They could find no evidence that the grizzly had gone either direction on the bank which was laden with a broad expanse of small rocks, so they waded across to the opposite bank, but could find no evidence there either, for the same reason.

Desperate to find Jordan's remains, they went back to the horses, put the jacket in a saddlebag, and rode up and down the stream on both banks until sundown. There was no sign of the grizzly's tracks nor of Jordan's body.

Both men wept as they headed down the trail toward the ranch, dreading to break the horrible news to Sylvia and Lorene.

"I'll ride into town first thing in the morning," said William. "I'll report this to Marshal Woodard and ask him to form a search party to help me find Jordan's remains."

At the Bar-S, Sylvia Shaw was in the parlor, upset over Jordan. Mark Hedren was there, trying to be a source of strength to both Lorene and her mother.

Knowing that no one in the Shaw household was going to be very hungry, Annie Colburn was in the kitchen, preparing a light supper.

She had already fed the ranch hands and knew that she could always fix more food if Knight and Mr. Shaw came home with Jordan. While her busy hands made quick work of the preparations, she was praying in her heart for a safe return of the men.

When the meal was ready, Annie left the kitchen and moved up the hallway toward the parlor. She could hear both Sylvia and Lorene weeping, and Mark talking to them in a low, soothing tone. Pausing when she reached the door, Annie observed the scene. Her own heart was still tender and sore over the loss of her adored husband. Tears of sympathy quickly flooded her eyes.

Dabbing at her cheeks with a hankie, Sylvia noticed Annie standing at the door, wiping tears. Mark and Lorene saw it and turned to look at her.

Finding her voice, Annie said, "I know it's getting late, and they're not back yet, but don't give up." She cleared her throat gently. "Supper's ready. It's quite simple: only bean and ham soup and brown bread and cheese."

Sylvia sniffed and said, "Annie, I'm sorry, but I just can't eat anything right now."

"I understand, honey," said Annie, "but you must keep up your strength for when your husband and son return."

Sylvia nodded, sniffed again, dabbed at more tears, and stood up. "You're right, Annie. I'll try. You're making tea, aren't you?"

"Yes. The kettle is boiling."

"Good. Hot tea does sound inviting." Then she said to the others, "How about you two?"

"Maybe we can get some of that soup down," said Mark, rising to his feet and offering Lorene his hand. "How about it, honey?"

"I'll try," she said, taking his hand.

At that instant, they heard the back door open.

"It's them!" Sylvia gasped, hurrying through the parlor door past Annie, and dashing down the hall toward the kitchen.

Annie followed, with Mark and Lorene on her heels.

When they entered the kitchen, they found a gray-faced pair

staring at them with sad eyes.

Sylvia felt her heart straining against the paralyzing terror that leaped into her chest. Her eyes were round in the ashen pallor of her skin. "Oh no! You found Jordan! He's dead, isn't he?"

William took Sylvia in his arms, and Knight went to his mother.

Holding Sylvia tight, William said, "We—we didn't find Jordan, honey, but we found evidence that something terrible happened to him."

"What? What happened to him?"

Guiding her to one of the kitchen chairs, William said, "Here. Sit down. I'll tell you about it." Then to his daughter he said, "Here, Lorene. You'd better sit down, too."

"Come on, Mom," said Knight, guiding Annie to another chair. "You sit down, too."

William sat down on a chair so he could look at Sylvia and hold her hands, and while Mark held onto Lorene and Knight kept a hand on Annie's shoulder, he told them the story.

When he finished, Sylvia gripped his hands. "It just can't be, William! It just can't be! Maybe the jacket is just one similar to Jordan's."

"No, honey," William said sadly, "it's Jordan's, all right."

"I want to see it!"

Shaking his head, William said, "Honey, no. You don't want to look at it. It'll just upset you worse."

"I want to see the jacket!" Sylvia said, tears coursing down her cheeks.

William sighed and started to rise.

"I'll get it, Mr. Shaw," said Knight, and dashed out the back door.

Annie moved to Sylvia, bent down, and kissed her cheek. "I'm here for you, honey," she said softly.

Sylvia patted Annie's hand. "Thank you."

Then turning to Lorene, Annie bent down and kissed her cheek, saying the same thing. Lorene wiped tears and thanked her.

William said, "This is all my fault, Sylvia. If I hadn't been so stubborn, and had shown our son more love and understanding, this whole nightmare wouldn't have happened. I'm sorry. So sorry. I hope you and Lorene can find it in your hearts to forgive me."

"Papa," said Lorene, "you were only trying to teach Jordan to do right toward others. Maybe you could have gone at it a little differently, but you were doing what you felt was best. Please don't punish yourself."

"She's right, dear," said Sylvia. "Don't punish yourself."

Knight's footsteps were heard on the back porch, and Sylvia tensed up. When he came through the door bearing the bloody, tattered jacket, she felt a cold prick her skin.

Moving up close to her, Knight held the jacket so she could get a sufficient look at it. He let her see the front, then turned it so she could see the back. Turning the front of the jacket toward her once more, he said, "It's Jordan's all right, ma'am." His voice was hollow, like the tail end of an echo.

Sylvia let out a wail and broke into deep, mournful sobs.

Supper was forgotten.

While the others stayed with Sylvia, Mark rode to town and brought Dr. Philip Warner back with him. The doctor immediately gave Sylvia a strong sedative, telling her it would take effect within half an hour and would help her to get some sleep.

The doctor told William to send for him again if he was needed.

Sylvia clung to her husband. Never once did she utter a word of blame toward him. She told herself William was blaming himself enough. She would not add to his misery.

Holding Sylvia tight, William ran his eyes to the others, then looked back at Sylvia. "I'll go to Marshal Woodard in the morning, show him the jacket, and ask him to form a search party to help me find Jordan's remains."

"I'll be part of that search party, Mr. Shaw," spoke up Mark Hedren.

"Good," said William. "Thank you."

"Mom," said Knight, "may I go along, too? I realize it will take me out of school for whatever time we're gone, but—"

"It's all right, son," said Annie. "If the tables were turned, Jordan would do it for you."

"Thank you, Mom," said Knight, patting her cheek lovingly. "I'll catch up on my schoolwork as soon as we get back."

"I appreciate your letting him go with us, Annie," said William. "Knight has proven over and over that he indeed was Jordan's best friend."

Sylvia was fighting the effects of the sedative, but the stronger force of the medicine was winning the battle. Everyone saw that Sylvia was getting drowsy.

Annie said, "Mr. Shaw, if you'll help Sylvia to the bedroom, I'll tuck her in."

Sylvia's eyes were droopy as William carried her to their room. Annie hurried ahead and turned down the covers. Lorene followed, and as her father laid her mother on the bed, she said, "I'll stay with her, Papa."

"No need for that, child," said Annie. "You and your papa need some time with each other. You go on back to the parlor. I'll stay with your mama."

Both William and Lorene thanked her and left the room.

Sylvia was already asleep. Annie pulled the covers up over her, then slid the rocking chair that sat by the window up next to the bed and eased into it.

As she rocked silently back and forth, Annie whispered to the Lord, praying for this family who so desperately needed Him. She and Buck had talked to the Shaws on several occasions after they were saved, trying to make them understand their own need for salvation, but they had politely told her they had their own ideas about life, death, and eternity.

"Please, dear Lord," Annie prayed aloud, "let this tragedy work in their hearts and minds so it will result in them receiving You as their Saviour."

Back and forth she rocked, her work-worn hands clasped tightly in her apron-clad lap.

Early the next morning, Marshal Mike Woodard held Jordan Shaw's tattered, bloody jacket in his hands with his young deputy, Bob Price, looking on.

Shaking his head, Woodard looked at William Shaw, Knight Colburn, and Mark Hedren. "There's no way Jordan can still be alive."

"We've accepted that, Mike," said William, his voice breaking. "Sylvia and Lorene had a hard time with it, but they know all we can hope for is to find Jordan's remains."

"I understand," said Woodard. "Not until the remains are found can it come to closure in your hearts and minds. I'll go to work on it right away. I'd say if we could get another four men, the search party would be the right size. I'll leave Bob here to watch over the town while I'm gone."

William nodded. "I'd say eight would be enough. It might get cumbersome if we have too many."

"Right. Since it might take a few days, you fellows pack up some food and bedrolls for yourselves and wait at the ranch. It won't take me very long to come up with four more volunteers. See you in a couple of hours or so."

At the same time William, Mark, and Knight were riding out of Elkton toward the Bar-S, Ace Decker and Keith Nolan were about to leave Jordan Shaw sitting on the floor of the room in their cabin they called his cell, and go to work at the sawmill.

Jordan's boots had been removed and his right ankle was chained to a post, with just enough length to allow him access to the food, water pitcher, and chamber pot close by. The chain was fastened securely to his ankle with a four-inch bolt through the links, and the nut was so tight it would be impossible to remove without pliers and wrench like the ones used by Nolan to put it on.

Since the room was on the front side of the cabin, Decker pulled the window shade down so anyone passing by on the road could not see in. He chuckled and said, "Well Jordan, ol' pal, we'll see you this evenin'. You have yourself an enjoyable day."

Holding the pliers and wrench, Nolan laughed. "This makes me feel good, Ace! In time, this kid's pa will give him up for dead."

"Yeah!" Decker laughed. "And the sufferin' that goes with it is our sweet revenge."

Jordan closed his eyes and bit down on his lower lip. It was of no use to remind them of how his mother and sister would suffer. As they left the room, he opened his eyes and looked that direction through a wall of tears. He heard one of them shove the bolt on the cabin's front door, then join his friend at the rear door. Jordan heard a padlock snap in place, and moments later, he heard Decker and Nolan trot their horses from the small corral toward the road.

As the sound of pounding hooves faded away, Jordan broke down and sobbed. He rued the day he first got into trouble with the law. "Jordan, you fool! None of this would have happened if you hadn't been so hotheaded."

He wept for a long time, his heart heavy for the suffering his family was going to bear. He thought of Lorene and Mark. Unless he could find a way to escape, he would not be there for their wedding on Saturday, June 18, which was less than two weeks away. And Mark had asked him to be one of his groomsmen along with Knight Colburn.

Gritting his teeth and shaking his head, he said aloud, "I've got to come up with a way to escape. I've got to!"

Late in the afternoon on the fourth day of leading his search party through forests and canyons, across streams, and into caves in the

Sawtooth Mountains, Marshal Woodard rendezvoused his teams of two at the base of Castle Peak.

His features were granitelike as each pair reported no sign of Jordan's remains. Woodard had kept William Shaw with him. Turning in his saddle to look at him, he said, "William, from the evidence I've seen: the tattered, bloody jacket; the grizzly's paw prints in the woods where Jordan was chopping wood; all the blood in the area; and the bear's tracks leading to higher ground, tell me that after the grizzly killed Jordan, it took the body to some remote spot and—well, enough said."

Wiping tears, William nodded. "I can see that it's futile to keep searching any longer, Mike. These men need to get home to their families. Mark, Knight, and I need to go home, too."

With heavy hearts, the men turned their tired horses southward and headed toward lower ground.

William Shaw was in the depths of despair, knowing that this horrendous tragedy was all his fault. If only he not had been so hardheaded and stubborn…

*How am I ever going to live with this?* he asked himself as he rocked in the saddle. *How am I going to face Sylvia and Lorene day after day from now on, knowing that Jordan was mauled by that grizzly because of me? And to add to my guilt, there is no way for closure for them. There is no body to bury…no way for them to say good-bye.*

Dusk was on the land as William, Mark, and Knight rode up to the Bar-S corral and dismounted. A couple of ranch hands were near, and after answering their questions about the search, William asked them to take care of the three horses. As the three of them headed for the back door of the ranch house, William was rehearsing in his mind what he was going to say to his wife and daughter.

When they stepped into the kitchen, the women were seated around the empty table. Sylvia slowly raised her eyes to meet her husband's as Lorene and Annie looked on. The grief etched on William's face was enough to bear the message, but Sylvia had to ask him.

Drawing a shallow breath, she said, "Find anything?"

Scrubbing a palm over his face, William said, "Not a trace."

Mark went to Lorene, and Knight went to his mother.

Rising slowly from the chair, Sylvia blinked at the fresh tears in her eyes. William opened his arms, and she stepped into them, collapsing against his chest. Sobs tore from her lips as she cried, "I can't believe it! I can't believe it!"

William's rehearsed words suddenly seemed inappropriate, and he dismissed them from his mind.

Lorene stood up, weeping, and Mark folded her into his arms.

Annie rose from her chair, and Knight locked her neck in the crook of his arm, holding her tight. As he beheld the sorrow of the Shaw family, he felt his own brand of sorrow. It was more than just the death of his closest friend. It was worse, knowing that Jordan had died without Jesus.

Annie thought of that, too, and of the many times she and Buck had talked to the Shaws about their need to be saved, but she decided that now was not the time to press them about it again. By previous experience with them on the subject, she knew they were not in a frame of mind to listen to her.

When Sylvia and Lorene had gained control of their emotions, Mark said, "Lorene, maybe we should postpone the wedding. You know, so as to let the natural period for mourning pass."

Moving her head slowly back and forth, Lorene said, "Mark, I don't think Jordan would want us to postpone it. I really don't."

"I don't either," said Sylvia. "And besides, even though you two have chosen to have a small wedding with just family and close friends, so much careful planning has gone into both the ceremony and the reception. Everything is set with the minister and the church in Ketcham, and he went out of his way to schedule it on June 18, which he said ordinarily he would only do just for his members. You remember, Mark."

Mark nodded. "Yes. I know he had already planned to take his family over to the Craters of the Moon area for an outing that day. They had set the date back in April. I just thought the three of you might rather put the wedding off a few weeks. But you're right. Too many things are already set."

"Not to mention that relatives on both sides of our family who live in the Midwest and back East have already purchased railroad tickets," said Sylvia.

Mark nodded.

"You will have to pick out another groomsman to take Jordan's place, darling," said Lorene. "But other than that, everything is in place."

"I think I'll ask Bart Collins," said Mark.

"Good choice," said Lorene. "Bart is certainly one of your closest friends. I'm sure he will be honored to do it."


As the days passed, Jordan remained in his cell and in chains when Decker and Nolan were away from the cabin. The more time that passed, the more discouraged he became. There was simply no way he could escape. He told himself he was going to have to wait until his captors took him into the mountains and tied him up in the cave just before they would leave Idaho.

He was glad, at least, that they were not going to kill him. When he was tied up with the ropes instead of bound with chains, he would eventually be able to free himself.


On Saturday, June 11, Decker and Nolan left Jordan shackled to the post in his room as usual, and rode into Elkton. They wanted to hear what was being said about Jordan's disappearance.

Arriving in town, they dismounted, moved slowly down the boardwalks and into one store after another. Often they heard townspeople talking about Jordan Shaw being killed and devoured by a grizzly; his bloody, tattered jacket being found; the search party led by Marshal Mike Woodard, trying unsuccessfully to find his remains; and the deep sorrow being experienced by the Shaw family.

As they rode back toward the foothills, Decker and Nolan laughed with glee, discussing the mental anguish their former boss was suffering. When they entered the cabin, they went into Jordan's cell and laughed heartily as they told him what they had heard the townspeople saying.

Jordan's heart was heavy, knowing he had done this terrible

thing to his family. He wished they would not have to wait so long to learn that he was alive.


At the same time Jordan Shaw was languishing in his cell at the cabin in the foothills, Knight Colburn entered the *Elkton Sentinel* office to find Claude Hayward smiling at him.

Hayward, who had recently turned sixty, said, "I'm sure glad it's Saturday. If I didn't have you in here once a week, Knight, I'd have to do all the work around this place."

"We couldn't have the boss under that kind of pressure, now, could we?"

Hayward laughed. "Not as old as I'm getting."

Knight shook his head, grinning. "You're not old, Mr. Hayward." He paused for effect, then added, "Compared to Methuselah."

Hayward made a mock scowl. "I'd fire you for that remark, but there's too much work that needs to be done around here."

They laughed together, then Knight said, "So, what's my first task, today?"

"I need to know about Mark and Lorene. Are they still getting married on the eighteenth or has the tragedy of Jordan's death caused them to postpone it?"

"They're going ahead with the wedding next Saturday, sir," said Knight. "Mark suggested that they put it off for a few weeks to give time for mourning Jordan's death, but Lorene and her parents felt that Jordan wouldn't want them to postpone it. So, as scheduled, the wedding will take place at three o'clock next Saturday afternoon at the church in Ketcham."

"Good. I want you to write a three-hundred-word article on the wedding and get it in my hands by six o'clock next Saturday if you can, and I'll print it on the front page of Sunday's issue. You can have it pretty well done before the wedding, then just add whatever you want when it's over. Can you do that?"

A wide smile spread over Knight's young face. "Oh yes, sir! I can do it! Thank you for the opportunity!"

"You're welcome, my boy," said Hayward, rubbing his silver mustache.

"I'm going to be giving you more writing assignments very soon. Enough practice. I want you doing the real thing each time from now on."

"I really appreciate that, sir," said Knight. "Now, what's my first job today?"

"The press needs cleaning. You can start there."

"All right," said the sixteen-year-old, "one clean printing press coming up!"


At the Bar-S on the next Saturday, there were mixed emotions in the big ranch house. Lorene and her parents carried the grief over Jordan's death, yet there was happiness because of the new life Lorene would begin as Mrs. Mark Hedren that day.

The Shaws, along with Annie and Knight Colburn, left the ranch for Ketcham just before one o'clock. Knight was astride his horse so he could ride back to Elkton immediately after the wedding reception was in progress, and place the final draft of the wedding article into Claude Hayward's hands. The others were in the Shaw carriage.

Lorene sat between Sylvia and Annie in the rear seat, each holding a hand as they tried to keep her mind on the wedding. When they arrived at the church, the women took Lorene to the room where she would put on her wedding dress. Bessie Hedren—Mark's mother—was there to offer her help. The two bridesmaids, who were close friends of Lorene's, were already there.

William went into the auditorium, where he met family members from the Midwest and the East who had been staying at the Ketcham Hotel, along with local friends. When he spotted Marshal and Mrs. Mike Woodard, he thanked the marshal once again for the effort he had put forth to try to find Jordan's body.

Knight went to the pastor's office, where he joined Mark, best man Lucas McSween, the other groomsman Bart Collins, and the pastor.

As Sylvia worked with Annie and Bessie to help Lorene get ready, she thought about Jordan, and with his death overshadowing the family, she was glad they had decided on a small, quiet wedding with only relatives and close friends.

Lorene, a pretty girl in her own right, glowed in the love Mark had for her as the finishing touches were put on her hair by her mother. The bride wore a lovely pale pink and white lace dress.

Sylvia, her heart aching over Jordan, painted a happy smile on her face and engaged her daughter in cheerful chatter. She fastened the last tiny button at the neck of the bodice and placed a filmy concoction of tulle attached to a white straw hat atop Lorene's shiny curls. She pinned it into place and stepped back to admire her.

Bessie, Annie, and the bridesmaids looked on as a mist of tears dimmed Sylvia's eyes. Taking Lorene's hands, Sylvia said, "You are so beautiful, sweet girl. Let this be the happiest day of your life."

Lorene's mind went to Jordan, but she pressed a smile on her lips and said, "I will, Mother. I will."


At the cabin in the foothills, Jordan Shaw was alone. Ace Decker and Keith Nolan had gone hunting in the mountains for the day. He was still chained to the post, leaning his back against the wall. As usual, the window shade was down and the cabin doors were securely locked.

Jordan's mind was on the wedding in Ketcham. It was almost noon, and he knew that in three more hours, his beloved sister would walk down the aisle to become Mark Hedren's wife. He wept as he thought of Lorene and his parents, knowing how hard it was going to be for them to get through the wedding, thinking he was dead.

He wondered who Mark had chosen to replace him as a groomsman and thought it was probably Bart Collins. Mark and Bart had been close friends for many years. Their friendship was second only to the friendship between Mark and Lucas McSween.

Noon came. Jordan looked at the food his captors had left him, but he had no appetite. A bit thirsty, he poured water from the pitcher into a cup and sipped it.

Time dragged by.

It was just after two o'clock when Jordan was picturing what he thought each person in the small wedding party was doing at that moment. Lorene was about to begin putting on her wedding dress with help from their mother, Bessie Hedren, and Annie Colburn. Mark, Knight, Lucas, and whomever Mark had chosen for his other groomsman were probably in the pastor's office.

Suddenly Jordan heard a horse whinny at the front side of the cabin, followed by another horse doing the same. His first thought was that his captors had returned home early, but this changed when he heard wheels grinding on the road, then a mixture of male voices. He could tell that the grinding wheels came to a halt, and he could hear footsteps on the ground.

He couldn't make out what the men were saying, but they apparently were having some kind of problem by the voices.

Jordan looked at the drawn window shade, and wished he could see out. The chain, however, was too short. His captors had made sure he couldn't reach the window.

*I've got to get their attention!* he thought, as he scrambled to his feet. *What can I—Wait a minute! Yes!*

Bending over, he picked up the nearly full water pitcher and hurled it at the window as hard as he could. It sailed through the air, hit the window shade solidly, and shattered the window with a loud crash. The pitcher also shattered, spilling water on the shade and the floor.

"Hey!" he shouted at the top of his lungs. "Help! Help me! Help me!"

Outside on the road, directly in front of the cabin some twenty yards away, four lumberjacks were carrying a load of logs on a large wagon, which they had cut down in the Sawtooth Mountains. They were headed for Fletcher's Sawmill near Ketcham, and had stopped because one of the ropes that secured the logs on the wagon had broken. They were attempting to adjust logs that had shifted and secure them with another rope.

All four stopped what they were doing when they heard the glass shatter and the voice call for help.

Jordan could hear them coming toward the cabin, talking among themselves about what kind of trouble the person inside the cabin might be having. "I'm here!" he called. "Front bedroom!"

Heavy footsteps sounded on the porch, then calloused hands reached through the broken window, pulled the shade aside, and four faces appeared. Jordan recognized them. "Hey, guys!" he shouted, relief evident in his voice. "It's me!"

All four of them stood aghast, eyes bulging.

"Jordan!" gasped Judd Cameron. "You're alive! We heard you were killed and eaten by a grizzly!"

Nick Ferigo pointed at the chain on Jordan's ankle. "Look! He's chained to that post!"

"We're coming in!" said George Bernay.

"Doors are locked." said Jordan. "You'll have to break one open."

"No problem," said Brandon Torveen. "I'll get an ax."

"You'll need a couple of wrenches or pliers to get the chain off me," said Jordan.

"We've got some," said Judd Cameron.

Less than a minute later, the front door was ripped to shreds with an ax, and within a minute after that, the chain was off Jordan's ankle.

"Now tell us about it," said Nick Ferigo. "Who did this to you?"

Quickly, Jordan told them about Ace Decker and Keith Nolan being fired by his father and of his kidnapping as a matter of revenge. He explained that they now worked at Fletcher's Sawmill, but were planning to depart from Idaho and leave him tied up in a cave in the mountains, where he could eventually work his way free.

Judd Cameron told Jordan they were taking their logs to that very mill. Jordan asked them not to say anything to them about having set him free. He would let the marshal deal with them. He then told them Lorene's wedding was about to take place, saying he wanted to get there before it was over.

Brandon Torveen said, "I've got my saddle horse tied on behind the wagon, Jordan. You can take him and return him to my house in Ketcham this evening."

"Oh, thanks, Brandon," said Jordan. "You're a lifesaver!"

At the church in Ketcham, Mark and Lorene left the platform after being pronounced husband and wife and headed quickly for the fellowship hall. The wedding party, family members, and wedding guests followed.

Though there was happiness in the hearts of the bride and groom and their families, there was a note of sadness because Jordan was not with them.

Knight Colburn felt the sadness as he watched Mark and Lorene start cutting the wedding cake. When the cake had been distributed and the wedding guests were passing by the bride and groom to congratulate them, Knight slipped up to them and said that he had to hurry and get to Elkton in time to give Claude Hayward his finished article.

Mark and Lorene thanked him for being a part of the wedding, then encouraged him to hurry. They definitely wanted the article on the front page of Sunday's paper.

Knight headed for the side door of the fellowship hall, waved to his mother and the Shaws, and hurried outside.

He was about to mount his horse when he saw a rider come galloping into the church lot at full speed. When he focused on the rider's face, his blood froze and his eyes bulged.

Skidding to a halt and sliding from the saddle, Jordan set steady eyes on an obviously stunned Knight Colburn. "I'm not a ghost, Knight. It's really me. In the flesh."

Tears gushed from Knight's eyes and he wrapped his arms around his best friend. Knight struggled to gain control of his emotions, then asked what had happened. Jordan gave him a quick but sufficient explanation.

Knight explained that the reception was in progress, then said, "Let's get you in there. Your family is going to be so happy to see that you're alive!"

Jordan was fighting his own emotions. "Shall I just walk in, unannounced?"

"Let me go in ahead of you and sort of prepare them."

Inside the fellowship hall, the bride and groom were still being congratulated while the wedding guests were enjoying cake and punch.

When Knight stepped in, the first to notice him was his mother. Annie hurried to him, noting that he had not closed the door tightly. "Son, is something wrong? I thought you were on your way to the *Sentinel* office."

"I was, Mom," he said, struggling to keep his voice level, "but…well, I have a surprise for everyone."

Annie's brow puckered. "A surprise? What?"

"Not what, Mom. Who."

Shaking her head, she said, "I don't understand."

"You will," he said, motioning toward William and Sylvia, who were looking at him.

They hurried to him, and as they drew up, William said, "What is it, Knight?"

"I have a wonderful surprise for you," said Knight, "and I want the two of you real close to this door. We'll let the bride and groom watch from where they stand by the table."

Sylvia looked perplexed. "Knight, what's going on?"

Smiling, he said, "I'll show you," and turned enough to shove the door open.

When Jordan stepped through the door, Sylvia gasped, throwing her hands to her mouth. "Jordan! Jordan! Oh, it's you! You're alive!"

Every eye in the room was drawn to the scene as William and Sylvia embraced their son, weeping for joy.

At the table, Lorene gripped Mark's arm and stared in shock, hardly daring to believe what her eyes and mind were telling her was true. Letting go of Mark's arm, she gasped her brother's name and slightly tripped on her long dress as she stumbled toward him.

William and Sylvia saw her coming—with Mark following—and moved aside enough to allow brother and sister to embrace.

"Jordan!" cried Lorene as she drew near, opening her arms. "Oh, Jordan! You're alive! You're alive!"

When Lorene's arms encircled her brother, he held her tight.

Squeezing him for fear he might disappear, she kissed his cheek, tears flowing.

"Sorry I'm not dressed for the wedding, sis," Jordan said, grinning at her, "but this is all I could come up with on short notice."

Lorene got a grip on him as she stepped back a little and looked at his filthy, dirt-caked clothes. "You look like a prince to me!" she said, and kissed his cheek again.

There was a joyous reunion as family and friends rushed to Jordan, and after much hugging, kissing, and happy tears, Jordan told his story.

When he had brought everyone up to date, Marshal Woodard stepped close and said in a thin voice, "Jordan, I'm going to Ketcham's marshal and take him with me to that cabin. I want you to draw me a map so we can find it easily."

"Sure, Marshal," said Jordan.

Running his gaze across the faces of the Shaws and their relatives, Woodard said, "I assure all of you that Ace Decker and Keith Nolan will be old men by the time they get out of prison."


That evening, after Knight had delivered his article to Claude Hayward, he and Jordan took a walk together into the fields on the Bar-S to have a little time together.

As the stars twinkled in the black, velvety canopy overhead, Jordan shared the fears and dismay he had suffered at the hands of the kidnappers, saying how good it was to be free and alive. They stopped beside the small brook that wound its way through the ranch, and listened to its pleasant sound.

Laying a hand on Jordan's shoulder, Knight said, "I can't tell you how happy I am to have you alive."

Jordan chuckled. "Thanks, ol' pal."

"But, Jordan…"

"Yes?"

"If that grizzly had come along and killed you while you were chopping wood, you would have died lost. Do you realize where you would be right now if that had happened?"

Jordan drew a deep breath and let it out slowly. "Knight, I'm really not ready to think about salvation right now."

"God has been good to spare your life in all of this," said Knight. "You know I've talked to you about repenting and receiving Jesus into your heart many, many times."

"Yes."

"It's because I care about you. But I can't force you to get saved."

Jordan smiled at him by the starlight. "Knight, you're the best friend a guy could ever have. I know you care about me and where I'm going when I die, and I appreciate it. But I'm just not ready to make that move, yet."

"Well, like I've told you many times before, death can come when you're not ready."

Jordan nodded. "I know. Thanks for caring. Like I said, you're the best friend a guy could ever have."

EIGHT YEARS PASSED.

On a cool, clear October day in 1872, twenty-year-old Tom Wymore entered the Richmond, Virginia, railroad terminal. He approached the large blackboard beneath a sign that said ARRIVALS and noted that the Boston train would arrive on schedule on track number five.

He was about to turn and head for the designated track when a familiar voice from behind said, "Hello, Tom!"

Pivoting, Tom smiled. "Well, Harry! I haven't seen you since we graduated from high school. How are you?"

"Just fine," said Harry Pointer, setting his heavy suitcase down and extending his hand. "And you?"

"Doing well," said Tom as they shook hands. "I knew you had left Richmond, but I didn't know where you went."

"I've been working for my uncle in Knoxville, Tennessee. He's in the construction business. He gave me a week off to come visit my parents. It's a surprise. They don't know I'm coming. I just got off the train. So what have you been doing?"

"Oh, just working. Duane Kitman at Richmond Hardware hired me full time as soon as I graduated."

"I recall that you were working there part time when you were in school."

"Right. I'm assistant manager, now."

"Well, great! I assume you're here to meet someone coming in on a train."

"Yes. My cousin Kent Wymore. He's a year older than me.

Lives in Boston. He could only come for two days, so we're going to spend as much time together as possible. We haven't seen each other for nearly four years."

Harry nodded. "You married?"

"Ah…no. You?"

Harry grinned. "Not yet, but I'm dating a sweet little Tennessee gal with red hair and big blue eyes. Her name's Ellie Trent. I really think Ellie and I will end up at the altar."

"I hope it works out."

"You have any prospects?"

"Well, not really. I've had my eye on a real nice girl. You may remember her—Diana Morrow. She was two years behind us in school."

"Oh, sure! Beautiful brunette with big brown eyes."

"That's her."

"You say you've had your eye on Diana. You mean it's gone no farther than that? You haven't dated her?"

"No. There are some complications."

At that instant, the clanging bell of an arriving train rang out through the terminal.

Tom pulled out his pocket watch and flipped the lid open. "Harry, I've got to get over to track number five. Kent's train is coming in. It sure has been good to see you."

"Same here," said Harry, shaking Tom's hand again. "I sure hope things work out between you and Diana, in spite of those complications you mentioned."

"Thanks," said Tom. "Now you get on home and surprise your parents."

With that, Tom turned and hurried toward the tracks.

The train was just chugging to a halt when he threaded his way through the crowd at track five. Soon passengers were moving out of all four coaches. Tom was positioned in front of the third car, and continually ran his gaze up and down, looking for his cousin.

Suddenly he spotted Kent descending from the rear platform of the first coach. Kent was off the steps and moving away from the train, overnight bag in hand, when he saw Tom. He smiled, waved, and headed for him.

Both young men were about the same size and build. When they drew up, Kent set his bag down, and they embraced, pounding each other on the back.

"Sure is good to see you, cuz!" said Kent.

"Same here, cuz!" said Tom. "This all your luggage?"

"Yes."

"I'll carry it for you. We're walking to my house."

Kent picked the bag up quickly. "Thanks, but I'll carry it."

Tom shrugged, grinned, and said, "Whatever makes you happy. Come on. Let's go."

As they stepped out of the terminal into the bright sunshine and headed for Main Street, Tom said, "I'm taking the next two days off so we can have as much time as possible together."

"Good! That's why I'm here!"

They reached Main Street and turned south toward the neighborhood where the Zack Wymore family lived. Moving down the boardwalk, they stopped frequently as they came upon friends of Tom's, and he introduced them to his cousin.

After having stopped for the fifth time, they hurried across an intersection between traffic, and moved once again along the boardwalk. Suddenly Tom stopped, eyeing a farm wagon that was just pulling up in front of the general store across the street. At the reins was a big muscular farmer in his early forties. Beside him was his wife, and in the wagon bed were their five children.

Kent was three steps ahead of him before he realized that his cousin was no longer beside him. He turned around and saw Tom peering across the street. Looking that way for an instant, he turned and walked back to Tom. "I assume you're looking at that wagon load of farmers."

"Yes," said Tom, without taking his eyes off them.

"You must know them."

Tom nodded, his eyes still fixed on them. "That beautiful eighteen-year-old girl in the back with the other young ones is Diana Morrow. I've had a crush on her since we were in school together. The family has a farm nine miles west of town."

Kent focused on the girl, admiring her long brunette hair as it adorned her magnificently sculptured features, then cascaded down in waves to her shoulders and down her back. Her dark brown eyes were soft pools, rimmed with sooty black lashes.

"She is quite good looking," said Kent. "Have you dated her?"

"No. But not by choice."

"She doesn't like you?"

"It's not that. It's her father. Take a look at the size of him."

"Yeah," said Kent. "He's a whopper."

"Stuart Morrow is a rough, bullheaded man, as well as a whopper. He won't let Diana date anyone. There are plenty of other young men in town and the surrounding area who would love to date her, but her father's mean temperament keeps them from trying. I've let the same fear keep me from trying, too. But... well, I've just about worked up the nerve to approach the man and ask him if I could take Diana on a date."

Kent smiled. "Well, she is a lovely girl. I hope you are successful whenever you get the rest of your nerve up."

Tom sighed, keeping his eyes on Diana. "Me too."


At the Morrow wagon, big Stu touched ground as his wife, Martha, began to climb down by herself, struggling with her long skirt.

Seventeen-year-old Derick hopped out of the wagon bed and offered his hand to his mother. While he was helping her down, ten-year-old Daniel moved to the tailgate, opened it, and hopped down. He offered his hand to Diana, and when she was out of the wagon, he helped thirteen-year-old Deborah down, then took his little five-year-old brother, Dennis, in his arms and placed him on the board sidewalk.

Dennis coughed, covering his mouth.

Diana's massive father stepped up to her and placed money in her hand. "Diana, go down to the pharmacy and pick up the cough syrup for Dennis. And hurry back. No dillydallying. Understand?"

"Yes, Papa," said Diana. She turned and headed down the boardwalk toward the pharmacy.

Across the street, Tom Wymore watched Diana while the rest

of her family filed into the general store. "Come on, Kent. I want to introduce you to Diana."

Kent hurried to keep up with his cousin as they angled across the street so as to intercept Diana before she got to wherever she was going. When Diana saw Tom coming toward her, she stopped and looked over her shoulder to make sure her father was out of sight.

Relieved that he was, she looked at Tom and a bright smile lit up her face. "Hello, Tom."

"Hello, yourself," he said, stepping up on the wooden sidewalk. "It's nice to see you. Diana, I want you to meet my cousin Kent Wymore. Kent, this is Diana Morrow. I've known her since I was in fourth grade and she was in second grade."

Being this close to the girl, Kent was struck anew at just how lovely she was. When she smiled timidly, saying she was glad to meet him, and offered her hand, Kent took notice of the two perfect rows of white, even teeth sparkling within her creamy complexion.

The smile was indeed pretty, but Kent saw that it did not reach her eyes. There was deep sadness hidden in their depths.

Kent also noticed that though Diana's clothes were neat and clean, they had a threadbare quality about them and her high-top shoes were scuffed and worn.

He stepped back after shaking her small, rough hand, and Tom moved up to take the place Kent had just occupied. "Guess we haven't talked for a month or so, Diana. That's too long. I'd really like to talk to you every day if I could."

"Really?" she said, glancing nervously over her shoulder, then turning back to him.

"Yes, really. I— Well, I—"

Tilting her head and blinking, she said, "What, Tom?"

Wymore swallowed with difficulty, cleared his throat, and swallowed again. "Diana, I—I've never told you, but I think it's time I do."

Her brow furrowed. "Tell me what, Tom?"

"Well, I—" He choked, then cleared his throat again. "Diana, I've liked you in a special way for a long time. I would really like to date you."

Diana's face stiffened, then softened quickly. "Tom...I would love to go on a date with you, but my father would never allow it." She took another look behind her, and sighed with relief when there was no sign of her father.

"I know your father is a hard man to deal with," said Tom, "but I have worked up the nerve to ask him...that is, if you will go on a date with me."

"Of course I would, Tom, but you don't understand just how hard my father is to deal with on this matter. It would really be a dangerous thing to—"

Tom's attention was drawn down the street past Diana, and she saw him flinch. She noticed Kent tense up.

Diana turned around and saw that her father had come out of the general store with a large sack of potatoes on his shoulder. He was standing there staring at her.

Tom knew it would only be a moment before Stu Morrow was on them.

Suddenly, the big man dumped the sack in the wagon and stomped up the boardwalk toward them, his face beet red.

Kent said hastily, "Tom, he looks real mad."

"Tom," Diana said, her voice quivering, "take Kent and go. Quick!"

Thinking there was no time like the present, Tom squared his shoulders and said, "Diana, it's time I talk to your father about dating you."

"No!" she said in a whisper. "You don't understand! He'll—"

"Diana!" bawled the man as he drew up. "How dare you talk to a man without my permission!"

Taking a step toward him, Tom said, "Mr. Morrow, I—"

"You shut your mouth!" boomed Stu in an eruption of anger. "I wasn't addressing you!"

Embarrassed, Diana said, "Papa, Tom and I went almost all the way through school together. He was two years ahead of me, but we became friends. I saw no harm in talking to him."

Scowling, Stu stuck out his palm. "Gimme the money for Dennis's cough medicine. You go immediately into the store with your mother and siblings."

Tom noted the people passing by, looking on, and decided to proceed with his plan. "Mr. Morrow," he said, "I've always liked Diana very much, and I'm asking you to allow me to take her on a date."

"She's too young to date anybody!" said Stu.

"But sir," said Tom, "many young women her age are already married."

Stu said, "Diana, get going!"

"Mr. Morrow," Tom proceeded, his heart pounding, "Diana deserves the opportunity to date young men. I'm asking you for permission to date her."

There was a dead silence as Stu weighed Tom with a sharp, penetrating glance. In that brief instant of time, Tom's and Diana's eyes met. Tom saw the pain and longing there; something akin to the longing in his own heart.

His beefy features suffused with a purplish red, Stu said in a dead level tone, "I'm gonna give you a chance to walk away in one piece, boy. You gonna take it?"

*I don't stand a chance against this big brute,* Tom thought. *Guess I better walk away and let him cool down.*

"Diana!" roared Stu. "Go!"

Not daring to look at Tom again, Diana handed her father the money and headed down the street. The small crowd that was observing the scene stood in silence, wondering what Tom was going to do.

Turning to his cousin, Tom said, "Come on, Kent. Let's go."

"You stay away from my daughter, boy, y'hear me!" said Stu, then stomped past them toward the pharmacy.

The crowd broke up.

"Sorry about the scene, cuz," said Tom. "Everybody in these parts knows the man is a brute to his family, but no one knows what to do about it."

Kent nodded silently.

Tom put an arm around Kent's shoulder. "Let's go."

They had only taken a few steps when Tom saw Diana standing at the door of the general store, looking at him. He smiled at her.

She smiled in return and moved inside.

—⁓— ⁓— —⁓—

At the Morrow farm two days later, Diana sat on a chair next to the kitchen table, holding a wet cloth to her mouth while a tearful Deborah looked on.

Potato soup was cooking on the stove, filling the room with its pleasant scent.

Martha was at the cupboard, taking iodine and salve from a shelf.

Turning about, she set them on the table and bent over a pale-faced Diana. "Let me look at it again."

Diana removed the cloth to expose the split upper lip that was oozing blood. Martha took the cloth from her hand and dabbed at the flow. "Now, tell me…why did your father hit you?"

"When I went in the barn to tell Papa lunch would be ready in half an hour, he was whipping Daniel with a belt. I was afraid he was going to seriously hurt Daniel. I asked him to stop. He stopped long enough to curse at me and hit me on the mouth with his fist. The blow knocked me down and stunned me. When my head cleared, he was still beating on Daniel, and blood was running from my lip."

Martha shook her head and wiped at the cut again. "Deborah, honey, wet another one of those pieces of cloth on the cupboard for me, will you?"

While a teary-eyed Deborah followed her mother's order, the three of them talked about the beatings Stu had given Martha and all the children when they made him angry. Martha commented that he was hardest on Diana because she was the oldest of the children, and on other occasions she had tried to interfere when her father was savagely beating on her siblings, and he had struck her for it as he had done today.

Handing her mother the freshly wetted cloth, Deborah sniffed and said, "And how about the times Papa has been beating on you and Diana tried to interfere, Mama? He hit her every one of those times, too."

Martha used the wet cloth to clean away the blood and applied iodine to the cut. "Diana, I'm so sorry for the way your father treats you."

Barely moving her lips as she spoke, Diana said, "If it weren't for you and my brothers and Deborah, I'd run away from home, Mama. I don't know where I'd go, but I would do it."

A look of pure terror crossed her mother's face. "Oh, please, Diana, don't even think that way! Your father would track you down, and—what he would do to you when he caught you is…is unthinkable."

Tears ran in rivulets down Martha's cheeks, and she brushed a shaky hand across her eyes in a futile attempt to stem the flow.

Diana's heart was immediately contrite at having caused her mother more pain. Martha was about to put salve on top of the iodine when Diana wrapped her arms around her and hugged her close. "I'm sorry, Mama. I didn't mean to upset you. I said if it weren't for you and my siblings, I would run away. Believe me, I would never do anything to cause this pitiful, hurting family any more grief."

As she spoke, Diana rubbed her hand over her mother's stooped back, trying to smooth away some of the pain. By her loving touch, the bond between the mother and her daughter grew stronger.

Deborah joined them, and all three held to each other for a long moment.

When their tears were dried, Martha went back to work on Diana's lip, coating it with salve. When she was finished, the bleeding was in check, and the three of them talked about the incident in town with Tom Wymore two days ago.

"I'm so glad Tom didn't push your father any further," said Martha. "He would have been in real trouble if he had."

"With Papa's temper," said Deborah, "that's for sure. Papa would have beaten him up good."

"That's what would happen to any of those young men who have shown interest in you, Diana," said Martha. "It's too bad. There are at least ten young men who have shown interest in you in the last couple of years, most you have known since you were quite young."

Diana nodded and wiped away a fresh tear. "Every one of them told me they would not make an attempt to date me because of

Papa. He has them frightened and intimidated. I...I especially like Tom. And he feels the same way about me. He proved that two days ago. But since Papa is so set against me dating, nothing can ever come of it."

"At least Tom showed that he wasn't afraid to ask Papa if he could date you," said Deborah.

"Yes. I admire him for that. But like Mama said, I'm glad he didn't push Papa any further."

Deborah looked at Martha, her brow deeply lined. "Mama, why is Papa so mean?"

Martha licked her lips, shook her head, and said, "Honey, I don't know. He wasn't like that when he courted me, or I never would have married him. He started showing his mean streak not long after your sister was born. But I can't tell you why."

Tears were trickling down Diana's cheeks. "Mama, it's only natural that I want romance, love, and marriage. But...but it will never happen as long as I live in this house. My only hope is to leave home and get away from the Richmond area altogether. In fact, I'll probably have to get clear out of Virginia."

Martha's features pinched. "Oh, honey, I can't stand the thought of your leaving home."

In her heart, Martha wanted to encourage Diana, but what could she say? Diana was right.

Deborah's voice trembled as she said, "It'll be the same for me, Mama, when I reach Diana's age. I'll have to leave home for any chance to fall in love and marry. Papa will never let it happen."

"The thing that frightens me about it is that if either one of you left home, your father would find you, and probably beat you half to death. You know how angry he—"

Martha's words were cut off by the sound of Stu and the boys climbing the back porch steps. All three looked toward the back door, eyes showing their intimidation.

The door came open, and Stu's huge frame appeared first, followed by Derick, Daniel, and Dennis.

"Lunch ready?" boomed the big man, removing his dirty old hat and tossing it on a wall peg by the door.

"Just about," said Martha, moving to the stove. "I was patching up Diana's lip. You men get washed up."

Stu's face took on a sour look as he stomped to the small table where the wash bowl sat beside a bucket of water.

While their father was washing his hands, Derick and Daniel slipped up close to Diana.

"I'm sorry Papa hit you, Diana," whispered Daniel. "I feel bad that you had to get hurt because of me. But thanks for trying to protect me."

Diana smiled in spite of the pain it caused. "I'd do it again," she breathed softly.

"That's the kind of sister you are," said Derick in a low voice. "You're the best sister a guy could ever have. But I'm sorry about your lip."

Stu whirled around with a towel in his hands and roared, "I'm not deaf! I heard what you boys said. Don't be feeling sorry for Diana. She had no business interfering when I was disciplining Daniel!"

The boys' eyes widened, fear etching itself on their young faces.

Fixing Diana with a hot glare, Stu pointed a stiff finger at her and shook it. "If you ever do it again, I'm gonna beat you within an inch of your life!"

The look in her father's eyes put a chill down Diana's spine.

7

ON WEDNESDAY MORNING of the following week, the Morrow family climbed into the wagon and headed for town to buy groceries for the family and grain for their cows and horses.

It was a beautiful fall day, with the sun shining down from a nearly cloudless sky, highlighting the brilliant colors of the leaves on the trees.

Dennis sat between his parents on the wagon seat, and the other four sat in the bed as usual.

As Stu guided the wagon onto the road and headed toward town, he turned his head so all could hear. "I'll leave you girls off at the general store with your mother, and I'll take you boys with me to the seed store. We should be able to wrap it all up in an hour or so."

Dennis looked up at his mother. "Would you get us some hard candy, Mama?"

Martha smiled down at him, patted his head, and said, "I think we can manage that."

Holding the reins with both hands, Stu jutted his jaw. "No candy, Martha."

Martha's brow furrowed as she looked at her husband. "Stu, I thought we settled this issue. The children haven't had candy for over a month. Didn't we agree that they could have some next time we went to the store?"

"Well, yeah, but I changed my mind after Daniel had to go to the dentist with that cavity two weeks ago. Candy makes cavities, and dentists cost money. No candy."

"Daniel's cavity couldn't have been caused by candy," Martha argued mildly. "He hasn't had that much. Neither have the rest of them. A little candy now and then isn't going to—"

"I said no candy!" he snapped.

Dennis laid his head against his mother's arm and began to sniffle.

"Enough of that, Dennis!" said Stu. "Dry it up! Right now."

At that instant, Stu looked up ahead and saw two wagons standing abreast in the road. One was headed toward town, and the other, the opposite direction. He recognized his neighbors, Shamus and Maggie O'Hearn, in the wagon that was headed toward town. He couldn't make out who they were talking to in the other wagon.

"Oh, look!" said Martha, pointing with her chin. "It's Shamus and Maggie. I can't tell who the other people are."

Derick—who was known to have extra keen eyes—was up on his knees, looking between his parents. "It's that Pastor Bradford and his wife."

Stu's countenance fell.

Martha saw it, and silently hoped he wouldn't make a scene. The wagons were blocking the road.

Soon the Morrows were drawing near, and Martha mentally released a sigh when she saw the Bradford wagon backing up. By the time they reached the spot, the Bradford wagon was in line with the O'Hearn vehicle, giving ample room for the Morrow wagon to get by.

Stu did not slow a bit.

As they passed the wagons, Martha called a greeting to their neighbors, as did the children, then she called out a thank-you to the pastor for giving them room to get by. Both the pastor and his wife smiled and waved.

Stu kept his eyes straight ahead, refusing to acknowledge any of them.

As the Morrow wagon continued on toward Richmond, Pastor Sherman Bradford pulled his wagon up beside the O'Hearn vehicle once more and said, "My heart is so heavy for that family."

"We know what you mean, Pastor," said Shamus. "I do believe

there would be a chance to reach Martha and the children if it weren't for Stu. He really has a high wall built up between himself and the Lord."

"I know," said the pastor. "I've been to their house on four occasions, wanting to give them the gospel and invite them to church. The first three, it was Martha or the oldest boy, Derick, who answered my knock. I could tell they were frightened just at my presence on the place. Each time, I was told that they didn't go to church and weren't interested in going—before I could get a word out.

"On the fourth occasion, which was about six months ago, Diana opened the door, but Stu came thundering up behind her immediately, and swore at me, telling me to get off his property and to stay off. He repeated angrily that I was never to step foot on the place again. So...of course, I haven't."

"It really grieves me," said Maggie. "I've known Martha a long time. She and I started first grade together at the old country school on Creighton Road. We were close friends until about two years after she married Stu. Something happened not long after Diana was born, and suddenly Stu got hard to live with. He wouldn't let Martha have anything to do with other people. It's still that way. The only time we get to see each other is if we happen to meet on the street in town or in a store."

"I know you've had opportunities to talk to Martha about the Lord in the five years that you and Shamus have been saved," said Lois Bradford. "You've mentioned a couple of them to me."

"Yes," said Maggie, her eyes misting.

"What kind of response have you gotten?"

"Most of the time, she just gets this frightened look in her eyes and politely changes the subject. I know it's because Stu is so mean and cantankerous. She's scared to death of what he would do if she became a Christian."

"And didn't she say something to you about if God loved her like you were saying He did, why did He let her life be so miserable?" asked Shamus.

"Yes. It was about a year ago, when she and I met on the street, and no one we knew was near. I was able to give her my complete testimony and explain to her what brought about my salvation and yours, too, dear. I quoted several Scripture verses on the subject of salvation and told her that God loved her so much he sent His only begotten Son to die on the cross for her, and that He wanted to save her.

"That was when she said, 'Well, Maggie, if God loves me like you say He does, why did He let my life turn out so miserable?' She went on to say that she couldn't provide for her children by herself if she left Stu, so she had to stay with him and live in misery."

"Bless her heart," said Lois. "It must be terrible living with a man like Stuart Morrow."

"You're right about that," said Maggie. "When Martha said that about having to stay with him and live in misery, she added that even if she tried leaving Stu, taking the children, and going elsewhere, he would come after them and when he found them, he would give her a good beating."

"We need to pray harder about this," said the preacher. "God can handle Stu."

"Right," said Shamus.

"I've had other brief opportunities since then," said Maggie. "With each one, I've quoted more Scripture and told her lovingly how much I want to see her come to the Lord. She has even thanked me for caring, but that same fear is always present in her eyes."

Shamus laid a hand on Maggie's shoulder. "We'll just have to do as Pastor says, honey, and pray more earnestly about the whole Morrow family."

"Yes," said Bradford. "I ran into Diana and Deborah on the street in town about a month ago. They were talking to the Meyer sisters, whom they knew from school. As you know, Betty and Barbara Meyer come to our church."

Shamus and Maggie nodded.

"At that time," the pastor proceeded, "I invited Diana and Deborah to come to church and Sunday school. They thanked me politely, but said nothing more. I met them on the street again a few days later, when they were alone. They told me then that they would like to come to church, but couldn't because their father would not allow it. Which, of course, did not surprise me. They also commented on how angry their father became each time I had visited the Morrow home. I could see the fear in their eyes. It's obvious. They live in constant fear of the man. It grieves my heart. They are such sweet girls."

"That they are," said Maggie.

"Well," said Bradford, "Lois and I need to make some calls on some of your other neighbors. See you Sunday."

"You sure will, Pastor," said Shamus, snapping the reins. "All right, Maggie, let's head for town."

Stu Morrow pulled the wagon up in front of the general store. He said to Martha, "The boys and I will be back in an hour or so."

Derick and Daniel hopped out of the wagon bed, and while Daniel helped his sisters out, Derick hurried up to the side of the wagon, took his mother's hand, and helped her down. Both boys jumped back in the bed, and Stu put the wagon in motion.

As mother and daughters stood on the boardwalk and watched the wagon blend into the traffic, Diana said dolefully, "It isn't going to take Papa and the boys an hour to get the grain, Mama. I know what else Papa's going to do."

Deborah sighed. "Me too. He's going to stop at one of the taverns."

Martha nodded solemnly. "I'm sure he is."

"Oh, Mama," said Diana, "I wish Papa wouldn't drink. It always makes him even meaner."

"I know, honey," said Martha, "but there's nothing we can do about it. I'm at least thankful that he never gets staggering drunk. He knows when to quit before that happens."

Deborah pointed down the street. "Look, Diana! It's Laura and Becky."

Their friends spotted them at the same time, and called to them, waving.

"You girls talk to your friends for a while," said Martha. "I'll go on in the store and get started."

"All right, Mama," said Diana.

The Morrow girls were chatting with their friends from school when they noticed the O'Hearn wagon pull up. Shamus and Maggie both smiled at them, and Diana and Deborah smiled back.

Shamus hopped out of the wagon, and as he helped Maggie down from the seat, she said, "Girls, is your mother in the store?"

"Yes," said Diana.

Picking up a pair of well-worn shoes from the wagon bed, Shamus told Maggie he would see her in a few minutes, and headed down the street toward the shoe repair shop.

Laura and Becky excused themselves and crossed the street to join their mother.

As Maggie O'Hearn moved closer to the Morrow girls, she noted Diana's black-and-blue mouth and the cut on her upper lip. "Honey, what happened? How did you cut your lip?"

Diana flicked a glance at her sister, then looked back at Maggie. "I…ah…fell down, Mrs. O'Hearn."

Deborah's mouth bent downward. "Diana, tell her the truth," she said flatly.

Diana cleared her throat, looked away, then faced Maggie again. "Well, I…ah…Papa hit me. He was severely beating Daniel, and I tried to stop him. It made him mad, so he hit me and knocked me down."

Maggie's eyes took on extra moisture and she lay a tender hand on Diana's arm. "Honey, I'm sorry you had to suffer because you were trying to protect your brother."

Diana shrugged. "That's just the way it is at our house."

At that instant three teenage girls came out of the general store and rushed up to Diana and Deborah, saying they had just talked to their mother in the store. Maggie saw that the Morrow girls were going to be talking to their friends, so she excused herself and entered the store.

It took only a moment for Maggie to spot Martha near the rear of the store at the fruit and vegetable tables. She waved, heading that way, and Martha waved back. When they came together, Martha greeted Maggie with a loving embrace. "I'm sorry we hurried past you and the Bradfords so fast. But as you know, Stu doesn't want anything to do with the preacher."

"Yes," Maggie said in a sad tone. "I wish it wasn't so. Shamus and I were just saying on our way into town, how much we would love to see your whole family come to church, and—"

"And be saved," Martha finished for her.

"Yes. Of course you don't have to come to church to be saved, honey. You could ask Jesus into your heart right here and now if you wanted to."

Martha nodded. "I understand that." She remembered all the times Stu had struck her in anger, and thought, *If I should ever become a Christian—as Maggie has so lovingly urged me to—Stu would beat me to death. No matter how wonderful salvation sounds, I could never do it. What would happen to my children if I weren't here to give them whatever protection I can?*

Sighing deeply within herself, Martha said, "Did you see my girls out front?"

Knowing her friend was avoiding the subject of salvation as she had done many times before, Maggie vowed in her heart to pray more earnestly for her. "Yes, and I saw that cut on Diana's lip. She tried to cover for her father when I asked her how it happened, but Deborah spoke up and told her to tell me the truth."

A crimson tide of embarrassment flooded Martha's lovely face.

Smiling, Maggie said, "Don't worry, honey. I won't let the cat out of the bag to anyone else. Except Shamus, of course."

Even as she spoke those last words, Maggie looked at Martha's left cheek and squinted at the fading purple mark there. "Did Stu hit you, too? Like the other times your face has had bruises?"

Martha's fingers went to the spot. Her face flushed again. "Well, ah—"

"Come on, honey," she said, laying a gentle hand on her arm, "this is your old friend, Maggie. You can tell me."

Martha's eyes filmed up. "Yes," she reluctantly admitted. "It was about ten days ago. Stu lost his temper and hit me."

Anger pulsed through Maggie like the steady beat of a clock. Eyebrows knitted together, she said stiffly, "He ought to have some big, strong man show him what it feels like."

At the feed and grain store, Stu and the two older boys finished loading feed sacks while little Dennis stood on his knees on the wagon seat and observed.

Derick and Daniel climbed in the wagon bed with the sacks while their father mounted the seat. Stu put the team in motion, and headed down the street in the direction of the general store, which was six blocks away.

After covering two blocks, Stu guided the horses to a stop in front of the Golden Lantern Tavern. Derick and Daniel exchanged fearful glances, knowing their father always became meaner than usual when he got liquor in him.

With a slight quiver in his voice, Derick said, "Papa, don't you think we ought to get on down to the general store? Mama will probably be ready soon."

Scowling, Stu said, "I'll only be a few minutes. You boys stay in the wagon. Don't be climbing down to look in store windows or something. Understand?"

"Yes, Papa," said Derick. "We'll stay in the wagon."

"Good," said the man, lowering himself to the ground. "You know what'll happen if you disobey me."

"We won't, Papa," Daniel assured him.

Stu gave each one a hard look, then made his way across the boardwalk and entered the tavern.


Down the street at the general store, Diana and Deborah finished talking to their three friends, and as they headed for the door, a female voice called Diana's name from across the street. She and Deborah turned to see two more of their friends from school threading through the heavy traffic to join them.


Inside the general store, Martha and Maggie had been joined by Shamus, and all three were enjoying their conversation when Martha's eyes strayed to the big clock on the wall above the back door. A little trickle of fear ran down her spine. There would be trouble if she hadn't finished her shopping when Stu returned. "Oh, dear!" she said. "I'm sorry, but I've got to finish my grocery shopping before Stu gets back. Nice talking to you Maggie, Shamus. Hope we can run into each other again soon."

"Real soon, I hope," said Maggie.

"Me too," chimed in Shamus. "And Martha…"

"Yes?"

"Maggie and I are here for you and the children if you ever need us."

Smiling nervously, Martha dipped her head in an embarrassed nod. "Thank you."

As they watched Martha hurry away in a fidgety gait, Shamus said in a low tone from the side of his mouth, "Such a pity, Maggie. Such a pity."


At the Morrow wagon, Derick and Daniel were trying to keep their active little brother occupied while their father was in the tavern.

Almost half an hour had passed when Stu emerged from the Golden Lantern. Though his walk was steady, the effects of the alcohol were already showing in his watery eyes and his reddened cheeks. The boys looked at each other in fear, dreading whatever might come their way.

Stu ran his whiskey-influenced gaze to his sons as he climbed onto the seat and growled, "You boys didn't get out of the wagon, did you?"

"No, Papa," said Derick. "We did as you said."

"Good," grunted Stu, taking reins in hand and putting the team in motion. "Saves you from being whipped."


On the board sidewalk in front of the general store, the third set of friends told Diana and Deborah good-bye, and as the sisters turned to enter the store, Diana saw Tom Wymore hurrying toward her, angling across the street, smiling and waving.

Her heart leaped in her chest, and her breath went tight in her lungs. "Deborah!" she gasped. "It's Tom!"

Following her sister's line of sight, Deborah said, "Looks like he wants to talk to you."

"What am I going to do? Papa will be showing up any minute!"

Deborah glanced up the street to see if the family wagon was in sight. "The traffic is heavy, but I don't see Papa and the boys right now," she said, her voice trembling.

Fear etched itself on Diana's face as Tom drew up. Seeing it, he said, "Is it all right if we talk?"

"Tom, I'm glad to see you," she said, "but Papa will be coming any minute. He went to the feed store. Since he told you to stay away from me, he will really be angry if he sees us together."

A serious look came over Tom's countenance. "Diana, I really like you a lot. I think about you all the time. Do…do you feel anything like that toward me?"

Diana managed a tiny smile. "I like you very much, Tom. And I would like to date you, but my father won't let me. You saw how he was when he saw us together before."

Tom rubbed his chin. "Diana, I want to date you more than anything in the world. I…would really like for us to become close. I don't mean to be too forward, but I'm very much attracted to you. I'll wait till your father shows up and try to reason with him."

Diana's lips pulled into a thin line, and she began to wring her hands. "Tom, I…I'm afraid for you."

"You mean, what your father might do to me?"

"Yes."

"Certainly he will listen to reason."

Diana was shaking her head as Deborah said, "Tom, you don't understand. Our father can get real mean when he's angry. And he will get real angry if you try to reason with him. Don't try to talk to him."

"But—"

"Please," Deborah said, "Papa's mind is made up. You won't be able to reason with him. He says Diana is too young to date. Nothing will change his mind."

Tom shook his head. "But most girls her age are either engaged or are already married."

"I have tried to get Papa to see this, Tom," said Diana. "And so has Mama. But he will not listen."

Tom sighed, shook his head again. "Well, has he told you how old you have to be before you can date young men?"

"He has never said."

"Hmm. Diana, I doubt you will ever be old enough in your father's eyes. He probably wants you to be an old maid."

Unknowingly, Tom Wymore had just stated what Diana had secretly feared for a long time.

When Tom saw her eyes mist up and her brow pucker, he said, "I'm sorry, Diana. I didn't mean to upset you."

Looking deep into his eyes, she said, "You don't have to be sorry, Tom. It isn't your fault my father is like he is. And I would love to be close to you, too. But it just can't be."

Tom took a deep breath and smiled. "That sure is a pretty dress you're wearing. It really brings out the brown in your eyes. I—"

"Diana!" gasped Deborah, grabbing her sister's arm. "Here comes Papa!"

Terror struck Diana's heart as she turned and saw the Morrow wagon pulling up. Her father's watery eyes were wild with anger as he saw Tom with Diana.

WHILE STU MORROW WAS CLIMBING DOWN from the wagon seat, Derick got Diana's attention and used signals as if he was holding a bottle and putting it to his lips, so she would know for sure that their father had been drinking.

Deborah saw it, too, and whispered, "He looks real mad, Diana."

Diana nodded, a sick feeling settling in her stomach.

Tom Wymore licked his lips nervously as Stu stomped toward him, his immense spread of shoulders twitching. Stu's face was flushed from whiskey and anger, and the hostility grew in his eyes as he fixed them on Tom. He swore at Tom and yelled at the top of his voice, "Didn't I tell you to stay away from my daughter?"

As Tom was opening his mouth to reply, Stu looked at Diana. "I told you I didn't want you in this hammerhead's company, didn't I?"

Diana was so frightened she couldn't speak. Deborah was gripping her arm with a trembling hand. The boys were climbing down from the wagon, their eyes fixed on their father, wondering if he was going to hurt Tom. They and their sisters knew how dangerous their father could be—especially when he had whiskey in him.

People on the boardwalk were stopping to look on, eyes wide.

Stu was running his hot gaze between Diana and Tom, waiting for one of them to reply.

Diana looked up at Tom, found her voice, and it came out with a tremor as she said, "Tom, it would be best if you leave right now."

Shaking his head slowly, Tom said, "Diana, I can't. My feelings for you are strong, and I can't wait any longer." Then to Stu, he spoke in a grave voice: "Mr. Morrow, can't we talk like gentlemen?"

Stu stiffened his back and rolled his wide shoulders. His reddened features remained solid as a stone image. "If you were a gentleman, you'd stay away from my daughter like I told you!"

"Sir, I have very strong feelings toward Diana. I know she likes me. She has said so. Please be reasonable. Diana is eighteen years old. She is a young woman, no longer a child. She has a right to male companionship. I would love to date her so if something is supposed to develop between us, it will have the opportunity. With all due respect, sir, you shouldn't stand in the way of Diana finding the right young man for her."

The crowd on the street was growing, and people were gawking at the potentially violent scene. Most of them knew Stu Morrow, and that he had an uncontrollable temper.

Stu stood there, looking at Tom with flaming eyes, his rage growing hotter. His mouth was dry, and his voice sounded as if it were coming from outside his own body as he bellowed, "Don't you get insolent with me, bub!"

"I'm not being insolent, Mr. Morrow," Tom said defensively. "I'm just trying to reason with you. You are not being fair to Diana."

Stu's big right fist struck out savagely. It connected with Tom's jaw and sent him sprawling into the dusty street.

Diana let out a tiny squeal, her hands going to her mouth. Deborah looked on, anguish twisting her young face. The boys stared, openmouthed, as did many in the crowd.

For a moment the world spun and blurred in front of Tom Wymore's eyes. There was extreme pain in his jaw. He gasped. His breath caught and his vision cleared, and he saw Stu Morrow—big as a mountain—coming toward him.

Tom tried to get up but before he could, Stu sent a swift, vicious kick into his ribs, driving the breath out of him. Cursing him, Stu kicked him repeatedly in the ribs, doubling him over with the pain.

People in the crowd stood frozen in place. Stu was too big and strong for any of the men present to take him on.

In desperation, Tom grasped Stu's foot when he was kicked for the seventh or eighth time and twisted it with all the strength he had left. Surprised, the big man went down, making a cloud of dust as he hit the street.

At the same time, Tom scrambled to his feet, holding his ribs.

While Stu was swearing and getting up, Tom said in a tight, pain-filled voice, "Mr. Morrow, fighting isn't going to settle anything. As Diana's father, you must realize that she has a right to a normal life, and to happiness."

Diana and her siblings were clinging to each other, fear evident in their faces.

Breathing hotly, Stu gained his feet and stood to full height. His big head settled into his shoulders until his neck was no longer visible, and there was a low, rumbling sound in his throat. He charged Tom like an angry bull, swinging both fists.

While Tom was trying to avoid the fists without striking back, one man said he was going after a constable. Even as the man hurried away, Stu overwhelmed Tom with one powerful blow after another. Diana let out a cry as Tom went down, sprawling on his back, obviously unconscious. He was bleeding at the nose and mouth.

By this time, Martha Morrow had come out of the store and was standing with her children, looking on in horror.

Suddenly Diana rushed to Tom, sobbing as she dropped to her knees beside him. "Tom!" she cried, while caressing his face. "Tom! Wake up!"

While the crowd observed the scene, Stu barked at his wife: "Martha, get the kids in the wagon!"

"But...but...the groceries," she said.

"Forget the groceries!" Stu boomed. "Do what I tell you!"

Martha said to the boys and Deborah, "Do as your father said."

While Derick was helping his mother up into the seat and Daniel was lifting his little brother into the wagon bed, Deborah climbed in on her own, weeping.

Stu stood over the sobbing Diana, and growled, "Get in the wagon, girl!"

Diana looked up through a veil of tears. "He's hurt, Papa! Can't you see he's unconscious? He needs a doctor!"

Stu grabbed her by the arm and jerked her to her feet. "I said get in the wagon!"

Wincing from the pain, Diana blinked against her tears. "But Papa! I've got to help him."

"Someone else can do that!" said Stu. "He should have stayed away from you like I told him. If he needs a doctor, it's his own fault."

"Papa, I can't leave him! I've got to make sure he's taken care of."

Stu swore, picked her up, carried her to the wagon bed, and roughly dumped her in. She was sobbing as he climbed into the seat beside a horrified Martha, snapped the reins, and put the horses in motion. When traffic cleared at the intersection in front of him, he put the team to a gallop.

As they left the outskirts of Richmond, Diana slumped over and continued to cry. Deborah, who sat beside her, took hold of her sister's hand, squeezing it tight. Derick moved to the other side and took hold of the other hand.

Martha reached back from the seat and laid a hand on her shoulder. "Don't worry, honey. Tom will be taken care of. Those people who were there will see that he gets to a doctor."

"It's his own fault!" growled Stu without looking back. "I told him in plain words to stay away from her! He defied me, he got hurt."

Martha looked at her husband. "You didn't have to hit him, and you didn't have to be so brutal."

Stu met her gaze coldly. "He got what he deserved. Maybe now he'll listen to me."

"But—"

"Don't argue with me, woman! I'm in no mood for it."

Martha bit her lower lip, looked back at her sobbing daughter, and patted her shoulder. Diana looked up at her, blinking at her tears.

Dennis crawled up close to his big sister. "Don't worry, Diana. Tom will be all right."

Diana released her hand from Derick's grip long enough to tenderly pat Dennis's cheek. "I hope so."

When the Morrows arrived home and entered the house, Diana was still weeping over Tom.

"That's enough bawling, Diana. Dry it up! You were as wrong as Tom was. You shouldn't have been standing there on the street, talking to him. You're supposed to obey me, and instead, you defy me."

Wiping tears, Diana said, "Papa, why are you so unreasonable? What Tom said was true. I have a right to a normal life and happiness. And you are keeping me from both. Why? Why can't I date like other girls? And don't tell me it's because I'm too young. You and I both know that isn't true."

Martha saw the rage building in her husband. She stepped up beside Diana, touched her arm, and said, "Honey, let's you and I get lunch started."

"Just a minute!" boomed Stu, the rage blazing in his eyes. "Diana, you've got no business talking to me like that! You need to learn a lesson!"

Stu raised a hand to strike her. Martha leaped between them to shield Diana from the blow. Stu swore, and swung his fist at Martha.

At police headquarters, Chief Constable Bob Perry was sitting at his desk, about to write a letter. He looked up at the calendar on the wall, noting that the date was Wednesday, October 16. He penned the date on the paper, then started writing the letter.

There was a knock at the door. He paused in his writing and called, "Yes?"

Officer Duane Cranford entered. "I need to talk to you, Chief," he said, pausing at the door.

"Certainly," said Perry, laying the pen down. "I was just writing a letter. Come in."

Moving in and closing the door behind him, Cranford said, "We had an incident down in front of the general store a little while ago."

Perry's brow furrowed. "Incident? What?"

"Stu Morrow beat up on young Tom Wymore."

"From the look on your face, I'd say it was bad."

"Yes, sir. I was on the corner of Main and Oak when I saw a man running toward me, waving his hands. It was Charles Malcolm. He was on his way here to headquarters to alert us about the beating Stu was giving Tom. I ran up there with Charles, and when we arrived at the scene, Stu had left with his family, and Tom was lying in the street unconscious. A couple of men picked him up, put him in a wagon, and headed for Richmond Hospital. I talked to people in the crowd that had seen it all, and they told me—every one—that Tom was calmly trying to reason with Stu about dating his daughter, Diana. They said Tom gave Stu absolutely no reason to hit him. It was just Stu's usual problem with his temper. I thought I'd better come on back here and let you know about it."

There was a knock at the door, followed by the officer on the desk sticking his head in. "Chief, I have Zack Wymore out here. He wants to see you."

"Certainly," said Perry, rising from his desk chair. "Send him in."

Wymore, who was in his late forties, stepped into the chief's office, his features drawn. "Chief Perry," he said, moving toward the desk, and nodding at Cranford, "have you heard about what happened between my son, Tom, and Stu Morrow?"

"Yes," said Perry. "Officer Duane Cranford was just telling me about it. He told me Tom was taken to Richmond Hospital. How is he?"

"He has two broken ribs and a fractured jaw," Zack said in a strained voice. "I want Morrow arrested on assault and battery charges. Witnesses will testify that Tom did nothing to anger Morrow. He was simply asking for permission to date Diana, and Morrow went berserk like a madman and assaulted him."

"This was the same thing people in the crowd told me," said Cranford. "They assured me that Tom did nothing to provoke Stu to attack him. When Stu punched him and he went down, Stu kept kicking him in the ribs. Tom grabbed his foot, twisted it, and caused Stu to fall. Even as Tom gained his feet, he tried to get Stu to listen to reason, but Stu went after him again. Tom tried to dodge his fists in an effort not to fight him back, but finally, Stu pummeled him into unconsciousness."

Perry shook his head, sighed, and said, "Mr. Wymore, I'll take Duane and another officer with me right now. We'll go out to the Morrow farm and arrest Stu for assault and battery on Tom. We'll jail him, and I guarantee you, the judge will not only give orders to keep him locked up for a while, but he'll also make Stu pay Tom's medical bills."

At the Morrow farm, Diana and Deborah bent over their mother as she lay on her bed where Derick had carried her after their father had beat her up. Their brothers stood motionless on the other side of the bed.

Martha's mouth and nose were bleeding profusely, and the girls were using wet cloths, trying to get the bleeding stopped. Her right eye was swelling, and it was obvious that it would soon be swollen shut.

Her right arm was dangling at an awkward angle, and Diana had told her siblings that she feared the shoulder had been dislocated. Martha was conscious but dazed.

Derick's mind went back to the moment when his father raised his hand to strike Diana and his mother leaped between them, trying to protect Diana, and his father hit her with his fist, knocking her to the floor. He then turned on Diana again, and his mother managed to get up and throw herself at him in an attempt to stop him. It was then that he grabbed her by the arm, wrenched it savagely, and hit her again. This time, when she went down, she was out cold...

As Martha lay limp on the floor, Stu ignored the weeping Diana and the other children, stood over his unconscious wife and bellowed, "That's what you get for standing in the way of my disciplining one of my children, Martha! Don't you ever do it again!"

With that, he stomped out of the house and headed for the barn.

For a timeless moment, the siblings stood frozen in terror, then finally gaining control of her senses, Diana bent over her mother and said. "Derick, will you carry her to her bed? She's bleeding badly."

Derick shook his head to clear away the stupor that had seized his brain, bent down, and picked up his mother. "I think we need to take her to the hospital, Diana."

"Papa wouldn't let us take her there," said Diana. "He wouldn't want people knowing he had done this to Mama. We'll have to take care of her."

As they followed Derick down the hall to the bedroom, Daniel sobbed. "Someday I'm gonna get big, and I'm gonna beat Papa good for this! I am! I'm gonna make him pay for what he did to Mama!"

As they neared the bedroom, Diana put an arm around her distraught brother and said, "Daniel, right now we have to do all we can for Mama."

"I know," said Daniel, "but I promise you, when I get big, Papa's gonna pay for this!"

Derick passed through the bedroom door and carried his mother toward her bed with his siblings on his heels.

Suddenly there was a knock at the front door of the house.

"I'll see who it is," said Derick, and hurried from the room.

Derick opened the door to find Chief Constable Bob Perry with two officers. "Hello, Chief Perry."

"Hello, Derick," said the chief. "These two men are Officers Duane Cranford and Lyle Hickman. We want to see your father. We are here in regard to his assault on Tom Wymore."

"Oh. Yes, sir."

"Did you see it?" asked Perry.

"Yes, sir."

"Did Tom do anything in your opinion to cause your father to assault him?"

"No, sir. Tom tried to talk to Papa in a nice way. He didn't want trouble. He just likes Diana, and asked Papa if he could date her."

The officers exchanged glances, nodding.

"Is your father in the house?" asked Perry.

"No, sir. He's out in the barn. He beat Mama up real bad and went out there."

Perry's eyebrows arched. "He beat your mother up?"

"Yes, sir. My sisters are trying to get her bleeding stopped. Diana thinks her shoulder is dislocated, too."

"May I see her, Derick?"

"Yes, sir. Come in."

"We'll wait in the parlor, Chief," said Officer Hickman. "You go ahead and take a look at her."

Derick led Chief Perry down the hall to the bedroom, where his mother lay on the bed with her other children around her. Diana and Deborah were working at getting the bleeding of her nose and mouth stopped.

Martha was still in a dazed state. She seemed aware that the chief was there, but made no attempt to talk to him. As Perry bent down and looked at her, he said, "Derick, you need to take your mother to the hospital so they can care for her properly. She doesn't look good at all."

"Papa will never let us take her to the hospital, Chief Perry," said Diana. "He wouldn't want people to know he had done this."

"Well, he's not going to be in a position to stop you," said Perry. "I have two officers with me. We're here to arrest him for what he did to Tom Wymore. He's going to jail."

"Good!" said Daniel.

"Then we'll take Mama to the hospital as soon as Papa's gone, Chief," said Derick.

"Yes, we will," said Diana. "I want her to have the best care possible."

"All right," said the chief. "I'll get my men. We're going to the barn right now and arrest him. You get your mother to the hospital right away."

When the chief had left the room, Diana said, "Papa's not going to go without a fight. He'll resist arrest, for sure."

"Well, I hope they clonk him good," said Daniel.

"Me too," put in Dennis.

As they heard the law officers go out the front door of the house, Diana dabbed at her mother's nose and said, "I think I have the bleeding in check now."

"Her mouth has almost stopped bleeding, too," said Deborah.

"I don't want her to go to the hospital," said Dennis. "Can't we keep her here?"

"No, honey," said Deborah. "She needs care that only the hospital can give her. You want her to get all well, don't you?"

"Uh-huh. But she's not bleeding bad, now."

"But she could start bleeding again," said Diana. "And she needs that swollen eye taken care of, and her arm."

Daniel pointed out the window as the officers passed by, hurrying toward the barn. "There they go."

Dennis began sniffling. "But Diana, if you take Mama to the hospital, maybe she'll never come home."

"Yes, she will," said Derick. "But she will be feeling good when she does."

Even as Derick was speaking, they heard their father's loud voice coming from the barn. They could not make out what he was saying.

Martha stirred slightly and opened her good eye. "He's going to fight them."

Suddenly there were loud clattering and banging sounds. It lasted only a brief moment, then all went quiet.

"He must have given up," said Deborah.

"Or they clonked him," said Daniel.

"I hope they didn't have to hurt him," Martha said with thick tongue.

"Look!" said Derick.

His siblings all peered through the window to see the law officers carrying their unconscious father with his hands cuffed behind his back.

Cranford and Hickman draped his heavy frame over the back of an extra horse they had brought along, while Chief Perry headed for the front of the house.

Derick ran down the hall and opened the door just as the chief was mounting the porch steps.

"We had to knock him out to subdue him, Derick," said Perry. "He isn't seriously hurt. It will be up to the judge how long he will be in jail for what he did to Tom Wymore. Someone will let you know. Now you get your mother to the hospital."

"I will, sir," said Derick. "I'll go out to the barn and hitch up the wagon right away. I'll take Diana along to take care of Mama in the back of the wagon, and I'll leave Deborah here to watch over Daniel and Dennis."

The other two boys came and stood beside Derick and watched as the officers put the horses in motion. Their father was starting to regain consciousness as they pulled away.

Martha's mind was clearing as Derick carried her outside with the other children following. Her right eye was a mere slit, but with effort, she focused on Derick's face with her good eye as he concentrated on trying to be as gentle as possible while he carried her to the wagon.

She tried to stifle a moan as her son's strong arms placed her in the back of the wagon, where Diana and Deborah had made a soft pallet of fresh straw covered with quilts. Diana climbed into the wagon bed, put a pillow under her mother's head, and covered her with a shawl, all the while speaking soothing words to her.

While Deborah, Daniel, and Dennis looked on, Derick closed the tailgate, hopped up to the wagon seat, and started the team toward the road.

When the wheels began to roll, Martha whimpered in pain. Diana braced herself against her mother's battered body, hoping to absorb as much movement as possible from the rocking wagon.

The three who were staying home moved to the rickety porch to watch until the wagon would pass from sight. Trying to see through the tears blurring her own vision, Deborah heard a loud sniff, and looked down at her youngest brother. Dennis was losing his valiant battle to stem the flow of tears, and rubbed his shirtsleeve over his runny nose.

Deborah bent down to his eye level, and blinking back her own tears, took his thin little body in her arms. This was all it took. Dennis forgot all about trying to be brave, and sobbed like any five-year-old would do under the same circumstances.

"Mama's going to be fine," Deborah assured him, squeezing him close.

"I just want her home!" came the shaky, young voice. "I'm afraid she'll never come back!"

Daniel looked on as Deborah guided their little brother to the porch swing, sat down, and lifted him onto her lap. "Hush, now, Dennis," she said, putting the swing in motion, running her hand over his blond locks and pulling his head tightly against her chest. "Mama will be back very soon. The doctors will make her all better."

Daniel moved off the porch silently, unnoticed.

Dennis sniffed. "Promise?"

"Yes, honey. I promise. And you know what?"

He sniffed again. "What?"

"If you'll be a big, brave boy, I'll make a mock angel cake to welcome Mama home."

Still sniffling, but his mind now on his favorite kind of cake, Dennis let his head rest on his sister's chest. Soon, the swaying of the swing lulled him to sleep.

Soon Deborah caught sight of Daniel walking past the house toward the barn, shuffling his feet and making dust clouds rise, his head bent low. She opened her mouth to call out to him, but closed it again. She knew the sound of her voice would awaken Dennis, and she didn't feel like dealing with him again so soon. She would let him sleep where he was for a while. Maybe Daniel could work out some of his own frustrations.

*I guess I can't solve everyone's problems,* she thought, her mind returning to the small, pitiful sight her mother had made, riding in the back of the wagon.

MAIL ORDER BRIDE SERIES
NO. 8
1872
USA
AL & JOANNA LACY

IN ELKTON, IDAHO—six days prior to the beatings Stu Morrow gave his wife and Tom Wymore in Richmond, Virginia—attorney Gage Pearsall left his office under a flawlessly blue sky and headed down the wide, dusty street. He happily swung the leather briefcase that he carried.

There was a touch of fall in the air as morning swelled across the land in waves of sunlight, and the soft breeze off the Sawtooth Mountains brought the scent of pine, thick and pleasant, upon the town.

Pearsall tipped his hat to the ladies in his usual friendly manner and greeted the men in the same way.

Soon he drew up to the front door of the *Elkton Sentinel* building and moved inside. He found the young couple, Dan and Erline Tyler, seated at their desks in the outer office, smiling at him.

"Good morning, Mr. Pearsall," Erline said. "We've been expecting you."

"And good morning to you, Erline," responded the attorney. "It's nice to see you."

"Good morning, Mr. Pearsall," said Dan, rising from his desk. "Knight is in Mr. Hayward's office at the moment. They are going over some important matters in connection with the sale. Mr. Hayward said if you arrived before they were through, to seat you and give you a cup of coffee."

Pearsall grinned. "Sounds good to me."

Erline went to the small potbellied stove where the coffeepot was giving off gurgling sounds and poured a cupful of the steaming liquid.

Dan sat the attorney down in the chair in front of his desk. Erline placed the cup before him, and sat down in the twin chair beside him. Dan eased back onto his desk chair.

"Well!" said Pearsall. "You two have been in Elkton about a month, haven't you?"

"A month and a week, sir," said Dan. "And we love it here."

"I'm glad," said Pearsall. "And let me tell you, Pastor Steele is plenty glad you came. He was really needing someone to take those two Sunday school classes since the Berrys left. He has commented to me on two or three occasions about what a wonderful job you are doing."

"We're delighted to each have a class," said Erline. "We both had classes at the church in Boise, but we never dreamed it would work out so well here. Dan loves his boys, and I love my girls."

"The Lord always has things well-planned in our lives," said Dan. "Better than we could ever plan them ourselves."

Gage Pearsall swallowed a mouthful of coffee. "For sure. Since He is already in our tomorrows, He can work things out perfectly for us if we will just follow Him as He says, rather than running ahead of Him."

"Right," said Dan. "Like when Erline and I were feeling that we were supposed to leave the newspaper in Boise. We almost got ahead of the Lord and took a job at the *Pocatello Free Press*. I'm sure glad we didn't. As you probably know, the paper went out of business just last week."

"Yes," said Pearsall.

"We would have been without jobs, and no place to go," said Erline.

"I'm sure glad we let the Lord lead us here."

"So your being hired by Claude Hayward five weeks ago was all because of the big transaction that's taking place today."

"Right," said Dan. "My becoming Knight's assistant as he becomes owner of the *Sentinel* is really a step up from what I had in Boise."

"And my being made secretary and bookkeeper is a step up for me, too, Mr. Pearsall," said Erline. "We're very happy to be a part of it. There is no doubt in our minds that Knight is going to make an even greater success of the paper as time goes on. And it's wonderful to know we'll have a born-again boss."

At that moment, the door to Claude Hayward's office came open, and both men came out.

"Ah, Gage!" said Hayward. "I hope you haven't been waiting long."

Pearsall chuckled. "Only about three hours."

Hayward laughed. "Oh, well, that's the way it is, sometimes."

Twenty-four-year-old Knight Colburn grinned and said, "More like fifteen minutes, Mr. Lawyer. I heard you come in."

Pearsall shrugged, chuckled again. "Oh, well. So you caught me giving false information."

"Just so you don't have any false information in those papers you've drawn up!" said Hayward. "Come on into my office, and we'll get this transaction done."

The Tylers watched the three men enter Hayward's office and close the door.

"Well, honey," said Dan, "in a few minutes, Knight will be our boss."

"Oh, dear," said Erline. "We'll have to start calling him Mr. Colburn, won't we?"

Dan laughed. "I doubt he will want us to do that. After all, he's only a year older than me, and two years older than you."

"Well, we'd better ask him, anyway."

Inside the office, Gage Pearsall guided the two men as papers were signed, which closed the sale of the *Elkton Sentinel* to Knight Colburn.

When the transaction was done, Knight grasped Hayward's hand and shook it. "Of course I'm glad to be the new owner of the paper, sir, but I sure am going to miss you. And I'm going to miss Mrs. Hayward, too."

"Well, Beatrice and I will miss you, and all of our friends in Elkton," said the man, "but we are really excited about moving back to Indiana where we can live close to our children and grandchildren."

"So you're leaving right away?" asked Pearsall.

"On this afternoon's train from Ketcham," said Hayward. "We'll be in Indianapolis before nightfall day after tomorrow. All I have to do is pack up my things in the office, put them in a box, and pick up Beatrice at the hotel, where we've been staying since we sold the house last week. Then we'll be off to Ketcham."

"Well, Claude," said the attorney, "I want to commend you for the way you've trained Knight in the newspaper business, and for selling the *Sentinel* to him for such a reasonable price."

Hayward looked at Knight, smiled, and said, "Well, Gage, there isn't another man in the world that I would want to have the paper. Knight is going to do well, I know."

Knight smiled back at him.

"And Knight," said Pearsall, "I want to commend you for the way you have worked and saved your money so you could buy the *Sentinel.*"

"It's been my big dream for a long time, sir," said Knight. "I'm really happy to see it come true."

Pearsall placed some of the papers in his briefcase and closed the lid. "Well, gentlemen, I'll be on my way."

Colburn, Hayward, and Pearsall shook hands, and moved toward the door.

As they stepped into the outer office, Dan and Erline both stood up at their desks, and Dan asked, "Is everything set?"

"All set," said the attorney. "You and Erline now have a new boss."

Dan's face tinted slightly as he looked at his new boss and said, "Erline and I were just discussing this. Should we call you Mr. Colburn now?"

Knight chuckled, shaking his head. "Please, no! You just go on calling me by my first name."

"Good!" said Dan. "I told Erline if you told us to call you Mr. Colburn, we'd just pack up and leave."

"Oh, sure!" Knight laughed. "You call me by my first name. All right?"

"All right!" said Dan, a broad smile on his face.

Knight looked at Erline. "All right?"

"Yes, sir!" she said. "I'll call you Knight."

"Now that we've settled that, there's something else."

Dan and Erline exhanged quizzical glances.

Knight put a deep authoritative sound in his voice and said, "Starting today, you will both have to work eighteen-hour shifts from now on."

Everyone had a good laugh.

Gage Pearsall shook hands with Claude Hayward, told him good-bye, and left. Hayward said a few words of congratulations to Knight, then returned to his office to finish packing up his possessions.

Just as Hayward closed his office door, the front door opened, and Annie Colburn came in off the boardwalk, smiling. She greeted the Tylers, then looked at her son. "Has the sale been made? I saw Gage Pearsall come out and head in the direction of his office a few seconds ago."

Folding his mother in his arms, Knight kissed her forehead. "It sure has, Mom. Your son is now the owner of the *Elkton Sentinel!*"

"Wonderful!" said Annie, rising on tiptoes to kiss his cheek.

Erline moved close to Annie and said, "Are you enjoying the new house Knight built for the two of you here in town, Mrs. Colburn?"

"Oh, I sure am," she replied, her eyes sparkling. "It's a beautiful house."

"Do you miss cooking for the ranch hands at the Bar-S, ma'am?" queried Dan.

"I miss it in some ways," said Annie, "but in other ways it is nice to get some rest. And I really enjoy the new house. Now, of course, I hasten to say that my son and I have an agreement about the house. When the Lord brings the right young woman into his life, and marriage is in the offing…he will buy me a small house here in town to live in."

"And if there isn't one available for sale," put in Knight, "I'll build her a little house of her own."

Dan chuckled. "Well, Knight, as handsome and dashing as you are, it won't be long till some beautiful young Christian gal will come into your life, and the two of you will fall head-over-heels in love."

Knight laughed. "I sure hope the Lord has that beautiful gal about ready!"

At that moment, Annie noticed a rider haul up in front of the office and dismount. "Knight, it's Jordan."

Knight and the Tylers turned to look out the window. Jordan was coming across the boardwalk.

"Sure enough," said Knight. "He's wanting to know if the sale has been closed."

Jordan opened the door, stepped in, and greeted the Tylers and Annie, then moved up to Knight with a sly grin on his face. "Well, ol' pal, is it done?"

"It sure is!" said Knight. "As of this day, Thursday, October 10, 1872, yours truly is the owner of the *Elkton Sentinel!*"

Chuckling, Jordan shook Knight's hand. "Congratulations! How about a job?"

Knight laughed. "Are you kidding? I couldn't pay you those humongous wages your father is paying you at the Bar-S." The others laughed, then Knight said, "Seriously, Jordan, how are the plans coming toward having your own ranch?"

"Well, it's probably a year or so away. My father is going to give me the money to buy a good spread when he feels the time is just right."

"Do you have some particular parcel of land in mind?" asked Dan.

"I have several," said Jordan. "There are some choice pieces, anywhere from ten- to twenty-thousand acres south, east, and west of here."

"I hope you get the very best parcel of land," said Dan.

"Thanks," Jordan said with a smile, then turned to his friend. "Knight, are you and I still set to go hunting together next Monday and Tuesday?"

"I'm sure planning on it. With Dan here to watch over the *Sentinel* for me, I can get away for those two days without a problem."

"Good! Well, I have to keep moving. See all of you later."

They watched through the window as Jordan Shaw mounted his horse and rode away, then Dan said, "Knight, are you getting anywhere witnessing to Jordan? You told me when we first came that he was still resisting the gospel."

"He still is," said Knight with a sad tone in his voice. "Just like he has for so many years. I talk to him about his need to be saved quite often, as I told you, but he keeps saying he just isn't ready to do anything about facing God."

"What a difference the Lord could make in his life," said Erline.

"Yes," said Knight. "At least Jordan hasn't been in trouble with the law since those two scrapes I told you about that happened eight years ago, but he still has a bit of a wild streak, and often gets himself into one kind of trouble or another because of his fiery temper."

"Mm-hmm," said Erline. "I've heard some people in town say they are wary of Jordan because of that wild streak."

"Jordan just needs to mature and to settle himself down," said Knight. "I think you've met his sister and brother-in-law, Lorene and Mark Hedren."

Both Tylers nodded.

"Mark and Lorene are not Christians, so they don't have the full picture. But Mark has taken genuine interest in helping Jordan to grow up and become more responsible, but so far, with little or no effect. Mark and Lorene have him in their home for a meal quite often in an attempt to spend time with him. William Shaw has been trying for years to make something of his son, but is also finding it difficult, no matter how old Jordan grows physically. There is still this immaturity and irresponsibility to be reckoned with."

"Jordan just won't grow up," said Annie. "It's like he wants to stay a little boy the rest of his life."

"That's about it, Mom," said Knight. "The reason William keeps putting off giving the money to Jordan so he can buy himself a ranch is because William knows he is too immature to make a success of it."

"Both William and Sylvia are hoping Jordan will fall in love with some solid young woman who can marry him and help mature him," said Annie. "There's a girl named Belinda Ashworth, and they're attempting to get Jordan interested in her. They like Belinda very much, and feel if Jordan would marry her, Belinda could help ripen him."

"So who is Belinda?" asked Erline.

"The Hyman Ashworth family are relatively new neighbors on an adjacent ranch to the Bar-S," said Knight. "They are very wealthy. They have two daughters: Belinda, who is twenty-one, and Jean, who is sixteen. Both Hyman and his wife, Dorothy, have taken a liking to Jordan. And no question, Belinda is quite attracted to him. Hyman and Dorothy are quite concerned that Belinda is almost twenty-two and not married. They would like for her to marry Jordan, which would keep her on the proper social scale, since the Shaws are equally as wealthy."

"Jordan hasn't shown any romantic interest in Belinda," said Annie. "I think he likes her as a friend. I'm told that he treats her kindly, but that's as far as it goes. He doesn't want her as a sweetheart. His parents are doing everything they can to cause romance to blossom between them. This past summer, they often encouraged the two of them to go riding together and on picnics. But Jordan is too interested in hunting in the Sawtooth Mountains and fishing in the Salmon River up there in the high country. He simply doesn't want to be with Belinda."

"He is quite a hunter," said Knight. "He has deer head and elk head trophies hanging on the walls in his room, and talks a lot about a certain big male black bear in the mountains he is determined to bag one day. He wants to have it stuffed full-body so it can stand in the corner of his room."

"So his interests all run toward hunting and fishing, eh?" said Dan.

"That's it," said Knight. "In itself, there's nothing wrong with that, but my main concern for Jordan is his lost state before God."

Annie patted Knight's arm. "Well, you just keep working on him, son. Once Jordan gets saved, everything in his life will change for the better."

"That's for sure, Mom," said Knight.

The door to Claude Hayward's office opened, and the former owner of the newspaper came out, carrying a box. "Well, it's time to say good-bye," he said with a somber note in his voice.

"Let me carry the box out to the buggy for you, sir," said Knight.

Hayward grinned. "All right. I'll just let you do that."

Annie stepped up and said, "Mr. Hayward, I want to thank you for making it possible for Knight to become owner of the *Sentinel.*"

"It is my pleasure, Mrs. Colburn," said Hayward. "Like I told Gage Pearsall, there isn't another man in the world that I would want to have it."

"I know he will do you proud," she said, glancing up at her son.

"I have no doubt about it, ma'am. I'll be writing now and then so I can keep up with the progress of the paper. I know the reports will always be good."

"Erline and I will be right here by Knight's side, Mr. Hayward," said Dan Tyler. "We are excited about the future of the paper as Elkton and the other towns around here grow. We have no doubt that with what you have taught him, along with his own talent and initiative, the *Elkton Sentinel* will become well known as a first-rate newspaper all over Idaho and into the territories around us."

Hayward grinned. "That's exactly what I'm expecting." He looked at the newspaper's new owner. "Well, Knight, I guess I'd better take that box to the hotel so Beatrice and I can have it transported to the depot in Ketcham, along with the other belongings we're taking with us."

The next day, Jordan Shaw was doing some minor fence repair with a young ranch hand named Guy Tabor. A few white clouds drifted overhead, kissed by the sun and propelled by the breeze. A flock of geese moved across the sky, heading south, squawking loudly as they followed their leader in V-shaped formation.

Both of their horses stood looking on, whipping their tails at pesky flies.

As Jordan was tamping dirt into a hole around a fence post in order to make it sturdy, Guy was holding the post steady. While Jordan was giving it a few final tamps, movement on the grassy land caught the corner of his eye. Guy set his gaze on a rider coming their way. "Someone's coming, Jordan."

Jordan looked up and focused on the rider. His back stiffened, and an unhappy look captured his eyes. "Oh no. It's Belinda."

Surprise showed on Guy's young features. "What do you mean, 'Oh no, it's Belinda'? I know a lot of fellas on the Bar-S who would love to have her come to see them."

"Well, I wish she would do exactly that."

"Really?"

"Really."

"I don't understand. Don't you like her? Everybody knows she really likes you."

Jordan sighed, leaned the tamping bar against the fence post, and said, "Guy, I like her as a person, yes. A friend, you know? She has a nice personality and is reasonably good-looking."

Guy frowned. "So what's the problem?"

"She's got romance and matrimony on her mind, that's what. And to make it worse, her parents and mine are crowding me like you wouldn't believe to get serious with her and marry her."

Guy looked back at her as she was trotting the horse and waving. "I think she's really quite the gal."

"Then why don't you pursue her? It won't make me mad. I flat do not see her as marriage material."

Guy shook his head. "Oh no, you don't. If your parents want you to marry her, I wouldn't go near her. Your father would fire me. I need this job like a turtle needs his shell."

Jordan glanced again at the approaching rider with her long red hair flowing in the breeze, and shook his head.

"Tell you what, Jordan," said the young ranch hand, "since this is the last post, and all that's left is to drive some staples to hold the barbed wire in place, I'll get on my horse and go. That way, you and Belinda can be alone."

Jordan frowned at him. "Deserter."

"Call me what you want," said Guy, hurrying to his horse and leaping into the saddle, "but I want to stay on your father's good side. Maybe if I'm gone, you and Belinda will have a better chance of falling in love."

Jordan shook his head. "I'm not falling in love with her, do you hear me?"

"Well, far be it from me to stand in your way if there's any chance at all."

Belinda drew rein and brought her horse to a halt. Smiling while setting admiring eyes on her prey, she said, "Hello, Jordie. I thought I'd ride out and see you." Then to his partner, who was about to gouge his horse's sides: "Hello, Guy. You leaving?"

"Uh…yeah. I'm leaving. Jordan's about to finish up there with the fence, so I figured I'd get on back and see if there's some work to do around the barn." He grinned at Jordan. "See you later."

With that, Guy Tabor put his mount to a gallop and headed over the rolling hills.

Dismounting, Belinda moved up close to Jordan with a sweet smile. "I dropped by the house to see you, and your mother told me where you and Guy were mending fence. She's such a nice lady."

Jordan nodded. "That she is."

"She always makes me feel so welcome. Just like your father does, Jordie. They're both such nice people."

"Real nice," he agreed, his stomach doing flip-flops.

"And Lorene and Mark. They both treat me so nice. They're really happy in their marriage, aren't they?"

"Uh…yeah. Real happy."

"That's what I've always envisioned for myself," Belinda said, moving even closer. "A happy marriage with just the right man."

"Mm-hmm. Well, I hope you find him. I've really got to get the rest of this repair job done, Belinda. Thanks for riding out to see me. It was nice of you."

With that, he bent over and picked up the hammer and a handful of staples that lay on the ground.

The redhead moved closer yet. "Jordie…"

He paused, looked her in the eye. "Uh-huh?"

She came very close, lifting her face toward his. "You're such a nice person. We need to do as your parents have so often suggested—spend more time together. I…I really like you." She raised her lips a little higher. "You like me, don't you?"

Jordan cleared his throat nervously. "Belinda, you are a nice girl, and I like you as a friend. But I have to be honest with you—I'm not ready to get serious with a girl."

"But most men your age are already married, and have been for at least two or three years."

"I'm not most men, Belinda. Like I said, I'm just not ready to get serious."

Feeling keen disappointment, Belinda Ashworth did not show it. Her mind was made up that she would eventually win Jordan to herself.

"Well," she said, "can't blame a girl for trying. I...guess I'll head on back home."

"See you later," he said, feeling relief. "Thanks for coming out to see me. You're a real friend."

Belinda moved toward her horse, telling herself that with patience, she would win Jordan over and would one day become Mrs. Jordan Shaw.

Suddenly she stopped as she saw William Shaw galloping toward the spot. Jordan saw him at the same time.

Belinda stopped, wheeled, and walked back toward Jordan. "Jordie, your father's coming. See him?"

"Yes. I see him."

Jordan hoped his father would not think he was interested in Belinda simply because they were there together.

## 10

AS WILLIAM SHAW DREW UP and pulled rein, he smiled. "Hello, Belinda! Nice to see you." There was a pleased look on his face. Jordan knew that was because he found the two of them together.

Running his gaze between them, William said, "Am I interrupting anything?"

"Of course not," said Jordan. "Belinda and I were just chatting. She was about to leave."

Swinging from the saddle, William looked around. "Didn't Guy come out here with you, son?"

"Yes, sir, but when we got down to just the barbed wire needing to be stapled to this post, he headed on back, saying he would see if there was some work needed to be done around the barn. I'm surprised you didn't run into him."

"I wasn't at the house. I came here from over at the Circle D Ranch."

"Oh."

"I just wanted to see how the fence repair was coming along."

"Well, gentlemen," said Belinda, "I'll excuse myself and be on my way. See you later, Jordie."

Feeling the pressure of his duty to be extra polite to Belinda in front of his father, Jordan took her arm and walked her to where her horse stood beside his. The two of them were contentedly munching on the grass.

William felt satisfied as he watched them together.

Steadying her as she stepped into the stirrup and swung into the saddle, Jordan said, "It was nice of you to come out and see me."

Belinda looked down at him, and smiled crookedly as she thought to herself, *My mind is made up. I am going to become Mrs. Jordan Shaw. You might as well prepare yourself for it, Jordie.*

Not knowing what to make of the strange smile that captured her lips, Jordan thought, *I wonder what that's about.*

William said, "Belinda, you're always welcome to visit Jordan here on the ranch anytime you wish."

Jordan saw the strange smile disappear from her lips as it was replaced by a normal one. "Thank you, Mr. Shaw." She looked at Jordan one more time, then put the horse to a trot.

While watching her ride away, Jordan told himself he might as well settle the Belinda matter with his father right now. He turned back, stepped up close, and was about to speak when William said, "Son, I'm glad to see things developing so favorably between you and Belinda. Let me tell you what I've got in mind."

"Father, I—"

"Let me tell you—" he raised a palm as if to keep Jordan from talking while he was informing him of his plan. "The day you and Belinda get engaged, I'll put the men to building the two of you a real nice log house here on the ranch, wherever you want it."

"But, Father—"

"Let me finish, boy. After you and Belinda have been married a couple of years, I'll buy you that big spread somewhere in the area that we've talked about, and you'll be on your own in the cattle business. How does that sound?"

Jordan's nerves stretched tight. "Father, I—"

"You know how much your mother and I think of Belinda, don't you? We both know she'll make you a wonderful wife." He chuckled. "I can't tell you how pleased I was to find the two of you together here."

William was taking a breath. Jordan plunged into the opening and said, "Father, I don't want to upset you or Mother…but there's something you have to understand."

Shaw raised his eyebrows. "And what is that?"

"I am not interested in Belinda for a wife."

William's eyebrows dropped and formed into a scowl. "What

are you talking about? She's perfect for you. She comes from good stock. She's on your social level. She's—"

"I like her as a friend," Jordan said levelly, "but I'm not interested in her romantically."

"Give it a little time," William said quickly. "Once you really get to know Belinda, you'll fall in love with her."

Jordan knew in his heart he would never fall in love with Belinda Ashworth. But he decided not to voice it to his father at that moment.

"Your mother and I have talked to Belinda's parents several times lately," said William. "They are quite anxious to see the two of you fall in love and marry. They really like you, son."

Jordan strongly disliked the pressure he was getting from both sets of parents but said nothing.

"Well! Let's get this fence job finished!"

Belinda Ashworth trotted her horse up to the rear of the Bar-S ranch house, dismounted, stepped up on the porch, and knocked on the back door. When the door came open, she put a big smile on her lips and said, "Hello again, Mrs. Shaw. I just wanted to thank you for directing me to the spot where Jordie was repairing fence."

"My pleasure, honey," said Sylvia. "Did you two have a nice time?"

"Oh, yes. Guy Tabor left shortly after I arrived out there, and left Jordie and me alone. He's so...so special. You have certainly raised a wonderful son, Mrs. Shaw."

"Why, thank you, dear. William and I have done our best. Won't you come in and visit for a while?"

"I have to be going, thank you. But I'll take you up on it soon."

"All right," said Sylvia. "You're welcome anytime."

Sylvia watched while Belinda mounted and rode away, then smiled to herself and closed the door.

Belinda was guiding her horse up the lane toward the road when she saw a wagon coming along the road from the direction of town. She recognized the Faulkner sisters, Althea and Bernadine, who were approximately her age. The Faulkner ranch was adjacent to the Ashworth Ranch on its far side, so she had gotten to know Althea and Bernadine quite well.

Belinda reached the road at the same time the Faulkner wagon was drawing near the Bar-S gate, and Althea drew rein.

Belinda halted her horse and smiled at the sisters. "Hello, Althea, Bernadine."

Bernadine grinned impishly. "Visiting somebody on the Bar-S, dearie?"

Belinda blushed and dipped her head slightly. "Yes."

Althea giggled. "We…ah…have heard little rumors that you and Jordan are getting serious about each other."

Bernadine playfully elbowed her sister in the ribs. "Althea, maybe they're not rumors."

Wanting to impress them, and having set her mind to become Mrs. Jordan Shaw, Belinda said, "They are definitely not rumors, girls. What you've heard is a fact. Jordie and I are getting very, very close. We just spent a couple of hours together, and found each other's company to be quite pleasant and satisfying."

"Has Jordan told you he loves you?" queried Althea.

Blushing again, Belinda replied, "Well-l-l-l…not in so many words, but his actions speak louder than words, anyway. He has made it quite clear how he feels about me."

The sisters giggled again, looking at each other, then Bernadine said, "I envy you, Belinda. Not only is Jordan very rugged, handsome, and charming, but he is also very rich. The Shaws are the richest of all the ranchers in this whole territory."

"I agree," said Belinda. "Jordie is indeed rugged, handsome, charming, and loaded with money."

"Honey, if you marry Jordan," said Althea, "you'll be even wealthier than you are right now. Much, much wealthier."

Belinda grinned and shrugged. "What can I say? But let me emphasize one thing. It is not if I marry Jordie. It is when I marry Jordie. There is no 'if' about it. We'll be engaged in another month or so. Mark my word."

Bernadine jabbed an elbow in her sister's ribs again and laughed. "It looks like Belinda knows what she's doing! She'll be

Mrs. Jordan Shaw before Christmas!"

Belinda laughed. "Honey, you can count on it!"


When William and Jordan stepped into the kitchen, Sylvia was working at the cupboard. Turning, she smiled and said, "Well, both of my men are back at the same time!"

"After I left the Circle D," said William, "I rode over to where Jordan was working on the fence. Guy had already headed back here, but I found Belinda with our son."

"Yes, I know," she said. "I told her where she could find him."

William grinned and looked at Jordan. "Anyway, after Belinda left, I helped him finish up there, so we rode on back together."

Sylvia moved closer to her son. "Honey, did you and Belinda have a nice time together?"

"Not in the way you mean, Mother," said Jordan. "I might as well tell you what I told Father. I have no romantic inclinations toward Belinda at all. None. She's a nice girl, and I consider us to be friends. But that's where it ends, Mother. That's where it ends."

Surprise showed on Sylvia's face. She looked at her husband.

William moved close to her. "I told him that once he gets to know Belinda, he'll fall in love with her."

"Of course," said Sylvia, turning back to her work at the cupboard. "She is such a delightful girl. Just a little more time spent with her, and he'll go head-over-heels. She's so perfect for him. She'll fit into this family excellently."

"No doubt about it," said William. "And it will be so good to have this tie with the Ashworths."

The parents' backs were now toward their son.

"Won't it, though?" said Sylvia. "I was thinking about that after Belinda was here today. A perfect situation."

William and Sylvia talked on, totally disregarding Jordan or his feelings. They were not even aware of it when their son left the room, shaking his head and mumbling, "I'm going to have to take this matter into my own hands."

He took the stairs to his room two at a time, in a hurry to escape the sound of their voices.

When Belinda arrived home and entered the big ranch house, she found her mother and sister in the kitchen, preparing to bake cinnamon rolls.

Dorothy smiled as she pressed the rolling pin over the dough. "Hello, honey. Were you able to spend some time with Jordan?"

Jean looked at her sister, waiting to hear what she had to tell them.

"Oh yes, Mama," said Belinda. "He was repairing fence out on the south section. Mrs. Shaw told me where he was, so I rode out there. He was so glad to see me."

"Of course," said Jean, smiling broadly. "He's in love with you, isn't he?"

Belinda managed to blush once more. "Well...you better believe it!"

Jean giggled and clapped her hands. "He told you he loves you?"

"Well, he didn't exactly put it into those words, honey, but Jordie has his own special ways of getting the message to me."

"That's wonderful," said Dorothy. "That's how your father was when we first began to show interest in each other. He didn't put it into words for a while, but he sure did show me how he felt."

"So things are really developing between you, huh, sis?"

"Most definitely," replied Belinda. "I'd like for them to develop a bit faster, but as long as I see progress, it's all right. I have no doubt that Jordie and I will end up at the altar together. I'm going to be Mrs. Jordan Shaw, sure as spring follows winter!"

Jean sighed. "I wish I could find a beau as handsome and rich as Jordan."

Dorothy smiled. "Well, honey, I hope you find one like Jordan, too. I want both of you girls to marry men who are on our social level." She paused. "How pleased William and Sylvia must be to see their son falling in love with you, Belinda."

Belinda smiled.

Jean stuck out her lower lip in a mock pout. "Too bad the Shaws don't have another son."

—⚭—          —⚭—          —⚭—

The next day, Jordan Shaw was riding toward Elkton and was some three miles from town when he saw a wagon coming toward him. When it drew near enough so he could see who was sitting on the seat, he groaned. "Oh no. The Faulkner sisters. Those two busybodies are the last thing I need right now."

They had recognized him and were waving.

Jordan knew they would expect him to stop and make polite conversation. He would have to do it or suffer the consequences. It would never do for his mother to hear that he had been rude. She would never let up on her lectures about proper etiquette and the place of good manners in the community.

As they were drawing abreast, Jordan stopped his horse and Althea drew rein.

"Hello, Jordan!" said Bernadine. "Nice to see you."

"And hello from me," piped up Althea.

Jordan touched his hat brim, nodded with a forced smile, and said, "Hello, ladies. Been to town already, eh?"

"Oh yes," said Bernadine. "We do a lot of the shopping for both our parents. Makes it easier on them."

Smiling broadly, Althea said, "We met up with Belinda as she was coming off your ranch yesterday, Jordan. She said she had spent a couple of hours with you, and that things really went well."

Jordan felt his blood heat up. Belinda had certainly exaggerated about the amount of time they had been together. He was tempted to set the record straight, but decided to leave it alone. "What do you mean, 'things really went well'?" he asked.

Althea giggled. "You know. Your romance."

Jordan felt something go sour in his stomach.

"We're so happy to hear that you and Belinda are falling for each other," said Althea. "You make a beautiful couple."

"You sure do," said Bernadine. "Belinda said the two of you are very, very close."

Anger welled up inside Jordan Shaw, but he covered it. "Well, ladies," he said, fighting to keep his voice level, "it's been nice chatting with you. I really must be going."

The Faulkner sisters bid him good-bye, and Jordan spurred his horse into a gallop. As he rode on into town, he told himself there had to be a way to stop this nonsense and still not irritate his parents.

But how?

He must find a way.

By the time Jordan had reached the outskirts of Elkton, he had pushed his horse into a lather, as well as himself. Anger burned within him toward Belinda. Being kind and polite to her was one thing…but Belinda was causing this situation to get out of hand. She was deliberately lying to people and making them think the two of them were falling in love. Jordan had told her plainly that he wasn't ready for any such thing, that he was not ready to get serious with a girl.

Riding into town, Jordan drew up where he needed to go, tied his horse to the hitch rail, and started down the boardwalk. "Belinda, you refuse to listen to what I tell you. All right, young lady…this calls for drastic measures. I'm not sure what they will be, but drastic measures are coming!"


At sunrise the next Monday, October 14, Knight Colburn was tying the bedroll behind his saddle at the small barn behind his house when he looked up to see Jordan come riding into the yard.

Jordan smiled as he reined in and said, "Well, ol' pal, are you ready for two days of hunting?"

Knight gave him a pleasant grin. "Sure am. It's been hectic at the office this past week. It'll feel good to get away. The Tylers are excellent at what they do. They'll keep things rolling without a hitch, I'm sure."

Jordan dismounted and helped Knight load his saddlebags with ammunition. Knight tied his knapsack full of food next to the bedroll, then slid his rifle into the saddle boot. As he buckled the strap that held the rifle in place, he said, "I suppose you'll have your eye out for that big black bear you're wanting to bag."

"I sure will. I've caught glimpses of him several times when I was staying at that same old cabin, but by the time I could grab my rifle and go after him, he was gone. One of these times, I'll get him." Jordan looked toward the house. "I think I can smell that Annie Colburn breakfast right now."

Knight chuckled. "Well, Mom's got it ready. Let's go!"

When they entered the kitchen, Annie smiled warmly and said, "Well, there's that boy who's like a second son to me! Ready for breakfast, Jordan?"

"I sure am!" said Jordan, taking in the sweet aroma through his nostrils with a big sniff. He bent down and kissed her on the cheek. "I'm always ready to eat your cooking. I sure miss it at the ranch. It isn't fair that Knight still gets to eat your cooking every day and I have to wait till I can make it in here once a week or so."

Annie laughed. "Well, you know you're welcome anytime you can come."

"I sure do, ma'am," said Jordan, "and I appreciate it more than I could ever tell you."

"Sit down, boys," said Annie. "It's all on the table."

Jordan endured the quiet moment as Knight offered thanks to the Lord, then enjoyed his breakfast.

When they had eaten their fill, both young men put on their hats and mackinaws. Jordan kissed Annie's cheek another time and thanked her for the good breakfast.

Knight hugged his mother and kissed her forehead tenderly. "Now, Mom, I'll be home tomorrow evening. If you need anything, just let the Tylers know. All right?"

"Yes. Don't worry about me, honey. I'll be fine."

Annie stood at the door and watched as her son and his best friend mounted up. They waved, and she waved back, saying in a low tone, "Dear Lord, take care of them."

Knight and Jordan rode out of the yard and headed for Main Street. They took a right turn and headed northward out of town. People on the boardwalk waved and called to them as they passed by. They returned the greetings, and soon were out in open country, aiming for the Sawtooth Mountains.

They kept the horses at a fast pace until they reached the foothills, then slowed them to a trot.

Jordan's thoughts were on Belinda Ashworth as he searched his brain for a solution. What could he do to end this mythical romance that was in her mind? Somehow he had to come up with a solution, and he had to do it in a hurry. Belinda's lies about him falling in love with her had to stop. But he couldn't just flat come out and tell her to shut her mouth. Whatever he did, he dare not upset his parents by treating Belinda in a rough manner.

"...don't you think?" came Knight's words filtering into his ears.

Jordan looked at his friend blankly. "I'm sorry. What did you say?"

"I said to me this is the most beautiful time of the year, with the brilliant colors of the leaves, especially the leaves on the aspen trees, don't you think?"

Jordan looked around at the colorful scene that surrounded them. The aspen leaves were turning golden and fluttering beautifully in the breeze, looking like flashing diamonds in the brilliant sunlight. "Yes. I agree, Knight. This really is the most beautiful time of the year."

A short while later, as they wound through the pines, birches, and aspens, Knight said something else to his friend. Again, Jordan was buried in thought, and Knight had to repeat what he had said.

Frowning as they guided the horses across a narrow stream, Knight said, "Ol' pal, is something troubling you?"

Jordan looked at him, blinking. "What do you mean?"

"Well, you seem to be quite preoccupied. Anything I can do to help?"

Jordan chuckled hollowly. "I'm sorry. Really, it's not important. Just have a lot on my mind right now." Brightening his face with a smile, he said, "When we're moving through the woods up there in the high country, stalking a deer or an elk, my mind will be on them, and I'll be concentrating only on hunting."

Two hours later, they reached the old abandoned cabin. As they dismounted, Jordan said, "Knight, I never come here without thinking about that grizzly that tore up my jacket eight years ago, and about Ace Decker and Keith Nolan taking me to their cabin and holding me their prisoner."

Knight patted his horse's neck and said, "I doubt you'll ever forget it, pal. And neither will Decker and Nolan. They've got twelve more years to sit in that prison and think about it."

Jordan loosed his knapsack and bedroll from behind the saddle, then looked around. "I wonder if that big ol' black bear has been around here lately."

"I would suppose he has. He seems to like this area."

"Yeah. And one of these days I'll get close enough to him to bring him down." A dreamy look captured Jordan's eyes. "In my mind, I call him Ol' Blackie. I can't wait to have him stuffed. He is going to look mighty good standing in the corner of my bedroom. And when I have my own ranch, I'll put him in my parlor so everyone who visits can get a good look at him. Ol' Blackie will make an excellent conversation piece."

Knight grinned. "I'm sure of that."

The two friends put their gear inside the old cabin, tied the horses to trees near the porch, and moved up the side of a mountain. Eyes peeled for any sign of big game, their rifles ready, they worked their way up through the forest to the sound of the wind in the trees and the singing of birds all about them.

Once again they were discussing the autumn beauty of the mountains when suddenly Jordan stopped, peering straight ahead through the dense timber, his hands tightening on his rifle.

At his side, Knight looked in the same direction. "See something?"

"Yeah. Movement of some kind. There's something sizable up there about fifty yards. Maybe it's Ol' Blackie."

There was a loud cracking sound from the area they were looking at then sudden movement. Both men saw a huge black shape, then it disappeared from view.

"It's him!" gasped Jordan, keeping his voice low. "Let's go!"

As they started running up the slope through the trees, Knight said in a subdued tone, "Jordan, be careful. Black bears are known to hide when they are being stalked by men, then suddenly jump out and attack."

Jordan was about to comment when the big black bear came into full view some thirty yards away, then moved into the shadows of the pines.

"It's him!" cried Jordan, and broke into a run toward the spot where the bear had been seen.

Knight was a few steps behind him.

Suddenly the huge beast appeared again. This time he was looking straight at Jordan, who was closing in on him. The bear roared threateningly and stood straight up, pawing the air.

Jordan stopped, shouldered his rifle, and fired before Knight got stopped. He had to sidestep quickly to keep from running into Jordan.

The bullet struck the bear's right paw, tearing away flesh.

The black beast ejected a loud roar, wheeled, and limped away at a fast run.

"I hit him, Knight!" Jordan cried with elation. "Come on! Let's close in for the kill!"

Jordan broke into a run, and Knight was beside him. As they dashed through the trees, Knight said, "Once a black bear is wounded, he is ten times as dangerous. We've got to be careful."

Panting as they hurried up the steep slope, Jordan said, "I'm not afraid. I've just got to kill Ol' Blackie so I can have him stuffed!"

When they reached the spot where the bear had been standing when the bullet struck his paw, they stopped and looked at the ground.

"Look!" said Jordan, dropping to one knee. The furry piece of paw that had been shot off lay on the grass, which was stained by its blood. Jordan picked it up.

Knight saw that two claws had been severed from the bear's paw, and said, "He'll really be dangerous now. He got a good look at you, Jordan, and bears have a good memory. You'll have to be doubly careful in these woods."

Rising to his feet, still holding the severed piece of paw, Jordan chuckled. "I'm the one with the rifle. Not Ol' Blackie. I'll get him, yet, Knight. Come on. Let's follow him."

Knight and Jordan spent the rest of the day searching for the bear, but to no avail. There was a blood trail for a while, but it finally faded out.

At sunset, Jordan grumbled all the way back to the cabin because he hadn't shot straight enough to kill the bear with the one and only shot he had been able to fire at him.

# 11

WHEN KNIGHT COLBURN AND JORDAN SHAW were eating supper in the cabin, Knight noticed that his friend was preoccupied again. Several minutes went by without Jordan saying a word.

Looking across the table at him by the light of the lantern that hung from a nail, Knight said, "Okay, what is it? The same thing that was bothering you this morning?"

It took a full five seconds for Knight's words to register. Jordan's head came up. "Uh…well, yeah. But actually what is bothering me the most is that I didn't shoot straighter when I fired at Ol' Blackie. I was too excited, I guess. A bullet in the brain or the heart would have brought him down in a hurry."

"I can understand that bothering you, my friend, but I know you well enough to deduct that it is the other thing that is bothering you the most. You have the same look on your face that you had this morning. I'm willing to listen if you want to talk about it."

There was still food on Jordan's plate, but he shoved it away. "The other thing will work itself out. What I'm most concerned about right now is the bear. Really. I should have hit him in a vital spot, not just shot off two claws."

Knight's plate was empty. He downed the last of his coffee and set the tin cup on the table. "You'll get another chance. I doubt that Ol' Blackie dies from that wound. But again, a word of caution. He may well remember you if he sees you again. Be careful. You're usually up here alone."

Jordan nodded. "Yeah. I'll be careful."

Later, when Jordan was slipping into his bedroll on one of the cots, Knight was at the table, reading his Bible.

Jordan was about to bid his friend good night, when he noticed tears on his cheeks. "Hey, pal, you all right?"

Knight looked at him, wiped his cheeks, and smiled. "I was just reading about the crucifixion in the twenty-seventh chapter of Matthew. It's so heart-gripping. May I read it to you?"

Reluctantly, Jordan said, "Well, all right."

"Listen to this. It covers several verses, beginning in verse 35: 'And they crucified him, and parted his garments, casting lots: that it might be fulfilled which was spoken by the prophet, They parted my garments among them, and upon my vesture did they cast lots. And sitting down they watched him there; and set up over his head his accusation written, THIS IS JESUS THE KING OF THE JEWS. Then were there two thieves crucified with him, one on the right hand, and another on the left. And they that passed by reviled him, wagging their heads, and saying, Thou that destroyest the temple, and buildest it in three days, save thyself. If thou be the Son of God, come down from the cross.

"'Likewise also the chief priests mocking him, with the scribes and elders, said, He saved others; himself he cannot save. If he be the King of Israel, let him now come down from the cross, and we will believe him. He trusted in God; let him deliver him now, if he will have him: for he said, I am the Son of God. The thieves also, which were crucified with him, cast the same in his teeth.

"'Now from the sixth hour there was darkness over all the land unto the ninth hour. And about the ninth hour Jesus cried with a loud voice, saying, Eli, Eli, lama sabachthani? that is to say, My God, my God, why hast thou forsaken me?

"'Some of them that stood there, when they heard that, said, This man calleth for Elias. And straightway one of them ran, and took a spunge, and filled it with vinegar, and put it on a reed, and gave him to drink. The rest said, Let be, let us see whether Elias will come to save him.

"'Jesus, when he had cried again with a loud voice, yielded up the ghost.'"

Jordan's eyes were fastened on his friend.

Knight wiped his cheeks clear of tears again. "Let me point out what that crowd said about Jesus in verse 42, Jordan. 'He saved others; himself he cannot save.'"

Jordan did not take his eyes off Knight, but remained silent.

Knight sniffed. "That crowd was so wrong. Jesus could have saved Himself if He so desired. He could have come down from the cross—as some of them challenged Him to do. But if He had, there would be no salvation for sinners. He stayed there, bore the sins of the world, and died to provide cleansing from sin and forgiveness for guilty, hell-deserving sinners. You understand that, Jordan?"

Jordan nodded without making a sound.

Flipping further back in his Bible, Knight said, "With what we've just seen, I want to point out a portion of another verse."

Stopping at Galatians chapter 2, he read verse 20: "'I am crucified with Christ: nevertheless I live; yet not I, but Christ liveth in me: and the life which I now live in the flesh I live by the faith of the Son of God, who loved me, and gave himself for me.'"

Jordan's gaze was still fixed on his friend.

"It's this part that I want to emphasize," said Knight. "The apostle Paul says here, the Son of God loved me and gave himself for me. Jordan, just as Jesus stayed on the cross and gave Himself for Paul personally, He also did it for Knight Colburn personally. And you know what? He also gave Himself for Jordan Shaw personally, so Jordan Shaw could be saved from his sins and the penalty of sin; eternity in hell. What love! What amazing love!"

Jordan's body was obviously stiffened, and his face was like granite. "I'm really very tired, Knight," he said. "I need to get to sleep." Even as he was speaking, he rolled over, covered his head, and lay still.

His heart heavy, Knight said, "Friend, you dare not keep putting this off. Eternity is coming. Don't die without Jesus."

There was no response.

Knight closed his Bible, prayed silently for several minutes, then put out the lantern and crawled into his own bedroll.

The next day, Knight and Jordan were moving through the high country just before noon when suddenly Knight saw a big bull elk off to his right between the towering pines. The elk was looking another direction and had not noticed them. Whispering from the side of his mouth as he laid a hand on Jordan's arm, he said, "Bull elk! Off to the right. Stand still."

Knight shouldered his rifle, and as he was taking aim, the elk spotted them and started to bolt. The rifle bucked against Knight's shoulder as it roared, and the elk went down.

Later, while they were carefully eviscerating the elk with its body hanging by a rope from a tree limb, Knight found his friend quiet once again. He decided to engage him in conversation. Pausing with the big sharp knife in his hand, he said, "Tell me something, ol' pal."

Jordan met his gaze. "What's that?"

"Well, I've been hearing some talk around town about you and Belinda Ashworth. Is it true that love is budding between the two of you and you haven't even told your best friend about it? You haven't said a word."

Jordan sighed. "So you were told that Belinda and I are in love."

"Mm-hmm. Three times."

Jordan's features hardened. He shook his head, meeting Knight's gaze. "It's not true. Belinda and I are not in love. But she's telling people we are."

Knight frowned. "Uh-oh."

"I might as well tell you. This is the thing that has been troubling me so much."

"Oh, so that's it."

"Yeah. Belinda's parents and my parents are putting pressure on me to marry her, and Belinda has been adding her own pressure—not only by pushing herself on me, but by telling her friends that we have fallen in love."

Knight nodded, and went back to work with the knife. "Don't you feel something for Belinda?"

"Only friendship. I have absolutely no romantic feelings toward her whatsoever. I am not interested in her as a possible wife. After Nellie Freeman dumped me for that other guy five years ago, I haven't found anyone who interests me. And Belinda is about to destroy even the friendship I feel toward her. Knight, I can't go anywhere in town or even among the ranchers without being bombarded with questions about when the wedding is going to take place. I'm trying very hard not to cause any trouble for Belinda or to embarrass her in any way. But if she keeps it up, I'll have to do something to put a stop to it."

Knight paused in his work again. "I can understand why you want it stopped."

"It's got to stop. The pressure from both sets of parents and the lies Belinda is telling are about to drive me crazy. I've got to do something about it, but I don't know how to do it without hurting their feelings—especially those of my own parents. I've come close to losing my temper with Belinda, and so far I've been able to keep from it. But you know my temper. Do you have any suggestions? This thing can't go on."

"Have you told your parents that you're not interested in marrying Belinda?"

"Yes. But they both want her for a daughter-in-law so bad, they say in time as I get to know her better, I will fall in love with her. So the problem is still there."

Knight shook his head. "You do have a problem, but I don't know what to suggest. It wouldn't be so complicated if your own parents weren't so adamant in their desire for you to marry Belinda. And I certainly admire you for wanting to spare them from being hurt. Wish I could help, but I'm drawing a blank on this one."

Jordan nodded. "I guess I'll have to figure it out for myself. It's my dilemma."

They finished cutting up the elk into relatively small pieces, put the meat in gunnysacks, draped them over the horses' backs behind the saddles, and headed for home.

While they were working their way down the steep slopes toward level land, Jordan said, "Ol' pal, we've talked about the lack of romance in my life. What about the lack of romance in your life?"

Knight was quiet for a brief moment, then said, "Well, it's like this. Even though there are a few eligible young women in both Elkton and Ketcham, I simply haven't found the right one."

Jordan chuckled. "Pardon me, but I happen to know that Christine Pfeiffer in Elkton and Kathleen O'Hara in Ketcham both admire you a whole lot. They're both lovely young ladies. Why don't you pursue one of them?"

"They are both nice girls, Jordan, but they're not Christians. I would never marry a girl who doesn't know the Lord. If I did, it wouldn't work. God calls that an unequal yoke, and commands His born-again children not to be unequally yoked to unbelievers."

"Oh. I wasn't aware of that. Makes sense, though."

Knight smiled. "Everything God says in His Word makes sense."


The following morning, Jordan Shaw walked into the Ketcham Bank and approached the closest teller's window.

"Good morning, Jordan," said the small, baldheaded man. "How are things at the Bar-S?"

"Couldn't be better, Edgar," Jordan replied with a warm smile. "In fact, it's so good, I'm here to make a deposit into the Bar-S business account." As Jordan spoke, he handed Edgar the checks and currency, along with a deposit slip.

Edgar looked at the deposit slip, then at Jordan. "It's not dated. Would you mind putting the date on the slip, please?"

"Of course not," said Jordan, taking a pen from an inkwell provided for the customers. He paused, looking toward the ceiling. "Uh…"

Edgar chuckled. "It's Wednesday, October 16, 1872."

Jordan laughed as he wrote it down. "Oh yeah! I've been so busy, the time gets away from me. The sixteenth, already. What do you know?"

Less than two minutes later, Jordan stepped out of the bank onto the boardwalk, tucking the receipt in his shirt pocket. He was heading for his horse when he heard a familiar female voice call his name.

His stomach tightened.

He halted, a frown etching itself across his brow. Before he turned to look at Belinda, he muttered to himself, "Oh no. What now?"

Then with effort, he replaced the frown with a fake smile and turned toward her. With Belinda were her parents, and a man and woman about their age. They were coming toward him with Belinda in the lead. All five were smiling broadly.

"Hello, Jordie," said a bright-eyed Belinda, drawing up. She turned toward the others, making sure her arm touched Jordan's. "Papa, I'll let you make the introductions."

Belinda's bold move to press herself so close to Jordan made him nervous.

Hyman introduced his brother and sister-in-law, Ralph and Claire Ashworth, to Jordan, saying they were from Lincoln, Nebraska. After Jordan politely greeted them, Hyman explained that they had just picked Ralph and Claire up at the railroad station. They had come to visit for a few days.

Both Ralph and Claire were friendly to Jordan, and his stomach tightened the more when a smiling Claire said, "Jordan, Belinda has written us several times about you. I'm so glad to see that my niece's young man is every bit as handsome as we've been told." Giggling in a girlish way, she ran her gaze between Jordan and Belinda. "Are you two engaged, yet?"

Jordan's stomach wrenched.

While he was trying to think of a way to react to the question without upsetting Hyman and Dorothy, Belinda slipped her hand into the crook of his arm. "Now, now, Auntie Claire. We mustn't rush things!"

Jordan's mind was racing. How was he going to bring this misleading "courtship" to an end? This horrid thing had to stop.

At that moment, Jordan's attention was drawn to a buggy coming from the direction of the railroad station, occupied by a young couple. Only the man was familiar. He was Del Forton. Jordan and Knight had gone all the way through school with Del, who had moved with his parents to the small town of Lost River, Idaho—some forty miles east—a couple of years after graduation. Jordan had seen Del only twice since then.

In order to get away from the Ashworths, Jordan called out, "Del! Hey, Del!" and waved.

Del heard him immediately, turned to see who was calling his name, and smiled as he pulled rein. "Jordan! Hey! Good to see you!"

Quickly, Jordan turned to the Ashworths. "I'll have to ask you to excuse me. This is an old friend I haven't seen in a long time."

"Of course," said Hyman.

Belinda let go of Jordan's arm, and he hurried across the street toward the buggy.

Del Forton jumped out of the buggy and shook hands with Jordan. "It really is good to see you."

"Same here," said Jordan, relieved to be away from Belinda and her family. He glanced at the lovely young woman. "And who's this, Del?"

"Someone I want you to meet. I just told her who you were. Jordan, I want you to meet Miss Sally Myers from Buffalo, New York."

"Proud to meet you, Miss Sally," said Jordan.

"Sally has come to be my mail order bride," said Del. "I just picked her up at the depot."

Jordan's eyes widened. "Your mail order bride?"

"Yes, sir."

"I'm pleased to meet you," said Sally. "Del told me just now that the two of you went all the way through school together."

"We sure did," said Jordan, then turned to his old friend. "Mail order bride, eh?"

"Mm-hmm. I simply hadn't been able to find a girl that suited me anywhere in this part of Idaho, so I decided to try the mail order bride system. I put ads in several eastern newspapers. I received a good number of letters answering the ads, but when I read Sally's letter, I knew she was the one."

"Well, well, well!" said Jordan. He set his gaze back on Sally. "I've heard about women coming west from mail order bride ads, but I've never met one."

While climbing back into the buggy, Del said, "Sally is going to be staying with some neighbors while the two of us get better acquainted. If everything works out like we think it will, we'll marry."

Rapid thoughts were flitting through Jordan's mind as he said, "I have a feeling it is definitely going to work out for you."

Del and Sally told Jordan good-bye, and as the buggy pulled away, Jordan turned around and headed back across the street. Deep in thought about his conversation with Del and Sally while threading through the traffic, Jordan failed to see Belinda standing outside the mercantile, a half block down the street from the bank. She was waving at him, trying to draw his attention.

She thought he looked her way a couple of times, but he proceeded across the street, mounted, and trotted his horse the opposite direction, heading north out of town toward Elkton.

A pucker formed between Belinda's eyebrows. *I wonder,* she thought. *Did he really not see me, or was he just pretending?* Giving horse and rider one last glance as they passed from view, she entered the store, seeking her mother and Aunt Claire.


Totally unaware of Belinda's presence in front of the mercantile, Jordan trotted his horse out of town, his mind still fixed on the chance meeting with Del Forton and Sally Myers.

"A mail order bride, hmm?" he mused aloud, with only the horse to hear. "Is this possibly the solution to my problem? But…could I marry someone I don't really know?"

He thought on it a moment.

"Well, I know Belinda, and I sure can't and won't marry her."

The bay gelding turned his head and rolled his eyes back as if to say, "Were you talking to me?"

Jordan laughed. "It's okay, ol' boy. I was just talking to myself. I…I think I might have the answer to my big problem."

Arriving in Elkton, Jordan hauled up in front of the newspaper building, excited about talking to his best friend. He slid from the saddle, tied the horse to the hitch rail, and entered the office.

"Hello, Jordan," said Erline Tyler with a bright smile.

"Hello, Erline. Is Knight in his office?"

"He sure is. Go on in."

Jordan could barely contain his excitement as he knocked on Knight's door and waited for a reply.

"Come in!" came the familiar voice.

The instant Knight saw the light in his friend's eyes and the wide smile on his lips, he knew something good had happened. Rising from his desk, he said, "You look happier than I've seen you in a long time."

"Can we talk?"

Piqued with curiosity, Knight gestured toward the chair in front of his desk. "Of course. Come sit down."

Jordan immediately began pacing the floor. "I'm too excited to sit, Knight. Go ahead. You sit down."

The pacing went on while a puzzled Knight Colburn returned to his chair behind the desk. "What in the world has got you so stirred up, pal?"

Still in motion, Jordan's words tumbled off his tongue one on top of the other. "I found the answer, friend. I found it! My Belinda problem is about to come to an end."

Knight jumped out of his chair, rounded the desk, and took hold of Jordan's arm. "Come on," he said, guiding him to the intended chair. "Sit down so we can talk."

With that, Knight pushed him down on the chair. Jordan remained where placed, and Knight sat on the edge of the desk. Lowering his head to look his friend straight in the eye, he said, "All right, now. Out with it. What's this wonderful plan that is going to solve your Belinda problem? Give it to me slowly."

Eyes dancing, Jordan held his words to a normal pace and said, "Guess who I just saw in Ketcham?"

"Uh...George Washington."

Jordan shook his head and snorted. "Come on. Be serious."

"All right. Who did you see?"

"Del Forton."

"Del! Well, how's he doing?"

"Just great."

"Is he married?"

"No, but that is exactly what I want to tell you about!"

"What's got you so excited? Has he asked you to be best man in his wedding?"

"Aw, nothing like that. Listen to me, now."

"I'm all ears."

"Del had a pretty lady named Miss Sally Myers with him. He had just picked her up at the railroad station. She's from Buffalo, New York, and has come to be his mail order bride!"

Knight left the desk top, sat down in his chair, and chuckled. "Well, isn't that something? A mail order bride."

Leaning over the desktop on his elbows, and looking Knight square in the eye, Jordan said in a level tone, "I want to place a mail order bride ad in several papers back east. You can wire them for me, can't you?"

"Why…ah…yes, but—"

"But what?"

"Well, this is all so sudden. I—"

"Knight, I ran into Belinda and her parents in Ketcham. They had picked up Hyman's brother and his wife at the depot. Belinda's aunt told me right off that Belinda had written to them about me several times…then she asked if we were engaged yet."

"Oh no."

"Oh yes. That's it! Knight, I want to order myself a bride from back east. That will solve the Belinda problem once and for all."

Knight frowned slightly. "You're really serious about this."

"I couldn't be more serious. When my mail order bride arrives, I'll strut down the streets of Elkton and let all the busybodies see her. It won't take long for word to get to Belinda, her parents, and my own parents. Nobody's feelings should be hurt, because I've made no commitment to Belinda, and no promise to her parents or mine that I would marry her. This will settle the whole thing without my hurting anybody."

"All right," said Knight, opening a desk drawer and taking out a sheet of paper. He picked up a pencil. "What do you want to say in the ad?"

Jordan thought on it for a moment. "Tell you what, Knight. You're the man of words. How about you write it for me?"

"If that's the way you want it."

"You're the newspaper man. That's the way I want it."

With Jordan looking on, Knight wrote the ad for him. When it was finished, Knight handed it to him and said, "Read it over carefully now and see if there are any changes you want."

As Jordan read the finished product, a smile spread over his face. Looking at his friend, he said, "Perfect! I like it very much. It'll catch many a female eye." As he spoke, he handed it back to him.

"Okay," said Knight, "I'll wire the ad to a dozen eastern newspapers. From what I know about the mail order bride system, you no doubt will get many responses from eager young women. The ads should be in the papers within a week, and you will probably start getting letters within two to three weeks."

"Good," said Jordan, rising to his feet. "What's the charge?"

"Nothing from the *Sentinel*. The newspapers back east will send their bills here to me. I'll turn them over to you when they come."

Jordan grinned. "You should charge me something, too."

"Friends don't do it that way."

"I appreciate it, ol' pal. Now, just one thing…"

"Mm-hmm?"

"This must be kept a secret. Just between you and me, all right?"

"Of course. Just between you and me."

As Jordan mounted his horse and headed for the ranch, he smiled to himself, knowing it would shock Belinda and both families when his new mail order bride arrived, but the stress he had suffered over the Belinda situation would be over.

ON WEDNESDAY, OCTOBER 16, at the same time Knight Colburn was writing the mail order bride ad for Jordan Shaw in Idaho, Martha Morrow was in the operating room at the Richmond Hospital in Virginia.

Derick and Diana sat close together on a threadbare sofa in the waiting room. Hands clasped in their laps, shoulders hunched, they tried to encourage each other, but often slipped into deep thoughts of their own.

Head bent low, Diana stared at the well-worn hardwood floor that had been paced and scuffed by countless feet over the years.

Outside in the hall, Chief Constable Bob Perry stopped at the nurse's station and was informed that the Morrow siblings were in the waiting room next to the operating room.

When Perry drew up to the door, he paused as he set sympathetic eyes on Derick and Diana, who were the only ones in the room. They were not yet aware of his presence.

*Children should not have to suffer at the hands of a father who is out of control,* he thought.

Taking a step into the room, Perry was still unnoticed. Both young people were bent over, staring at the floor. The chief constable coughed lightly to get their attention.

Both heads came up, and when Derick and Diana saw him, they rose to their feet in anticipation of the news he was bringing them in regard to their father.

Perry moved up to them. "Hello, Diana, Derick. How is it going with your mother?"

"Her shoulder is definitely dislocated, Chief Perry," said Diana, "and the bone in her upper arm is fractured. They should be through working on her soon from what a nurse told us about twenty minutes ago. Of course, it will be some time before she is awake so we can see her."

Perry nodded.

"So what about our father?" asked Derick.

"He's going to spend a month in jail for assaulting Tom Wymore, and Judge Weathers has ordered him to pay all of Tom's medical bills."

Brother and sister exchanged glances.

Derick released a weary sigh. "We don't even have the money to pay Mama's medical expenses. How will we ever pay for Tom's as well?" he muttered. "And with Papa in jail, he can't even earn any money."

Diana patted his arm. "We'll make it somehow, Derick. Right now our biggest concern is Mama. Somehow we must protect her from this horrible thing ever happening again."

Derick set his jaw, rolled his narrow shoulders, and said in a brave, determined voice, "Papa better never touch her again, or he's gonna answer to me."

Discreetly hiding a grim smile, Perry laid a hand on the boy's shoulder. "Judge Weathers told me if your mother will press charges against him, Derick, he'll sentence him to a year in jail."

Derick looked at his sister again, then at the chief constable. "Mama won't do that, sir. I know it."

"Right," said Diana. "She knows if she did, when he got out, he would come after her with a vengeance."

Perry sighed and shook his head. "Well, I guess the best you can wish for is that the month in jail will be enough time for your father to realize his mistakes, and not let himself repeat them."

"We can only hope so," said Diana.

At that moment, the doctor who had been working on Martha came through the door. All three turned to face him.

"Hello, Chief," said the doctor.

"Hello, Dr. Bates."

To Derick and Diana, Bates said, "We were finally able to get your mother's nosebleed stopped. The puffiness around her eye has made it close completely, but it will heal in time. We put her shoulder back in place, and we set her arm. She has a cast on it and will carry the cast in a sling. It's going to be quite a while before she's back to normal again. She won't be able to do much in the way of cooking and housework until the cast is off."

"We'll see that she has all the help she needs," Diana assured him.

"Good. She is bound to get a little discouraged at times, so she'll need all the encouragement you can give her."

The doctor turned to Perry. "Something has to be done about Mr. Morrow, Chief. Martha can't take any more of this kind of punishment."

"I understand," said Perry. "Stu can be jailed for a year if Martha will press charges. But that's as far as the law can go. I'm glad, at least, that her injuries are not worse."

"So are we," said Derick.

Perry ran his gaze between brother and sister. "I'll come back and see your mother tomorrow. I must, by law, ask her if she wants to press charges."

The siblings both nodded silently. Perry excused himself and left.

Dr. Bates said, "You can see your mother in an hour or so. She will be in a room by then, and the anesthetic will be wearing off. One of the nurses will advise you as to what room they put her in."

Almost two hours had passed when a nurse came into the waiting room, approached Derick and Diana, and said, "You are Mrs. Morrow's children, right?"

"Yes, ma'am," said Derick.

"She's in room 212. You can go down there now, but you should only stay ten minutes or so. She needs to rest."

They assured the nurse they would make it a short visit, thanked her, and hurried to room 212. As they stepped into the room, they saw their mother in the first bed, and another woman in the bed by the window.

Martha was still groggy from the chloroform, but she managed a weak smile. "Hello, sweet babies," she said.

They both greeted her quietly, saying they loved her, and bent down one at a time to kiss her cheek.

Diana laid a hand on her mother's good arm. "Dr. Bates said you will be fine. It'll just take a little time."

Martha nodded slowly.

"When you get home," said Derick, "you are going to be a lady of leisure. You're going to sit and rest while your daughters cook and your sons clean house."

Martha managed another weak smile, then looked toward her roommate. "Laura, this is my daughter, Diana, and my son, Derick. Children, this is Mrs. Laura Thomas."

Both greeted her politely, then Laura said, "I am recovering from surgery that I had three days ago. Your mother hasn't been awake very long, so about all we've done is introduce ourselves to each other. I'm wondering what happened to her."

Brother and sister looked down at their mother questioningly.

"You might as well tell her," Martha said. "She will hear the nurses talking about it, anyway."

Derick stepped to the side of Laura's bed, and in brief, explained that his father had lost his temper and beat his mother severely.

Laura's facial features tightened, and a compassionate look showed in her eyes. "Oh, I'm so sorry, Martha. I didn't know. I didn't mean to pry. Please forgive me."

"You weren't prying," said Martha. "You were only being kind enough to show interest. There's nothing to forgive."

"Chief Perry came to see us in the waiting room, Mama," said Diana.

"He told us Papa will be in jail a month for what he did to Tom."

Martha closed her eyes, opened them again. "A month."

"Mm-hmm."

"And Judge Weathers says he has to pay all of Tom's medical bills," added Derick.

"Chief Perry told us that the law says he has to present you with the opportunity to press charges against Papa," said Diana. "He's coming to see you tomorrow."

Martha's already pallid face went sheet white. "Oh no! I can't. You know what he would do when he got out."

"We told him you wouldn't press charges, Mama," said Derick. "And we told him it was because of what Papa would do to you. But he still has to come in his official capacity as chief constable and give you the opportunity to press charges. He said if you did, Judge Weathers would sentence him to a year in jail."

"A year?" Martha said, her voice quivering. "It would only make things worse."

The trepidation that was in Martha's eyes touched Laura's heart. She wanted to say something encouraging, but she couldn't find what she felt were the proper words.

Diana said, "Mama, the nurse told us not to stay but ten minutes or so. We need to go so you can get some rest."

"Right," said Derick. "We're going to Tom's room and see him before we head for home."

"I hope he gets well soon," said Martha.

Diana bent down and kissed Martha's cheek. "I love you, Mama. You rest, now."

Derick kissed her cheek also. "We'll see you tomorrow, Mama. I love you."

Martha said, "I love both of you so much. Tell Deborah, Daniel, and Dennis I love them, too. I wish the hospital didn't have the rule that a child has to be at least sixteen to visit someone here. I'd love to see them."

"You'll be coming home soon," said Diana in a soothing tone. "It was nice meeting you, Mrs. Thomas."

"Yes," said Derick. "It sure was."

Laura smiled warmly. "Since your mother is in that cast, I'll ring the bell for her anytime she needs a nurse."

Both of them thanked her, then started toward the door, heartsick over their mother's condition. They paused at the door and looked back at her tired, bruised, and battered face. She looked so pathetic in the cast and with the black-and-purple eye that was swollen shut. Their faces showed the anguish they were feeling.

"Please go on home and take care of the younger children for me. Like you said, Diana, I'll be home soon."

Derick and Diana, still reluctant to leave her, held onto each other, looking at her with sad eyes.

Summoning up all her strength, and making an effort to smile again in spite of her battered mouth, Martha said, "You will do me more good by taking care of them than by staying here—as much as I love having you. I'll be fine, and when you come back tomorrow, I'll look much better. I promise."

"All right, Mama," said Diana. "We'll do as you say."

Both took a lingering look at their mother, then left.

Laura's gaze was fixed on Martha as she released a pent-up sigh, and a pained look etched itself on her features. "Martha, you're hurting. Would you like for me to call a nurse? I'm sure they can give you something to relieve the pain."

Martha swallowed hard and turned her face toward Laura. "Yes, please," she said in a strained whisper. "Even the light makes my head and eyes hurt."

When Derick and Diana entered Tom Wymore's room, they found his parents there, standing beside the bed. Zack and Ruth Wymore gave them a cold look.

"Hello, Diana, Derick," said Tom through the slit in the bandage on his face and jaw. "Nice of you to come by."

"Tom is supposed to rest," Zack said curtly.

"That's right," came Ruth's frigid agreement.

Diana stepped ahead of her brother, drew up close to the bed, and said, "We'll only stay a moment. Tom, I just want you to know how sorry I am for what my father did to you."

Ruth's face flushed red. The veins stood out prominently on her neck as she said bluntly, "It would be best, Diana, if you and Tom don't see each other anymore. If the two of you hadn't been talking there on the street, this wouldn't have happened."

Tom reached out and touched his mother's hand. "Mom, I told you it wasn't Diana's fault. It was I who approached her."

Zack said grimly, "Tom, since Stu Morrow feels toward you as he does, it really is best that you stay away from Diana."

Diana said, "Mr. Wymore, it isn't Tom in particular that my father dislikes. He doesn't want me in contact with any young man."

"I told both of you," said Tom, "that Diana warned me about

her father when I approached her. But I thought I could reason with him, so I went against Diana's warning and tried to talk to him. Please don't blame her. It's my fault."

"Well, trying to reason with him didn't work, Tom," said Ruth, "so you should avoid any contact with Diana from now on."

Feeling quite uncomfortable, Diana turned to her brother and said, "We need to be going, Derick. Tom needs to rest."

Derick nodded. "All right."

Looking back at Tom, Diana said, "Again, I'm so sorry."

Tom closed his eyes and nodded. "Like I said, Diana, it was my fault."

Diana walked ahead of her brother, and as both of them stepped out of the room and started down the hall, they heard footsteps and looked over their shoulders.

Ruth's face was flushed again as she rushed up and said tartly, "Diana, I want you to stay completely away from my son. I mean it. Do you understand?"

Tears welled up in Diana's eyes. "Mrs. Wymore, it was Tom who approached me. Didn't you hear him?"

"Tom wouldn't have approached you if you hadn't led him on, and you know it!"

Derick's eyes flashed fire. "This is not true, ma'am! My sister did not lead him on."

Ignoring him, Ruth pointed a stiff forefinger at Diana, shook it threateningly, and hissed, "You stay away from my son, or you're going to be one sorry girl! Do you hear me?"

With that, she wheeled and went back into the room.

Derick put an arm around his weeping sister. "Come on, Diana. Let's go home."


Stuart Morrow was lying on his bunk when he heard the door that led to the office come open and heard a prisoner two cells down the row say, "Are you here to let me out, Chief?"

"No, Harold," said Perry. "I don't think you're going to get out till tomorrow."

"How come?" said Harold. "I thought—"

"Judge Weathers had some other things to tend to today. I think he'll get to your case tomorrow."

Stu turned his big head so he could see the chief, and realized he was coming toward his cell. He gave Perry a sour look as he drew up to the bars, but stayed on the bunk and waited for the chief to speak.

Peering through the bars, Perry fixed Morrow with stern eyes and said, "I just came from the hospital."

Stu sat up, rolled his wide shoulders, then rose to his feet and stepped to the bars. "Yeah?"

"Yeah. Your wife's in pretty bad shape. If you don't get that temper of yours under control, mister, you'll probably kill her next time."

Stu frowned and jutted his jaw. "Whattaya mean?"

"You practically crippled her this time. You dislocated her right shoulder and broke the bone in her upper right arm. Who knows how long it will be till she can use her shoulder normally again. She lost a lot of blood because you bloodied her nose. I saw her at the house just before we had to coldcock you. Both her nose and mouth were bleeding profusely. They finally got the bleeding stopped at the hospital, but it took a while. I talked to Diana and Derick, and to Dr. Walter Bates in the waiting room. They said her right eye is swollen shut and her face is badly bruised."

Stu drew a sleeve across his mouth. "So what did the judge say about me?"

"That's the main reason I came to see you. He's giving you a month in this cell, and you are to pay all of Tom's medical bills."

Stu's mouth fell open. "Yeah? Well, just how am I supposed to pay those bills? I can't earn any money sitting in here."

"That's your problem, mister," Perry said tightly. "But it could get worse."

"Whattaya mean?"

"It's my duty as chief constable to talk to Martha and tell her if she wants, she can press assault and battery charges against you. Judge Weathers says if she does, he will sentence you to a year behind bars, in addition to the month that you are already going to serve."

Stu gripped the bars till his knuckles turned white. "She wouldn't dare," he growled.

Perry shrugged. "It's up to her. I'll be talking to her tomorrow and offer her the opportunity."

Stu's features turned a deep crimson. He opened his mouth to speak, thought better of it, and moved back to the bunk. He looked back at Perry, shook his head, and sat down without another word.

When Diana and Derick reached the hospital's parking lot, Derick helped her climb onto the wagon seat, then climbed up and sat down beside her. Diana took a hankie from her dress pocket and dabbed at the fresh tears that were spilling down her cheeks.

As Derick took the reins in hand, he looked at her with pity in his eyes and said, "Sis, are you all right?"

Diana sniffed and blinked against a fresh supply of tears. "I'll be okay in a minute." She sniffed again. "Derick…"

"Uh-huh?"

"Maybe we should go to the jail and see Papa."

His eyes widened. "What for? He'll probably just cuss you out for talking to Tom."

"Maybe so, but he is our father. We should go visit him."

Derick sighed, put the horses into motion, and said, "If you insist."

When brother and sister walked into the police station, they approached the sergeant on the desk. He gave them a weak smile and said, "What can I do for you young people?"

"Sergeant," said Derick, "our father, Stuart Morrow, is one of your prisoners."

"Yes?"

"I'm Derick Morrow, and this is my sister, Diana. We would like to see our father."

Sergeant Ben Chasen slowly shook his head. "We have a rule, here. No one your age can visit a prisoner unless they are accompanied by someone twenty-one or over."

"Our mother is in the hospital, sir," said Diana. "We have no one to accompany us."

Chasen scratched at an ear. "I…I'm acquainted with your situation. Tell you what. I'll take you to Chief Perry's office. He is the only one who has the authority to bypass the rule."

When Bob Perry looked up from his desk and saw Chasen leading Diana and Derick into his office, he rose to his feet and smiled. "Hello Diana, Derick."

"They want to visit their father, sir," said Chasen. "Since they are both obviously under twenty-one, I explained the rule to them. I…thought maybe you'd bypass the rule because of the circumstances."

Running his gaze between brother and sister, Perry said, "I'm a bit surprised that you would even want to see him after what he did to your mother."

"Well, sir," said Diana, "we felt we should come and visit him in spite of what he did, since he is our father."

Perry sighed and said, "I hope someday Stuart Morrow realizes just what a special son and daughter he has. All right. I'll take you to him."

As they followed the chief down the narrow hall that led to the cell block, Derick took hold of Diana's hand, gripping it firmly. She smiled at him, and her eyes told him how very much she appreciated him.

Perry led them into the cell block, and while the other prisoners looked on, he ushered them up to their father's cell.

The big man was lying on his bunk once again, his eyes closed.

"Morrow," said Perry, "there's someone here to see you."

Stu opened his eyes, glanced through the bars, and when he saw his oldest two children, he got up from the bunk.

Looking at the young pair, Perry said, "You can stay fifteen minutes, maximum. I'll be back to get you."

As the chief constable walked away and passed through the hall door, Stuart Morrow set fiery eyes on Derick and Diana and stepped up to the bars. The anger in those eyes put chills down both their spines.

WHEN RUTH WYMORE RETURNED to her son's hospital room, she heard Tom say to his father, "But how will he ever be able to do that?"

Drawing up, Ruth ran her questioning gaze between both men and asked, "How can who do what?"

Zack said, "Since we were interrupted by Diana and her brother before we could tell Tom about our visit at home from Chief Bob Perry just before we came to the hospital, I was telling him that Perry told us Judge Weathers was going to make Stuart Morrow pay all of his medical bills."

"I was asking Dad how Mr. Morrow could pay my bills," said Tom. "For one thing, he is a farmer who doesn't even own the farm he lives on. He rents it. I know the Morrows don't have much money. And for another, if he's in jail for a month, things will get tighter for him."

"I don't know what he will do," said Zack, "but according to Chief Perry, Judge Weathers is going to make him pay."

"That's Morrow's worry," Ruth said. "If he hadn't beat you up, he wouldn't be facing this problem."

Tom sighed and used a hand to adjust the bandage on his jaw. "Diana warned me not to try talking to her father. If I'd listened, I wouldn't be in this condition, and there wouldn't have been any trouble for her. I just felt sure I could reason with him. I really do like her. She's a sweet girl, and until this trouble started with her father, she's always shown a keen sense of humor. The fear of what he might do if she breaks his unfair rules has clouded that sense of humor. I hope he will start treating her right so she can be her old self again. She's always been very pleasant to be around."

Ruth pulled her lips into a thin line. "Tom, when I went out there in the hall, I told Diana to stay away from you. I don't want you to have anything to do with her anymore."

"Mom, I'm not a child. If I want to see her some more, I—"

"You what?" Ruth said crisply. "You want to end up in the hospital again? You like to be beat up, do you?"

"Well, no, but—"

"How may times do you have to be pounded to a pulp before you realize that Diana is poison? Hmm?"

"Mom, it's not Diana's fault. I told you...it was my fault. She tried to get me to walk away when her father saw us together. Like I said, I thought I could reason with him. I got pounded because I wouldn't listen."

"Come on, son. She led you on. That's why you're lying here in this bed."

"She did not lead me on!" Tom said quickly. "This was my doing. Why won't you listen to me?"

"Tom," said Zack, "that's enough. Let's drop it. Diana is not for you. If you'll stay away from her and find yourself another girl, everything will turn out all right. Now, let's talk about when you get out of here."

At the Richmond jail, the blaze of anger in Stuart Morrow's eyes against the crimson flush of his skin was a wicked thing as he stared through the bars at Diana and lashed out at her. "I'm surprised at your gall, girl! What are you doing here?"

Diana's features lost color. Her lips trembled as she tried to form her words.

"She wanted to come and see you," spoke up Derick, his own eyes showing the ire that he felt. "Why can't you be civil to her?"

Stu's face flushed a deeper crimson. "You stay out of it, boy! I wasn't talking to you!" Then to Diana he said, "This whole thing is your fault! If you hadn't disobeyed me and talked to Tom Wymore, none of this would have happened! I wouldn't be in jail, and your mother wouldn't be in the hospital."

Tears filmed Diana's eyes. With face white and strained, she said, "Papa, I didn't approach Tom. He approached me."

"Oh? Then why didn't you send him on his way? Tell me that, girl!"

"I tried, Papa, but—"

"Don't lie to me!" boomed Stu.

The men in the other cells were looking on in muted awe.

Diana's blood heated up, sending courage through her. "I'm not lying!" she retorted. "When you sent me after Dennis's cough syrup, I told Tom you wouldn't let me date him. And when I saw you coming, I told him to take his cousin and go. But he wouldn't listen. He insisted on asking you if he could date me."

"Bah!" said Stu. "Says you!"

"It's the truth, Papa. You just won't believe anything I say."

"She's telling the truth, Papa," said Derick in her defense. "Diana wouldn't lie to you."

"Oh no?"

"No. This morning when you were drinking at the Golden Lantern and we were going to meet Mama and the girls at the general store, Diana told Tom to leave. Deborah told me so."

"Oh, sure," Stu said in a tone of disgust. "Deborah would lie to cover for her sister."

Diana's anger at her father's derogatory words about Deborah filled her with more courage. Her eyes flashed as she took a step closer to the cell door and said, "What is it, Papa? Why can't you take any of us at our word?"

"Don't you speak to me like that," said Stu. "I'm your father. When I get outta here, you're gonna get it! This whole mess is your fault! Me in jail, and your mother in the hospital!"

"What are you talking about?" Diana said tartly. "It's your fault! I didn't beat up on Tom. You did. And I didn't beat up on Mama. I didn't dislocate her shoulder, break her arm, and bruise her face. You did."

Swearing at Diana, Stu thrust an arm through the bars to grab her. But she stepped out of reach.

Derick's own anger flared. "Papa, what you did was dead

wrong! Diana is right. This whole thing is your fault. You need to face it and admit it."

Stu's upper lip pulled back over his teeth in a feral gesture, and he swore vehemently as he attempted to grasp Derick through the bars, but the youth was just out of reach and knew it. "How dare you talk like that to me, boy! I'm your father."

The other prisoners still gawked at the scene silently.

"You're my father, yes, " said Derick, "but that doesn't make you free of fault. Why don't you face it? You shouldn't have beat up on Tom. And what you did to Mama was worse."

Stu's breathing was hot and heavy.

"It sure was, Papa," said Diana. "Mama was only trying to protect me from you when you were going to hit me. And she took that violent beating for it. You should be ashamed of yourself for what you did to Mama."

Fixing the girl with a deadly glare, Stu hissed, "The day I walk out of here, girl, you're gonna get the beating of your life. D'you hear me? And Derick, if you try to interfere, you'll get the beating of your life. I've had enough of this insolent back talk! You two are out of line!"

"But putting Mama in the hospital isn't out of line?" said Diana.

"Enough, girl!" said Stu. "You're in for it. You just wait and see."

Diana met his gaze without showing fear. She knew the only reason she had no fear at the moment was because of the bars that separated them.

"You can give me that look now, girl!" said Stu. "But when I get outta here, I'll teach you some fear."

The thought of his threat changed Diana's countenance, and he saw a touch of dread capture her eyes.

"I'm sure you've thought of running away from home to escape what's coming to you, girl. Well, if you ever do, I'll track you down, and you'll get a beating like you've never imagined. The world isn't big enough for you to hide from me."

The thought of running away from home had just passed through Diana's mind and when her father so quickly brought it up, it was like she was a trapped animal with no way to escape. Tears welled up in her eyes. She drew a ragged breath and broke down, weeping.

Derick took her hand and said, "Come on, sis. We're leaving right now."

"You can get away from me at this point, girl," said Stu, "but I won't always be locked up. I'll beat you till you beg me to stop, and when I do, you're gonna apologize for your insolence. You too, boy!"

Derick softly pushed a sobbing Diana toward the door, ignoring his father's latest threat.

As Derick opened the door, Stu's big voice thundered, "Payday will come for both of you! I mean it. Especially you, Diana. Just you wait and see!"

Derick paused, gripping his sister's hand, looked back, and said, "We came because Diana wanted to see you, Papa. She said you are our father, and we should come and see you. I warned her that you'd cuss her good when you saw her, but she still said we should come because you are our father. Boy, did we make a mistake."

Stu's beefy face was a mask of wrath as the hot breath sawed in and out of his lungs and he glared at them.

Suddenly, Sergeant Ben Chasen appeared in the hall, having heard Stu's latest outburst because the hall door was open.

"What's going on, here?" he asked, noting Diana's tears and Stu's flushed features.

"Papa's mad at us," said Derick. "We came to see him because we wanted to show him respect as our father, but he doesn't appreciate it. He's blaming my sister for his being in jail, and he's making all kinds of threats of how he's going to give her a real beating when he gets out of here."

"You two go on," said Chasen, stepping out of the way so they could move down the hall.

With an arm around his weeping sister, Derick hastily guided her toward the door that led to the police department offices.

Chasen waited till they were through the door, then while the other prisoners looked on, he stepped up to Morrow's cell. "So you like our jail, eh, Morrow?"

Stu's jaw jutted and his neck stiffened. "Whattaya mean?"

"I heard you threatening both of them…especially Diana. 'Payday' was the word you used. If you beat that girl like Derick said you were threatening to—or him, either—you'll be right back in here. And I remind you of what Chief Perry told you. If Mrs. Morrow presses charges against you for the beating you gave her, you'll get a year in jail. And with what we know about you now, if you beat those two young people like you were threatening to, you could end up in prison for twenty years. Or longer."

Stu only stared at him, breathing hotly.

Frowning, Chasen said, "Are you listening to me?"

The big man pivoted, swinging a fist through the air, and sat down on his bunk.

When Derick and Diana moved outside and walked toward the wagon, which was parked down the street a distance, Diana wiped tears from her eyes and said, "I wish Mama would press charges against him. Maybe in that year he was locked up, we could find a way to move where he couldn't find us."

Derick let a few seconds pass. "He'd find us, sis. You heard his threat about what would happen if you tried to run away. Mama knows he'd find us, too. That's why she's afraid to press charges."

They reached the wagon, and both horses whinnied at them.

Derick helped Diana up into the seat, rounded the wagon, and climbed up beside her. She was still crying as he put the team in motion, pulled into traffic, and started down the street.

Holding the reins with his left hand, Derick took hold of her hand with the other and squeezed it. "This is why I wasn't keen on the idea of coming to see him, sis. I was sure he'd light into you for talking to Tom."

Diana nodded. "So much for trying to show him respect as our father."

"Well, at least we tried."

"Yes," she said, sniffling. "We tried."

Diana kept sniffling and wiping tears as they passed through Richmond, and when they reached the outskirts and headed into the country, she said, "Derick, I'm really scared. When Papa gets out of jail, he'll probably beat me to death. With that temper of his, once he gets his hands on me, he won't stop pounding till I'm dead. If we all left as a family, we'd be easy to find. But if I go alone, since I'm the one he's really wanting to chastise, I could probably find someplace to hide till he gave up looking for me. Then, of course, I would have to go on through life without ever coming back here."

Derick sighed. "I'm afraid that he'll beat you to death. I see no other choice for you but to run away."

Diana thought on it while the wagon bounced along the road between the open fields of tawny grass. "Derick, where do you think I could go so Papa can't ever find me? I know he said the world isn't big enough for me to hide from him, but even this country is big enough to hide me, if I can find the right place."

Derick rubbed his chin and shook his head. "I'll have to think on that, sis."

"And of course, I'll have to find a way to make a living, wherever I go," said Diana, a quiver in her voice. "And the problem is, I don't have much time to figure out where to go and what to do to make a living. Papa will be out in a month. I've got to leave soon. Real soon."

"I'll put my mind to it," said Derick. "I'll think of something, I'm sure. There has to be a solution. You sure can't stay here."

"I was thinking about relatives who might take me in," said Diana, "but that would be the first place Papa would look. Like Uncle Gerald and Aunt Bertha in Minneapolis. Or Uncle Charles and Aunt Evelyn in Atlanta. But it wouldn't be right to put them in the line of fire of Papa's temper."

"You're right about that," said Derick. "It can't be relatives. And we don't have friends elsewhere, so that's out. Besides, if we did, Papa would look there. It has to be somewhere he would never think to look."

"Right. Let me think on it. I'll come up with something."

As they drew near the Morrow farm, Diana dried her tears. "Derick, we mustn't tell Deborah, Daniel, or Dennis about Papa's threats. We'll just tell them we went to see him."

"Right," agreed Derick. "There's no reason at this point to upset them about that. Of course, when the day comes that you leave, we'll have to tell them why you're going away."

Diana nodded. "And we must appear positive about Mama's condition at all times before them."

"Yes. We'll do that."

That night as Diana lay in her bed in the girls' room, her thoughts went to the escape she must make before her father got out of jail. While Deborah lay sound asleep in the other bed, Diana wiped tears with the sheet and wondered where she could go that her father would never find her, and what she would do to earn herself a living. She would be willing to do washings, or clean houses, or clerk in a store.

Fear ran its icy fingers through her mind. She wiped more tears and thought of God. She didn't know much about Him, but she did believe He was up there in heaven looking down on people around the globe.

While fresh tears scalded her cheeks, she whispered, "God, I think You can hear me if You want to. And I hope You want to. I've heard people talk about how much You love us...especially Shamus and Maggie. I—I'm really scared, God. Shamus and Maggie say You know everything, so You know what Papa has done to Mama and Tom. And You know that he would probably beat me to death if I was here when he got out of jail. I...I have to run away. I have to go somewhere he won't ever be able to find me."

Using the sheet once more to mop tears from her face, Diana swallowed hard and whispered, "Dear God, it really hurts to think about leaving. I'll probably never be able to see Mama, Derick, Deborah, Daniel, or Dennis again."

This brought her emotions fully to the surface. She broke down and sobbed, muffling her cries by covering her mouth with the covers. When she was able to bring herself under control, she drew a shuddering breath and whispered, "Please, God. Please help me. I wouldn't see Mama and my sister and brothers again if Papa killed me, either, so I have to go away. Would You help me to know what to do? Derick is trying to think of something, too. Please help me to be gone before Papa gets out of jail."

Diana dabbed at her tears again. "Dear God, I've heard Shamus pray at the table when we've eaten at their house. I want to do this right. He always prays in Your Son's name, so I ask these things in Jesus' name. Amen."

The next morning, Martha Morrow and Laura Thomas were talking about the problems the Morrows were facing.

Laura said, "I don't want to wear you out by causing you to talk too much, Martha, but if you knew the Lord, He could help in ways that no one else—"

Laura's words were cut off by Diana and Derick coming into the room.

Both greeted Laura, then bent over their mother, kissing her cheek and asking how she was feeling.

"I'm doing better," Martha assured them.

"You look better, Mama," said Diana.

"You sure do," said Derick.

"Laura has been such a help to me. She's very encouraging about our problems, and every time I've needed a nurse, she's rung her bell for me."

Diana stepped to Laura's bed and said, "Thank you so much, Mrs. Thomas, for being so kind to Mama."

"Yes," said Derick. "Thank you, ma'am."

Laura smiled. "I'm happy to do anything I can. You have a very sweet mother."

"And so do your children," Diana said softly. "That is, if you have children."

"I sure do. I have two daughters and a son. Of course, they're adults and married now, but they're still little children in my eyes."

Diana returned to her brother's side. Martha looked up into their faces and said, "Are your sister and brothers all right?"

"They're fine, Mama," said Derick. "They told us to tell you that they miss you and love you and are looking forward to the day you can come home."

Tears misted Martha's eyes. "Me too."

Derick flicked a glance at his sister. "Do you want me to tell her?"

"We agreed she has to know right now," said Diana. "It isn't right to keep it from her. I'll let you tell her."

"Tell me what?" said Martha.

Derick took a deep breath, glanced at Laura, and said, "I really don't like talking about our troubles in front of Mrs. Thomas because it may make her uncomfortable, but you have to know what happened at the jail yesterday, Mama."

"Don't worry about me," said Laura. "I'm fine. You tell your mother whatever it is she needs to know."

Derick gave Laura a thin smile, and was about to speak when Martha said, "Is this something you heard about, or did you two go to the jail when you left here?"

"We went to the jail because I told Derick I wanted to go," said Diana. "I felt we should go see Papa because he is our father."

"That was kind of you," said Martha. "So what happened?"

Derick gave his mother a detailed explanation of the incident at the jail, how their father had blamed Diana for everything that had happened because she was talking to Tom Wymore against his orders; and the threats he had made against Diana.

"Mama," he said, his face grim, "I'm afraid Papa is so mad at Diana that if he started beating on her, he wouldn't quit till she was dead."

Martha put a shaky hand on Diana's arm. "With his temper, he just might do that. "

"We've been talking about it, Mama," said Derick. "Diana can't be home when Papa gets out of jail four weeks from now. She's got to go somewhere he can never find her."

Martha's lips quivered and her brow furrowed. "I hate to see it like this, but I agree. If she's here when he gets out, it could be real bad."

Diana gripped the hand that was on her arm and said, "I'm terrified of what Papa will do to me if I'm here when he gets out of jail, Mama, but how am I going to leave you and my sister and brothers? You need me."

"I'm old enough to take care of them, sis," said Derick.

"Yes," agreed Martha. "We'll make it all right, Diana. We can't take the chance that your father might beat you to death. We've got to come up with a place for you to go."

"It'll have to be a long way from here, Mama," said Derick. "As I told you, Papa said yesterday that if she tried to run away, he would find her no matter where she went."

Diana trembled as raw emotion squeezed her heart. She leaned over the bed, carefully embraced her mother, and said, "Oh, Mama, why does Papa have to be so mean? Why doesn't he love his family like other men do?"

"I don't know, honey," said Martha, sniffling. "That's just the way he is. As I've told you before, he wasn't that way when I married him. It was after you were born that he started getting mean, and with each child that came along, he just got worse."

Diana kissed her cheek. "Mama, we'd better go. We're wearing you out. We'll be back tomorrow."

"In the meantime," said Derick, "we'll try to come up with an idea for someplace for Diana to go."

Once again, both Derick and Diana thanked Laura for being so kind to their mother and left.

As soon as they had passed through the door, Martha broke down and sobbed.

Laura was not yet able to get out of bed, but she spoke to Martha in soothing tones, trying to comfort her. When Martha's weeping subsided, Laura said, "Honey, this is a horrible thing you've got to deal with. My pastor could be a real help to you. He's been out of town for a few days, but he's due back today, and he said he would be in to see me when he got back. If you'll let him, I know he can be a comfort to you."

Martha managed a smile. "Who is your pastor, Laura?"

"Sherman Bradford."

"Oh, I've met him. Our neighbors, Shamus and Maggie O'Hearn, speak highly of him."

Laura's eyes lit up. "My husband and I know Shamus and

Maggie quite well, Martha. We often get together for meals. Picnics in the summertime. They are dear people. I'm sure you've found them good neighbors."

"Oh yes. Stu won't let me see them very often, but—"

A distinguished looking man came into the room, carrying a Bible.

"Pastor!" said Laura. "We were just talking about you. You know Martha Morrow? She lives on a neighboring farm to Shamus and Maggie O'Hearn."

Smiling warmly, the preacher said, "Yes, we've met. How are you, Mrs. Morrow? You know the O'Hearns well, do you?"

"Yes, sir. Very well. Both of them have bragged about your preaching. They really love you."

"Well, I really love them, too," said Bradford. "Shamus and Maggie are some of my most faithful members, as are Laura and her husband, Glenn."

"Glenn has been here twice since I was put in the room with Laura yesterday," said Martha. "I like him very much. And, of course, I really like this dear lady very much, too."

Moving up to the side of Laura's bed, the pastor chuckled and said, "I sort of like her, myself. How are you doing, Laura?"

"Quite well, Pastor," said Laura. "My doctor says I should be able to go home in another four or five days."

"Marvelous! How about my reading you one of the Psalms?"

"I'd love that. How about Psalm 77? I love them all, but that's one of my favorites."

Bradford opened his Bible and read the requested Psalm to Laura, and Martha took it all in, listening intently.

When he had finished, Bradford commented on verse 13 and read it again.

"'Thy way, O God, is in the sanctuary: who is so great a God as our God?' And the answer is," he said, smiling, "there is no God like our wonderful God."

Bradford prayed with Laura, asking the Lord to heal her quickly for His own glory, and praised Him that she had come through her surgery so well.

Martha observed the tender moment as Laura's pastor prayed with her, thinking she had never seen anything like this. She was very much impressed with the pastor's demeanor. Her opinion—as well as Stu's—had been that all preachers were in it for the money, and taught their people to be fanatics about the Bible and its contents. Somehow, this man impressed her as being genuine and sincere in what he was doing. He wasn't acting or speaking in a fanatical manner at all.

When he closed his prayer, Sherman Bradford turned back to Martha, ran his eyes over her cast and bruises, and said, "Do you mind my asking what happened to you, Mrs. Morrow?"

At first, reluctance welled up in Martha, but she decided she might as well tell him, since Laura knew. She told him the story, shedding tears in the process.

Bradford was very sympathetic, saying how sorry he was that this had happened to Martha and her children. Then he looked her in the eye and said, "Mrs. Morrow, I'd like to ask you something."

"Yes, Pastor Bradford?" She afforded him a weak smile as she wiped tears from her cheeks.

"Let's say the beating your husband gave you had been worse, and you had died from it. Would you have gone to heaven?"

Martha's brow puckered. She ran her eyes back and forth. "I…I hope so, but I can't say for sure."

"Do you understand that a person can know they are saved from the penalty of their sins, and that they are going to heaven?"

"Shamus and Maggie have talked to me about it several times, Pastor. They have even quoted Scripture verses about salvation and forgiveness of sin. I…well, even though I deeply respect them, I have always felt that their beliefs border on fanaticism."

"I can understand that, ma'am," said Bradford. "Many people come from a background where they were taught that faith in the Lord Jesus Christ for salvation and living for Him is fanaticism. But if you just let God speak to you through His Word, it will change your way of thinking."

At that point, the preacher began to quote passage after passage about the Lord Jesus Christ and His sacrificial death on the cross of Calvary for hopeless sinners.

When he paused for a moment, Martha said, "Pastor, may I ask you something?"

"Of course."

"If God loves me as the Bible says He does, why has He let my life be so miserable? You've just heard what my children and I are suffering at the hands of my husband. Why does God let us suffer this misery?"

"There are many things about life that are mysteries, ma'am," said Bradford. "We don't always understand things that come our way that make our lives miserable, but in time, I can help you to understand some of them from the Scriptures. But more important than the misery you are facing right now with your husband is the misery you will face in hell forever if you die without Jesus as your personal Saviour. May I show you some more things in the Bible?"

Martha nodded, noticing that Laura had her head bowed, her eyes closed, and her lips were moving silently.

The preacher then took Martha to additional passages in the four gospels, showing her how much the Lord loved her. He laid out salvation's plan plain and clear, and showed her the consequences she would face if she rejected Jesus.

As tears coursed down her cheeks, Martha said, "Pastor, what I thought was fanaticism is the most wonderful thing I've ever heard. Shamus and Maggie helped prepare me for this moment by quoting so many Scripture passages. God did so love me, Martha Morrow, that He gave His only begotten Son on the cross to die for my sins."

She took a ragged breath. "I want to be saved, Pastor. Will you help me to know how to call on the Lord?"

"It will be my pleasure, Mrs. Morrow."

Laura wept silently while her pastor was leading Martha to Jesus, and when it was done, the three of them rejoiced together in Martha's salvation.

Wiping happy tears, Martha said, "I'm so glad to know that I am now a child of God, and am going to heaven. Now, I am concerned for my family. I want my husband and my children to be saved."

Bradford and Laura exchanged smiles, then he said, "That is one of the first signs of genuine conversion: a burden for loved ones to be saved. Let me show you one more thing, then I'll leave for now, and give both of you ladies a chance to rest."

The pastor then showed Martha in Scripture that as soon as she was able, she should obey the Lord's command, be baptized, and unite with the church.

Martha's first thought was what Stu would do when he found out she had become a Christian, and had been baptized and become a member of the church. At first there was a stab of fear, then a sweet peace flooded her heart. Looking up at the preacher, she said, "It will depend on when this cast comes off, Pastor, but as soon as it does, I'll do as the Lord has commanded me."

*14*

As Derick and Diana Morrow were driving out of town toward home, Diana said, "Derick, I think we should stop and tell Maggie and Shamus about Mama being in the hospital. Since Papa is in jail, he won't know about it. They would go see Mama, and I'm sure it would help her. Especially since Maggie and Mama have been friends for so many years. She needs all the encouragement she can get."

Derick thought on it a few seconds, then turned on the wagon seat to look at Diana. "You don't think Mama will care if we tell the O'Hearns about all that's happened, do you?"

"Mama needs a friend right now. I'm sure she won't mind. Maggie is the best friend Mama has. I think she would want her to know."

"Let's do it," said Derick.

When they arrived at the O'Hearn farm, Maggie told them Shamus was helping a neighboring farmer build a new toolshed and wouldn't be home till suppertime. Seeing the serious looks on the faces of Derick and Diana, Maggie asked if there was something wrong.

Together they told Maggie about the beating their father had given Tom Wymore and why. Then they told her about their father's anger toward Diana, how their mother had tried to protect Diana from being struck by him, and had ended up in the hospital as a result of the beating she received.

They explained that their father was in jail for beating up on

169

Tom Wymore, and also shared with her the threats he had made against Diana.

Maggie wept as she heard the story and said she was going to hitch up the buggy and go see Martha immediately.


At the hospital, Martha and Laura were both dozing when a nurse came in and told Martha that Chief Constable Bob Perry was there to see her. Laura looked on as Perry entered the room and stood over the bed. "Mrs. Morrow, I want you to know that I am very sorry for what your husband did to you."

Martha adjusted the sling on her arm and winced slightly from the pain it caused. "Thank you, Chief."

"The law says I must advise you, ma'am, that you can press charges against Mr. Morrow for beating you, and Judge Weathers says he will sentence him to a year in jail if you will. This will be added to the month he is in jail for beating up Tom Wymore."

Perry saw an expression of fear flit across Martha's face as she shook her head in tiny movements. "No. I can't, Chief. I'd live in terror for that year, counting down the days until he would get out. I don't dare press charges against him."

Perry saw the compassion in Laura Thomas's eyes as she looked at Martha. Nodding, he said, "I understand, Mrs. Morrow. There's nothing the law can do about his intimidating you. We can only act after he has already done something—like this beating he gave you." He sighed. "But as chief constable, I must at least advise you of your right to press charges. Thank you for allowing me to do that. I'll be going now."

"I appreciate your coming, Chief," said Martha.

He smiled, started to leave, then checked himself. "I do want you to know that I have talked straight to him about what he did to both you and Tom. I hope that my words and the month in jail will cause him to get a grip on his temper and never do this kind of thing again."

Martha smiled thinly. "Me too."

When Perry started through the door, he stopped to allow Maggie O'Hearn to pass by him, then hurried away.

Both women saw Maggie, whose eyes widened when she noticed Laura in the bed by the window. "Well, isn't this something? Martha, your roommate is a very close friend of mine."

"I know," said Martha. "We've already talked a lot about you."

Maggie smiled, then looked at Laura. "How are you doing, honey?"

"Just fine," said Laura. "I'll be going home in a few days."

"Good." Then letting her gaze take in the cast, the swollen eye, and the facial bruises, Maggie said, "Martha, Diana and Derick stopped by on their way home from the hospital and told me the whole story."

Martha nodded.

"Honey, this is terrible. I'm so sorry. And all because you tried to defend Diana."

Martha closed her eyes and nodded again.

Maggie bent down, kissed her forehead, and said, "Bless your heart. You did what any good mother would have done."

"She sure did," agreed Laura.

Tears misted Martha's eyes.

"Derick told me about Stu's threats against Diana," said Maggie. "I'm concerned for her, Martha. From Stu's past behavior, I'm afraid he might—well, might—"

"Yes," said Martha, thumbing tears from her eyes. "Me too. Did they tell you we're trying to come up with a way to send Diana somewhere Stu can't find her?"

"No. They might have if we'd had longer to talk, but they needed to get home, and I wanted to hurry in here to see you. But I can't blame you. She's got to be protected somehow. Any idea where you might send her?"

"Not yet. First we've got to get our hands on some money. Wherever we send her, it's going to be expensive. If we owned the farm, I would somehow borrow against it, but since we only rent it, I'll have to come up with the money some other way."

Maggie drew a deep breath, and as she let it out, she said, "If Shamus and I had the money, we would give it to you. But we don't."

Martha took hold of her hand. "I know you and Shamus

would help if you had the money. But you know what?"

"What?"

"I have some good news for you in the midst of all this trouble."

"Does she ever!" said Laura.

A questioning look captured Maggie's features as she ran her gaze to Laura, then back to Martha. "Well, tell me!"

Martha let go of Maggie's hand and brushed more tears from her eyes. "You know how many times you have talked to me about being saved?"

Maggie's eyes widened. "You…you—"

"Yes, honey! I've been in the family of God for almost two hours now! Pastor Bradford came to see Laura and led me to Jesus!"

Happy tears filled Maggie's eyes. "Oh! Glory to God! That's wonderful." She bent down and kissed Martha's cheek. "Shamus and I have prayed for this so many times!"

Laura said, "I'm so happy for her. Glenn will be too, when he finds out!"

Martha told Maggie that she was going to be baptized as soon as the cast was off, which thrilled her again.

Maggie had a passing thought that Stu would probably be out of jail before the cast could come off. "I'm so glad, honey. This is the best news I've had in a long time. I can't wait to tell Shamus. Martha, we'll be praying about Diana's situation. The Lord will give you the solution, I know."

Maggie prayed with her friends, kissed them both on the cheek, and headed for home.


The next morning, Pastor Sherman Bradford returned to the hospital for another visit. He was glad to see Martha rejoicing in her salvation, and after spending a few minutes talking to Laura, he turned to Martha and asked how she was feeling.

After saying she was feeling better physically, Martha shared her burden with him over Stu's bad temper, explaining that he felt toward Jesus Christ, the Bible, churches, and Christians just like she had.

A deep frown lined her brow as she said, "Pastor, how am I going to bear up under Stu's anger when he gets out of jail and learns that I have become a Christian and will be uniting with the church upon my baptism? I think you can understand my concern."

"Of course," said the preacher, opening his Bible and flipping pages. "One of the blessings of being a born-again child of God as you are now, Martha, is that your heavenly Father is always with you to help you. Let me read a couple of verses to you. First, here in 2 Corinthians chapter 12, Paul is going through great suffering. God speaks to him in verse 9 and says, 'My grace is sufficient for thee: for my strength is made perfect in weakness.' God's grace would be sufficient for Paul, no matter what the circumstances, because God's strength is perfected in His children in their weaknesses. This is one of the marvels of being a Christian."

Clinging to every word, Martha kept her eyes fastened on him, waiting for more.

"The Lord is fully aware of your situation, Martha," Bradford went on. "And He is fully capable of helping you to handle it. He says His grace is sufficient, right?"

"Yes, but Stu can get so mean, and there's no telling what he might do."

"Let me help you with this," the pastor said, giving her an assuring smile. "Yesterday, you placed your full trust in the Lord to save your soul, keep you from ever going to hell, and to finally take you to heaven by His grace, didn't you?"

"Yes."

"Do you have any doubts that He will keep His promises?"

"Of course not."

"Good. Then if you can fully trust Him to save your soul, keep you from ever going to hell, and to take you to heaven by His grace when your life is over here on earth, can't you trust Him to supply sufficient grace for your needs while you're still here on earth?"

A new light showed in Martha's eyes. "I hadn't thought of it that way, Pastor. You're right."

"Don't feel bad," said Bradford. "Many Christians who have been saved for decades haven't thought of it that way; or if they have, they still have a hard time trusting the Lord with problems in this life. God is well able to meet this problem with your husband with the measure of grace you need. Let me read another verse to you."

Bradford flipped forward a few pages. "I'm going to read Ephesians 4:7 to you. Keep in mind what I just said, and I repeat: God is well able to meet this problem with your husband with the measure of grace you need. Speaking of born-again people, it says: 'But unto every one of us is given grace according to the measure of the gift of Christ.' Because you belong to Jesus, He will meet every problem you bring to Him with the measure of grace you need."

Martha smiled. "I understand, Pastor. Since I can trust the Lord to take me to heaven by His grace, I can also trust Him to get me through this life by His grace, come what may."

"Right. Jesus told us we would have tribulations while here on earth, so we can expect to face many trials and hardships. But He is always with us, and His grace is sufficient to meet every need. Just trust Him for the measure of grace you need for each trial."

"Thank you for showing me this truth in the Bible, Pastor," Martha said softly. "I…I have something else to say."

"Yes?"

"I want my children to be saved. Of course Dennis is too young, but the other four are old enough."

"I'll talk to them," said Bradford, "and do my best to lead them to the Lord."

Martha touched her temple, thought a few seconds, then said, "Tell you what, Pastor. Since their minds have been conditioned to disdain the Bible and its message by both Stu and me, it would be best if I talk to them first. I'll tell them I'm saved, and how wrong I was to teach them what I did. I'll let you know when you can come to the house and talk to them."

"All right. I can see it would be best to do it that way. Now, before I go, let me say this: God's ability to give the measure of grace we need doesn't mean we throw caution and good sense to the wind. If you believe that you are going to be in danger when your husband gets out of jail, the church will provide a place of safety for you and the children."

"I appreciate that, Pastor," Martha said. "We have almost a

mouth. Let me see how things go between now and then, and if I feel we need a hiding place, I will let you know."


The workload on the Morrow farm was heavy for the children with both of their parents away, but from oldest to youngest, they pitched in and did the chores, wanting to have everything in order when their mother was released from the hospital.

In the early part of that morning, Diana was busy, baking several loaves of bread while her siblings were doing the outside work. Deborah was sweeping both the front and back porches of the house, and the boys were at the barn. Diana was hurrying with the bread so it would be done before she and Derick needed to head for the hospital.

She was deep in thought, as always when there was a quiet moment, trying desperately to come up with a workable plan to get her safely away from the Richmond area without making a hardship on anyone who might offer help.

Suddenly a small, pitiful sound penetrated her thoughts. Her hands, buried in bread dough, came to a stop. Tilting her head to one side, she listened for the sound to come again. When there was nothing, she was about to chalk it up to her imagination.

Then she heard it again.

"Someone is crying," she whispered to herself.

Taking her hands from the sticky dough, she wiped them on a nearby dish towel and headed toward the front of the house where the weeping was coming from. Stopping to listen every few steps, she soon found herself entering the boys' bedroom.

She found her five-year-old brother sitting on the floor in a corner, sobbing. His head was pressed against his drawn-up knees, with gulping sobs escaping his mouth.

Diana wondered when Dennis had come in the house. She told herself it must have been when she was in the pantry. Hurrying to his huddled little form, Diana bent down, took him in her arms, and carried him to one of the beds. Sitting on its edge, she sat him on her lap and folded him in her arms. "Honey, what's the matter?"

Dennis pressed his face against her shoulder and wailed loudly, no longer trying at all to curb the flow of tears. For several minutes, Diana held him, gently rubbing his shaking little shoulders, speaking soft words in the attempt to quiet him so he could tell her what was bothering him.

When the sobs finally ceased, and only small sighs and hiccups were being released, Diana gently pushed him away from her shoulder, tilted his tear-stained face upward, and looked him in the eye. "Honey, what is it?"

"I...I'm s-sorry," he said, stuttering through tears that were threatening to spill down his cheeks again.

"You don't have anything to be sorry for."

"I d-don't mean to upset you."

"You haven't upset me. Please. Just tell me what's wrong."

Lips quivering, Dennis said, "Diana, why is Papa so mean? And why does he hate all of us?"

Diana's heart felt like it was turning over inside her chest. *How do I explain this to such a little child?* she wondered as she looked down into his expectant face.

"Dennis, listen to me. Papa doesn't hate us. He is just—well, he's sick in his mind. He has a very bad temper, and he doesn't know how to control it. This is what makes him mean. But he doesn't hate us. When Mama comes home from the hospital, we're going to do everything we can to make things better."

Dennis's expression took on a deeper look of inward pain. "Is Mama really coming home?" he asked with his chin quivering and tears pooling in his eyes.

"Of course she is."

"Are you just telling me an' Deborah an' Daniel she's coming home to make us feel better 'cause Mama's really dead?"

Diana looked at him with surprise. "Oh no. Dennis, baby, I promise. Mama is not dead. In fact, she is getting better every day and will be coming home very soon."

"You really promise?"

"Yes."

A broad grin beamed on his wet cheeks. "Really?"

"Yes, really. Mama will be just fine. I wouldn't lie to you."

"Oh boy!" Dennis said with elation. "I thought Mama was

dead. I want her to come home. I love you, Diana, but…but I need Mama to tuck me in and tell me a story at bedtime."

"I understand, honey. And I love you. Believe me, Mama will be home soon to do just that!"

Giving his big sister a tight hug, Dennis jumped down from his perch on her lap.

"Would you like to help me make bread, honey?" asked Diana.

"Sure," he said, taking her hand. Together they made their way toward their kitchen.

It was just past ten o'clock when Martha looked up to see her two oldest children enter the room.

When they had both kissed her and were told that she was feeling better, Diana noted Laura's empty bed and asked, "Where's Mrs. Thomas?"

"They have her in the examining room to check her over where they did the surgery. She may be going home tomorrow."

"Oh. I wish we could take you home tomorrow."

"It'll be soon, now, I'm sure. I want both of you to pull those chairs up and sit down beside the bed. I have something very important to tell you."

Eyeing their mother curiously, they sat down. Martha explained that Pastor Bradford had shown her from the Bible about heaven and hell, and how Jesus Christ had died on the cross of Calvary to provide salvation for sinners. To be saved, she must repent of her sin and receive Jesus into her heart as her own personal Saviour. When she went on to tell them that she had done this, they were shocked.

While Derick stared at his mother in astonishment, Diana said, "Mama, I'm surprised at this because you and Papa have always taught us that this is foolish fanaticism."

"Well, honey, we were wrong. I see it so plainly now. All these years, we've had Christmas at our house, but we were missing the whole point of God's Son coming into the world by a virgin birth. It wasn't just to give the world a holiday. It was to provide salvation for all of us, because all of us are sinners before God. It's so wonderful to know that my sins are forgiven, and I will go to heaven when it's time for me to leave this world."

"I'm still stunned, Mama," said Derick, "but I have to say that you have a sparkle in your eyes I've never seen before. I'm glad to see it."

"Me too," said Diana.

At that moment, there were pronounced footsteps, and all three looked up to see Dr. Bates enter the room.

Smiling, he said, "Hello, Diana, Derick. I'm here to check your mother's condition. If she's improved since I checked her yesterday, you can take her home tomorrow."

Both young faces brightened as they left their chairs and moved them to give the doctor room to work.

Five minutes later, Bates smiled. "Just as I thought. She's well enough to go home tomorrow. Is there someone who can look after her?"

"Yes, Doctor," said Derick. "Us!"

"We'll take care of her and give her all the help she needs, Dr. Bates," said Diana, her own eyes sparkling. "We won't let her do anything she shouldn't do."

"Sounds good to me," said the doctor. "You can pick her up after nine o'clock tomorrow morning."

Diana patted her mother's cheek. "We'll be here with bells on!"


The next morning, Dennis was sitting on the steps of the front porch of the house, where he had been since Derick and Diana drove away toward town. Deborah and Daniel were in the parlor, giving it a last minute touch-up in anticipation of their mother's return. Dennis had his eyes fixed on the road, eagerly waiting for the first sign of the wagon and team. Twice, he had started to celebrate, but saw immediately that they were wagons belonging to neighboring farmers.

Suddenly there was movement on the road and a horse whinny. Dennis jumped to his feet and focused on the approaching wagon.

"Deborah! Daniel!" he cried. "It's them! They have Mama in the wagon!"

Brother and sister joined him on the porch, and as the wagon turned off the road, the little boy jumped up and down, shouting, "It's Mama! It's Mama! Mama's come home!"

Moments later, a smiling but obviously uncomfortable Martha Morrow beamed as she looked at her three youngest from the wagon seat. Dennis bounded off the porch as the wagon came to a halt near the porch and raced toward her. "Mama! Mama! I'm so glad you're home!"

Hopping out of the wagon, Derick intercepted his brother, gripping his shoulders, and said, "Dennis, you wait right here. Mama's arm is in a cast, and you must be careful not to hurt her."

"I'll be careful," the child assured him, his eyes dancing. "I just need to hug her."

Smiling, Martha allowed Derick and Daniel to ease her to the ground from the wagon seat. "Deborah and Daniel are next, but Mama will hug her baby first!"

Quickly enfolding her youngest child in her good arm as happy tears flowed freely down her bruised cheeks, Martha bent over and kissed the top of his blond head. Dennis hugged her arm and said, "I love you, Mama. I'm so glad you're home!"

Martha chuckled. "I love you, honey, and I'm glad to be home!"

Dennis let go of the arm, and stepped back to allow Deborah and Daniel to greet their mother with kisses and careful hugs.

Diana had prepared the couch in the parlor for her mother to sit or lie on during the day. When Martha was comfortable on it, she said, "Daniel, Deborah, yesterday I told Derick and Diana about something wonderful that happened to me at the hospital the day before. When they picked me up this morning, I asked if they had told you about it, and they said they hadn't. They felt I should be the one to tell you."

Martha proceeded to tell Deborah and Daniel about having received the Lord Jesus as her own personal Saviour. Dennis listened, but Martha knew he was too young to grasp what she was saying, especially since he had not been exposed to anything about the Lord or the Bible.

When she finished, she saw the skepticism in the eyes of Deborah and Daniel, and assured them that she had seen the error of her ways. She made it clear that what she and their father had taught them on the subject was dead wrong. Though Deborah and Daniel were stunned, they too saw a light in their mother's eyes they had never seen before.

Martha told herself she would have to go slow with all four of the older children because of what she and Stu had taught them all of their lives.

At midmorning the next day, Derick hitched the horses to the wagon at the barn and headed for the front of the house. He was going to town to buy groceries, and he was taking his brothers with him.

In the parlor, Deborah was standing at the window while Diana sat beside Martha on the couch, and her younger brothers stood over them, talking about when their father would get out of jail. When Deborah saw Derick pull up in the wagon, she turned and said, "Okay, boys. Kiss Mama and hurry out the door. Derick just pulled up."

Diana joined her sister at the window while Dennis and Daniel kissed their mother and darted out the door.

They watched the boys drive away, then Deborah turned back to her mother.

Diana stayed at the window, staring blankly through the glass. Soon tears began to course down her cheeks. Deborah was busy making her mother more comfortable on the couch, but Martha noticed her oldest daughter wiping tears. "Diana, honey, what are you crying about?"

Diana slowly turned. "I'm so afraid, Mama. I know I've got to leave home before Papa gets out of jail, but...but I'm afraid he will do what he told me. That he will track me down."

"Honey," said Martha, "we're going to find a place for you where he won't be able to track you down. Since I've been saved, I've been praying and asking Jesus to help us."

Diana sniffed and blinked at more tears. "But Mama, even if we find such a place, Papa will make you tell him where I am."

"Honey, wherever you go, no one in this family will tell Papa."

"But he will probably try to beat it out of you."

"Don't you worry about it, Diana," Martha said softly. "The thing we have to concentrate on now is where you're going. And you need to be gone as soon as possible. It may be a great distance from here."

"But where, Mama? And with no money, how will I get there?"

Before Martha could say more, Deborah noticed movement in the yard. "Maggie is here."

Martha and Diana looked out the parlor window and saw Maggie O'Hearn pulling her buggy to a halt at the front of the house.

Maggie was met at the front door and ushered into the parlor. Smiling happily, Maggie took a beautiful Bible out of a cloth bag and presented it to Martha as a gift from Shamus and herself.

Holding the Bible in her free hand, Martha thanked Maggie, then laid it in her lap and opened it. The flyleaf held a note of love from the O'Hearns, saying how glad they were that Martha had become a Christian and that they looked forward to happy days in church together.

Looking up at Maggie, Martha said, "I hate to do it, but when Stu comes home, I'll have to hide this beautiful Book from him. I'm afraid he would tear it up."

Diana said, "Mama, Maggie, if you will excuse us, Deborah and I have work to do."

When the girls were gone, Maggie sat down beside Martha and tried to encourage her about the situation with Stu.

Martha told Maggie about the Scriptures Pastor Bradford had shown her concerning the measure of grace God gives His children in their trials, and they talked about it for a few minutes.

Maggie gave her some examples of times in her own life when burdens and trials had been heavy, and how the Lord had given her His measure of grace each time she had let Him do it.

"Honey," said Maggie, "Shamus and I are praying that the Lord will bring Stu to Himself, and of course, your children. We want to see the whole family saved."

"Oh, Maggie," said Martha, "what I wouldn't give to see Stu become a Christian, but I have to admit my faith is pretty weak in that direction. I can visualize my children being saved, but Stu…that would be one great big miracle."

"Well, it was a great big miracle when you got saved, wasn't it?"

"Y-yes. I would have to say it was."

"Well, God has a vast supply of miracles in His storehouse. Let's believe Him for Stu…and your children."

Martha's eyes glistened. "Yes. Let's believe Him for that."

"Let's have prayer right now, honey."

"All right."

Maggie then prayed with Martha, asking the Lord to bring Stu to Jesus, and also their children. She closed by thanking God that He would answer their prayers.

Martha silently thought on it. She had faith to believe that her children would be saved. But doubts assailed her about the big, hot-tempered, profane man who at the moment was behind bars.

IN RICHMOND, THE MORROW BOYS came out of the general store, carrying boxes of groceries. Even Dennis had a small box of paper goods and was proud to be helping his brothers. A slight breeze was plucking at their hair as they moved onto the boardwalk.

The wagon was a few paces down the street, and as the boys started that direction, Daniel's attention was drawn to a newspaper that lay on a bench where people sometimes sat and talked while watching the traffic pass by. Its pages were flapping in the breeze.

When they reached the wagon and were putting the boxes in the back, Daniel said, "Hey, Derick, you know how much Mama loves to read newspapers, but she doesn't get to do it very often because we can't afford to buy them."

Derick eyed him quizzically. "Yeah. What about it?"

Pointing at the bench and the flapping paper with his chin, Daniel said, "See the paper?"

"Yeah."

"How about if I go get it and we'll take it to Mama?"

"Sure. It'll be all right to take it, since whoever bought it just left it there."

Daniel was already in motion. He ran to the bench, picked up the paper, saw that it was that morning's issue of the *Richmond Chronicle,* and dashed back to the wagon, smiling gleefully.

Derick and Dennis were already in the seat, and Derick had reins in hand, ready to go. Daniel climbed up into the seat, plunked down, and sighed. "This will make Mama very happy."

Derick put the team in motion, and soon they were leaving the town behind and rolling along the bumpy country road.

Dennis really didn't understand why his mother liked newspapers so well, but he felt positive that it would make her happy. He was excited to get home and see the expression on her face.

The time seemed to drag to the five-year-old, but finally they were on the home place. He climbed over the back of the seat and dropped into the bed of the wagon. Almost before the wagon came to a halt at the back porch of the house, Dennis jumped out over the tailgate and went running into the house.

"Bless his little heart," Derick said as he and Daniel watched him go. "He's always so eager to make Mama happy."

"That proves he didn't inherit Papa's traits," Daniel said.

"Mama! Mama!" said the little boy as he sped through the kitchen and dashed up the hall toward the parlor.

Suddenly, Diana came out of the girls' bedroom and intercepted him.

"Whoa there, little man!" she said, laughing as she quickly grabbed him by the shoulders, bringing him to a sudden stop. "What's the big hurry?"

"I got something special to tell Mama, Diana!" Dennis said as he tried to wrest his way out of her grasp.

"Okay, but slow down. You might hurt Mama's arm if you go charging in there like a galloping horse and run into her."

"I won't do that, Diana," Dennis said. "I promise. I just want to tell her about the surprise we have for her."

By then, the other boys had carried the grocery boxes into the kitchen and heard Dennis's words. Placing the boxes on the cupboard, they stepped back into the hall.

Diana looked back over her shoulder at Derick and Daniel, her eyebrows raised in question.

Daniel lifted the folded newspaper above his head so Diana could see plainly what it was. "This is what he's so excited about. Let him go, so he can tell Mama. He's been beside himself all the way home."

Diana looked down at her youngest brother. He grinned up at her, a happy light dancing in his eyes. "All right, Dennis. But just slow down a bit, and go tell Mama your good news."

Dennis grinned at her slyly, and with exaggerated slowness in each step, tiptoed into the parlor.

When Martha saw him, she said, "Well, there's Mama's little man. What's all the excitement about?"

Still sporting a sly grin, Dennis sidled up to where his mother was sitting on the couch. He stopped in front of her, careful not to touch her.

Martha noted that her son was standing first on one foot, then the other, the happy gleam still dancing in his eyes. "Whatever is it, Dennis, that has you so excited?"

"Oh, Mama!" he said. "We found a present for you in town, and Derick and Daniel say you're gonna love it!"

Even as Dennis was speaking, the two older brothers came into the parlor with Diana, and now Deborah, on their heels.

Martha ran her gaze to the older children, fixing it on the boys. "Well, what is this present you got for me, anyhow?"

Daniel, who had the newspaper behind his back, waggled his head slowly. "Aw, Mama, it isn't all that great, but I know you'll enjoy it. I found it on that bench in front of the general store. Somebody had left it there."

"Hurry, Daniel!" said Dennis. "Give it to her!"

Grinning, Daniel brought the folded paper into his mother's view and placed it in her lap.

Martha's eyes shone as she realized what they had brought her. She laid her free hand on the paper, gave all three a smile of gratitude and said, "Thank you, boys, for being so thoughtful. I will enjoy it very much."

Pressing against his mother's knees, Dennis asked, "Did we do good, Mama?"

"You did real good, sweet one," Martha responded, then leaned over and hugged him with her good arm. Reaching to the small end table beside the couch, she lifted her Bible up so they could see it. "I got another nice present while you were gone. Maggie and Shamus bought this Bible for me."

Dennis looked at it with puzzlement. "What's a Bible, Mama?"

"It's God's Book, honey. It tells all about God and His Son, Jesus."

Dennis frowned. "But—"

"But what, honey?"

"Those are bad words that Papa uses when he's mad. God an' Jesus. You said we weren't supposed to talk like that."

Martha's face crimsoned. "Well, honey, those aren't bad words when we use them in the right way."

"Oh. But Papa uses 'em in the wrong way?"

"Yes. I'll explain it to you when you get a little older."

"All right."

Martha swung her gaze to the other two boys. They were trying to appear pleased about the Bible, but Martha could read it in their eyes. They were afraid what their father would do when he saw it.

The next morning, Derick drove the spare wagon to school, accompanied by Daniel and Deborah as usual. Each of the three bore a note for their teacher—written by Diana—explaining that their absence had been because their mother had been in Richmond Hospital.

Diana made her mother comfortable on the couch, for which Martha thanked her. Martha said, "Honey, I'd like to read you some verses from the Bible about salvation. The same ones Pastor Bradford showed me."

"All right, Mama," said Diana, sitting down beside her. "Before you do that, would you pray that God would show us where I'm supposed to go before Papa gets out of jail? I'm really scared."

"Sure, honey."

Martha held her daughter's hand as she stumbled through a prayer, asking the Lord to show them in some positive way where Diana should go, and to somehow provide the money for the trip and a place to live. "And she'll need a way to provide for herself, Lord," Martha tacked on. "In Jesus' name. Amen."

Diana then sat silently and listened as her mother read several passages of Scripture. Her heart was touched when she heard about Jesus dying on the cross for sinners, and she felt an uncomfortable stabbing in the same spot when she heard about her sinful condition before God.

When Martha had given her plenty to ponder on, she closed the Bible and said, "Well, what do you think?"

"It is all so new to me, Mama," Diana replied. "I'm going to need some time to think about it."

Nodding, Martha said, "I understand, honey. We'll talk more about it after you've had time to think on it."

At that moment, Diana's line of sight fell on the folded newspaper, which lay on the small table nearby. "Did you get to read the paper yet?" she asked.

"Yes, I read all of it that I wanted to," said Martha, picking it up and extending it to Diana. "You can throw it out."

Taking the paper, Diana stood up and said, "I've got work to do in the kitchen. You rest. And if you need anything, just call."

"I will, honey. And you be sure to give some earnest thought to those Scriptures I read to you."

Diana nodded and left the room. When she entered the kitchen, she decided to take a look at the *Chronicle* before doing the work she had laid out for herself.

Sitting down at the table, she began running her gaze over the front page, reading the particular articles that interested her.

After a short time of scanning the pages as she turned them, Diana came to the classified section. Since the two full pages of this section didn't interest her, she started to turn to the last page but her eye caught a column among the classified ads headlined: MAIL ORDER BRIDES.

Diana had heard of the mail order bride system, but was surprised to see that there was still a shortage of women on the western frontier.

Suddenly an idea flashed into her mind. This would be a perfect means to get away from her father and to have a living provided!

*Yes!* she thought. *A husband out west. That's big country out there. Papa would never be able to find me.*

An excited Diana let her eyes slowly run down the column, reading each ad carefully. Out of fourteen ads, there was one that arrested her attention more than the others. Slowly and precisely, she read it again.

Hardworking and adventurous twenty-four-year-old partner of profitable ranch near Elkton, Idaho, seeks bride of high moral character between the ages of eighteen and twenty-one who values family, has at least a basic education, and who loves children and enjoys working with animals. Anyone interested may write to Jordan Shaw at: Bar-S Ranch, General Delivery, Elkton, Idaho. The young woman chosen will be sent money for travel expenses. It is requested that no photographs be sent in order that the applicant may be chosen for her personality and content of her letters only. Applicants may expect a reply within a few weeks, with more details regarding the prospective groom. Please expect no photograph for the above mentioned reason.

Diana's heart pounded as she contemplated the possibility that lay before her. Taking a deep breath, she read the ad slowly a third time, being careful not to overlook anything.

Laying the paper down, Diana thought on it, asking herself what her chances might be that Jordan Shaw would choose her. *He might get hundreds of responses,* she thought. *He sounds nice enough, but how will I know what he is really like? What if he turns out to be just like Papa?*

The excitement she had felt at first seemed to slowly seep out of her heart. Picking up the paper, she read each ad once more. When she finished, she told herself the only one that captured her interest at all was Jordan Shaw's ad, and certainly he wouldn't be like her father.

Laying the paper down again, she put her elbows on the table and dropped her head into her hands. "What should I do?" she said in a whisper. "Do I stand any chance at all? Well, I'll never know if I don't try. I may never hear back from him, but it sure can't happen if I don't try."

Rising from the chair, Diana picked up the newspaper and carried it down the hall. When she entered the parlor, her mother was stretched out on the couch, and her eyes were closed.

Thinking she was asleep, Diana told herself she would not disturb her. As she was about to turn and leave the room, Martha opened her eyes. "I'm not asleep, honey. I was just praying for you.

I was asking God to give us an answer very soon on where you should go."

Diana swallowed hard. "I think maybe we have our answer, Mama."

Martha's eyes widened, then her attention went to the newspaper Diana was holding. "Tell me."

"Well, I decided to read through the paper like you did, and—"

Martha frowned. "And?"

"Well, I happened to notice the mail order bride section in the classifieds. I…ah…I read the ads. There is one I want you to read."

Martha sat up, adjusted herself on the couch, and blinked. "Mail order bride? I never thought of that. Let me see it."

Handing her the paper, which was folded with the mail order bride ads in plain view, Diana put her finger on Jordan Shaw's ad. "This one."

With the paper in her free hand, Martha supported it with the arm in the cast and began reading. Raising her eyes to her daughter's face when she finished, she said, "Quite impressive. You don't like any of the other ads?"

"No. This is the only one that interests me. What do you think, Mama? Should I answer him?"

Martha let a smile curve her battered lips. "Honey, it might indeed just be the answer we've been looking for. Jordan sounds like a nice young man. His requirements are in good taste. I especially like the part about moral character, valuing family, and loving children. And we wouldn't even have to come up with any money. That would have been the hardest part of getting you away. Your very life is at stake. Seems to me those are my prayers being answered. I hate to see you go so far away, but if you can marry and be happy, this is what I want for you."

Suddenly the excitement was back in Diana's heart. A smile broke across her face. "All right, Mama. I'll write the letter as soon as I get some of the work done in the kitchen. I'll take one of the saddle horses into town so I can mail it today."

"Good!" said Martha. "I have a feeling this is going to work, no matter how many replies young Mr. Shaw gets to his ad."

Diana closed her eyes and took a deep breath. "Papa will never be able to find me way out in Idaho."

In little more than half an hour, Diana had the work done and sat down at the kitchen table with pen, ink, paper, and envelope before her.

Trying to still her shaking hands, she clasped them together in a tight squeeze and formulated the letter in her head. She told herself she would make a rough draft, make whatever adjustments she found necessary, then write the real thing.

Picking up the pen, she dipped it in the inkwell and began. She paused after two lines as a random thought crossed her mind. *This one letter could change my whole life.*

"Please, God," she whispered. "Let it work."

Having worked on the letter for over an hour, Diana entered the parlor to find Dennis sitting on the couch next to his mother. Diana stopped and said, "I'm…ah…finished, Mama."

Martha noted the letter in Diana's hand and said, "Dennis, why don't you go back outside and play for a while? Mama and Diana need to talk."

"Okay!" said the little boy, hopping off the couch. "I'll come and see you later, Mama." With that, he put on the jacket that lay on a nearby chair and bounded out of the room.

Diana sat down next to her mother, handed her the letter, and said, "See what you think."

Taking the letter, Martha said, "I wish this didn't have to be. But your father has made it imperative."

Diana eased back and watched her mother's face as she read the letter silently.

*Dear Mr. Jordan Shaw,*

*I am writing to express an interest in your ad for a mail order bride that was placed in the* Richmond Chronicle. *I am almost nineteen and have lived on a farm near Richmond, Virginia, my whole life. I have always been fascinated with the west. I have read many books about it, and have dreamed of living there for a long time. I have found that cities are conve-*

nient, but often noisy and dirty. A ranch surrounded by the tranquillity of open range sounds almost too good to be true. I admit that the mention of a ranch, which I have always romanticized, was one reason why I responded to your ad, but not the only.

The way you described yourself as adventurous was definitely intriguing. I also respect the qualities you want in a wife. You were very adamant about wanting a wife with good character, which makes me believe that you have good character and high morals yourself. The fact that you do not want any photographs also spoke well for you. Most women are judged only on looks, and as a woman, I have to appreciate your search for something that will last longer than physical beauty. What I liked best about your ad, though, was the fact that you specifically mentioned children and family. Being a wife and mother has been my cherished dream for a long time.

As to the rest of your ad, I do have a fair amount of education and excel at my favorite hobby, which is reading. I love animals, and most seem to respond well to me, most likely because they can sense that I have no fear of them. Well, no fear of most of them, at least. I am not known to be temperamental, and though I'm no angel, I try to always live my life in a way that will help and not hurt others, which is what I hope you will consider as good character.

I enjoy cooking and have been told I do a creditable job of it. I don't honestly care for housework, but I dislike clutter more, so the housework is always done. I have a good sense of humor and I love to explore. I haven't had a great deal of adventure in life, but I think I could be very adventurous with the right person by my side.

I know you must have had many young ladies respond, so I won't take up any more of your time. My mailing address is below, in case you are like me and rip up envelopes getting them open.

Sincerely,
Diana Morrow
General Delivery
Richmond, Virginia

There was excess moisture in Martha's eyes as she said, "Honey, I'm sure Jordan will love the way you express yourself, and by the very spirit of the letter, he will fall in love with you."

Suddenly Diana's eyes misted up. She embraced her mother, being careful not to hurt her, and sniffling, said, "Mama, I want to get away from Papa, but I can't leave you."

"Honey, you have to go away. If you're not gone by the time your father gets out of jail, your life will be in danger. I'd rather have you alive in Idaho than to see you buried in Virginia. Please. Go saddle one of the horses and get this letter to the post office in town as fast as you can. Time is of the essence. I want this letter in Jordan's hands before he replies to some other young woman, asking her to be his mail order bride. And I want you out of here on your way to Idaho as soon as possible. These letters are going to take a week or more both ways. Hurry, honey."

Martha's words caused her daughter's mixed emotions to settle into one single goal. She sealed the letter in the envelope, saying she would be back later, and rushed out the door.

At the same time Martha was commenting on Diana's letter to Jordan Shaw at the Morrow farm, Pastor Sherman Bradford entered the Richmond police department and approached the sergeant on the desk.

"Hello, Pastor Bradford," said Sergeant Ed Cantrell. "What can I do for you?"

"I would like to visit Stu Morrow," said the preacher.

At that instant, Chief Constable Bob Perry came out of his office, spotted Bradford, and headed for him. "Pastor Bradford! Nice to see you."

"I was about to take him back to visit Stu Morrow, Chief," said Cantrell.

"I'll take him back, Ed," said Perry.

The sergeant nodded. "All right, sir."

When Perry and Bradford stepped into the cell block, the chief pointed to two prisoners in separate cells. "Those guys are both sleeping off drunken stupors. The curse of alcohol. My job and yours would both be a lot easier if that curse was never invented."

"You're right about that, Chief," said Bradford.

Leading the preacher up to Stu Morrow's cell, they saw the big man lying on his bunk, hands interlaced behind his head.

"Morrow," said Perry. "Pastor Sherman Bradford is here to see you."

Stu sat up, a dark scowl capturing his face. Rising from the bunk, he approached the bars and swore vehemently. "Well, I don't want to see you, preacher!"

"Enough of that, Morrow." said Perry. "Mind your manners."

The door to the hallway opened, and Sergeant Ed Cantrell said, "Chief, Lieutenant Dirk Bowers needs to see you right now. It's very important."

Perry nodded at Cantrell, then pointed a stiff finger at Morrow. "You listen to what Pastor Bradford has to say. And watch your mouth." With that, he wheeled and left with the sergeant.

Fixing Bradford with eyes like pinpoints, Stu growled, "I'm not interested in a thing you've got to say, Bradford. So go waste your time elsewhere."

Taking a step closer to the bars, Bradford said, "How do you like being locked up?"

Snarling, the big man said, "I hate it."

"Then you wouldn't want to be locked up forever, would you?"

"Whattaya mean?"

"Like all human beings, Mr. Morrow, you are a sinner before a holy God, and the Bible says if you die in your sins, you will spend eternity in the blazing prison called hell. You'll be locked up forever. No escape. Nothing but burning in the flames and begging for water for all eternity."

While Stu stared at the preacher wide-eyed, Bradford went on to tell him about God's Son going to Calvary's cross to provide salvation and forgiveness for Stuart Morrow.

Stu broke into a cold sweat and swore again, angrily telling Bradford to get out and never come back.

Tears welled up in the preacher's eyes as he said, "I can't force you to listen, Mr. Morrow. But I want you to think about this. If there were no eternal prison house called hell, the Lord Jesus would never have come from heaven to sacrifice His life and His blood to give us the way to miss it. If you die without Him as your Saviour, you will go to the prison from whence there is no escape."

Morrow's beefy features were set in a harsh mold. His eyes blazed as he swore. "Get outta here! I don't want to hear any more of that. Y'hear me? Get out!"

The preacher wiped tears from his cheeks, turned, and left the cell block.

Stu Morrow cursed the preacher's name and plopped back down on his bunk.

# 16

AN ICY NORTH WIND HOWLED down off the snowcapped peaks of the Sawtooth Mountains, whipping across the hills and through Elkton as Jordan Shaw rode into town late in the afternoon on Monday, October 28. The raw chill of the wind was beginning to bite through Jordan's boots and his heavy mackinaw, sending a periodic shiver through his body.

Pulling rein in front of the post office, he saw a familiar face on the boardwalk. It was his brother-in-law, Mark Hedren.

Mark smiled, tugged his coat collar up tighter around his neck, and stepped up close to the hitch rail as Jordan dismounted.

"Feels like January instead of October," Mark said, glancing toward the mountains. "Old man winter is already having a heyday up there. Plenty of snow, already."

"I don't mind the snow," said Jordan, wrapping the reins around the rail. "Makes for good hunting."

"Oh, yeah." Mark chuckled. "You love that hunting, don't you?"

"Sure do."

Mark looked him square in the eye. "You bringing Belinda to Lorene's birthday party?"

It was all Jordan could do to keep his voice warm and friendly. "Not planning on it."

"But you'll be there with your parents, won't you?"

"Oh, of course. I wouldn't miss my sister's birthday party."

"Jordan, I'm sure Belinda would come with you if you'd ask her."

"Oh, I don't doubt it. But I'd rather come alone."

Mark gave him a quizzical look. "I don't understand you."

"What do you mean?"

"Here's a very pretty girl available and yearning to be your one and only, and you let her dangle. She's really a nice girl, Jordan. You'd better latch onto her before some other guy does."

*I wish some other guy would,* thought Jordan. Belinda was still pushing herself on him, and the pressure was still on by his parents and hers for nuptials. Both Mark and Lorene still put in their little digs about it, too. Irritated by it all, Jordan wanted to just spout off to the whole bunch, telling them to mind their own business, but he especially didn't want to upset his parents. He wanted the new ranch his father had promised him, as well as the log house that was to be built on it.

Eager to get inside the post office, Jordan said, "Well, Mark, if I don't run into you in the next few days, I'll see you at the party."

"Okay," said Mark. "I'll tell Lorene you won't be bringing Belinda."

Heading for the post office door, Jordan looked over his shoulder. "You do that."

Inside the post office, there were two long lines at the counter. Jordan got in the shortest one and prepared himself for the wait. A few people were gathered around the potbellied stove that stood in the middle of the floor not far from where the lines were formed.

A fidgety Jordan Shaw shifted his weight from one foot to the other, wishing the clerks would work faster. Since Knight Colburn had placed the mail order bride ads for him in the eastern newspapers, Jordan had made sure he was the one from the Bar-S to pick up the mail when it arrived three times a week by stagecoach.

It had been nearly two weeks since Knight had wired the ads eastward, and so far, there had been no replies. Jordan was hoping it would be different today.

The lines moved slowly, but finally, Jordan stepped up to the counter and forced a smile. "Howdy, Clete. Need the mail."

"Sure enough, Jordan," said the elderly clerk. "I'll get it for you."

While Clete was behind the wall, Jordan looked around and

noted that there were few people left in the building. Only a handful stood in both lines, and two elderly men who had been sitting by themselves in chairs near the potbellied stove were preparing to leave.

Clete returned with a small stack of mail. "Here you go, Jordan."

"Thanks," said Jordan, taking the stack. When he turned around, the two elderly men had vacated the building, and no one else was near the stove. Sitting down on one of the chairs, Jordan quickly sifted through the mail. He barely got started when he found an envelope from a Betty Sandell of Dayton, Ohio, addressed to him.

His heart began to pound. He started to open it, then decided to check the rest of the mail first. He set the letter aside and continued sifting. His heart seemed to skip a beat when he found a second letter addressed to him. This one was from a Marianne Wilson of Jersey City, New Jersey.

Laying that one aside also, he flipped through what was left, and was pleasantly surprised to find a third letter addressed to him on the very bottom of the stack. It was from a Diana Morrow of Richmond, Virginia.

Nervously, Jordan used his pocketknife to open the first envelope, and took out the letter from Betty Sandell. When he finished reading it, he moved his head back and forth slowly, and put the letter back in the envelope. Next he read the letter from Marianne Wilson. Like Betty Sandell's, it too was disappointing. Both young women showed themselves to be quite shallow, and only interested in the fact that he had money.

Stuffing Marianne's letter back in the envelope, he picked up the letter from Diana Morrow. "Well, here goes," he said, slitting the envelope and taking out the letter. He scanned it quickly, fully prepared for another disappointment.

But it wasn't like the others.

He smiled as he perused it slowly, and his smile broadened as he carefully read each word. *Yes!* he thought as he folded Diana's letter and slipped it back into the envelope. In a whisper, he said, "You could very well be the one, Diana. I can tell that you are a sweet young lady with a tender heart. You never once mentioned my wealth, and you have a good sense of humor. I like you very much already."

Placing Diana Morrow's letter in the pocket of his mackinaw, he gathered up the rest of the mail and moved outside. Quickly, he stuffed the mail in a saddlebag, mounted, and trotted down the street to the *Elkton Sentinel.*

Erline Tyler was at her desk when Jordan stepped in. "Hello, Jordan. I assume you want to see the boss."

Jordan grinned. "Yes, ma'am. Is he busy?"

"Not that busy. He's alone in his office. As always, he'll be glad to see you."

"Thanks," said Jordan, pulling the envelope out of his mackinaw pocket as he headed for the office door. Tapping on it, he called out, "Is the big newspaper magnate in there?"

He heard Knight laugh and say, "No, but come in anyhow."

Jordan stepped in, closed the door behind him, and rushed up to Knight's desk, waving the envelope. "Look what I got!"

"Your first response to the ads?"

"Well, actually there were three letters in today's mail, but I've already ruled two of the women out. They seemed more interested in my wealth than myself. Ah, but this one! I want you to read it, Knight. She's just what I've been dreaming about! Not one time does this girl mention my money. She's really something. I think I've found her."

"Hold on there, my friend," admonished Knight, knowing how impetuous Jordan could be. "Not too fast, now."

Extending the envelope to him, Jordan said, "Here. Read it for yourself. You'll see what I mean."

Knight grinned at him, took the letter from the envelope, leaned back in his desk chair, and began reading. The further he read, the more he was impressed with Diana Morrow.

When he finished reading the letter, he smiled and said, "I like this girl, Jordan. You're right. I think you may just have found her. So what next?"

"I want you to word a return letter to her for me."

"Be glad to."

"Good! I want to tell Diana that she sounds like just the girl for me. And I want you to use the most captivating words you can think of. I want to say in the letter that if after receiving it, Diana wants to come as my prospective bride, I want her to let me know as soon as possible and I'll send her the money for her travel expenses."

"All right," said Knight, taking paper from a desk drawer. "Let's see if I can get it down in a way that pleases you. Have a seat."

Jordan sat down on one of the chairs in front of the desk and watched as his friend took pen in hand, dipped it in the inkwell, and began to write.

When Knight was finished, he blotted the ink and handed it to Jordan. "See what you think."

The look that came into Jordan's eyes as he read the letter told Knight that he was pleased.

Smiling broadly, Jordan looked at Knight and said, "Ol' pal, it's perfect! Thank you."

"You're welcome. I hope it works out for you. New subject."

"Mm-hmm?"

"Are we still going hunting together tomorrow?"

"I'm sure planning on it."

"Good. I was hoping nothing would come up on the ranch that would keep you from going."

Jordan laughed. "It would take something really drastic to keep yours truly from going hunting! Should be good hunting, with all the snow that's fallen in the mountains the past few days."

"Yes," said Knight, glancing out the window. "Looks like it's starting to snow out there right now."

Looking at the fat flakes coming down from a heavy sky, Jordan said, "Sure enough. That north wind has sent us some snow right here in town." He rose from the chair. "Oh. I need you to address an envelope for me."

"Sure."

When the envelope was addressed to Diana Morrow, Knight handed it to Jordan, was thanked again, and Jordan hurried out to post the letter. The stagecoach that had come in from Ketcham that afternoon would carry his letter to the railroad the following morning.

The next morning, it was still snowing lightly as Knight and Jordan rode into the Sawtooth Mountains. The wind had dwindled to a slight breeze, for which they were thankful.

When they reached the high country, they left the horses and pack mule tied to trees and began plodding through the eight-inch depth of snow in the forest on foot, rifles in hand.

Keeping his voice just above a whisper, Knight said, "I'm really glad for you. The more I've thought about Diana Morrow's letter, the more convinced I've become that she's the right girl for you." His warm breath was forming small clouds on the cold air as he spoke.

The excitement Jordan was feeling showed in his shining eyes as he said with his own breath clouds riding the icy air, "I can't wait to hear back from her. I hope she'll still be interested after she reads my letter."

"I have no doubt that she will. Sounds like she's just what you need in a wife."

They came to a small, gurgling stream, which was ice-edged, and after they hopped to the other side, Jordan said, "Speaking of what I need in a wife, what are you doing about finding yourself a wife? You're twenty-four too, you know, and should be getting married."

As they pushed aside snow-laden pine branches so they could keep moving, Knight said, "The Lord will send the right girl along when it is His time for it to happen. As a child of God, I can rest in His plan for my life. And I can also rest in His care when I die and leave this world, Jordan. I know when I take my last breath on earth, I'll find myself looking into the face of my Saviour in heaven. But you—"

"I think you should try the mail order bride system, Knight," said Jordan, purposely cutting off the direction of the conversation toward repentance and salvation. "Looks like it's going to work for me. You might very well find this right girl that way."

Knight was about to comment when they both saw a big buck deer some forty yards ahead of them in an open area. Both raised their rifles quickly, took aim, and fired. The echoes of the shots went rattling away among the peaks and were fading into the distance when the deer's knees buckled, and he fell flat in the snow.

"Come on!" Jordan said gleefully. "We'll both have venison on our tables tonight."

As they were plodding through the snow toward the dead deer, suddenly a big black male bear lumbered out from between two towering, thick-trunked conifers. He rose on his hind legs and stretched his full length, pawing the air. Looking directly at Jordan, he ejected a wild roar and shook his head angrily.

"It's him!" cried Jordan, raising his rifle. Just as he squeezed the trigger, he slipped in the snow. The rifle spit fire, and the slug chewed into the tree closest to the bear, splattering bark in every direction. The bear roared again, pivoted, scurried into the dense forest, and disappeared.

Jordan started to run after him, but slipped again, and fell on his face in the snow. Knight grasped an arm, and as he was helping him up, he said, "I think it's the same bear you shot. It looked like part of his right paw was missing."

"I hope so," said Jordan, brushing snow from his rifle. "I've just got to track that big boy down, kill him, and get him stuffed."

Knight followed as his friend hurried toward the spot where the bear had appeared. They arrived at the same time, and Jordan pointed at the bear's tracks in the snow, saying, "Look, Knight! It's him, all right. Two claws are missing from the right paw."

"Sure enough," said Knight. "He's the one you shot, all right."

Jordan looked in the direction the bear had run and sighed. "He's probably a long way from here by now. You know how fast they are."

Knight nodded. "Plenty fast."

Staring at the spot where he had last seen the bear, Jordan said, "I've got to come back up here as soon as I can. I've got to find him, Knight. I want him! I want him!"

Knight lifted his hat, ran fingers through his thick, wavy hair, and said, "It might be the other way around, ol' pal. Maybe it's him wanting you. He was looking straight at you when he stood up and roared. It was like he remembered you. He may think of you every time he looks at his disfigured paw."

"You're serious. You really think he remembers me?"

"Yeah. You'd better be careful when you're tracking him. Let's get this buck dressed out."

On Tuesday, November 5, Diana Morrow was putting a stew together for supper with her mother sitting at the kitchen table, looking on. Dennis was playing in the boys' room.

While working on the stew, Diana said, "Maybe this will be the day, Mama. There's been enough time now since I mailed the letter. Maybe when Derick, Deborah, and Daniel get home from school and bring the mail, there'll be a letter from Jordan."

"I hope so, honey," said Martha. "Your father will be getting out of jail in nine days."

Cold terror, like an icy hand, squeezed Diana's spine. Her voice quivered as she said, "I…I've got to be gone before then."

"You will be, honey. I've prayed so hard. You will be."

Diana stirred the ingredients of her stew, and trying to keep her mind off her impending danger, said, "It was really a time for mixed emotions when we told Derick, Deborah, and Daniel about my replying to the mail order bride ad, wasn't it, Mama?"

"Mixed emotions for sure," said Martha. "Your siblings fear for your safety if you're still here when their father is released from jail, yet they can hardly stand the thought of their big sister living so far away."

At that moment, they both heard the pounding hooves of the team and the rattle of the wagon as it passed by the kitchen window on its way to the barn. Diana glanced through the window, and her heart quickened pace as she said, "Oh, Mama, they've just got to have the letter!"

"We'll see, honey. Maybe this is the day."

Moments later, footsteps were heard on the back porch, and when the door came open, Deborah entered, smiling. "It came, Diana!"

Diana drew a sharp breath. "Really? Jordan's letter came?"

"Sure did. Derick has it."

Even as Deborah was speaking, the boys came in with Derick

waving the envelope. "Here it is, sis!" he said gleefully. "The letter from your future husband."

Diana dried her hands on her apron, snatched the envelope from his fingers, and turned toward her mother. "I…I've got to read it in private, Mama. I'll go to my room. Be back in a few minutes."

"All right, honey," said Martha. "I understand."

"Hurry," said Deborah. "We want to know if Jordan wants to marry you."

"Yeah," said Daniel. "Hurry back."

Diana gave them a weak smile and dashed out of the kitchen. When she entered the bedroom that she and her sister shared, she closed the door, and with trembling fingers tore the envelope open and took out the letter. Taking a deep breath, she unfolded it and began reading.

*Dear Miss Diana Morrow,*

*I confess that when I placed my ad for a mail order bride, I suffered from serious doubts. I began to wonder what sort of woman might answer that type of ad, and I began to imagine the very worst. I also began to worry over what kind of life could be built with someone who is a stranger. I lost some sleep over these doubts, believe me.*

*Miss Morrow, I must tell you. Your letter dispelled every doubt. Your way with words is entrancing, and the manner in which you described yourself left me longing to truly know you. Your letter was by far the most personable, and as I finished reading it, I sensed that I had caught a glimpse into your very heart. I hope this letter may spark similar feelings in you.*

*I am a partner in my father's ranch and I love it. Ranch life is the only life I can imagine truly offering happy living. There is a freedom that can't be described. It can only be experienced in the everyday workings of a ranch. You can never anticipate what tomorrow will hold. Even the ordinary can one day catch you totally off guard with its simple, yet majestic, beauty. From the birth of a new colt to a fast ride on a bronco, ranch life can exhilarate you like nothing else, with the wonder of just living.*

*It is at such moments that I wish for someone to share my wonder and happiness. I am an ordinary, simple man. I like to fish, hunt, and ride. I love order, a good story, starry nights, and laughter, more than anything, if you can compare those things. I esteem women highly. I do not drink, and after several years of learning the hard way, I have learned to keep my temper in check. I will be the first to tell you that I am not perfect, but if you would consider me, I would try to always make you happy. You would have a nice home, plenty of food and clothing, as many animals as you could wish for, books upon books, and hopefully many children.*

*I believe you are someone with whom I could build a good life. Please write back soon and tell me if you think you might be able to ever feel the same. If, however, you do not think we are suitable for each other, please be honest and say so. I await anxiously for your answer.*

*Yours with all sincerity,*

*Jordan Shaw*

*P.S. If after reading this letter, your decision is to come as my prospective bride, please let me know as soon as possible, and I will send the money for your travel expenses. Included will be directions on the best way to reach Elkton.*

With her heart thundering in her chest, Diana reread the letter. Elated, she took a deep breath and left the room, hurrying down the hall.

Martha and her other children—minus Dennis, who was still playing in his room—were waiting with bated breath as they heard Diana coming toward the kitchen. They knew by the look on her face that she had good news.

"Well, come on," said Martha. "What did he say?"

Placing the letter in her mother's hands, Diana said, "I'm having trouble breathing. You read it to them, Mama."

Diana's siblings listened intently as their mother read Jordan Shaw's letter to them. When she finished, it was evident that everyone, including Martha, was touched by the letter.

First to speak was Deborah. "Wow, Diana! I hope someday I can find a man who writes letters like that."

"He sounds like the right one for you, sis," said Derick.

"Sure does," agreed Daniel.

Martha swallowed the lump that had risen in her throat, and said, "Honey, he sounds like a fine young man. You need to write the answer in a hurry. I'm afraid we're going to have to hide you somewhere nearby until you hear back from Jordan and have the travel expense money in your hands."

"Mama," said Derick, "I'm afraid we won't be able to hide her anywhere near Richmond where Papa can't find her. We've got to think of something before a week from Thursday."

"I've been praying very much about it, Derick," said Martha. "God will show us what to do."

Derick, Deborah, and Daniel exchanged skeptical glances, but remained silent.


That evening, while the rest of the family were in the parlor, Diana wrote to Jordan in her room, saying she would come to Elkton as his prospective bride if he knew for sure he really wanted her.


Alone in her bedroom that night, Martha lay in the darkness and said, "Dear Lord, I am still quite new at this, but I'm asking You to work out a way for us to hide Diana in a safe place until she receives Jordan's letter with the money in it, and she can get a train out of Richmond."

As she continued to pray, another concern filled her heart. "Lord," she said, fighting tears, "as much as I want Diana safe on this earth from her father, I so much more want her soul safe in Your care. Please help me to know what to say to her. I'm so sorry for leading her astray from You and Your saving grace for so many years. Please use me now to bring her to Your saving power. Help me not to falter before any of my children, nor before Stu when he is released. Oh, heavenly Father, give me that special 'measure of grace' and use me for Your glory.

"Thank You for being so patient and long-suffering with me. Help me now, as I wait upon You. I am having moments of fear. But as I read in Your word just yesterday, help me to say: 'What time I am afraid, I will trust in Thee.' It seems to me that one of the hardest things for a new Christian is to learn to trust in Thee. Help me, dear Father, not to live in doubt and fear, but to fully trust You. Thank You, Lord, for Your understanding of this humble servant. And thank You, again, for saving me."

When Martha had finished praying, a peace stole over her soul.

Diana's letter to Jordan was mailed at the post office early the next morning.

At supper that evening, Martha talked to her four oldest children about salvation, as she had done periodically since becoming a Christian. They listened politely, but each one was having a hard time with it because of what both parents had taught them for as long as they could remember.

Martha did not push them, but once more told them how wrong she had been to teach them not to believe the Bible. She also told them that she had prayed hard last night, asking the Lord to show them what to do about Diana before their father was released from jail a week from Thursday.

When Tuesday of the next week came, and Martha and her children were still without a satisfactory place to hide Diana while she waited for Jordan Shaw's letter containing the travel money, they were on the verge of panic.

As the children climbed in the wagon after breakfast, ready to head for school, Diana was standing close while Martha looked on from the front porch.

Derick looked down at Diana from the wagon seat and said, "Sis, if nothing else, I'll take you to Petersburg tomorrow and we'll tell the police there about the danger you're in. We'll ask them if they can put you someplace where you will be safe until you can leave for Idaho."

From her place on the porch, Martha said, "Derick, that's a good idea. You plan to do that. How does it sound to you, Diana?"

Diana looked over her shoulder. "It's the best idea yet, Mama. I'll go along with that."

Derick put the horses in motion, and Diana moved onto the porch, standing beside her mother. As they watched the wagon pull out of the yard, Martha said, "Honey, somehow, as good as Derick's plan is, I am getting a feeling down deep inside that the Lord has some better plan for you to escape your father's anger."

They were about to turn and enter the house when they saw a rider coming toward the house from the road.

"Who do you suppose that is, Mama?" said Diana.

Squinting, Martha said, "I can't tell yet, but another few seconds will answer your question."

Diana was first to make out the man's face. "It's Chief Perry, Mama. I wonder why he's coming here."

Martha shrugged. "I have no idea, but I guess we're about to find out."

DIANA MORROW OPENED THE FRONT DOOR just as Chief Perry started up the porch steps. The air was quite chilly, and there was a stiff breeze.

"Good morning, Chief Perry," she said with a smile. "Please come in."

"Thank you, Diana," said Perry, stepping past her and removing his hat. "I think winter may come early this year. That air has a bite to it."

"You may be right about an early winter," said Diana, wondering what kind of weather they were having in Idaho.

Unbuttoning his coat, Perry asked, "Is your mother up to talking to me? There's something I need to tell you both."

"Yes, sir. She's in the parlor. Let me take your coat."

Perry thanked her, handing her the coat. She also took his hat, and hung them on hooks next to the door.

Martha gave the chief a pleasant look as he followed Diana into the parlor. "I overheard what you told Diana, Chief. I assumed this was more than just a social call when we saw you coming."

"Yes, ma'am," he said, obviously a bit nervous. "May I ask how you are feeling? You look much better than you did when I saw you last."

A small grateful smile flitted across Martha's face, which still carried some bruise marks. "Each day I feel a bit better, thank you. This cast is a hindrance at times, but I'm learning to live with it. Might as well. I've got several weeks to go before it can come off."

"Chief, we've got hot coffee on the stove," said Diana. "Would you like some?"

"Sounds wonderful!" said Perry.

"I'll be right back," Diana said as she rushed into the hall and disappeared.

In an attempt to fill the time until Diana returned, Perry said, "I met up with your older children on the road. I assume they were on their way to school."

"Yes."

"We waved to each other, but didn't stop to talk."

"Mm-hmm."

Looking around, he said, "Your little guy—"

"Dennis."

"Yes. Dennis. He around?"

Martha grinned. "He's a late sleeper. No sounds from him yet."

"Oh. Dennis is how old?"

"He's five. Four months to go before he turns six. And I can wait."

"I understand. My children grew up too fast."

Diana entered the parlor carrying a tray with three cups of steaming coffee. "Here we are!" she said cheerfully.

When all three were seated, each holding a cup, Martha and Diana looked at each other questioningly and waited for the chief to state his business.

After taking tentative sips of coffee, Perry cleared his throat nervously and said, "I...I don't know if what I have to tell you will come as good news or bad. It's about Stu."

Both women kept their eyes on him, waiting for further information.

"Stu, as you know, has a very flinty temper."

Both women nodded.

"Well, yesterday we had an incident. One of my deputies, Johnny Galloway, carried the prisoners' food trays to their cells as usual. You may have noticed, Diana, that there is a six-inch space under the cell doors."

"I hadn't noticed," commented Diana.

"Well, anyway, when Johnny slid Stu's lunch tray under the

door, his hand slipped and some of the coffee slopped out of the cup, soaking Stu's sandwich. Before Johnny could say he would take the tray back and get more coffee and another sandwich, Stu swore at him, calling him a clumsy—well, a name I wouldn't say in front of you ladies.

"Johnny held his own temper, apologized, and said he would take the tray and bring him another sandwich. But Stu wouldn't leave it alone. In a temper fit, he swore at Johnny again, called him a worse name, bent down and picked up the coffee cup and flung the hot coffee in Johnny's face."

"Oh, my," said Martha. "I'm sorry."

"The sorry one is your husband, Mrs. Morrow. Judge Weathers added two more weeks to Stu's sentence for his deed. If he behaves himself, he'll be released on November 28." Perry took a deep breath. "I…don't know whether this is good news or bad. Given the circumstances, I figured it might be a relief to you, but on the other hand, this keeps Stu away from the work he ordinarily does here on the farm."

Mother and daughter looked at each other with relief.

This answered Perry's question for him.

"Did your deputy get burned by the coffee, Chief?" asked Martha.

"No, ma'am. He's fine."

"I'm so glad. Thank you for riding out here to tell us. We really appreciate it."

Perry finished his coffee, and moments later as Martha and Diana stood at the parlor window and watched him ride away, they held onto each other with tears flowing.

Sniffling, Martha said, "Oh, honey, God indeed has answered my prayers. Do you see it? There was no way you could have been out of here and headed for Idaho before your father was released from jail. Now, instead of finding a place to hide you till you could be on your way to join Jordan Shaw, the Lord simply let your father's temper cause him to get time added to his sentence. I just know you'll at least be on your way to Idaho when he gets out."

"I see it all right, Mama," Diana said softly. "Thank God for answered prayer!"

On the same day Diana and her mother were visited by Chief Perry with his good news—Tuesday, November 12—Jordan Shaw rode into Ketcham, Idaho, and dismounted in front of the post office. Since the stagecoach only came to Elkton three times a week, Jordan was making the trip to Ketcham daily to pick up the mail. He was eager to hear back from Diana and didn't want any time wasted.

Four other letters from hopeful young women had come, but Jordan had dismissed each one, telling himself Diana Morrow was the girl for him.

Entering the post office, he approached the counter. One of the clerks looked up from something he was reading and smiled. "Well, if it isn't Mr. Shaw again. Whatever you're expecting in the mail must be mighty important!"

"It is, Barney," said Jordan. "Very important."

Barney disappeared for a moment, then returned with a small stack of mail. Jordan thanked him, went to a table that was provided for customers, and hurriedly sifted through the mail. His heart thudded his rib cage when his eyes fell on an envelope with his name on it and the return address was from Diana Morrow of Richmond, Virginia.

Nervously licking his lips, he pulled out his pocketknife and carefully opened the envelope. Taking out the letter, he unfolded it and let his eyes take in Diana's written words.

*Dear Mr. Jordan Shaw,*

*I was very surprised by your letter. I had never replied to a mail order bride ad before, and I was sure that I had made a dreadful mess of it. I too had serious doubts about this method of finding a life partner. I suppose it is rather frightening for both parties in a situation like this.*

*As soon as I opened your letter, every trace of fear melted away. You call yourself an ordinary, simple man, but I sincerely doubt that you are. No one who can write as you do could ever be considered just an ordinary man. Everything you say about yourself fascinates me, and your letter really did make me want to truly know you, too. I believe you and I could build a good life together. We seem to be similar in heart and mind.*

*I will offer you a few warnings, though. I cannot bear being around snakes. They scare me more than answering newspaper ads for brides! Also, I have been known for speaking my mind at times. (This may make you rethink your proposal.) I usually freckle in the summer, and I bite my bottom lip when I'm upset. I believe that marriage is a partnership, and I cannot abide overbearing men who assume the role of dictators over their wives. If after reading all of this, you still think I'm the one for you, then I happily accept your proposal. If you are having second thoughts, as you may well be, please do not hesitate to be honest with me.*

*I am looking forward to receiving your next letter. If you are absolutely sure that I am the one you want as your bride, I request that you send me any information I may need for traveling to Elkton, Idaho.*

*Please write to me soon, no matter what you must tell me.*
*Rather anxiously,*
*Diana Morrow*

Smiling in elation, Jordan whispered. "Diana, there's nothing to be anxious about. I am absolutely sure you're the one for me!"

He read the letter again, feeling stronger yet about Diana with each word. While placing the letter back in the envelope, he felt gratitude toward the railroad people for running their trains day and night across America so a letter could get from Virginia to Idaho in seven or eight days.

Hurrying out the door, Jordan swung into the saddle and put his horse into motion through the fresh blanket of snow that was on the ground.

Knight Colburn was at Erline Tyler's desk, discussing an article she had written, when the door opened and with the rush of cold air came Jordan Shaw.

Both greeted Jordan, then Knight said, "What can I do for you, ol' pal?"

"Need a little private time with the big newspaper magnate," said Jordan.

Knight laughed. "Sorry, but Dan Tyler isn't here right now."

Erline giggled.

"Will I do?" asked Knight.

"Sure," said Jordan. "I'd wait for the big magnate, but I'm in a hurry."

Erline grinned to herself as the two friends entered Knight's office and the door went shut.

As Knight closed the door, he looked at Jordan with anticipation and said, "You got your reply from Diana!"

"Yes!" said Jordan, pulling the envelope from his coat pocket. "Here. Read it. I need another letter to her immediately."

Knight sat down in his chair behind the desk and took the letter from the envelope. Jordan eased onto one of the straight-backed chairs and watched his friend's face as he read it.

When Knight finished, he looked at Jordan with a smile. "She's quite the little gal, isn't she?"

"She sure is! Now let me give you what I want to say slowly, so you can get it just right."

After nearly an hour, Jordan held the finished product in his hand after reading it through three times. "Beautiful, Knight! You have such a way with words. You really should put your own ad in the eastern newspapers and get yourself a mail order bride."

Knight smiled. "I know in my heart that a mail order bride ad isn't necessary. My heavenly Father has given me peace about it. He is going to send the bride He has chosen for me in His own way, and in His own time."

Not wanting to get into another discussion on God and His Son, Jordan shrugged his shoulders and stood up. Taking out his wallet, he said, "If you'll address an envelope for me, I'll put in sufficient money for Diana's trip, and ride back to Ketcham so I can get it in the mail right away."

A few minutes later, sealed envelope in hand, Jordan thanked Knight once again for helping him, and hurried out the door.

On Tuesday afternoon, November 19, Diana and her mother were in the sewing room next to the girls' bedroom when they heard the back door open.

"They're home from school," said Martha.

Rapid footsteps could be heard in the hall, and Derick's voice pierced the air as he shouted, "Diana! Diana! Jordan's letter is here!"

Jumping up from the table, Diana rushed to the door just in time to find her excited brother skidding to a stop on the wooden floor. The others drew up as Diana took the envelope from Derick and ripped it open. As she turned back toward her mother while pulling out the letter, several bills of currency slipped from the letter and fluttered to the floor. While her siblings dropped to their knees to retrieve the money, Martha said, "Read it quickly, honey, so you can tell us what he says."

Biting her bottom lip, Diana nodded and stepped to the window where she read the letter while her heart pounded so hard, she could feel the pulse in her neck and temples. As she read it, tears filled her eyes and a smile lighted up her lovely face. She ran her gaze to her mother, then to Derick, Deborah, and Daniel. "He wants me to come and marry him!"

Martha's brow formed deep lines and her eyes misted as she put a hand to her mouth.

"I sorta figured that when I saw all that money." Derick chuckled.

"Read it to us!" said Deborah.

"Yeah!" chimed in Daniel.

Diana looked at her mother. "We would all like to hear it, honey," said Martha.

Diana took a deep breath in an attempt to ease the fluttering of her heart and holding the letter with trembling hands, read it slowly:

"*Dear Miss Diana,*

*I was overjoyed to receive your letter accepting my proposal. From the moment I began reading your first letter, I knew you were the one I wanted as my wife. I only hope that I will not disappoint you. I'm not at all concerned that you will disappoint me.*

*As to your warnings, I have a freckle or two, myself. And if I learn there is a snake around, I am the first to run! I agree that partnership in marriage is absolutely essential, and an overbearing husband is blind to the fact that he is building a wall between himself and his wife. Someone you are not afraid to share everything with is the ideal life partner. I would never be the overbearing kind to you because I know that dictating husbands miss out on the true happiness marriage can hold. And, Miss Diana, as for speaking your mind, what is that but honesty? I would not expect less. By all means, I want you to always be honest with me. As long as it is not cruel, honesty could never be considered to be wrong.*

*Enclosed is more than enough money to cover all your traveling expenses, and as you will see, at the bottom of this sheet, I have explained about the railroad line to Ketcham and the stage line to Elkton. I will pay for a room at an Elkton boardinghouse for you to stay in until the wedding. I am sure you will agree that we need to have an ample courting period so we can get to know each other better before we make a lifelong commitment.*

*Please come as soon as you can. Of course, I want you to have sufficient time for packing and saying your good-byes, but needless to say, I am more than eager to meet you in person. Please let me know as soon as possible when to expect you.*

*Yours most sincerely,*
*Jordan."*

Both Martha and Deborah were crying.

"Oh, Diana," said Deborah, wrapping her arms around her sister, "I'm so happy for you! I'll miss you terribly, but you'll be safe from Papa, and you'll be with the man who will love and cherish you. You deserve that."

Martha embraced Diana with her good arm, and the boys followed, showing their joy for this marvelous change in her life.

Martha wiped tears from her eyes. "All right, here's the plan.

Since school is out for the rest of the week for the Thanksgiving holiday, we'll have Derick drive all of us to the railroad station in Richmond first thing tomorrow morning so Diana can set up her train and stagecoach schedules and buy her tickets. We need to have her on that train as soon as possible. Your father gets out of jail in just over a week."

Derick set soft eyes on his mother. "Mama, your prayers really worked. God timed this all out to perfection, didn't He?"

Happy to hear these words coming from her oldest son, Martha said, "Yes, He did, honey. Everything God does is perfect." She ran her gaze over the faces of the others. "All of you need to learn that."

"Mama, what about Dennis?" said Deborah. "Since he's taking his nap as usual right now, he still doesn't know what's going on. We can't keep it from him much longer."

"He need not know but the bare essentials," said Martha. "We dare not let anyone but those of us in this room know where Diana has gone. We must keep it a secret. No matter what, your father must not learn where Diana has gone."

"Mama," said Diana, "even though Jordan and I will have a courtship, I really don't think it will be very long until we marry. Once I am his wife, there is nothing Papa can do, even if he should somehow find out where I am. I will be Jordan's wife then, and no longer under Papa's rule. Jordan sounds like the kind of man who would protect me from my father."

When Martha and her children drove away from the railroad depot in Richmond the next morning, they went directly to the post office. Diana had brought along paper and envelope.

While the rest of the family stayed close to the potbellied stove, Diana went to one of the tall tables and penned her letter.

*Dear Jordan,*

*I feel almost as if I have been dropped into the middle of a fairy tale. I think the reality of it has yet to hit me. It seems far too good to be real, and I catch myself wondering if I am about to awake from a dream and find out that's all it was. Since nothing of the sort has happened as yet, I have given you my travel schedule below. You will know me when you see me. I will be the one who looks like she has butterflies in her stomach.*

*Other than that, all I have to tell you is how happy I am, and how much I am looking forward to getting to know you. I am still not certain why you chose me, but I am very glad you did. You are offering me everything I ever wanted and never thought I would have. I can hardly wait to look into your eyes and touch your hand. I think that is the only way this will truly seem real to me. It seems insane, yet so right to totally put my hope and trust in a man I only know through a few short letters. I have never felt this strongly about anyone before, and I don't even know you...and yet, I do.*

*I am in full agreement with the courtship and the boardinghouse, and thank you for being the good man that you are.*

*I will be leaving Richmond this coming Friday, November 22, and am scheduled to arrive in Elkton by stagecoach on Thursday, November 28, at 3:00 P.M. So, with my luggage, sweaty palms, aforementioned butterflies, and much hope, I prepare to set out on my journey. I hope you are as excited as I am. I can hardly believe I am going to see you soon.*

*There is nothing in the world I want more.*

*Happily,*
*Diana*

Diana read the letter through three times to make sure it was exactly the way she wanted it, and then sealed it in the envelope, stepped to the counter, and handed it to a postal clerk to be mailed.

On Thursday, Diana kept herself busy cleaning, cooking, and baking. She wanted everything to be caught up before she left, knowing that with the broken arm, her mother was still limited as to what she could do. Staying occupied also kept her from having too much time to think about how much she was going to miss her mother and siblings.

That evening, Diana prepared a special dinner with Deborah's help. At the table, everyone worked hard to keep a light and happy atmosphere, but their faces were showing the heaviness of their hearts. Martha tried valiantly to lighten the mood by bringing up happy times from the past.

Soon all of the children were joining in. Downturned lips were lifted into smiles, and the meal ended on a happy note.

As the family was rising from the table, Deborah looked at her sister and said, "Diana, you've worked hard today. I know you're tired. You've got some packing yet to do. I'll clean up the kitchen and do the dishes. You go on and get your things ready."

Diana wrapped her arms around Deborah and hugged her tight. "Thank you, sweetie."

"You're quite welcome, sis. And I don't want you worrying about this household when you're gone. I'll take care of things. Understand?"

Diana hugged her again, fighting tears. "Yes."

Diana hugged her mother and brothers, then went to the room that she and Deborah had shared since Deborah was very small.

A small trunk which was partially packed sat open and waiting on the floor, and a satchel had been placed on Diana's bed.

Emotions arose within her. She sat down on a chair and gazed around the room taking in its sparse furnishings, and said to herself in a whisper, "This is my home. This is my family. How—how am I ever going to leave them?"

She could feel hot tears welling up in her eyes and running down into her throat. She gulped them back, rose to her feet, and while the tears ran down her cheeks, went to work to finish packing.

The task was quickly accomplished. She stood looking at her meager belongings. "Guess that's one good thing about being poor. You don't have much to take with you when you move to a new location."

Movement at the door caught her eye. "Oh. Mama."

"May I come in?" asked Martha.

"Of course. I just finished packing."

Martha went to the bed, sat down on its edge, and patted the spot next to her. "Come sit down, sweetheart."

Struggling to keep from crying, Diana sat down beside her mother and met her loving gaze.

Martha took hold of her daughter's hand and drew a deep breath. "Sweetie, I can only imagine how very difficult this is for you. Here you are, leaving your home and family and going someplace strange and new to meet a young man that you only know by the words he has written in a few letters. We are going to miss you terribly. This house will never be the same without you, but none of us could live with ourselves if we stood in your way of going then your father came home and beat you to death."

Blinking at the tears that filled her eyes, Diana squeezed her mother's hand. "We both know that I have to leave here, Mama, but I worry about you and my sister and brothers. I'm afraid Papa will come home and be like always. He may take out on you what he would like to do to me."

"I honestly don't think so, dear," Martha said. "For whatever the reason, it is you he seems to take out his frustrations on. I'm optimistic that his six weeks in jail will provide good cause to make him think about his actions and bring about a change in him. This is why I'm not afraid he will try to beat out of us where you've gone. He has established a record with the law by being jailed for assault and battery on Tom Wymore. Chief Perry is aware of the way he has beat on you children and myself before. Your father knows he's walking on thin ice with the law. So don't you be worrying about us."

"I can't help but worry, Mama," Diana said.

Letting go of Diana's hand, Martha caressed her cheek tenderly and said, "This mail order bride thing is all new to you, honey. It is going to bring about a dramatic change in your life. I know you don't understand about my new life in Jesus, but I have put you in His mighty hands, and He has given me perfect peace that He will protect you and that He will protect your siblings and me."

Diana wrapped her mother's fragile body in her own young arms and kissed her cheek. "Thank you, Mama, for loving me, and wanting what is best for me. I hope someday I can be a wise and loving mother to my own children just as you have been to all of us."

Easing back in Diana's embrace, Martha looked her in the eye and said, "Please promise me that you will find a Bible-believing church and go to it."

"I promise."

"Thank you. Now how about we gather everybody in the kitchen and each of us have a piece of that marvelous chocolate cake you baked?"

"Sounds good to me."

It was an emotional moment at the Richmond railroad station the next morning as Martha and her other children stood beside the train with Diana to tell her good-bye, not knowing if they would ever see her again.

Martha looked at her with misty eyes. "Honey, we haven't had a moment to discuss this it seems, but I want you to write to us, so we'll know how it is going for you."

"But Mama," protested Diana, "if I do that, and Papa gets hold of an envelope with my return address on it, he'll know where to find me."

"I've already figured out how to keep that from happening. Address the envelopes to Shamus and Maggie. I'll explain the whole thing to them. They'll see that I get every letter you send."

"Oh. That's a good idea," said Diana. "I'll do it."

Each one except Dennis told Diana they would write to her after her first letter came and they had the address of the boarding-house.

Martha reminded Diana of her promise to seek out a Bible-believing church. Diana assured her she would.

Many tears were shed as good-byes were said, and each one embraced Diana, then watched her board the coach as the conductor was shouting out his last call for everyone to get aboard.

Soon they saw her take a seat next to the window. She forced a smile as the train pulled away, and waved to them, trying to hold her tears in check.

*18*

DIANA MORROW HAD A LUMP IN HER THROAT as she pressed her face to the window, trying to keep her beloved family in view as long as possible. When the train made a curve as it left the depot, the last she saw of them they were waving.

She burst into tears, glad at least that there was no one sitting beside her. People across the aisle were looking at her, and not wanting to make a scene, Diana took a linen handkerchief from her small handbag and pressed it to her face. She cried as softly as possible into the handkerchief for a few minutes, then finally gaining control of her emotions she wiped her cheeks and blew her nose.

Gulping back the tears that still wanted to be shed, she forced herself to contemplate the future that lay ahead of her. She felt great relief, knowing she would not be home when her father was released from jail. *I can only hope Mama is right,* she thought. *That Papa will be a different man once he is out of jail and I am out of the picture.*

Diana was still jittery about meeting Jordan, and a bit on edge at the thought of marrying a man she had never met. Knowing Jordan was wealthy helped a lot, however. She had known nothing but a poor farmer's existence all of her life.

Drying her eyes and adjusting herself on the seat with the soothing rumble of the wheels beneath her, she concentrated on what life would be like on a sprawling cattle ranch in the west. After a few moments of this, she switched her thoughts to Jordan Shaw, trying to picture what he might look like.

Was he tall and slender? Or short and stocky? Or maybe tall and stocky? Or short and thin? Was he dark or fair? She would have to wait until that moment she met him when she stepped off the stagecoach for the answers to these questions. But one thing she knew. Any man who had a way with words like Jordan did was quite intelligent and had a tender heart.

The coach rocked slightly as the train began a long curve. Instantly, her head began to pound. Pressing fingertips to her temples, she knew the headache had come as a result of the mental anguish she was suffering because of leaving her beloved family.

Closing her eyes, Diana leaned her tired head back on the seat, and after a few minutes, was asleep. Soon she was dreaming about a handsome young man who stood in front of the Wells Fargo station in Elkton, heading toward her with a smile as she was about to step down from the stagecoach. She sighed in her sleep and a gentle smile curved her lovely lips.


Late the next night, Diana arrived in Kansas City, Missouri. She left the train and waited in the depot until the train came in that was bound for Portland, Oregon. This train would take her as far as Boise, Idaho, where she would board another one for Ketcham.

Early the next morning—Sunday, November 24—Diana boarded the Portland-bound train. She was alone on the seat once again and let her thoughts trail to her mother and siblings. Her heart ached for them, but the pain of the ache eased when she remembered that if her father behaved himself, he would be released from jail on Thursday. She was thankful for the way God had worked it so she would be gone by then.

After eating breakfast alone in the dining car, Diana returned to her seat, looked out the window at the sun-drenched plains of Nebraska, and thought about the moment when she would first lay eyes on Jordan at the stage station in Elkton.

By the time she sat down at the small table in the dining car for lunch, the sun had disappeared behind heavy clouds. When she returned to her seat, she saw windblown flecks of snow smashing against her window. With each hour that passed, the storm grew stronger. When she arrived late that afternoon in Cheyenne City, Wyoming, it had developed into a blinding snowstorm.

Diana watched several passengers leave her coach, bending their heads against the blowing snow, and soon new passengers were boarding, doing the same thing. She heard them talking about the storm, which had come down from Canada and hit the Cheyenne City area some forty-eight hours previously. They were saying it was the worst snowstorm to hit that part of the country in ten years.

Soon a woman in her late fifties drew up to where Diana was sitting. "Anyone occupying this place next to you, dear?"

Giving her a warm smile, Diana said, "No, ma'am."

The woman brushed snow from her coat, laid it in the overhead rack, then sat down, placing her handbag on the floor by her feet. Sighing, she said, "Some storm."

"Sure is," said Diana.

Other new passengers were moving by in search of seats as the woman said, "I'm Cora Zeller. My home is in Portland, Oregon. I've been visiting my son, daughter-in-law, and three grandchildren here in Cheyenne City."

Diana nodded, giving her another smile. "My name is Diana Morrow. I'm from Richmond, Virginia, on my way to Elkton, Idaho, to become the mail order bride of a young cattle rancher. His name is Jordan Shaw."

Cora's eyebrows arched. "A mail order bride. Well, I've heard of lots of them, but this is the first time I've ever met one."

"I've never met one either," Diana said, chuckling.

The whistle blew and soon the train was chugging out of the station, heading due west. While the wind hurled snow against the windows, Cora and Diana discussed the mail order bride system and how much it was being used by men in the west to provide themselves with wives.

"Diana, may I ask you something?"

"Of course."

"Do you find it difficult facing the prospect of marrying a man you have never met and know very little about?"

"Well, I have to admit, Mrs. Zeller, it is a bit frightening, but it isn't as frightening as the thought of staying in Richmond."

Cora saw the hint of fear in Diana's eyes, but did not pry.

Soon the train was climbing into the Rocky Mountains on a steep incline. The storm was relentless as it continued to batter the sides of the coach, making it difficult for anyone to see out the frost-edged windows.

Diana laid her head back and closed her eyes. Moments later, she felt Cora moving on the seat and opened her eyes to see her pulling a big Bible out of her handbag. She closed her eyes again, then after a few minutes, looked at the Bible as Cora was reading it.

From the corner of her eye, Cora noticed Diana looking at the Book in her hands. After several minutes passed, and Diana still had her eyes on the Bible, Cora smiled at her and asked, "Do you know the Author of this Book, honey?"

"Well, ah, no, I don't. As far back as I can remember, both of my parents taught my siblings and me that these born-again, Bible-reading Christians were nothing but fanatical fools."

"Oh, really?"

"Yes. Then quite recently, my mother went through a very difficult trial, and the pastor of a Richmond church talked to her, showed her some things in the Bible, and she was born again."

"Oh, wonderful!" Cora's face was suddenly beaming.

"Mama's trying to lead her children the same way. She made me promise that when I get to Elkton, I will find a Bible-believing church and attend it."

"Well, good for her. But you haven't been born again."

"No, ma'am. With all the things my parents taught me against the Bible, I'm very confused. Mama admits that she had been wrong to teach us what she did."

"And what about your father?"

"Well, he's still of the same opinion he always was."

"I see. Well, I'm so glad to hear that your mother is now a Christian. Diana, I would be very glad to show you right here in the Word of God how to be born again."

Diana drew a short breath and swallowed hard. "Thank you, ma'am, but with all the confusion in my mind from what I was taught in the past, I think it would be best if I wait till I get settled in Elkton then go to church and learn about it."

"But what if you were to die before then? According to what the Lord Jesus said in John chapter 3, you can't go to heaven unless you have been born again. There is only one other place you can go, and that is the awful burning place called hell. Do you understand that?"

"Well, yes. Mama made sure I did."

"Diana, your mother was right to do so. Do you understand that God's Son came into this world for the express purpose of shedding His blood and dying on the cross to pay the penalty for sin, so we could be saved if we would come to Him for salvation?"

"Mama made it clear about that, ma'am."

"Honey, Jesus allowed Himself to be crucified because it was the only way He could provide salvation. He died and they put His body in the tomb. But death couldn't hold Him. He did just what He had predicted He would do. Three days after he was buried, He came back from the dead. And He is alive to save all who will come to Him in repentance of sin and ask Him to save them. If you die without receiving Him into your heart as your Saviour, you will spend eternity in hell."

Diana's face had paled significantly. "M-Mrs. Zeller, I…ah… am very tired. I need to get some sleep. I don't mean to be rude, but I'm really very weary."

Cora nodded. "I understand that, honey, but you need to seriously consider your lost condition before God. It isn't something to put off. I'll be very happy to show you from the Bible exactly how to be saved so you can clearly understand it."

Faking a yawn, Diana put a hand to her mouth, made her eyelids look heavy, and said, "I will seriously consider it, ma'am. Right now, I need to get some sleep." As she spoke, she slid down a bit on the seat and closed her eyes.

"All right, dear," said Cora.

The train continued to make its way higher into the Rockies while the storm howled outside. Cora read her Bible for a few minutes, then lay her own head back, closed her eyes, and silently prayed for wisdom and power that she might be able to lead the girl to Jesus.

Diana was dreaming that the stagecoach was pulling into the Wells Fargo station in Elkton when she was rudely jarred awake by the wheels of the train screeching on the tracks as it slid to a sudden halt.

At first, she was unable to make the correlation between dream and reality as she sat up and rubbed her eyes. She frantically looked around her, and realized she was aboard the train, and her dream was just that. A dream.

Shaking her head to clear away the cobwebs, Diana saw the passengers trying to see out the snowy windows while they talked in low, worried tones, wondering why the train had come to a halt while they were still in the mountains. The snow was pelting the windows, driven by a savage wind.

They were in the midst of a blizzard.

Diana looked at Cora, who was listening to two men across the aisle discussing the sudden stop, and said, "Mrs. Zeller…"

Cora's head came around to see the girl's eyes wide with fear. "Yes, honey?"

"Why have we stopped?"

"I have no idea. But don't be afraid. God is in control, as always."

Diana was amazed that she saw no fear in Cora's eyes. Peace and control were reflected there.

Taking the girl's trembling hands in her own, Cora gave her a cheery smile. "It will be all right, dear. It's probably just something to do with this terrible storm. I was really rather surprised that they didn't keep the train in Cheyenne City until the storm had passed. We may be delayed here for a while, but the Lord always knows best."

Feeling somewhat better, Diana tried to look out the window into the dark night, shivering with each blast of wind that sent blinding icy pellets against it.

The two men across the aisle rose from the seat, and one of them looked around at the confused passengers and said, "Folks, my name is Dale Manning. My friend is T. J. Smith. T. J. and I are going to go and see if we can find out why we're stopped."

Even as both men headed for the door at the front of the coach, there was a thundering roar toward the rear of the train. It went on for two to three minutes, then all was quiet.

Quickly, Manning and Smith left the coach.

Time dragged as they awaited some word on the situation.

Soon the front door opened. The engineer and the fireman hurried through the coach, each carrying a burning lantern. There was a sudden babble of voices as people asked what was going on, but the two men moved on out the rear door without making a reply.

Only seconds passed until the door at the front opened and the conductor came in, hurrying toward the rear of the coach. Passengers asked him what had happened, but he only shook his head, saying he didn't have time to stop and tell them. Some were shouting angrily at him as he moved out and closed the rear door behind him.

Immediately, the two men who had left the coach earlier came in the front door and stopped. Dale Manning ran his gaze over the confused, frightened faces of the passengers and said, "We only had a brief moment with the conductor, folks, but he told us the engineer stopped the train when the headlight on the engine showed him that an avalanche had occurred, and the tracks ahead were buried under tons of snow. There are steep slopes above us on the right, and the snow simply slid down the mountain and covered the tracks. The roar we all heard after the train was stopped was an avalanche behind the train. We are now trapped between two avalanches."

Women gasped and some of them began to whimper, as did some of the children.

At that moment, the engineer, the fireman, and the conductor came through the rear door. Again, there was a babble of voices as people began asking questions.

One frightened woman's voice rose above the others as she cried out, "Tell us! Are we in danger?"

"Now, ma'am," said the conductor, "just settle down. We're not in any real danger. We just have to get a grip on ourselves and—"

"Why don't you tell them the truth?" said Dale Manning.

"They all have a right to know just what danger we're in."

Diana grabbed Cora's hand, trembling. Cora patted her arm, attempting to calm her.

All eyes were on the conductor. He choked up.

The engineer cleared his throat and said, "Ladies and gentlemen, we...ah...we are on the edge of a deep canyon. The fireman and I saw this before we ever left the engine. We went to the rear to see just how bad the avalanche is behind us. It's dark out there, but it looks every bit as bad as the one in front of us. I...ah...hate to tell you this, but an avalanche could come down on the train any minute and shove it over the edge into the canyon."

There was instant panic. Women and children who were old enough to understand the engineer's words began weeping, and many of the men were close to it. The railroad men tried to calm them, but to little avail. The three men hurried out the front door of the coach, heading toward the front of the train. The crying and wailing went on.

Frozen in terror, Diana still had a grip on Cora's hand. She saw Cora close her eyes and bow her head. Her lips were moving in silent prayer.

Suddenly, a silver-haired man who was seated near the front of the coach stood up and stepped into the aisle. Lifting his voice above the din of wails and cries, he said, "Listen to me! Everybody listen to me!"

He had the attention of about half the people at once. It took him a minute or so to talk to them and reduce the frightened voices to the point that everybody could hear him. "Folks," he said, "we need to pray for God's protection on us. He made this world. He can keep the snow above us from coming down. I will lead in prayer, if you will allow it."

One woman spoke up. "This is the most sensible thing I've heard. Please, sir, lead us in prayer."

Cora squeezed Diana's hand and whispered, "Bless him!"

The elderly man prayed in the name of Jesus Christ that God would keep the snow from coming down the side of the mountain and shoving the train into the canyon, and tactfully wove the gospel into his prayer.

When he finished, there was definitely a calmer atmosphere in the coach.

Diana looked at Cora through a mist of tears. "Mrs. Zeller, I—"

"Yes, dear?"

"I realize how afraid I am to die. I know if God should see fit to let this train go over the edge into the canyon, I would die lost and go to hell. I've been a fool to put off salvation. I've been using what my parents had taught me in the past as an excuse to put off dealing with it in my life. Would you show me what to do? I want to be saved. I didn't listen when Mama tried to show me, but I'll listen now."

Breathing a silent prayer of thanks to the Lord, Cora said, "All the Lord wants is a willing heart, honey." With that, she took her Bible from the handbag, opened it, and carefully took Diana from passage to passage, dealing with repentance, faith, and the new birth. Soon the girl was weeping.

When Cora asked if she understood, Diana assured her that she did. Cora had the joy of leading her to the Lord.

Wiping tears after calling on the Lord to save her, Diana said, "Oh, Mrs. Zeller, thank you! My mother is going to be so happy when she learns that her oldest daughter has been saved. That is, if she learns it here on earth. She may have to wait till we meet in heaven."

Cora hugged her and said, "Honey, I believe the Lord is going to answer the gentleman's prayer and deliver us from this predicament safely."

Shortly thereafter the wind eased, and the conductor came into the coach explaining that the passengers were invited to go to the dining car in shifts, so everyone could eat.

By the time everyone on the train had eaten, it was past midnight.

Cora put an arm around Diana and led them in prayer, thanking the Lord for bringing Diana to Himself and for keeping His mighty hand on the train. She thanked Him that they indeed would get out of the mountains safely and asked Him to bless the gentleman who had calmed the people in their coach by his words of faith.

With peace in their hearts, Cora and Diana dropped off to

sleep with only a slight breeze touching the snow-caked window next to them.

When dawn came, the sky was clear and there was still just a slight breeze.

The passengers waited while the train's crew went outside to assess how much snow was piled up in front of the engine. Entering each car, they gave their report.

When they came into coach number three, the engineer said, "Ladies and gentlemen, we have taken a look at the avalanche in front of us, and it is not as large as we thought it might be. If all the able-bodied men aboard will help us, we should be able to have the snow cleared from the tracks in no more than two days."

There were happy cheers in the coach.

The engineer grinned and said, "If the rest of you don't mind letting the men eat breakfast first, we can be removing snow from the tracks while you're eating breakfast."

When all the men who were going outside on snow removal duty had eaten and followed the crew to the avalanche in front of the engine, the rest of the passengers took their turns eating in shifts as usual.

Potbellied stoves were burning in each coach, keeping the women and children warm. After they had eaten their breakfast, Cora and Diana returned to their coach and sat down.

Cora opened her Bible and said, "Diana, I want to show you some verses concerning your new life in Christ. These are very important things that are vital to your spiritual growth and your walk with the Lord."

Diana listened intently and eagerly as Cora showed her the verses and told her that she needed to find the right kind of church and be baptized. Diana assured her she would.

Cora then said, "Honey, there is something else I need to show you."

"Yes, ma'am?"

Doing her best to be tactful, Cora said, "Honey, you are going to Idaho to marry Jordan Shaw."

"Yes."

"You're a Christian now."

"I sure am." Diana's eyes were shining.

Opening her Bible again, Cora said, "Let me show you what God's Word says about Christians and unbelievers."

Diana's brow furrowed. She studied Cora's face for a few seconds, then let her eyes fall on the Bible in Cora's hands.

Having her Bible open to 2 Corinthians 6, Cora put her finger on verse 14. "Look at this, honey. 'Be ye not unequally yoked together with unbelievers: for what fellowship hath righteousness with unrighteousness? and what communion hath light with darkness?' There are other Scriptures on this subject, Diana, but this is enough to show you that a born-again child of God should not marry a person who is not saved. It can only lead to much heartache because a child of God is walking in God's light, whereas an unsaved person is in darkness like you used to be, and there is no communion between light and darkness."

Diana bit down on her lower lip.

"To put it plainly, honey," said Cora, "you shouldn't marry Jordan Shaw if he is not a born-again man. I assume he didn't stipulate in his newspaper ad that he wanted a born-again bride."

"N-no," said Diana, her voice weak. "Mrs. Zeller, what should I do?"

"When you get to Elkton, you need to explain to Jordan that you became a Christian on the trip west, and you would like for him to become one, too. First, for the sake of his own soul; and secondly, because the Bible tells you to only marry a believer. It will be best if you find a good Bible-believing pastor to help you with this."

Diana nodded, but did not tell Cora this frightened her. If Jordan rebelled at this, there would be no wedding. She would be in a strange place among strange people, and would have to find a way to support herself or return to Richmond and face the wrath of her father. The prospect of the latter sent cold chills slithering down her spine.

Suddenly she remembered her father's words to her that day in the jail, when he said if she ran away, he would track her down and give her a beating like she had never imagined. The world wasn't big enough for her to hide from him.

Fear was an icy claw on her heart as she contemplated her helpless situation. If she and Jordan did not marry, she would have no one to protect her from her father.

Diana said in her heart, *Dear Lord, I saw what You said in Your Word about believers not yoking up with unbelievers, and I will obey You. But I will need Your help with these problems that lie ahead of me.*

ON MONDAY, NOVEMBER 25—while the train crew and the male passengers were working to remove the snow from the tracks high up in the Rocky Mountains of Wyoming—Jordan Shaw rode into Ketcham, Idaho, at midafternoon and dismounted in front of the post office. The Wells Fargo stage would be carrying the mail to Elkton on Tuesday, but Jordan was eager to get his hands on the expected letter from Diana if it should arrive in Ketcham on Monday.

As he was dismounting, he heard a familiar voice call his name. Turning that direction, he saw Althea and Bernadine Faulkner coming up the street in their wagon. Guiding the wagon at an angle toward him and pulling the team to a halt, Althea said, "Nice to see you, Jordan."

"Yes," said Bernadine. "We had to come to Ketcham to pick up some things that we can't buy in Elkton. We didn't expect to see you here."

"Well, we Bar-S folks have to do that now and then, too."

"So we hear you're taking Belinda to Lorene's big birthday party," said Althea.

Jordan's stomach flipped. "Oh? Who told you that?"

"Why, Belinda, of course."

"Well, Lorene's birthday is almost two weeks away. I don't recall even talking to Belinda about it."

The Faulkner sisters exchanged glances and giggled, then Bernadine said, "I guess Belinda's so sure of herself with you that she knows your invitation to go to the party is forthcoming."

Althea sighed. "Oh, Jordan, I hope someday the man will come into my life who will sweep me off my feet and show me the kind of love you show to Belinda."

Jordan frowned. "I guess Belinda has told you some of our innermost secrets, eh?"

Althea's face flushed. "Well, I— that is, Bernadine and I never pry. Belinda just feels she can share some things with us."

"I hope Belinda hasn't told you that we have wedding plans."

The sisters looked at each other again and giggled.

Bernadine said, "Althea, we'd better not tell him all we know about that!"

"We dare not," said Althea. "Belinda would have our hides for spilling the beans."

Jordan laughed. "You probably know more than I do. Well, ladies, I have business to attend to in the post office. Nice chatting with you."

With that, Jordan headed across the boardwalk. The Faulkner sisters were giggling as they pulled away.

Before opening the post office door, Jordan set his gaze on the Faulkner wagon as it moved along the street. "Go ahead, girls. Laugh it up. But the last laugh will be mine."

Entering the building, Jordan found three short lines, and stepped into the one in front of his friend, Barney Koval. In less than five minutes, it was his turn. He stepped up to the counter and smiled. "Hello, Barney. Need the Bar-S mail."

Barney chuckled. "Still haven't received that important piece of mail you've been looking for, Jordan?"

"Not yet, but I'm hoping you've got it for me today."

Barney went behind the wall, and when he returned, he had a small stack of mail. Laying it on the counter, he said, "Well, I most certainly do hope it's here."

Jordan grinned and started sifting through the stack. The third envelope he came to made his grin spread into a bright, broad smile.

"Yes! Here it is. Barney, you're a good man. Thanks a lot!"

Barney laughed. "Well, whatever it is, I hope it makes you happy."

"You can count on it," said Jordan as he turned and walked away.

Moving over by the potbellied stove, an anxious Jordan sat down on a chair and used his pocketknife to slit the envelope open.

He took out Diana's letter and was thrilled to learn that she was coming for sure with the prospect of becoming his mail order bride and would arrive in Elkton on the three o'clock stage on Thursday. *Just three days,* he thought, *and I will be rid of Belinda and all the pressure from her family and mine to marry her!*

When Jordan was in the saddle again and heading out of Ketcham, he told himself that tomorrow he would go hunting again in the mountains.

His first stop would be at Mattie's Boardinghouse in Elkton, then he would go by the newspaper office, let Knight know that Diana was coming, and see if he wanted to go hunting with him.

The lowering sun was putting a golden glare on the snowy land as Jordan rode into Elkton, turned off Main Street after two blocks, and rode two more blocks west. Hauling up in front of Mattie's Boardinghouse, he mounted the steps that led to the porch. There was another boardinghouse in Elkton, but Jordan chose Mattie's because it was better kept, and Mattie's cooking was better than the cooking at the other one.

Not wanting to give his plan away to anyone, Jordan had worked at coming up with a plausible reason as to why he would want to reserve a room. With his scheme intact, he stepped into the small office and found Mattie Herndon at her desk. Mattie, who was fifty, rotund and rosy-cheeked, smiled as she left the desk and stepped to the counter. "Why, Mr. Shaw, it's nice to see you. What brings you here?"

"I want to reserve a room for a young lady, Mattie," he said. "She's actually a friend of Knight Colburn's, but he's very busy, and he asked me to handle it for him."

"I see," said Mattie, opening her record book. "What is the lady's name?"

"Miss Diana Morrow. D-I-A-N-A M-O-R-R-O-W."

Mattie wrote the name. "And when will Miss Morrow be arriving?"

"This coming Thursday, the twenty-eighth. She'll be coming in on the three o'clock stage."

"All right," said Mattie, penning it down. "And how long will she be staying?"

Pulling out his wallet, Jordan said, "Knight gave me enough money to pay for a month. So put her down for a month."

Jordan figured he and Diana would be married at least by December 28, but hopefully a week or two ahead of that.

"That will be twenty dollars even, Mr. Shaw," said Mattie, "which covers two meals a day."

As Jordan handed Mattie a twenty-dollar bill, he saw a sly grin curve her thick lips. Lowering her voice, she said, "Is this—well, some new lady friend of Mr. Colburn's? I mean…he is past the age that most men get married."

Leaning close to her, Jordan matched her voice level. "Now, Mattie, you have got to stay mum about this. You mustn't tell anybody that Miss Morrow is here as Knight's guest. As far as you're concerned, she paid you for the room, herself. Understand?"

"Oh, of course. I won't breathe a word."

"Good. Thank you."

As he turned away to leave, Mattie said, "Ah…Mr. Shaw…"

Jordan stopped. "Yes?"

"You're past the age that most men get married, too. When are you and Belinda Ashworth getting married?"

"What makes you think we are ever going to get married?"

Mattie ducked her head, grinning sheepishly. "Oh, there are rumors going around."

Once again moving toward the door, he said over his shoulder, "Can't believe all the rumors you hear, Mattie."

A tiny thrill of anticipation ran through Jordan. "Just three days!" he said aloud. "Just three days!"

Knight Colburn was in conversation with Dan and Erline Tyler at Dan's desk when Jordan stepped through the door. All three looked at him as he smiled and moved toward them.

"He looks happy," said Erline.

"Couldn't be happier," said Jordan. "It's just been a good day. Knight, ol' pal, I need to talk to you."

"Sure," said Knight. "Come on into my office."

"Nice to see you," Jordan said as he followed his friend into his private office.

Knight held the door open till Jordan had moved past him. "Have a seat."

Jordan waved the envelope at him. "Guess what this is!"

Knight chuckled. "It must be from Diana, saying she's coming."

"Sure is! It's a little too personal for me to let you read it, but she's coming, all right. She'll arrive on the three o'clock stage on Thursday."

Knight shook his head, grinning. "Well, ol' pal, it looks like your bachelor days are about over."

"Yeah! Isn't it wonderful? I stopped by Mattie's Boardinghouse just before coming here, Knight. I reserved a room for Diana and paid Mattie a month in advance. I figure we'll be married well inside of that, but she's covered for a month, anyhow."

Knight wrapped his arms around his friend and pounded him on the back. "I'm happy for you."

As they parted, Jordan said, "I'm going hunting in the mountains tomorrow. Want to go with me?"

"I'd like to," said Knight, "but the workload won't allow it. Got too much going on right now."

"Oh," said Jordan, a slight touch of disappointment in his voice. "I'd sure love to have you with me, but I understand."

Knight chuckled. "Of course once your little gal gets here, you'll probably give up hunting and fishing altogether."

"Oh no, I won't. I'm taking Diana with me. But you can come along, too."

"All right."

"If you'd get busy and find yourself a wife, Knight, we could go as a foursome."

"In God's time," Knight said softly. "So, are you going to try to track down that big black bear tomorrow?"

Jordan laughed. "You mean Ol' Halfpaw?"

"Ol' Halfpaw? When did you give him that name?"

Jordan laughed again. "Just now. And to answer your question,

I most certainly am. I want Ol' Halfpaw stuffed so I can put him in the foyer of the new log house my father is going to have built for Diana and me after we get married."

"You told your parents about Diana?"

"Of course not. But my father said whenever I get married, he will buy my wife and me the ranch property he and I have agreed on, and build us a log house on it. He just doesn't know how very, very soon he's gonna have to put wheels to his promise."

Knight ran fingers through his dark, wavy hair. "And William Shaw figures when it does happen, it'll be you and Belinda."

"Yeah. It'll be a shock for him all right, as well as for my mother and the rest of the family. And for Belinda and her family, too. But it can't be helped, Knight. It's Diana I want, not Belinda."

"I understand."

Rising to his feet, Jordan said, "Well, I've got to head for home. I'm looking forward to introducing you to Diana."

"I'm looking forward to meeting her," said Knight, leaving his chair to walk his friend to the front door of the building.

That evening during supper, Jordan Shaw looked at his father across the table and said, "I've got my work all caught up, so I'm going to take tomorrow off and go hunting in the mountains."

"Fine," William said, nodding. "Bring us home a big elk this time, okay?"

"Whatever you say," Jordan said with a smile.

"Is Knight going with you, dear?" Sylvia asked.

"Not this time, Mother. I asked him, but he can't get away from the paper right now."

"Isn't there someone else who could go with you? I feel better when I know you're not out there alone."

"I'll be fine, Mother. Don't worry about me."

"I'll try, but you know how mothers are."

"Sure, and I love you for it."

There were a few minutes of silence as they continued eating, then William said, "Son, I haven't seen you with Belinda for a while. You two haven't broken up, have you?"

Jordan had to bite his tongue to keep from saying there was nothing to break up, but he silently shook his head, then said, "Would you pass the gravy, Father?"

William and Sylvia looked at each other questioningly. William handed his son the gravy bowl.

"Thanks," said Jordan. He wanted to tell his father they should go ahead and purchase the ranch property they had agreed on, for him and Diana, but he knew it was best to wait until his parents had met her and knew she was his bride-to-be.

Excitement coursed through Jordan as he anticipated bringing Diana to the house to meet them. The event was only three days away!

The next morning there were two inches of fresh snow on the ground, but the sky was clearing as Jordan mounted his horse at sunrise and rode north with his rifle in the saddleboot.

Soon he was winding his way among the leafless willows and blue spruce of the foothills, squinting into the sun glare that came off the towering peaks above him. He had one goal in mind. Find Ol' Halfpaw and kill him. If he did, he would have to ride back to the ranch and get a few men to bring a wagon and help him load the bear so he could take him to the taxidermist in Ketcham.

As the horse carried him higher, Jordan's thoughts were on Diana Morrow. He tried to picture in his mind what she looked like. He told himself that as sweet as she was, she just had to be pretty. Was she blond? Brunette? Redhead? He could hardly wait to find out.

"Just two days," he said with a sigh, then tried to imagine the look that would be on the faces of his parents when he introduced Diana to them Thursday afternoon as his prospective mail order bride.

He grinned to himself as he pictured the look that would be on Belinda's face when she found out he was getting married to someone else.

Soon Jordan hauled up in front of the old abandoned cabin where he had spent so much time in the past several years.

Dismounting, he took the rifle from the saddleboot and looked around for pawprints in the snow, knowing that the big black bear often moved through the area.

He had seen Ol' Halfpaw's prints in the snow around the cabin twice since he had shot off the two claws. But this time, there were only the small, deep prints which gave evidence that deer had passed by the cabin since the last snowfall. Since the snow was calf deep, Jordan decided to ride his horse rather than wear himself out plodding higher on foot.

"Okay, boy," he said, swinging into the saddle. "Let's go see if we can find that big black beast."

The sun was almost to its apex in the cobalt blue sky when Jordan was slowly making his way through a snowbank a few hundred yards below timberline.

Suddenly, movement among the shadows of the trees just ahead caught Jordan's eye. He stiffened in the saddle, focusing on the spot as he jacked a cartridge into the chamber of his rifle. There was more movement, and his heart leaped in his chest as he saw a black bear in the deep shadows.

He quickly slid from the saddle and tied the reins to a birch tree. Looking back toward the area where he had seen the bear, he began plodding up the steep slope as quietly as possible, moving stealthily among the trees.

The bear had vanished from view, but Jordan's determination to find and kill Ol' Halfpaw was a living thing in his heart. His back stiffened when the black bear moved from the shadows into the sunlight, sniffing the air. He quickly shouldered the rifle, but as he took aim, he saw that the bear was much smaller than Ol' Halfpaw. It took only a few seconds to tell that it was a female.

Disappointment flooded through him.

He had hoped that the day had finally come when he could bag his most desired trophy.

Then he jumped as he heard his horse eject a shrill whinny, and wheeled around to see what had frightened him. His heart leaped in his chest when he saw a huge male black bear no more than thirty yards away. The beast was looking straight at Jordan, and when he rose up on his hind legs and released a threatening roar,

Jordan clearly saw that half of the right paw was missing.

*It's him!* he thought, as his whole body began to shake from the sheer excitement he was feeling.

His moment had come!

Ol' Halfpaw released a loud, angry roar, tossing his head with nostrils flaring and eyes bulging, and lurched directly toward the man he had chosen as his prey.

Jordan lifted the rifle to his shoulder with trembling hands—not from fear, but from eager anticipation of fulfilling his dream of killing and stuffing the huge beast so he could display him as his prize trophy.

Ol' Halfpaw was propelling his massive body through the snow with shocking speed.

Jordan tried to steady his hands as he squeezed the trigger. The rifle bucked against his shoulder as it spit fire, but the bullet missed its mark, whizzing past the bear's big, wide head. This infuriated him, and he ejected a bloodcurdling roar as he bore down on his prey.

Hurriedly, Jordan jacked another cartridge into the chamber and raised the weapon to his shoulder.

When suppertime came at the Bar-S ranch, Sylvia stood at the kitchen window, looking toward the barn, hoping to see her son come riding in.

William stood behind her and said, "Now honey, don't let it worry you. Jordan is an experienced hunter. He's fine. He'll show up any minute."

Sylvia turned to face her husband. "I just wish he wouldn't go hunting alone."

"But he's been hunting by himself since he was sixteen. He knows what he's doing."

"I know, but I just like it better when he has someone with him. Especially Knight."

"Come on," said William. "Supper's getting cold."

By the time the meal was over and Sylvia was carrying plates, bowls, and cups to the cupboard, she was almost in tears.

William slipped up behind her, put an arm around her waist, and said, "Honey, maybe Jordan bagged that elk I told him to get, or even a deer, late in the afternoon. And rather than drag it all the way home behind his horse in the dark, he's probably staying at the old cabin for the night and will come home in the morning."

Looking up at him with tears in her eyes, Sylvia said, "You really think that's it?"

"Could very well be. Like I said, he's an experienced hunter."


At noon the next day, when William came into the house for lunch, he found his wife pale and quite upset.

Taking hold of her husband's upper arms, Sylvia said, "I can't stand this any longer, William. I want you to send a couple of ranch hands up to the cabin to see if Jordan is there."

"Honey," said William, patting her cheek, "we mustn't panic, here. Our son can handle himself. Maybe he didn't get anything yesterday, so he's going after his game today. Let's give it a little time. He'll probably be home before sundown."

After lunch, William drove a wagon into Elkton to buy supplies, and as he was pulling the wagon up in front of Crum's Feed and Grain, he saw Knight Colburn coming his way on the boardwalk.

Hopping out of the wagon, he lifted a hand to Knight. Knight said, "Howdy, William. Did Jordan bag anything yesterday?"

"Well, I don't know. He hasn't come home yet, so I figure he must not have. He's probably trying again today."

Knight chuckled. "Good ol' Jordan. He's got determination, I'll say that for him."

The two men chatted for a few minutes, then Knight moved on down the street, and William entered the feed store.


When William returned home and entered the house, he found Sylvia in their bedroom weeping.

Sitting down beside her, he said, "Honey, you mustn't let Jordan's tardiness upset you so."

"I can't help it," she sobbed, looking up at him with red-rimmed, tear-filled eyes. "I'm just worried sick. I'm afraid something has happened to him. It just isn't like him to be this long getting home."

"Hey, wait a minute, Mother Shaw," William said, playfully clipping her jaw lightly with his fist. "Aren't you forgetting something?"

"What?"

"How many times in the last six or seven years has Jordan gone hunting alone for what was supposed to be a day, and the day turned into anywhere from two to four days?"

Sylvia sighed and shook her head. "You know, I must have pushed those times somewhere into the back of my mind. Of course. You're right. I shouldn't be getting so upset. He's done this before, actually more times than I can say."

William leaned down, kissed her cheek, and said, "That's my girl. You just keep a grip on that. Jordan will probably come riding in here tomorrow sometime, dragging an elk carcass behind him."

When Knight Colburn was shaving the next morning, he thought about Diana Morrow coming in on the stage that afternoon at three o'clock. He told himself that Jordan no doubt was home by now.

As he splashed his face with cold water, picked up a towel, and began to dry it off, he said to himself, "Knight, why don't you ride out to the Bar-S and make sure he's back?"

Stopping by the newspaper office, Knight told Dan and Erline he was riding out to the Shaw place and would be back in a couple of hours.

William Shaw opened the front door of the big ranch house in response to the knock, and smiled when he saw Jordan's best friend standing there.

"Well, hello, Knight. Come on in."

Stepping into the foyer, Knight said, "Is Jordan around? I need to talk to him."

William looked at the floor, rubbed the back of his neck, and said, "He hasn't come home yet."

The news hit Knight hard. *Why isn't he back?* he asked himself. *Diana is arriving today!*

William saw the concern on Knight's face and said, "Now don't let it worry you. I had to remind Sylvia last night that over the last six or seven years, Jordan has done this many times: turning one day of hunting into two, three, or four. He's just repeating it again."

Knowing he was not at liberty to tell William about Diana's pending arrival that afternoon, Knight decided he would have to go along with what he had just said. Pressing a grin on his lips, he said, "Oh, sure. I hadn't taken that into consideration, either. I'm sorry to have bothered you. He'll probably show up before noon."

"No bother, Knight," said William. "You're welcome here anytime."

William followed Knight out onto the porch, watched as he mounted, then gave him a smile and a friendly wave as he rode away.

WHEN WILLIAM SHAW TURNED and circled the house, he found Sylvia standing just inside the door.

"I overheard your conversation with Knight, dear," she said. "I hope he's right and Jordan does show up here by noon. But if he doesn't, don't you think you ought to send a couple of the ranch hands up to the cabin to check on him?"

"Honey, I remind you again of Jordan's little adventures, making a three- or four-day hunting trip out of what was supposed to be one day. He's only been gone a little more than two days. Let's give him till tomorrow evening. If he isn't back by then, I'll take Mark with me and ride up to the cabin on Saturday."

Worry lined Sylvia's pale features. "How about if he doesn't come home by tonight, you and Mark ride up there to the cabin tomorrow?"

"Can't," said William. "Have you forgotten there's a directors' meeting at the bank tomorrow? As a director, I must be there."

"Oh. I did forget. What time is the meeting?"

"It starts at ten o'clock, and if it's typical, it won't be over till sometime in late afternoon. Honey, Jordan is probably pulling another one of his long stays. Let's not get too worked up about it."

Sylvia sighed. "All right, but will you promise me that if our boy isn't home by tomorrow night, you will take Mark and ride up to the cabin on Saturday?"

Taking her in his arms, William kissed her softly. "Yes, sweetheart. I promise."

While working on an editorial in his office at the *Elkton Sentinel* as the morning passed, Knight Colburn had a difficult time concentrating. Jordan kept coming to mind. Laying his pen down, he eased back in the chair and said in a low voice, "Jordan, ol' pal, where are you? You know Diana is arriving here at three o'clock this afternoon. There's no deer, or elk, or—or big black bear with half a paw shot off that's worth missing Diana's arrival at the Fargo station when that stage pulls in."

It was just past noon when Knight sat at the kitchen table with his mother's hot beef stew on his plate.

While eating her own lunch, Annie noticed that her son was absently picking at his food. Clearing her throat, she said, "Son, is something wrong with the stew?"

It took a few seconds for his mother's voice to filter through his thoughts. Raising his head, he blinked. "What did you say, Mom?"

"I asked if there is something wrong with the stew."

"Oh. No, of course not. It's as good as always."

"Well, I'm glad to hear that. Something at the paper bothering you?"

"No. Everything's fine."

"Well then, what's got your attention? Something's wrong."

Knight sighed and laid his fork down. "It's Jordan, Mom."

"Oh no. What's he done now?"

"Well, he went into the mountains on Tuesday to go hunting, and was supposed to be back that evening. He didn't show up. Nor did he show up last night. I rode out to the ranch this morning to see if he was back yet. He isn't. I'm concerned about him."

Annie chuckled. "Honey, you know how Jordan is. How many times in recent years has he gone hunting for what was supposed to be a day, and he didn't come back for several days?"

"That's the same thing William brought up this morning, Mom. He's not concerned about Jordan at this point, so I guess I shouldn't be, either." *But Diana's coming to Elkton at three o'clock today!* his inner voice was screaming.

Returning to the *Sentinel*, Knight went back to the editorial he was writing, and even though he had intermittent conversations with Dan and Erline, he masked the concern he was carrying about Diana Morrow arriving on the stage with no Jordan there to meet her.

When two-thirty came, and there was no indication from anyone in the Shaw family that Jordan had returned, Knight decided to go to the stage office just before three o'clock and see if Jordan was there. If he wasn't, Knight knew it would be up to him to meet Diana and tell her Jordan went hunting in the Sawtooth Mountains on Tuesday and hadn't returned. The only thing he could do was take her to Mattie's Boardinghouse.

At a quarter to three, Knight stepped out of his office, his hat lopsided on his head, shouldering into his coat. He glanced at Dan, who had the press rolling with his back toward him, then moved up to Erline's desk and said, "I have an errand to run. I'll be back shortly."

"All right," said Erline, smiling. There was a twinkle in her eye. "If President Ulysses S. Grant drops in to see you, I'll tell him you'll be back shortly."

Knight snorted, shook his head, and as he went out the door, he said, "You do that."

Greeting people along the way on the boardwalk, Knight hurried toward the Wells Fargo office. As he drew near the building, there was no sign of Jordan, nor a Bar-S buggy.

Moving inside, he looked around, hoping somehow Jordan was there in spite of the fact that no Bar-S buggy was parked outside. There were two men at the counter, talking to Fargo agent Vern Morton. By what they were saying, Knight knew they were purchasing tickets on the three-thirty stage to Ketcham.

Vern smiled at Knight and said, "Hello, Mr. Colburn. Are you here to meet someone on the three o'clock stage?"

"Yes. There is someone on the stage that I'm meeting for a friend."

"Far as I know, it'll be on time," said Vern.

"Thanks," Knight said.

Unable to sit still, Knight paced restlessly around the office, stopping each time he came to the window to glance out into the street. His mind was racing as he tried to come up with some reasonable answer as to Jordan's absence at this crucial moment. When he came to the window again, he stopped, looked out at the traffic in the street, and said in a low whisper, "Something has happened to him. The last time I saw him, he was beside himself with excitement, knowing that Diana had consented to come with the prospect of becoming his bride. I know he'd be here if he could. As soon as I get her settled in the boardinghouse, I'm going into the mountains to look for him, myself.

"No one else knows about Diana, so they can easily chalk all of this up to typical Jordan behavior, but I know differently. Wild Indians couldn't keep him from meeting Diana when she comes in on the st—"

Knight's words were cut off as the stagecoach rolled into view.

Knight took a deep breath and headed toward the door. "Well, here goes," he said to himself.

As he stepped outside, Knight saw driver and shotgunner climbing down from the seat. He halted a few steps from the side of the coach and looked inside. The passengers were only silhouettes, but he could make out two men and a woman.

When the driver opened the door, he said to the passengers, "All right, folks. End of the line. Welcome to Elkton."

One of the male passengers moved out first, then turned and offered his hand to the woman. Knight's heart sank when he saw that she was silver-haired and estimated that she was in her late sixties. She thanked the man, then turned and said something to the silver-haired man who came out behind her. By her words, Knight knew the man was her husband.

When the three passengers had stepped away from the stage, Knight moved up and looked inside. *What now?* he thought, then went to the driver, who was taking small pieces of luggage out of the boot at the rear.

"Pardon me, sir," he said. "Wasn't there supposed to be a Miss Diana Morrow on the stage?"

"There was supposed to be another female passenger and two other male passengers," replied the driver. "I don't know the lady's name, but she wasn't at the Ketcham station when it was time to leave and neither were the men, so the agent told us to go on."

"Oh. I see. Thanks."

The driver nodded and continued his work.

Knight walked slowly back down the street toward the *Sentinel*, a deep frown of concern creasing his brow. No Jordan and no Diana.

What was going on?

Jordan had definitely told Knight that Diana was coming to Elkton on the three o'clock stage on Thursday. The missing female passenger the driver spoke of had to be Diana.

"Lord," he said as he drew near the front door of the *Sentinel*, "You know where Jordan is, and You know where Diana is. Please help me to know what to do."

When Knight stepped into the office, Erline was at the file cabinet near her desk. She turned to see who had come in, and her gaze fastened on her boss's ashen face. "Knight, what's wrong?"

Pausing, he said, "What do you mean?"

"You look like you're worried or upset about something."

"Somebody," he said.

Erline frowned. "What somebody?"

"Jordan. He went into the mountains alone on Tuesday morning. Hunting. He was supposed to be back by that evening, but he wasn't. I rode out to the Bar-S this morning to see if he had come home. He hadn't. I'm afraid something has happened to him."

"Maybe he's home, now. He might not have thought about stopping here in town to let you know."

Knight couldn't tell Erline about Diana and the three o'clock stage, but he just had to ride back out to the ranch and talk to the Shaws. "You're right, Erline. You and Dan close up shop, will you? I'm going out to the Bar-S right now."


The sun had dropped behind the rugged hills to the west of the Bar-S as Knight knocked on the front door of the big ranch house.

"Knight!" said William, swinging the door wide. "Come in."

Sylvia was standing a few steps behind her husband as Knight moved inside. "I can tell by your faces. He hasn't come home."

Tears filmed Sylvia's eyes. "No. He hasn't."

William explained that he had a directors' meeting at the bank the next day, but that he had promised Sylvia if Jordan wasn't home by tomorrow night, he and Mark would ride up to the old cabin on Saturday.

"I have some important business at the land office in Ketcham early on Saturday morning," William said, "but I'll be back between ten and eleven o'clock. Mark and I will head out for the mountains at that time."

"I'd like to ride with you," said Knight.

"We'd be glad to have you with us," William said, laying a hand on Knight's shoulder.

"Thank you, Knight," said Sylvia. "I appreciate your offering to go along."

"I wouldn't have it any other way," said Knight. "I'll be here by ten o'clock Saturday morning. Now, if that scalawag comes home before then, you make him ride into town immediately and let me know he's back. Otherwise, you'll see me no later then ten."

William worked up a smile. "Thanks, Knight. You're a true friend."

Smiling back, Knight said, "That's the only kind to be." He also gave Sylvia a smile then returned to his horse and rode away.


Early on Saturday morning, Diana Morrow hired a buggy at the railroad depot in Ketcham to take her to the Wells Fargo station. Upon leaving the train, she had inquired at the railroad ticket office when the next Wells Fargo stage would be going to Elkton. She learned that there were three stagecoaches a week from Ketcham to Elkton, and that Saturday's stage arrived in Elkton at 9:30 A.M.

As the buggy moved down Ketcham's main thoroughfare toward the Fargo office, she asked the driver to wait while she checked to see if she could get a seat on the Elkton stage, saying if not, she would need him to take her to Ketcham's hotel where she would wait until she could get a seat on the first available stage.

As they drew up to the Fargo office, a stagecoach was parked in front, and two men were hooking a harnessed team to it. The buggy driver told her it was the stage that would be going to Elkton. He helped Diana from the buggy, and as she hurried toward the door, she saw the conductor from the Boise train coming out. Recognizing her, he spoke politely, held the door open for her, then hurried back toward the depot.

Inside, Diana found two men at the counter, whom she had seen on both the Kansas City and Boise trains. The Fargo agent was at the desk behind the counter, tapping out a coded message on the telegraph key.

Recognizing Diana, the two men both smiled at her. One of them said, "Miss, are you here to take the Elkton stage, too?"

"Yes," she said, returning the smile.

The men looked at each other questioningly as the Fargo agent finished his telegraph message and returned to the counter. Noticing the lady, the agent said, "Were you on the Kansas City train, too, ma'am?"

"Yes, sir."

"And you were wanting to get to Elkton?"

"Yes. I was scheduled on the stage that went Thursday afternoon, but the train was delayed by an avalanche in the Rocky Mountains of Wyoming."

"So I just learned from the conductor, and from these two gentlemen," said the agent. "You must be Miss Diana Morrow."

"Yes, sir."

The agent scratched his head. "Well, Miss Morrow, we have a problem. I already have four passengers from right here in Ketcham who are scheduled on this morning's stage. Mr. Williams and Mr. Baxter here were also supposed to have been on Thursday's stage and are needing to get to Elkton this morning. That makes seven, and we can only seat six in the coach."

Diana's face went pale. "Oh."

"Miss Morrow, I could put you on Tuesday's stage," said the agent. "That's the next one to Elkton."

"I have a problem, sir. There is a young man who was expecting me on Thursday. And…and now, if I'm not on this stage—"

"I just wired the Fargo agent in Elkton to advise him about the train's delay in Wyoming, so he could tell the people who were to meet Mr. Williams and Mr. Baxter on Thursday that they will be on today's stage. There's nothing I can do now but schedule you for Tuesday."

Noting the look of deep disappointment on Diana's face, Victor Williams said, "Miss Morrow, I assume you are not from Elkton. Returning home, I mean."

"No, sir. I'm from Virginia. I'm coming to…well, I—"

"I think it must be very important, miss," said Williams.

Diana cleared her throat nervously. "I…ah…well, sir, I am on my way to Elkton to become a…a mail order bride."

Williams and Baxter looked at each other. "I can wait till Tuesday, Mr. Baxter," said Williams. Then to the agent he said, "Put Miss Morrow on today's stage in my place. I'll stay at the hotel till then."

Diana said, "Oh, sir, I can't let you do that. I—"

"It's settled, dear," said Williams. "I'm from Cheyenne City. My youngest son just married himself a mail order bride less than a month ago. I know the kind of excitement he had when he went to the depot to meet his prospective bride. I'm sure your young man has been on pins and needles since Thursday, when you weren't on the stage, and at that point, nobody there knew about the train being detained by the avalanche. You go to your young man. I insist."

Tears welled up in Diana's eyes. "Oh, Mr. Williams, I don't know how to thank you. This means more than I could ever put into words."

Williams spread a smile from ear to ear. "Words in this case are not important, little lady. You can thank me by marrying that young man and having a very happy life."

"Yes, sir. That's what I plan to do."

The Fargo agent, touched by the scene, said, "Tell you what, Mr. Williams. How about if I let you ride up in the box between the driver and the shotgunner? It's against company policy, but in this situation, I can make an exception."

Williams smiled again. "That's fine with me."

"All right," said the agent, "that's the way it will be. And, Miss

Morrow, I'll wire the agent in Elkton again and tell him you are on this stage. That way your future groom will know you're coming. Before you arrive in Elkton, he will be told why you weren't on the Thursday stage."

"Thank you, sir," said Diana. "I've got to go out and tell the driver of the buggy I hired that I will be going on this morning's stage. I have a small trunk and a suitcase in the buggy. Shall I tell the driver so he can put it on the stage?"

"I'll put them on the stage for you, miss," said Albert Baxter.

"And I'll help him," said Williams.

"Fine," said the agent. "I'll go send that wire right now."

At 9:15 that morning, the stage driver called down from the box to the passengers inside: "Elkton, fifteen minutes, folks. Fifteen minutes till we arrive in Elkton!"

The butterflies in Diana's stomach came alive. Feeling rather disheveled from the lengthy time on the train and the swaying stagecoach, she removed her gloves, reached up, took hold of the hatpin that held her hat in place, removed it, and lay the hat and pin in her lap.

The other passengers looked on as she tried to smooth her hair into place. When she was satisfied she had done the best with it that she could, she placed the hat back on her head and firmly secured it once again with the hatpin.

She tried in vain to brush the deep wrinkles from her dark wool coat and pulled her scarf up close around her throat. Her hands were trembling as she worked her gloves back on.

*I hope Jordan keeps in mind how long I've been on this trip and doesn't expect too much on first sight,* she thought, as the butterflies seemed to multiply. She clasped her shaking hands together and laid them in her lap.

Diana had enjoyed the ride and told herself she would love living in this rugged country with its mountains, hills, and wide-open spaces.

When the town came into view, she had to silently tell her pounding heart to settle down. She took comfort, knowing that the Ketcham agent had wired the Fargo agent in Elkton that she would be on the nine-thirty stage. She told herself that since she hadn't been on the stage as scheduled on Thursday, certainly Jordan had kept in touch with the Fargo agent in Elkton so he would know that she was on this stage.

"Lord," she whispered, barely moving her lips, "help me. I have a real task ahead. Please guide me and give me wisdom as I talk to Jordan about being saved. And give me a preacher who will help me."

The stage rolled into Elkton on schedule, and Diana was busy looking the town over as much as possible from her window. Her heart was thudding in her chest as the stage stopped in front of the Wells Fargo station.

There was a scrambling up in the box as driver, shotgunner, and Victor Williams climbed down. One of the male passengers hopped out of the coach, offered Diana his hand, and helped her down. She stepped aside to allow the other passengers to get off, and looked at a small group of people who were standing about.

There was no young man Jordan's age in the group.

The group apparently was waiting for two of the other passengers, for they rushed to them, embracing them.

Victor Williams joined Albert Baxter, each carrying his overnight bag. As they were about to head down the street for the Elkton Hotel, Williams stepped up to Diana. "Good-bye, Miss Morrow. I wish you the very best in this new chapter of your life."

"Thank you, sir," she said. "And thank you for what you did for me."

The two men walked away briskly.

The air was cold, and a chilly breeze was whipping through the town.

Pulling her scarf up tighter against her throat, Diana looked around for Jordan, but the area had cleared. The driver and shotgunner were unloading her small trunk and suitcase.

Stepping up to them, she said, "Could I prevail on you gentlemen to carry those into the office for me, please? The person who is to meet me isn't here yet."

"Be glad to, ma'am," said the driver.

Carrying the luggage, they followed Diana into the office. The elderly agent stood behind the counter and greeted the stage crew warmly as they sat the luggage down near the door.

"The person who is to meet the lady hasn't shown up yet, Clarence," said the driver. "She asked us to bring them in here for her."

"Fine," said Clarence Hubbard, who was bald, except for a white fringe over his ears. "You've got four passengers for Ketcham. They should be showing up soon."

"We'll go ahead and feed the horses," said the shotgunner.

Diana thanked them as they headed out the door.

"You must be Miss Diana Morrow," said Clarence. "The Ketcham agent wired to tell me about the avalanche, and that you'd be on this stage. Who's coming to pick you up?"

"His name is Jordan Shaw, sir," said Diana, moving closer to the counter.

"Oh, sure. Of the Bar-S Ranch."

"That's right. As you know from the wire, I was to have been here on Thursday. I assume Jordan was here to pick me up."

Clarence shrugged. "I don't know, ma'am. I wasn't here on Thursday. I'm not the regular agent. Used to be, but I retired two years ago. Fella named Vern Morton is the agent now, but he's gone to Boise for a few days, so I'm filling in."

"I see. Well, I'm sure Jordan was here to pick me up on Thursday. So you've had no contact with him about this morning's wire, then."

"No, ma'am. I haven't seen him. I was here all day yesterday, too. Didn't see him then, either."

"Hmm. Is there a buggy I could hire to take me to the ranch?"

"Oh, sure. But we just got a new eight-inch blanket of snow last night, so it'll probably be a sleigh. I'll send the shotgunner down the street to fetch Willie Akins. Willie'll take you out there."

Fifteen minutes later Diana sat beside middle-aged Willie Akins as the sleigh glided over the snow, heading out of town. Soon they were in the country, and Diana drank in the beauty of the snow-covered scenery around her. She kept looking northward, taking in the majesty of the Sawtooth Mountains with their white peaks reaching for the sky.

Perplexed as to why Jordan had not stayed in contact with the

Fargo agent concerning her delayed arrival, she told herself it was probably because for some reason he had not received her letter, and had no idea if or when she would arrive.

*Oh, dear!* she thought. *Maybe Jordan did get the letter, but he thinks because I wasn't on the stage Thursday that I had changed my mind and wouldn't be coming. Well, if that's the case, I can soon straighten that out!*

The cold air put a rosy glow on her cheeks, and the anticipation of soon meeting the man she had come to marry put a lively sparkle in her eyes.

It was almost ten o'clock when Knight Colburn was drawing near the Bar-S Ranch and heard a shout behind him.

Turning around in the saddle, he saw William Shaw trotting his horse through the snow, waving at him. Pulling rein, Knight halted his horse and waited for William to catch up.

As William drew up, Knight said, "I assume Jordan didn't come in sometime last night."

"He didn't," said William.

When the two men entered the ranch house together, they found Mark and Lorene in the kitchen, having coffee with Sylvia.

All three greeted Knight, then Mark said, "I'm sure glad you're coming along with Dad and me."

"I couldn't do anything else," said Knight. "I have to be with you so we can find him together."

Sylvia poured coffee for Knight and her husband, saying it would warm them up for the cold ride.

Some twenty minutes later, the coffee cups were just about empty, and the three men were eager to get in the saddle and head into the mountains.

Suddenly there was a knock at the front door.

"You boys finish your coffee," said William. "I'll see who it is."

When William opened the door, he found a lovely young brunette on the porch and the sleigh near the house with luggage on the backseat. He waved to the driver. "Hello, Willie!" He met the young lady's probing gaze.

"You are Mr. William Shaw, I presume," said Diana, with a warm smile.

"I am."

"I'm Diana Morrow," she said, thinking her name would bring on a welcoming smile.

Puzzlement showed on William's face. Squinting, he said, "I'm sorry, Miss—I assume it's 'Miss' Morrow. Am I supposed to know you?"

It was Diana's turn to show puzzlement. "Yes. Miss Diana Morrow from Richmond, Virginia."

Still, William looked confused.

"You are Jordan Shaw's father?"

"Well, yes, but—"

"You must know that I'm here to be Jordan's mail order bride."

William was shocked into silence as he stared at the pretty young woman with the hint of a soft Southern drawl in her speech. Suddenly aware that she was still standing out in the cold air, he stepped back and motioned for her to come his way, trying to find his voice.

When she was in, and he pushed the door shut while still staring at her, eyes wide, Diana noted the perplexed expression on his face. "Have I come at an inconvenient time, Mr. Shaw?"

William's mouth quivered as he found his voice. "Ah  ah...no. No. I'm just stunned, is all. Please forgive my bad manners."

"Is Jordan here?"

"Uh...no. He went hunting in the Sawtooth Mountains on Tuesday and has not returned."

"Oh. May I—may I have Mr. Akins bring my luggage in?"

"Certainly," said William.

Diana opened the door and motioned to Willie.

When the luggage was placed on the floor just inside the door, Diana reached into her purse. "Thank you, Mr. Akins. I appreciate your bringing me out here."

William stepped up, waved her off, and said, "No, no! Let me take care of Willie."

He pulled out his wallet and placed more than enough money to cover the cost of Diana's ride to the Bar-S in Willie's hand.

Willie thanked him, told Diana he hoped she would enjoy living in Idaho, and left.

When the door was closed, William looked at Diana, befuddled as to how this could happen without anybody in the family knowing about it.

Drawing in a short breath, he said, "May I take your coat?"

"Oh yes. Thank you."

When the coat was hanging on a peg next to the door, William took another short breath. "M-Miss Morrow, let me take you back to the kitchen, where the rest of the family is having coffee."

# 21

KNIGHT COLBURN AND MARK HEDREN instantly rose to their feet at the table when William ushered the lovely dark-haired woman into the kitchen. Sylvia and Lorene looked at her, wondering who she was, where she was from, and why she was there. They could tell that Mark was having the same thoughts. The ranch seldom had visitors in the dead of winter.

They were also confused at the look on Knight's face. He didn't look perplexed, but rather, seemed awed by the young woman.

Running his gaze over the four faces, William said, "I would like to introduce Miss Diana Morrow from Richmond, Virginia. She just came in on the nine-thirty stage. Miss Morrow, this is my wife, Sylvia—Jordan's mother."

Sylvia smiled, though the mention of Jordan added more puzzlement to the situation. "Happy to meet you, Miss Morrow." Her brow furrowed. "How do you know Jordan?"

"I'll explain in a moment," said William. "Miss Morrow, this is Jordan's sister, Lorene, and this is Lorene's husband, Mark Hedren."

Both Hedrens greeted Diana in a friendly manner.

Gesturing toward the tall man, William said, "And this is Knight Colburn, Jordan's best friend."

Knight swallowed hard as he looked into Diana's dark eyes. *So this is Diana,* he thought.

Knight was closest to her. She offered her hand, and he took it, noting that it was trembling a bit. "Ma'am," he said, pressing a smile on his lips.

William scrubbed a palm over his mouth nervously. "Miss

Morrow told me at the door that she has come to be Jordan's mail order bride."

The look of puzzlement on the faces of Sylvia, Lorene, and Mark changed quickly to shock.

"H-his m-mail order b-bride?" said Sylvia.

"Yes, ma'am," said Diana.

Sylvia's face was white. "He…he never said anything about a mail order bride. This comes as a jolt to all of us." She stood up quickly, pulled back a chair that had not been occupied, and said, "Please s-sit down, Miss Morrow. Would you like some coffee?"

"Ah…not right now, Mrs. Shaw, thank you. But I do need to sit down." As she spoke, she eased onto the chair and set her purse on the floor next to a chair leg.

The three men sat down.

Sylvia muttered, "I don't understand why Jordan would do this and not even share it with his family. Miss Morrow, are you sure you have this right?"

"Why, yes. Jordan put an ad in some newspapers back east, saying he was looking for a mail order bride. I don't know how many newspapers, but one ad was in the *Richmond Chronicle*. I read the ad, and…well, I answered it."

Sylvia shook her head. "I just can't believe it."

Knight's stomach was in knots.

Diana picked up her purse, opened it, and took out the clipped newspaper ad and the two letters she had received from Jordan. Handing the ad to Sylvia, she said, "Read this and pass it around, Mrs. Shaw."

While a stunned Sylvia read the ad, Diana looked around at the others and said, "Jordan sent me the money for my travel expenses."

Blinking and shaking her head at what she had read in the ad, Sylvia handed it to Lorene. Both she and Mark read it, then Lorene handed it to her father. When William had read it, he said, "Well, the ad has the name and address correct. It was Jordan's ad, all right." He then passed it on to Knight.

Knight took it and recognized the ad he had written.

Diana then handed Jordan's first letter to Sylvia and the second letter to William. "These are the letters he sent me in reply to the ones I sent him."

Sylvia's head bobbed as she looked at the letter. She picked up the envelope and looked it over. "Well, something's wrong here," she said. "This is definitely not Jordan's handwriting."

William hadn't started to read yet. He looked at the handwriting on the envelope, then opened the letter and examined it. "Same here, honey," he said. "This isn't his handwriting, either."

The pulse in Diana's temples throbbed. A flicker of emotion skittered across her pale face. Stunned, she ran her eyes between Jordan's parents. "I...I don't understand. If somebody is pulling some kind of joke, they certainly parted with a substantial sum of money to get me here."

At this point, Knight knew he had to tell all of them what had happened. Adjusting himself nervously on the chair, he said, "Well, it's time for me to shed light on all of this confusion."

Every eye went to him like metal to a magnet.

They listened intently as Knight told how Jordan had come to him, saying he wanted to put a mail order bride ad in some eastern newspapers, and asked him to word the ad for him because he had a way with words. He went on to explain that for the same reason, at Jordan's request, it was he who had written the letters to Diana, with Jordan giving him basically what he wanted to say.

This news left everyone at the table speechless, including Diana.

"But why did our son want to advertise for a mail order bride, Knight?" asked Sylvia. "He could marry Belinda anytime he wanted to. She's in love with him."

Diana's eyes widened.

Knight eased back on the chair, rubbed his chin, and said, "That's just it, Sylvia. Jordan has never had a romantic interest in Belinda, but from what he has told me, he has been under pressure from her to develop a romance, and from her parents and from you and William as well. He felt like he was being pushed into marriage with a girl he didn't love. He didn't know how to just come out and tell Belinda he wanted nothing to do with her without hurting your feelings. He came up with the idea of a mail order bride, believing that when he brought his prospective bride to you, it would make everything easier.

"He came to my office at the *Sentinel*, told me about his mail order bride idea and asked me to send the ad to several eastern newspapers for him. He swore me to secrecy. He was so excited about Diana coming."

Sylvia burst into tears, "Then something has happened to him! His not being here when Diana arrived is proof of it."

William left his chair, bent down, and put an arm around Sylvia. "Don't despair now, honey. We can't give up."

When Sylvia's sobbing subsided, Diana said, "I should explain that I was actually supposed to arrive on the three o'clock stage last Thursday, but an avalanche in the Rocky Mountains in Wyoming held up the train, making it a day and a half late getting to Boise, where I was to catch the train to Ketcham. Mr. Shaw, you told me at the door that Jordan went hunting in the mountains on Tuesday."

"Yes."

"So he did intend to be back before Thursday."

"Mm-hmm. He was to return Tuesday evening. Over the past several years, we have had him go hunting in the mountains alone, saying he would be back in a day—and then he has stayed up there sometimes three or four days. We figured this was another one of those incidents. But now we see that it isn't."

"Oh, my," Diana said, putting a hand to her mouth.

Standing to full height but keeping a hand on Sylvia's shoulder, William said, "Diana—I mean, Miss Morrow, I—"

"Please, sir. You can call me Diana."

William nodded, smiled, and said, "All right, Diana. I am about to take Mark and Knight with me to see if we can find Jordan. There's an old abandoned cabin in the high country where Jordan stays when he is up there hunting. He always hunts in that area so he can stay in the cabin at night. We'll start there, first. If he's not there, we'll search for him."

"May I go along with you?" asked Diana.

"Oh, honey," said Sylvia, "that's rough country up there. It's no place for a woman. You can stay here with Lorene and me."

"Right," said Lorene. "You'd have to ride a horse. For a young lady from Richmond, that would be quite difficult."

"I'm actually from a farm a few miles outside of Richmond," said Diana. "I've ridden horses since I was a child. I really want to go. I feel I should, since Jordan wanted me to come as his potential bride."

She looked at William with pleading eyes. "Please, Mr. Shaw."

William rubbed his chin, ran his gaze to the other men, and said, "What do you think, boys?"

"Well, since we've met this fine young lady, and have learned that Jordan wanted her for his wife," said Mark, "I think we should take her with us."

William looked at Jordan's best friend. "Knight?"

"It's fine with me, in view of the circumstances."

"All right, Miss—I mean, Diana," said William, "you can go with us."

"Thank you!" she said, smiling. "I'm sure you're wanting to go right away. I have a split skirt with me, which is more suitable for riding. I'll need a few minutes to get changed, and then could I have five minutes to write my mother a letter? I promised her I'd write as soon as I arrived, so she would know I got here safely. It wouldn't be out of the way, would it, to let me post it in town on the way to the mountains?"

"It's faster getting to the mountains if you bypass the town," said Lorene. "I'm going into town a little later today. I'll mail it for you."

"Oh, thank you," said Diana. Then to William: "Can I have a few minutes?"

"Of course."

Diana turned to Sylvia. "Is there a room I can use to change into more appropriate clothes?"

It took Sylvia a few seconds to respond. "Oh! Of course, child. Forgive me. I'm just so upset right now."

"I understand, Mrs. Shaw. I'm rather in a state of shock, myself."

"I assume you want her in the front guest room," said William.

"Yes," said Sylvia.

"First, let's read these letters that Diana got from Jordan," said William, "then I'll carry her luggage up there. While she's getting ready and writing the letter to her mother, the boys and I will saddle her a horse and load up the packhorses."

Diana waited quietly while both letters were read by each of the four family members. Lorene commented on how well Knight had worded the letters and the others agreed. When they were finished, Diana put the letters and the newspaper ad back in her purse.

"How many pieces of luggage do you have, Miss Morrow?" asked Knight.

"Only two. A small trunk and a suitcase. They're just inside the front door."

"How about helping me, Mark?" said Knight.

"Sure."

"Well, since you boys insist," said William, "I'll be at the barn." All three men hurried away.

"Let's go on up to the room, dear," Sylvia said to Diana.

"I'll start cleaning up the kitchen, Mom," said Lorene.

"Fine, honey," said Sylvia. "Follow me, Diana."

As Sylvia and Diana moved down the hall toward the staircase, Sylvia said, "Again, I apologize for not responding to you immediately a moment ago, dear. I should have offered you the room when you said you needed to change. You must think we are totally without manners around here."

"Nothing of the kind," said Diana. "I can imagine what a shock my arriving here like this must be to all of you. I'm sorry for hitting you with it all of a sudden. I had no idea Jordan was keeping me a secret from his family."

Knight was halfway up the stairs, carrying the trunk, and Mark was ahead of him with the suitcase.

As the two women started up the stairs, Sylvia said, "That had to be a shock for you, honey. I can see why you would naturally assume Jordan was sharing the news with his family that he had a mail order bride coming."

"Looks like this has been a shocking day for all of us, Mrs. Shaw."

"To say the least."

"I do hope Jordan is all right—that it's just some unforeseen problem that is hindering his coming home."

"Me too," said Sylvia, her voice quivering.

As they topped the stairs, Knight and Mark were coming out of the first door on the left side of the hall.

"We put both pieces of luggage on the bed, Miss Morrow," said Knight.

"Thank you," she responded with a smile.

"We'll see you in a little while," said Mark, and the two of them moved down the stairs.

Sylvia led Diana into the room, which was beautifully decorated. "Please make yourself at home, dear. I'll have Lorene bring up some hot water. I'm sure you would like to freshen up a bit after your long trip."

"That would be nice."

"Also, there is paper, pen, and ink in the top desk drawer. You'll find envelopes in the bottom drawer on the left. I'm glad you're going to get the letter to your mother in the mail today. I wouldn't want her to be sick with worry over her child like I am over mine."

Diana's gentle heart went out to the distraught woman. Laying a hand on her shoulder, she said, "It just has to be that some kind of problem came up that is hindering him, Mrs. Shaw."

A small smile creased Sylvia's cheeks. "Oh my dear, I hope you're right. I'll leave you now. Lorene will be up with the hot water in a few minutes."

"You're very kind. Thank you."

"And Diana…"

"Yes, ma'am?"

"Please feel free to leave your things here. And consider this your room for as long as you need it."

Diana thanked her again, and Sylvia closed the door behind her as she left.

As Diana approached the comfortable-looking bed, she thought, *What I wouldn't give to be able to crawl under the covers and take a long nap.* Giving herself a mental shake, she uttered in a soft voice, "First things first."

Opening both the suitcase and the trunk, Diana took out

everything, spreading it on the bed. Quickly sorting through it, she laid the split skirt and a blouse on a chair. She picked up a small bag and put what she figured she would need for the mountain trip in the bag.

Then sitting down at the desk, she hurriedly penned the letter to her mother, telling her that she had arrived late, because of the avalanche, but safely. Saying she would fill her in on details in her next letter, she tells her mother of Cora Zeller leading her to the Lord on the train between Cheyenne City and Boise. She gave praise to the Lord, saying how wonderful it is to be born again and to know she is going to heaven.

Quickly she addressed the letter to Shamus and Maggie O'Hearn, using the general delivery address of the Bar-S Ranch under her name in the upper left-hand corner.

As she was sealing the envelope, there was a tap at the door. She opened it to find Lorene with a steaming kettle of hot water. Taking the kettle, she thanked Lorene, then gave her the letter, saying she would pay her for the postage when they got back from the mountains. Lorene told her she would gladly pay the postage and hurried away.

Diana carried the kettle to a table where a washbasin sat and poured the larger portion of the water into the basin. She removed her wrinkled travel clothes, then taking a soft cloth from the table, she washed herself as thoroughly as possible for the short time she had in which to do it. Drying off with the towel, she put on the blouse and split skirt for her trek into the mountains.

Taking a deep breath and looking with longing at the comfortable bed, she picked up the small bag and left the room.


By eleven-thirty, the group was mounted and on their way with two packhorses following on lead ropes. Diana was wearing a heavy black coat supplied by Sylvia, along with a black hat with a ribbon that tied under her chin.

While they were climbing into the mountains, Mark and Diana listened as William and Knight talked about the time they went in search of Jordan eight years ago when they thought he had been killed and eaten by a grizzly.

Diana shuddered at the thought and said, "I'm sure glad it wasn't so."

"So were we," said William. "What a relief when Jordan showed up at Lorene and Mark's wedding, alive and well."

"Oh, I want to hear about that," said Diana.

While William and Mark were telling her the story, Knight thought about Ol' Halfpaw and the grudge the bear might have toward Jordan for shooting off part of his right forepaw. He would keep this to himself. William, Mark, and Diana didn't need that to worry them.

When they reached the old abandoned cabin in midafternoon, they were disappointed to see no sign of Jordan nor his horse. The only tracks in the fresh snow around the cabin were those of deer and elk.

Sliding from the saddle, Knight said, "I'll go inside and take a look. Be right back."

Knight plodded through the snow, stepped up on the porch of the cabin, opened the squeaky door, and went inside.

Mark said, "Where do we go now?"

"No particular place," said William. "He could be anywhere. We'll just have to start searching."

Looking around at the towering mountain peaks and the massive forests, Diana said, "I hope he's holed up somewhere dry, warm, and safe."

"Me too," said William.

At that instant, Knight came out the door, stepped off the porch, and approached his companions. "Someone has been staying in the cabin recently. I can tell by the ashes in the stove and fireplace, and the lack of dust on the cupboard and the table. But there's no way we can be sure it was Jordan. There's plenty of firewood, so we'll be able to warm it up good when we come back tonight."

"I'm glad to hear that," said William. "Tell you what. I think we should pair off so we can cover twice as much territory."

"Good idea," said Knight. "I'll take Miss Morrow with me."

William nodded.

Looking at Diana, Knight said, "This all right with you?"

"Sure is."

"Let's do it like this," said William. "Mark and I will go up through the forest to the west, and you two head due east toward those peaks over there. I think we should call out Jordan's name loudly as we ride, so if he's in trouble somewhere near, he can hear us and hopefully respond.

"If one pair finds him, they are to fire three successive shots into the air, then bring him here to the cabin. The other pair will then make a beeline this direction. If no shots are fired, we'll meet here at the cabin at dusk."

"Sounds like a good plan to me," said Knight.

"Okay," said William. "If we haven't found Jordan by nightfall, we'll cover other areas tomorrow."

"That's fine," said Knight. "Well, Miss Morrow, let's move out."

As Knight and Diana rode through the woods together, with Knight periodically shouting out Jordan's name, he asked questions about Diana's family in Virginia. She told him about her siblings and her mother, but when he asked about her father, she became reluctant to go into any details.

Noting that the mention of her father stiffened her face, he said, "I'm sorry, Miss Morrow. I didn't mean to be nosy."

"You're not nosy, Mr. Colburn," she said, smiling at him. "You're simply showing interest in my family, and I appreciate it. Suffice it to say that I took Jordan up on his offer and left home because of some deep heartaches involving my family. I'd just rather not talk about it right now."

"Of course," Knight said, smiling back. "I understand."

They rode on in silence for a while—except for Knight's calling out Jordan's name every few minutes.

Diana was thinking if they found Jordan to be all right, how fearful she was going to be to tell him she had become a Christian on the trip and could not marry him unless he became one, too.

To her surprise, Knight said, "Miss Morrow, did you attend church in Virginia?"

"No, I didn't. My father hates churches and never took us. He wouldn't let us go without him, either."

"Have you ever heard that when Jesus Christ died on the cross, He paid the price for all of sinful mankind to be saved from hell and the wrath of God if they would come to Him by faith and let Him save them?"

Diana's heart leaped in her chest. Turning to look at him, she said, "Not until quite recently. My mother was in the hospital, and a pastor came into her room with his Bible. He showed her how to be born again, and she received the Lord Jesus into her heart as her own personal Saviour. Because of the reason she was in the hospital, she hasn't been able to be baptized yet, but she's going to do so as soon as possible."

Knight's eyes lit up. "Well, wonderful!"

"And you know what?"

"What?"

"Mama tried to talk to me about being saved, but I wouldn't listen. But I know she's been praying for me because when I was on the train between Cheyenne City and Boise, a dear, sweet lady from Portland, Oregon, named Cora Zeller began talking to me about being saved and led me to Jesus."

Knight's face took on a bright beam. "Oh, Miss Morrow, I'm so glad to hear that! Praise the Lord!"

Knight called out Jordan's name loudly a few times, and as his voice echoed over the mountains, Diana said, "Mr. Colburn, since you're Jordan's best friend, you know him well, I'm sure."

"Yes. We've been friends since we were small boys."

"I...I need to know if he is a Christian."

Knight's brow furrowed. A touch of sadness showed in his eyes. "No, he isn't. I've been trying to lead Jordan to the Lord since I got saved eight years ago. But he won't have anything to do with the Lord. He's a moral and sincere person, but he's not a Christian."

Diana nodded silently.

Knight went on to tell her of his father's sudden death eight years ago, which came a very short time after he was saved. He explained how it came about that he and his parents were saved, then told her that his mother now lived with him in his house, and would one day live in a house of her own whenever he found the right girl and got married.

Diana let a brief moment of silence pass, then asked, "Are you seeing someone?"

"No. I'm just waiting for the Lord to send that right girl into my life."

"I'm sure that's the right thing to do."

"Sure is. Don't want to get the wrong girl."

Again, Diana let a brief moment of silence pass, then said, "What is your job at the *Elkton Sentinel,* Mr. Colburn?"

"I…ah…I own the paper," he said.

Diana's mouth dropped open. "Well, isn't that something? A man as young as you are! That's wonderful. I'm impressed."

Knight chuckled. "Well, you're good for a man's ego, Miss Morrow."

She was smiling at him as he cupped his hands around his mouth and called out Jordan's name a few more times.

By the time dusk was falling over the mountains, Knight and Diana had heard no gunshots. They returned to the cabin as darkness was settling in. William and Mark had not yet returned.

Knight took Diana into the cabin, and while he was building a fire in the fireplace, he said, "We won't be able to eat until William and Mark return, since the food is in the knapsacks on the backs of the packhorses."

Diana was tired beyond belief, both physically and mentally. Taking one of the chairs from the table, she placed it in front of the fireplace and sat down. "Well, until they get here, I'm going to soak up some heat."

Knight picked up another chair and sat down beside her. Soon the fire was blazing.

Diana thought back to earlier that day when she first met Knight. She had felt an unexplainable magnetism toward him. But now she knew it was because he was a brother in the family of God. She felt so comfortable in his presence—as if she could talk to him about anything.

Glancing at him in the flickering light of the fire, she said, "Mr. Colburn, I'm sorry if I seemed abrupt today when you were asking about my family, and I said I didn't want to talk about them."

"I didn't feel that you were abrupt at all. I understand how those kind of things can be very upsetting."

"Thank you, Mr. Colburn," she said softly. "I…I would like to talk about them. You seem to be such an understanding person, and when there are a good pair of listening ears, sometimes it helps to share the heartaches."

"I'll be glad to listen on one condition," he said, looking her square in the eye.

"Yes?"

"That you call me Knight. I believe we are becoming friends, and as your friend, Mr. Colburn sounds so formal. Okay?"

Diana warmed him with a smile. "All right. Then you must call me Diana."

"It's a deal," he said. "Now, these ears are ready to listen."

With the dual warmth of her new friend and the crackling fire soothing her nerves, Diana told him the story of her father's brutalities to the family, of his being in jail for beating up Tom Wymore, and of his threats toward her. She explained in detail why she replied to Jordan's ad in the newspaper, and of the relief she felt being where her father could not find her.

"Diana, my heart goes out to you. I'm so sorry you've had to leave the rest of your family because of the fear you have of your father. And now you've come here to find refuge with Jordan, and he has disappeared."

"That brings up something else," she said, then told him that Cora Zeller had shown her in the Bible what God says about believers not marrying unbelievers.

"She did the right thing by showing it to you, Diana. So many Christians have messed up their lives by going against God's commandment about that. Some by ignorance. Others by rebellion."

"I have to admit that I've been very nervous about having to tell Jordan I won't marry him unless he becomes a Christian," said Diana. "I don't know what I'll do if something has happened to Jordan, or if we find him, but he doesn't get saved. I can't possibly go back to Virginia and face the wrath of my father."

Knight was about to tell her that he would help find some solution for her when they heard a horse whinny.

Both of them stood up, and Knight started for the door. Before he could reach it, the door came open and William and Mark stepped in, holding the knapsacks.

"Well," William said dolefully, "it appears that you two found no sign of Jordan, either. We'll get an early start in the morning."

Diana prepared a hearty meal for the weary group, and even though none of them had much appetite, they ate as much as they could hold, knowing they would need strength for the next day.

Before they got into their bedrolls, Knight took his Bible from his pack and asked William and Mark if they would like to join Diana and him for Bible reading. Both men politely declined, removed their boots, and slipped into their bedrolls.

Sitting close to the fire, Diana listened as Knight read an encouraging portion of Scripture.

Sometime during the night, Knight Colburn awakened and felt the chill of the air on his face. Opening his eyes, he saw that the fire had dwindled to a few flickering flames, which were barely putting out heat.

Moving as quietly as possible, he eased out of his bedroll and rose to his feet. William and Mark were sleeping soundly near the table. Diana's bedroll was near the fireplace, and as Knight stepped that way, he saw that she was asleep but twisting beneath the covers and tossing her head back and forth fitfully.

He quietly placed more logs on the fire, then turned to head back to his bedroll. He noted that Diana was still quite restless, and as she was rolling her head back and forth, she was moving her lips and making a moaning sound.

It was obvious that Diana was having some kind of bad dream. He was trying to decide whether to awaken her or not when suddenly she let out a loud cry and sat bolt upright, gasping.

William and Mark were both stirring as Knight knelt beside Diana, grasped both shoulders and said softly, "Diana, are you all right?"

The effect of the nightmare was so powerful, Diana threw her arms around Knight's neck without thinking. Knight's natural reaction was to put his arms around her.

She gripped his neck tightly. "Oh, Knight! It…it was so awful! So terrible!"

Trembling, she clung to him for a moment, then suddenly let go and said, "I'm sorry. Please forgive me for hanging onto you like that. I…I had a horrible nightmare."

"You don't need to apologize," said Knight, releasing his hold on her. "I could tell you were frightened."

Both Mark and William were sitting up, sleepy-eyed.

"What was the nightmare about, Miss Morrow?" asked Mark.

Diana swallowed hard, put fingers to her temple and said, "I was dreaming that a man was beating me. Please forgive me, all of you. I'm sorry to have awakened you."

"It's all right," said William. "You had no control over what you dreamed."

"You didn't wake me up," said Knight. "I had just put more logs on the fire and was heading back to my bedroll when you cried out and sat up. Do you think you can get back to sleep?"

"I'm sure I can," she said. "Thank you."

Knight went back to his bedroll, fully aware that the man in Diana's nightmare was her father.

In the stillness of the night, Diana lay there, thinking how secure she felt in Knight's strong arms. No one had ever held her like that before. She thought about how she had felt an attraction to him upon learning that he was a born-again man. His tall frame and good looks didn't hurt her image of him, either.

In his bedroll, Knight was thinking about how Diana seemed to belong in his arms. There was just something there that clicked…

Suddenly, he felt a pang of guilt, and barely whispering, said, "Lord, I'm sorry. Please forgive my thoughts. Even though Diana told me she would not marry Jordan until and unless he became a Christian, I know I shouldn't desire her for myself."

MAIL ORDER BRIDE SERIES
NO. 8
1872
USA
AL & JOANNA LACY

# 22

AFTER BREAKFAST THE NEXT MORNING, both pairs rode out again in opposite directions, agreeing to fire the three successive shots as planned if they found Jordan. They were to meet at noon at a certain spot higher up that Knight and William both knew.

Once again riding alongside Diana and periodically calling out Jordan's name, Knight led the search for his friend.

As they guided their horses up a steep slope through two feet of snow, Knight said, "Sure feels odd not to be going to church today, but I just had to come up here and do what I could to help find Jordan."

"Oh, my, this is Sunday, isn't it?" said Diana. "December 1."

"Sure is. Another month and it'll be 1873."

"Hard to believe. Time sure has a way of passing quickly."

"Mm-hmm. And they tell me the older you get, the faster it seems to go."

"I've heard that, too."

They reached a temporary plateau, and Knight pulled rein. "Let's stop here and give the horses a breather."

When Diana halted her horse, Knight cupped his hands around his mouth and called out Jordan's name loudly four times, allowing a few seconds to pass between each one.

As his voice echoed across the high country, he looked at the lovely brunette and said, "Diana, this nightmare you had last night. Have you had nightmares like it before?"

"Yes. Many times."

"Do you have them often?"

"About twice a week."

"Is it the same nightmare each time?"

"It varies a little, but it's always the same man who is beating on me."

Knight studied the fear in her eyes. "I believe I know who the man is."

Tears surfaced in Diana's eyes. "You're right. It's my father."

"Would it help you to talk about it? We need to let the horses catch their breath for a few minutes."

Finding her heart reaching toward this kind Christian man, Diana nodded, took a shuddering breath, and sniffled.

Sliding from his saddle, Knight went to the left side of Diana's horse, lifted his hands toward her, and helped her down. As her feet sank into the snow, she blinked at the tears. "I didn't even think about the date as I told you last night about Papa's threat against me. It just hit me. Papa is out of jail, now. He was released on Thursday."

"But you're here and he's there," Knight said, trying to encourage her.

"Yes, but I'm afraid that in spite of Mama's determination to keep him from finding out where I am, he will find out and come after me. He said he'd find me, no matter where I went if I ran away. When I left, I felt that as Jordan's wife, I would be protected from my father if he showed up. But...but now, I'll not be Jordan's wife unless he becomes a Christian, and if he doesn't, I'll have no protection."

Before he knew it, Knight found himself thinking, *I'd love to protect you for the rest of your life, sweet girl.* Mentally chastising himself for having the thought, he said, "You're God's child now, Diana. He will watch over you."

"I have much to learn about my new life in Christ, Knight. Right now, I'm so frightened, I don't think I can stand it. The fear of my father is about to tear me apart."

Stepping to his horse and unbuckling a saddlebag, he said, "I keep a Bible in here, as well as in the canvas pack. Let me show you some Scripture verses that will help you."

When he had Bible in hand, for a safety measure Knight also

slipped his rifle from the boot and said, "Let's go sit down on this fallen tree over here."

Leaning the rifle against the tree, Knight brushed the snow off as best he could and helped Diana sit down. Then sitting down beside her, he opened the Bible and showed her Ephesians 4:7 and 2 Corinthians 12:9, commenting on the measure of grace God gives His born-again children, then took her to James 4:6 and said, "Diana, read this verse to me."

Fascinated with what she was learning, Diana focused on the verse. "'But he giveth more grace. Wherefore he saith, God resisteth the proud, but giveth grace unto the humble.'"

Knight looked deep into Diana's eyes. "We just learned that our heavenly Father gives a measure of grace to His children when they need it, right?"

"Yes."

"Now, read me that first sentence in James 4:6 again."

Diana looked at the verse. "'But he giveth more grace.'"

"See that, Diana? When the circumstances in a Christian's life demand a greater measure of grace, our Father gives us more grace."

"Oh, Knight," she said, smiling at him, "that's beautiful! Thank you for being such a help to me."

"My pleasure," said Knight, closing the Bible. "Keep that in mind, won't you?"

"I sure will."

Knight stood up. Offering his hand, he said, "We'd better get back to searching for Jordan."

When Diana stood up, their eyes locked for a timeless moment.

In her mind, Diana found herself wishing she could be in Knight's arms again.

In Knight's mind, he found himself wishing he could take her in his arms and kiss her—then silently asked the Lord to forgive him. He lashed himself inwardly, telling himself that Diana was in Idaho because Jordan sent her the money to come with the prospect of becoming his bride.

They walked to the horses, and Knight put the Bible back in the saddlebag.

While he was doing so, Diana's attention was drawn to a huge bald eagle that was making circles in the sky and swooping down near the treetops about a hundred yards away.

Fastening the buckle, Knight turned and saw Diana staring up the gentle slope. "What are you looking at?" he asked.

Pointing to the swooping eagle, she said, "I've seen pictures of them, but I've never actually seen an eagle before."

Knight caught sight of the eagle quickly. "They're a sight to behold, especially when they're in flight," he said, taking hold of her arm. "Let's go over here to the clearing, where you can see him better."

He guided her to the nearby clearing, where there were no trees to obstruct their view of the great bird as it continued to circle and make dives toward the distant treetops.

Fascinated, they watched the magnificent sight.

Suddenly both horses ejected shrill whinnies, which were followed instantly by a wild, ferocious roar that came from directly behind Knight and Diana.

Both of them pivoted at the sound and saw a huge black bear standing on his hind legs some sixty feet away.

Diana felt her heart lurch in her chest, and her blood curdled at the sight of the beast.

Knight recognized Ol' Halfpaw as the bear roared again, angrily waving both forepaws as a means of frightening his intended victims before charging.

In abject terror, Diana gasped.

Knight jacked a cartridge into the chamber of the rifle, saying, "We can't outrun him, Diana. Stand absolutely still."

Diana's mind was a pulsating maze and her breaths were coming in short gulps as Knight stepped in front of her, offering what protection he could from the bear, who was now charging full speed.

Shouldering the rifle, Knight took careful aim, knowing he would have to be dead accurate for Diana's sake as well as his own. The black beast was within thirty feet when Knight squeezed the trigger. The rifle barked, sending a sharp, echoing sound over the mountains.

Ol' Halfpaw went down into the snow with the slug dead center between his eyes. He released a death roar and struggled to get up. Looking over Knight's shoulder, Diana screamed as he worked the lever again, took aim, and drilled another slug into the bear's head. Ol' Halfpaw dropped lifelessly into the snow.

Diana was trembling. Knight put his free arm around her, squeezed tight, and said, "It's over. He's dead."

Pressing her head to his chest, Diana clung to him until the terror of the experience subsided. When they let go of each other, Diana eyed the beast warily, then looked up into Knight's eyes. "You placed yourself between me and that charging bear. Thank you."

Knight found himself wanting to say he would like to be her protector, but kept it to himself, and silently asked the Lord to forgive him once more for feeling that way. Taking her hand, he led her to the spot where the bear lay and showed her the damaged forepaw, telling her that one time when he and Jordan were hunting together, the bear had appeared at a close range, and Jordan had shot the forepaw while trying to hit him with a lethal shot.

Then he said, "Let's get back to the horses."

Just as they drew near the horses, Knight and Diana saw William and Mark riding toward them. William said, "We're glad to see that you're all right. We heard one shot, then after a few seconds, another one. It wasn't the signal, but we had to come and see if you were okay."

Knight pointed at the dead bear lying in the snow. "That big boy came after us. I had to drop him. He's the same bear that Jordan shot in the right forepaw one time when we were hunting together. He's missing two claws. We saw his tracks a time or two after that. They were easily identifiable. Jordan dubbed him Ol' Halfpaw."

"He never told us about it," said William. "Well, now that we know you two are all right, we'll get back to our task."

Both pair resumed their search.

At noon, they met at the agreed spot and ate lunch. They were discouraged that there had been no sign of Jordan, but were determined to keep searching until they found him.

As Knight and Diana rode together, they traded questions and answers about their lives. Jordan Shaw, though absent, stood between them.

Darkness was falling that evening when Knight and Diana arrived at the cabin. He built a fire in the fireplace, and as they sat close to each other to gain warmth from the flames, Knight drank in Diana's beauty as the flickering shadows danced on her lovely face.

They were sitting silently, when Diana said, "Knight, those two letters you wrote for Jordan…"

"Yes?"

"I have to tell you that it was the spirit of those letters that told me I could fall in love with Jordan when I met him. I was so surprised when I learned that it was you who had written them."

Knight let a grin curve his lips. "Well," he said, "Jordan basically told me what to say. I just put it in words and phrases that sounded best to me."

Diana warmed him with a smile. "Well, you did a beautiful job."

He grinned again. "Thanks."

As the flickering shadows continued to highlight her loveliness, Knight Colburn was fighting a battle in his heart. He knew he was falling in love with Diana, but felt he was betraying Jordan. In his heart, he told the Lord they must find Jordan soon. The longer he was in Diana's presence, the stronger he felt about her.

Unknown to Knight, the identical battle was going on inside Diana. Even though she had only known this wonderful man since yesterday, she had fallen in love with him. *Lord, can love be limited by time? I've only known him two days, but I feel like I've known him all my life. I know he likes me, Lord, and I think he could learn to love me, given the chance. But…but what about Jordan? It was his ad I answered, not Knight's. But Knight is a Christian—*

Diana's silent talk with the Lord was interrupted by the arrival of William and Mark.

Supper was eaten, with a discouraged William about to give up hope of finding his son. Knight, Mark, and Diana tried to encourage him, saying maybe they would find him tomorrow.

On Monday morning, December 2, in Richmond, Virginia, Chief Perry unlocked Stu Morrow's cell door while men in the other cells looked on. "You could have been out on Thursday if you hadn't mouthed off to Deputy Barnes, Morrow. I hope you learn to control that temper before it really gets you into trouble."

Stu glared at him in silence.

"Two things before you go."

Stu looked him square in the eye, waiting.

"Number one, you'd better pay Tom Wymore's hospital and medical bills, or you'll be right back in here. Understand?"

"Yeah."

"And number two, if you beat on any member of your family again, I guarantee you'll get no less than five years in the Virginia State Prison. Got it?"

Stu nodded glumly. "Yeah. I got it."

"Let me make sure you understand," said Perry, his lips drawn into a thin line. "Next time you beat on your wife, she won't have to press charges. I know the reason she didn't do it this time is because she's scared to death of you. Well, next time it'll be different. You are now on record with this office for what you did. You so much as lay a hand on her and it's off to prison. If she tells us you have gone beyond reasonable discipline of your children, it's off to prison. Is this sinking in?"

Stu nodded. "Yeah."

"All right. Before you go home, you go to the hospital and to Tom's doctor and make arrangements to pay them. I want to see it on paper today. Any questions?"

"No."

"All right. Go."

Stu Morrow walked out of the jail into the crisp December air and headed for the hospital. An hour later, he entered the police building and handed Chief Perry the necessary papers to prove that he had made arrangements with the hospital and the doctor to pay them over an agreed period of time.

The sunny kitchen of the Morrow house was scented with the savory fragrance of yeast as Martha took four loaves of hot bread out of the oven one at a time with her good hand, and set them on the cupboard to cool.

There was a prickling at the back of her mind as she covered the loaves with clean cloths. Martha was aware that her husband was to be released from jail that morning. As she worked about the kitchen with little Dennis observing, her ears were attuned to the sound of Stu's imminent arrival. He would be walking from town.

Nervously, she glanced at the clock on the wall. 10:20.

Dennis was playing on the floor with a small hand-carved horse that Shamus O'Hearn had made him, and knowing that his father was to come home today, was full of questions. Martha tried valiantly to follow his train of thought and answered them as best she could.

Also at the front of her mind was Diana. She had told herself upon waking that morning that certainly a letter would arrive at the O'Hearn place for her in a few more days.

Suddenly Martha's heart leaped in her chest when she heard the front door open and Stu's big voice bellowing, "Martha, I'm home!"

Dennis's head came up, and fear showed in his eyes. Leaving the wooden horse on the floor, he rushed to his mother, wrapped his arms around her legs, and hid his face in her apron. She nervously adjusted the cast in its sling, then lay her good hand on the child's trembling shoulder. While heavy footsteps were heard in the hall, Dennis peeked up and saw the terror in his mother's eyes, then quickly pressed his face into her apron again.

Martha patted his shoulder. "It's all right, honey," she said, "Papa isn't going to hurt you."

Dennis gripped her tighter, keeping his face hidden.

When Stu came into the kitchen, he looked at Martha, then at Dennis, then back at Martha and snapped, "Why didn't you come and see me while I was in jail?"

She met his gaze, but did not answer.

Stu huffed and shook his head. "I suppose Derick, Deborah, and Daniel are in school."

"They are."

Stu looked around. "Where's Diana?"

Martha swallowed with difficulty. "She isn't here."

"Where is she?"

Squaring her shoulders, Martha said evenly, "I can't tell you."

A deep scowl bent Stu's face. "What do you mean you can't tell me? Don't you know where she is?"

Martha cleared her throat nervously, asking the Lord in her heart for protection. "What I mean is—I won't tell you. Diana has her own life to live, and you are not going to interfere."

The huge man's features flushed. He stepped closer to her while a terrified Dennis clung to her legs. "You tell me where she is, or I'll beat it out of you!"

"I happen to know that Chief Perry warned you what would happen if you ever beat me or one of my children again. It'll be a lengthy sentence in state prison, Stu. Is that what you want?"

"How do you know what he told me?"

"He was here Saturday and explained it all to me. That's how I know."

Stu rasped, "Diana's my daughter! I want to know where she is!"

"You mean so you can give her a beating like she can't even imagine? Well, Derick, Deborah, Daniel, and I promised Diana we will never tell anyone where she is. And Dennis doesn't know. You lay a hand on any of us, and you'll be behind bars in a hurry."

Stu regarded her with hot eyes for a long moment, then stomped toward the back door, went out, and slammed it behind him. Turning with a weeping Dennis still clinging to her, she looked out the window and watched her husband as he headed for the barn.

That evening, when the family was at the supper table, Stu ran his hard gaze over the faces of Derick, Deborah, and Daniel, and said in a gruff voice, "I want to know where Diana is. Now out with it!"

Derick looked at his father across the table. "Papa, we were here Saturday when Chief Perry came to tell us that if you ever beat on Mama or any of us again, you will go to prison for a long time. We love Diana, and I was there at the jail with her when you threatened to give her a beating. All of us love Diana. We don't want you to ever touch her again. We know what you'll do if you find her, so we've agreed not to tell you. If you want to try to beat it out of us, we can't stop you. But one way or another, if you do, you'll go to prison."

Stu dropped his eyes to his plate, and silently finished his supper.

At bedtime, when Stu and Martha were alone in their room, she sat down on the edge of the bed while he was removing his shoes, and with her heart thudding against her rib cage, said, "There's something I need to tell you, Stu."

"Yeah? What?"

"When I was in the hospital, I found out that my roommate was a member of the same church Shamus and Maggie are. Pastor Sherman Bradford came into visit her regularly. One day he talked to me about being saved. He showed me things in the Bible I never knew were there. I learned how terribly wrong you and I have been about the Bible. To put it short and plain, Stu, I received the Lord Jesus Christ into my heart as my Saviour. I am now a Christian. I have such wonderful peace knowing that I'll never go to hell, but that I am going to heaven. The children and I went to church yesterday, and will be going regularly from now on. I am going to be baptized as soon as this cast comes off."

Stu's mind flashed back to the day Pastor Sherman Bradford came to the jail and warned him of hell…the eternal prison. Ice-cold needles seemed to dance down his backbone.

Dropping the shoe he had just removed, he looked at Martha.

Expecting to see fire in his eyes, Martha had steeled herself for the onslaught. But instead of fire in his eyes, there was a softness she hadn't seen in years.

Stu mumbled in a low tone, "It's all right with me if you and the kids go to church, as long as you don't expect me to go."

Martha blinked and nodded. *Thank You, Lord, for this measure of grace.*

When the sun was slanting toward the high peaks in the Sawtooth Mountains on Monday afternoon, December 2, Knight Colburn and Diana Morrow had spent another day together in their search for Jordan Shaw. They had no success in their search, but the time in each other's presence had served to cause both to secretly fall deeper in love.

The sky was a brilliant blue and the light of the lowering sun made the snow on the mountains glisten like diamonds as Knight pulled rein. "Well, it'll be almost dark by the time we get to the cabin. We'd better head on down there."

No sooner were the words out of his mouth when they heard three rapid shots cut through the cold air.

Diana felt her heart jolt inside her body and put a hand to her mouth as the shots echoed. They looked at each other, eyes wide.

Jordan had been found!

Looking into Knight's eyes, she saw reflected there what appeared to be the same feelings that she was experiencing.

But she couldn't be sure.

*I know I have no choice,* she thought. *Even if it means living alone, I must tell Jordan of my salvation. Lord, I will not go against the plain command in Your Word. I will not marry a man who is an unbeliever. Please give me the courage and wisdom that I need to handle this situation.*

Holding each other's gaze for a brief, silent moment, Knight and Diana turned their horses and began their slow descent down the snowy slopes toward the cabin and to whatever the future held.

As they rode, both of them had mixed emotions. They were glad and relieved to know Jordan had been found, but for Knight, it meant Jordan had claim on the young woman who had captured his heart.

For Diana, it meant she must tell Jordan immediately that unless he became a Christian, she would not marry him. She had no idea what his response would be, but from what Knight had told her about Jordan's rejection of Christ all of these years, she figured it would probably be negative. Stiffening her legs and pressing her feet hard against the stirrups as they moved down a steep embankment, she told herself that even if Jordan did get saved, it still would be wrong to marry him. She was in love with Knight. Again, she prayed for God's help.

They reached ground that was relatively more level, and within a few minutes, they were drawing near the cabin. Suddenly Diana caught sight of movement among the trees off to her right, and focusing on the spot, she pointed. "Knight, there they are."

William and Mark were riding toward them. "I don't see Jordan," Knight said, frowning.

"I noticed that right away," she said.

Knight and Diana reached the cabin first, and dismounted. As William and Mark drew near, they saw that William was weeping.

"Oh no," said Knight. "Looks like bad news."

Diana nodded, her eyes fixed on William.

As they drew rein, William was now sobbing so hard he couldn't speak.

Mark slid from the saddle, helped his father-in-law down, and looked at Knight and Diana. "We found a cave up at about ten thousand feet. By the tracks we saw in the snow all around the mouth of the cave, it had to have been the lair of Ol' Halfpaw. The right forepaw definitely had two claws missing. As you said, Knight, the tracks were easily identifiable."

Mark choked up, swallowed hard, and blinked at the tears in his eyes. "We...ah...we found Jordan's torn-up coat and clothing inside the cave, along with what was left of his body. We buried the remains under some large rocks outside the cave."

Even though Diana had never met Jordan, and even though in her mind, she had already given her heart to Knight, she gasped at Mark's words. Stepping up to William, who was now weeping silently, she touched his arm and said, "Mr. Shaw, I'm so very, very sorry."

William looked at her and said, "So am I, Diana. So am I."

Knight stepped up and silently embraced William for a long

moment, then stepped back, allowing Mark to give what comfort he could.

Knight's heart was heavy over his friend's death, but he hurt the most, knowing Jordan had died without Christ.

# 23

IT WAS LATE MORNING THE NEXT DAY, when the solemn, silent foursome—each deep in their own thoughts—arrived at the Bar-S Ranch and broke the news to Sylvia and Lorene, whom they found in the parlor.

William sat beside Sylvia on a couch as they wept together, and Mark sat beside Lorene on a second couch, holding her in his arms as she wept. Knight and Diana were sitting in adjacent chairs, facing the others.

When the weeping had subsided, William looked at Diana tenderly and said, "Diana, I'm so sorry that you came all this way to meet such a shocking disappointment. I'll pay your way back to Richmond."

Knight saw the fear that leaped into Diana's eyes at the mention of her returning to Richmond. "I think, William, that after all she's been through since arriving here, she shouldn't travel for a week or so."

"I agree, Knight," said Sylvia, dabbing at her wet cheeks with a hankie. "Diana can stay here with us as long as she wants."

"That's fine with me," said William. "We'll be glad to have her. After all, she was almost our daughter-in-law."

"Maybe it would be better," said Knight, "if Diana stays in town, just in case all of this should have an effect on her nerves and she needs to see a doctor. She can stay at my house with Mom and me."

"Well, that's up to her," said Sylvia. "What do you think, Diana?"

Just the thought of being near Knight a little longer brought peace to Diana's mind. Speaking to the Lord in her heart, she told Him she was already sensing that promised measure of grace. Then to the Shaws, she said, "I very much appreciate you dear people offering to let me stay here, but I think Knight's idea would work best for me."

When Knight and Diana arrived at his house in town, he took her inside and introduced her to his mother, explaining that Diana had been saved during her trip from Richmond to Elkton. Annie Colburn was happy to learn this, and when she heard the entire story as told by Knight, her heart went out to the girl, and she welcomed her into their home. She told them both that she was sorry to hear about Jordan's death and spoke her greater sorrow that he had never received the Saviour into his heart.

Diana was given the room next to Annie's, which was on the second floor at the front part of the house. Knight's room was on the second floor at the rear.

After Knight had carried Diana's trunk and suitcase up to the guest bedroom, he told the women he had to get to the *Sentinel* office and see how everything was going with Dan and Erline. He was also going to write an article on Jordan's untimely death to go on the front page of tomorrow's edition of the paper.

As he was going out the front door, Annie led Diana up the stairs and into the guest bedroom. Hugging her, she said, "I'm so sorry you've had this terrible tragedy in your life, honey. I'm sure the Lord has someone else for you. He never makes mistakes."

"I know He doesn't," said Diana. "The Christian life is all so new to me as yet, but I'm learning."

Annie showed Diana around the room, then said, "I'll leave you alone so you can unpack. You can come on downstairs whenever you want to."

Diana thanked her, and when Annie was gone, she gave the room a thorough examination. It was quite cozy and beautifully furnished. Her room at home that she had shared so many years with Deborah was a far cry from this one, she told herself. She thought of the near-poverty she had come from, and as she looked at the white iron bed, she lovingly caressed the quilted coverlet.

Sitting on the edge of the bed, Diana bowed her head and said, "Dear Lord, thank You for saving my soul, and for keeping Your hand on me. Thank You for letting me escape Papa's wrath. But…but Lord, the rest of my family is in danger. Please protect them and don't let Papa hurt any of them. I don't really know how to say this exactly, but since You're God, You have known what Papa is like all along. Would You…would You do a work in his heart like You did in Mama's, and show him how wrong he is about You and Your Son and Your Word?

"I ask for guidance from You concerning my situation here. I can't go back home, Lord, unless I hear that You have brought Papa to salvation. You know what I would be facing. I have to do something about where to live. I just don't know what to do. I know You are able to help me, and show me where to live and how to make a living for myself. I know You have a plan for my life. Lead me, please, and help me to fully trust Your faithfulness. I love You, Lord Jesus. I ask all of this in Your precious name. Amen."

Sweet peace flooded Diana's heart. A small smile curved her pretty mouth as she left the room to join Knight's mother downstairs.


That night after Annie had gone to her bed, Knight and Diana sat on a small couch in front of the fireplace in the parlor.

They talked about Jordan's violent death and the tragedy of his leaving this world unsaved, then Diana told him how very much she liked his mother.

"She's a sweetheart," Knight said, looking at Diana by the flickering light of the fire. "The more you get to know her, the better you'll like her." He paused. "Diana…"

"Yes?"

"It was very kind of William to offer to pay your way back to Richmond. You don't really want to go, do you? I mean, with your father's threats to face?"

Instantly he saw the fear in her eyes. "No. I can't go home."

"Would you consider staying here permanently?"

A bit shocked at his question, Diana said, "What do you mean?"

"May I be perfectly honest with you?"

"Of course," she replied softly, noting the reflection of the fire dancing in his eyes.

Knight rubbed a palm over his mouth. "Diana, I've known you less than a week, but I feel like I've known you all of my life. I...I don't know how else to say this. I have fallen head over heels in love with you."

His words stunned her.

While she was trying to catch her breath, he said, "Diana, I am certain you are the one God has chosen for me to be my wife. If you will stay and give Him time to put the same kind of love in your heart for me, I'll get you a room at Elkton's nicest boarding-house and provide your every need."

Tears welled up in Diana's eyes. "Knight, I don't need time to fall in love with you. I already have...and I know you are the man the Lord had for me all along."

Knight's heart was pounding so hard he could hear it thunder in his ears. He leaned his face closer to hers, and his gaze seemed to be devouring her beautiful features.

A pulse jumped nervously in her throat.

He brought his face closer. They were only inches apart, and his breath fluttered warmly on her upturned lips. As if by instinct, his strong hand reached out and closed protectively over hers. The magnetism between them was powerful, bringing their lips together in a sweet, tender kiss.

When their lips parted, Knight looked deep into Diana's eyes and said, "Since we're both sure the Lord made us for each other, we might as well make plans to marry."

"We might as well."

After another kiss, Knight said, "Do you remember that I told you when God sent the right young woman into my life that I would get Mom a house to live in so my wife and I could live in this one?"

"Yes."

"Well, a small house came up for sale on the south end of town just before we went into the mountains to look for Jordan, and I noticed it is still for sale when we rode in today. Since we need to tell her about us in the morning, I'll talk to her about the house, and I'll buy it for her right away."

"Are you sure she'll like it?"

"Positive."

"Well, you know your mother."

"And I know she likes the house. She has commented on it several times since we moved into town."

Diana smiled. "I just want her to be happy."

"So do I. And she will be, believe me."

"Knight," she said, "I'm truly sorry about Jordan being killed by the bear. I wish he could have had a long, happy life."

"I do too. But no matter what, God made you just for me. Even if Jordan had not been killed, the Lord would have put you and me together. It has been His plan since before we were born. I'll put you in the boardinghouse tomorrow, where you'll stay until we marry. It's the same one Jordan had arranged for you to stay in. I went by today and explained to the lady who owns it what happened with Jordan, and I...uh...well, I told her I'd bring you there tomorrow because you needed a place to stay."

Diana grinned, looking him in the eye. "Knight Colburn, I think you knew how this was going to turn out."

He chuckled. "Well, I sort of felt the Lord had it all arranged. And I was right. Praise His name."

"You wonderful man," she said. "I love you."

"And I love you." They kissed again, then Knight said, "We'll go see Pastor John Steele tomorrow and set the date for the wedding."

"All right. I'll talk to him also about being baptized on Sunday."

They kissed one more time, then went to their rooms for a night's rest.

At supper the next evening, there was great joy in the Colburn house. Annie was thrilled about the way the Lord had worked in her son's life, and about the house he had bought for her that very day. The wedding was set for Saturday afternoon, January 11.

Though the Colburns had many friends in the valley, both Knight and Diana had decided on a small, simple wedding.

Annie was known to be an excellent seamstress, and told the happy couple over supper that she would make Diana's wedding dress. She assured them she could get it done in plenty of time.

Diana shed happy tears as she thanked Annie and hugged her.


On Wednesday, December 11, in Virginia, Martha Morrow opened the front door of the farmhouse to find a smiling Maggie O'Hearn on the porch.

Flashing an envelope, Maggie said, "Look what I have here! It's a letter from Diana."

"Well come in this house!" said Martha, snatching the envelope from her friend's hand and stepping back so she could enter.

As Maggie closed the door, Martha eyed the return address in the upper left-hand corner. "Elkton, Idaho. She's there. I'm glad, but it's so far away."

"I knew it was all right to come," said Maggie. "I saw Stu heading for town in the wagon a few minutes ago, so I hurried over."

"Thank you," said Martha, opening the envelope carefully. "Dennis is playing in his room."

Maggie waited while Martha began reading the letter. Suddenly, Martha burst into tears. "Oh, Maggie! Oh, praise the Lord!"

"What, honey?"

"Diana got saved!"

"Oh, glory to God! How'd it happen?"

"She says a lady named Cora Zeller led her to the Lord on the train between Cheyenne City and Boise!" Pressing the letter to her heart, Martha let the tears stream down her cheeks and said, "Oh, thank You, Lord! Thank You!"

When she brought her emotions under control, she finished reading the letter and frowned.

"What's the matter?" asked Maggie.

"Well, she tells me about arriving late into Elkton because the train was delayed in the Rocky Mountains by an avalanche. But she doesn't mention Jordan Shaw. All she says is that she'll fill me in on the details in her next letter. I can tell she wrote this in a hurry. She must've been squeezed for time to get it in the mail and wanted to let me know that she got saved and that she arrived in Elkton safely."

"I'm sure you'll be getting another one soon, honey," said Maggie. "Then—as she said—she'll fill you in on the details."

"Yes! But more than anything, I'm so glad she got saved."

When the three older children came home from school, their father had not yet returned from town. In Dennis's presence, Martha let the older children read Diana's letter. They were impressed that their older sister had become a Christian, and all three commented to their mother that after hearing the sermons on Sunday, they were beginning to understand it better.

This pleased Martha. She had been praying harder than ever for them to be saved.

While driving the wagon home from town, Stu was boiling inside over the fact that Diana was gone and he couldn't find out where she was. He told himself he would beat it out of his religious fanatic wife if it weren't for Chief Perry's stern warning. Perry would see that he went to prison, for sure.

Stu figured Diana had to be somewhere nearby, but promised himself he would find out her whereabouts some other way. No more jail cells for him.

This thought stirred his memory about another warning. The one that came from Pastor Sherman Bradford that day in the jail. The graphic picture of the blazing prison called hell emblazoned itself in his mind.

After a brief struggle with it, Stu shook it from his thoughts.

Arriving home, Stu pulled the wagon up to the barn door, then headed for the house. He would have Derick and Daniel unload the grain sacks he had purchased in town and get Martha alone. He would tell her that he had been wrong to threaten Diana, and say he wanted to go to her and ask her forgiveness. Maybe this approach would work. Then when he found Diana, as much as he would like to give her a good beating, he would at least throw a scare into her like she'd never known before. She had defied him, and she needed to pay one way or another.

Inside the house, Derick and Daniel were doing homework in their room, and Martha and Deborah were cleaning the parlor together before it was time to start supper.

At the same time, five-year-old Dennis was alone in the kitchen. He had seen his mother stash Diana's letter in the pantry—the one place in the house his father never went. Curious to see it for himself, Dennis climbed up on a stool in the pantry, grasped the hidden envelope, took the letter out, and was looking at it when he heard the heavy footsteps of his father coming in the back door.

Frightened, Dennis jammed the letter in the envelope so he could put it back where he found it, but lost his balance and fell to the floor. Whimpering, he started to get up with letter and envelope in his hand when he saw his father, like a monstrous giant, standing in the open door of the pantry, looking down at him.

"What're you doing in the pantry, boy?" Stu said gruffly. He bent over him. "And what have you got here?"

Dennis's features went white. He was too frightened to speak.

Stu snatched the envelope from Dennis's trembling hand, noted first the return address under Diana's name in the upper left-hand corner of the envelope, then read the letter.

Martha and Deborah came into the kitchen at the same moment and froze when they saw Stu standing by the pantry door, holding Diana's letter in one hand and the envelope in the other.

Dennis bolted past his father, ran to his mother, and wrapped his arms around her legs, burying his face in her apron.

Martha's eyes widened as Stu moved toward her, an evil sneer on his face. "So she's in Elkton, Idaho, eh? Long way from home. She says she's now a religious fanatic like you, Martha, but there isn't any indication here as to what she's doing there. What did she go to Elkton, Idaho, for?"

Martha and Deborah looked at each other, then Martha licked her lips nervously and said, "She answered a mail order bride ad that she found in the *Richmond Chronicle*. She went there to marry a rancher."

"What's his name?"

"Jordan Shaw. She'll be happy now, Stu. Jordan is quite wealthy. Just be glad for her."

"Glad for her?" His face reddened. "You think I'm gonna just sit here and be glad for her? I've got some money stashed away. I'm going after her on the next train west! I'm saddling my horse and riding into town to the railroad station to get my tickets right now. There are four or five westbound trains outta Richmond every day. I'll be on one of them tomorrow."

Martha's face pinched. "Please, Stu. Leave her alone. Let her have some happiness."

"Leave her alone? Hah! I'm bringing that girl home whether she's married or not!"

Stu pivoted and dashed out the back door.

When Martha saw him gallop past the kitchen window, she took her coat and scarf off a hook by the door and said, "Deborah, I'm going over to the O'Hearn place. I've got to let Shamus and Maggie know your father has found out where Diana is and that he is going after her. I want them to pray."

Dennis looked up at his mother with tears in his eyes. "I'm sorry, Mama. It's my fault."

Having already figured out what happened, Martha patted his face tenderly. "We can't change it now, honey. Mama loves you."

Martha was back by the time Stu returned from town, and had a late supper on the stove. Stu announced that he was leaving at ten o'clock in the morning. He would ride into town with the children when they went to school.

At ten o'clock the next morning, Stu Morrow settled back in his seat as the train chugged out of the Richmond station. Closing his eyes, he reflected on how hard Martha and the children had worked at keeping Diana's whereabouts a secret. But Dennis's curiosity in wanting to see Diana's letter for himself had turned the tide in Stu's favor.

Stu was alone on the seat. Grinding his teeth, he mumbled to himself, "Even if she has married this fancy cowboy, I'm gonna give her the thrashing of her life. If this Jordan Shaw tries to intervene, he'll end up a bloody mess like Tom Wymore did. Way out there in Idaho, there's nothing big mouth Chief Perry can do about it!"

In Elkton, on Thursday morning, December 19, a saved, baptized, happy Diana Morrow was enjoying her room at Mattie's Boardinghouse.

The room was comfortable and pleasant. A bright winter sun flowed into the room past crisp white curtains and made a pool of sunlight on the highly polished oak floor. She sat by a window in an overstuffed chair and read a chapter in the new Bible Knight had given her. She closed the Bible, breathed a word of thanks to the Lord for the blessing it was to her, then let her eyes wander around the quaint room.

"Oh, how Deborah would love a room like this," she murmured. "Mama and the kids do the best they can with the crowded conditions and their meager belongings in the old farmhouse. They have been so good to me by helping me get away and sacrificing their own well-being to keep me safe."

Diana thought about the letter she had sent her mother some two weeks ago in care of the O'Hearns. She was hoping for a reply soon. She had told her mother in the letter about Jordan Shaw's death, and explained about Knight Colburn and how the Lord had brought them together. She also told her about her baptism and about the wedding which would take place at their church on January 11, saying she wished her mother and siblings could be there.

Tears filled Diana's eyes. She folded her hands in her lap, bowed her head, and prayed that the Lord would watch over her mother and her siblings and keep them safe from harm. "Show me, dear Lord," she said, "if there is anything in my power I can do for them. I have a wonderful man who loves me, a beautiful home to move into, and a heart full of joy and gladness. Please somehow let my mother, sister, and brothers benefit as I have. I feel so guilty that I have so much, and they have so little."

She went on to pray that the Lord would make a way that she could share her blessings with them, and that He would get a hold of her father's heart. She thanked the Lord that He would hear her prayer, and once again expressed her gratitude for the salvation He had given her.

Feeling encouraged after having cast her burdens once again on her heavenly Father, Diana took her coat out of the small closet, then walked out the door. She would spend some time at Mrs. Colburn's new home with her, and talk about future things while she watched her work on the wedding dress. When it was coming up on noon, she would go to the *Elkton Sentinel* office as she had been doing every weekday. She would spend a few more minutes getting to know Dan and Erline Tyler better, then have lunch at one of Elkton's cafés with the man she loved.

With a happy heart, Diana walked to Annie Colburn's house and was welcomed as always by her future mother-in-law.

Annie hustled her inside, and while hanging up her coat and hat, Diana said, "The sun is bright today, but certainly isn't giving off any warmth."

"Well, come into the kitchen, honey," said Annie. "It's toasty warm in there. I've been sewing on your wedding dress all morning, and I'm just about to the place where I need you to try it on."

"Oh, really?" said Diana.

Annie followed Diana into the kitchen, bid her sit down at the table, and poured each of them a bracing cup of hot tea.

Diana looked at the beautiful white dress with adoring eyes, and gently caressed it, saying, "I can hardly believe it, Mrs. Colburn. This is my wedding dress! So much has happened in such a short time, starting with my wonderful salvation."

Placing the cups on the table, Annie sat down and picked up the dress. Taking tiny stitches in the soft fabric, she said, "I'm sure, my dear, you must feel as though you have been caught up in a whirlwind. But you just enjoy every minute of it. You are making beautiful memories."

Diana took a sip of tea and smiled. "Thank you, Mrs. Colburn. You always seem to know just the thing to say."

Annie smiled in return. "Honey, since you and my boy are getting married in less than a month, I'd like to ask you to call me Mom. That's what Knight calls me. You call your mother Mama. So, could I be Mom from now on?"

Diana rose from her chair, bent down, and hugged Annie. "All right, Mom. That's the way it'll be from now on."

Annie kissed her cheek. "Thank you. I love you, Diana."

Diana kissed her cheek in return. "I love you too, Mom." Returning to her chair with tears in her eyes, Diana sat down. "Could I ask a favor of you, Mom?"

"Of course."

"Would you pray with me? I feel so burdened for my mother and my siblings. I've told you about Mama being saved when she was in the hospital, but unless things have changed, my sister and two oldest brothers are not. Also, I've escaped my father's wrath, but they still have to live in fear."

Diana gulped down a sob as she finished speaking.

Annie laid the dress down, took both of Diana's hands in her own, and said, "We'll pray about this right now, and I'll make it a part of my prayers every day."

Both women bowed their heads, and Annie led in prayer, asking for God's mercy and grace on Diana's family.

As Diana walked toward the newspaper office, she thanked the Lord for bringing Knight and his mother into her life. She was enjoying God's blessings every day.

She was glad that she was no longer having the nightmares, though at times the fear that her father might somehow find out where she was and come after her arose in her heart. Each time, however, the Lord had given her the measure of grace she needed, and she was able to concentrate on the upcoming wedding and her happy new life with Knight.

Though Diana missed her mother and her siblings, she found God's grace sufficient in this matter, too. She had thoroughly enjoyed every church service so far, and was glad to be learning more of God's Word.

On Friday afternoon, December 20, Diana had just returned from having lunch with Knight and was about to write another letter to her mother when there was a knock at her door.

Happily humming "Amazing Grace," she crossed the room, wondering who it might be. She turned the knob, swung the door open, and the sight she beheld filled her heart with horror and dread. She drew a quick, sharp breath and her mouth instantly lost all its moisture. "Papa! I—"

A smile broke over Stu Morrow's usually turned-down face. "Hello, sweet Christian daughter," he said in a cheerful tone. "I won't blame you if you slam the door in my face, but I'd like to ask if you would let your brand-new, born-again father come in and talk to you."

Diana could hardly believe her ears, but she was noting the soft look in her father's eyes—a look she had never seen—and the smile, which she could only remember vaguely from somewhere in her childhood. Indeed, something good had happened to him.

Struggling to find her voice, she choked, swallowed, choked again, and said, "C-come in, Papa."

The numbness in Diana's limbs and the horror in her heart drained away as she closed the door. Her father was a different man.

Eyes glistening with tears, Stu's lips quivered as he said, "Diana, honey, please forgive me for being the terrible father I've been. I beg of you to forgive me for the beatings I gave you."

As she stared in awe, he dropped to his knees, weeping—something she had never seen him do. Looking up at her, he said, "Please, Diana. Please say you will forgive me!"

Diana felt like she was dreaming. She was trying again to find her voice when he said, "When I get back home, I'm going to seek forgiveness from your mother, Derick, Deborah, Daniel, and Dennis; as well as from the many people in and around Richmond that I've wronged. But if you don't forgive me, I think I'll just die!"

Tears coursed down Diana's cheeks. "I forgive you, Papa! I forgive you!"

Stu rose to his feet, and she opened her arms to him. For the first time in her memory, he hugged her.

When the emotion of the moment had subsided, Stu kept an arm around his daughter as he told her of Pastor Sherman Bradford visiting him at the Richmond jail, preaching the gospel to him, and solemnly warning him of his destination in eternity...the prison called hell.

He went on to tell her how the horrid thought of eternity in hell kept haunting him.

Stu sniffed and wiped tears from his cheeks. "Then, honey, when I boarded that train in Kansas City, guess who the Lord put on the seat beside me."

"Who, Papa?"

"A Bible-thumping preacher!"

Diana could see God's hand in answer to prayer.

"Honey, that preacher said the same things to me that Pastor Bradford had said about hell being an eternal prison, and he didn't even know I'd ever been in jail! He read the gospel to me...and he led me to the Lord!"

"But God knew you'd been in jail, Papa!" she said.

"He sure did, honey. Oh, I can't wait to see your mother's face when I tell her about this!"

Father and daughter were in each other's arms again, shedding happy tears.

When their emotions had settled again, Diana sat her father down and told him of Jordan Shaw's death. She explained how she and Knight had fallen in love during the search for Jordan, and of their wedding date set for January 11. She went on to explain that Knight—at twenty-four—was owner of the town's successful and growing newspaper, the *Elkton Sentinel*.

Even while Diana was speaking, there was a knock at the door. She opened the door to find her smiling fiancé.

"Come in, darling," said Diana. "There's someone I want you to meet. Papa is here."

Knight's smile drained away as he stepped in and laid eyes on the big man, who was now on his feet.

Feeling the rush of a need to protect Diana from the cruel man, Knight put a strong arm around her waist, set steely eyes on Stu and said, "What are you doing here?"

"It's all right," Diana said, taking hold of his arm. "Papa isn't here to hurt me or to try to take me back home. He was coming here for that purpose, but a preacher led him to Jesus on the train. He's a new creature in Christ, just like Pastor Steele preached about on Sunday night. Isn't that wonderful?"

Still holding Diana close against his side, Knight took a good look at her father for the first time. He saw, not an angry, hate-filled man, but a humbled man with soft, gentle eyes.

"Let's sit down, darling," said Diana. "I want you to hear the story from Papa. It all started when the pastor who lead Mama to the Lord visited Papa in the jail."

They sat down, and Stu told Knight the whole story. When he finished, Knight leaned forward, shook his hand and said, "This is wonderful, Mr. Morrow. Praise the Lord for answered prayer."

"Amen," said Stu. "Amen."

Diana informed Knight that she had just told her father about Jordan's death, and how the Lord had led the two of them together.

Stu told Knight he was glad the Lord had given his daughter such a fine Christian man, and he was also a successful newspaper-man. He asked about the *Sentinel's* growth, and Knight explained that with Elkton growing, it was helping, but the paper was getting circulation in towns all around, including Boise. Stu said he was glad to hear it.

"Mr. Morrow, I have an idea. How about you and your family moving here? I'm at the place where I need to hire a man to run the printing press full time. Right now, my assistant Dan Tyler works the press, but more and more I need him out gathering news."

Diana's eyes lit up. "Oh, Papa, you should consider it. Since the farm is only rented, you wouldn't have to be concerned about sell-ing it."

The excitement she felt at such a prospect caused her words to almost tumble out as she said, "Shamus would buy your livestock, I'm sure. And…and…the money from that would no doubt cover the cost of travel expenses for the family. And Elkton has a wonder-ful church and a great pastor."

Stu set loving eyes on his daughter. He was dumbfounded. Not only had she so freely and willingly forgiven him, but now she wanted him to live near her. "Precious Diana," he said, tears surfacing once again, "it sounds very appealing. And I would love to learn how to run a printing press and to work for my new son-in-law, but I owe the hospital and the doctor for what I did to Tom Wymore. I also owe the hospital and doctor for your mother's bill. I'm paying them a little at a time, but I have a long way to go."

Knight asked, "How much do you owe, Mr. Morrow?"

Stu cleared his throat. "A total of almost four hundred dollars."

"Tell you what," said Knight, "Dan can teach you how to run the press in no time. If you'll take the pressman's job, I'll cover those bills for you as a bonus. There is a two-story house for rent in Elkton that I just learned about today. I'll rent the house for you and your family, and pay the first two months."

Diana stared at him, eyes wide, mouth open. "Knight Colburn, you are the most wonderful and generous man I know!"

Knight smiled at her. "Thank you, sweetheart, but should I be any less generous since God gave His only begotten Son on Calvary's cross for me?"

Diana leaned close and kissed his cheek. "Like your mother, you always know just what to say."

Stu shook his head in wonderment. "I feel so unworthy of your generosity, son, and of yours, too, sweet daughter. Only God could give both of you the grace to forgive me for what I've done, and only God could give both of you such charitable hearts."

Suddenly Knight snapped his fingers. "Oh! Diana! I have something for you."

While she looked at him in astonishment, Knight reached into his inside coat pocket. "I picked up my mail at the post office a while ago, and the clerk handed me a letter for you from your mother."

WITH TREMBLING FINGERS, Diana opened the envelope, took out the letter, and said, "Excuse me, Knight, Papa. I'll read it through, then I'll tell you what Mama says."

Both men nodded, then watched Diana while she read her mother's letter.

When she finished, she smiled at them and said, "Mama says she got both letters I sent her. She's very happy to know the Lord has led you and me together, Knight, and she's putting her blessing on our upcoming marriage. She wishes that she and my siblings could be here for the wedding."

Knight smiled.

Tears filmed Diana's eyes as she looked at her father and said, "Papa, they can be here if you will take Knight up on his offer. You haven't actually said you will."

"Oh, honey," said Stu, "I've just been so overwhelmed at his offer, I can hardly think straight." Then to Knight: "Son, I accept your most generous offer!"

Diana rushed to her father, wrapped her arms around him, and hugged him tight. "Thank You, Lord! Thank You for going above and beyond my greatest expectations. And thank you, Papa, for accepting Knight's offer."

Stu kissed her cheek and said, "Sweet daughter, I'd be a fool not to. Of course, it's not final until your mother says she is in agreement with moving here."

"I can already tell you that she will, Papa. I know she will!"

Diana then went to Knight, kissed his cheek, and embraced

him. "And thank you, darling, for being everything you are. God has truly blessed me."

He kissed the tip of her nose. "Not as much as He has blessed me."

She smiled at him, her eyes filled with love.

"We can go to the Western Union office right now and send your mother a telegram," said Knight. "I'll pay for it. Will the telegraph office in Richmond deliver it to your farm?"

"They will," spoke up Stu.

"All right. Let's go get it sent."

As they were putting on their coats, Knight told Stu what his starting salary would be. Diana's head bobbed in astonishment.

Stu's eyes filled with tears. "I...I've never made that much money before. How can I ever thank you?"

"Just do a good job and keep your family happy, sir," said Knight. "Then there's only one other thing I want you to do."

Stu buttoned his coat. "Name it."

"Okay. I want you to walk that beautiful lady down the aisle in the wedding and give her to me officially."

"You've got it."

The three of them hurried off to the Western Union office, and a lengthy telegram was sent, advising Martha of Stu's being saved on the train, and of Knight's entire offer.


The next afternoon, Stu left his room at the Elkton Hotel, and walked to the boardinghouse to spend some time with Diana. He had only been there a few minutes when the Western Union deliveryman arrived with a telegram from Martha.

They read it together.

Martha was rejoicing in Stu's salvation, and told them that Derick, Deborah, and Daniel were saved in the morning church service last Sunday and were baptized. Dennis did not understand it all yet, but was showing genuine interest. She and the children were all for the move. Martha had talked to Shamus that morning, and he would buy their livestock for the going price. He would be able to pay them half the price up front, and would have to send the rest a little at a time until it was paid in full. There would be more than enough in the up-front money to pay the family's travel expenses to Elkton.

Stu and Diana hurried to the *Sentinel*, and in Knight's office, Diana let him read the telegram. Knight shed happy tears as he read it and gave praise to the Lord.

Diana hugged Knight, then hugged her father, saying, "Oh, Papa, I'm so glad you're going to be here to walk me down the aisle and give me away to Knight."

"Me too, sweetie," said Stu. "God has been so good."

After a while, they were drying their tears when Stu said, "I'll go home as soon as possible, take care of the bills and the livestock sale, and bring the family to Elkton."

"Let's go over to the bank," said Knight. "I'll draw out the money so you can pay those hospital and doctor bills, and you can buy your tickets to get home. Then we'll go rent that house I told you about. After that, we'll go to the Western Union office and send a telegram to your wife so she'll know it's all settled, and when to expect you."

The next day, as Knight and Diana watched the stagecoach pull away, they waved to her father, then she squeezed his arm and said, "Darling, the Lord indeed provided His measure of grace in my life—and when I needed it, He gave me more grace."

"That's our wonderful God," said Knight as the stagecoach vanished from view.

Holding onto his arm as they started down the street together, Diana said, "I'm so thankful that even as a young Christian I've learned so many precious truths from God's Word. I've been memorizing some passages since you gave me my new Bible."

Knight smiled down at her. "Like what?"

"Like, 'Ask, and it shall be given you; seek, and ye shall find; knock, and it shall be opened unto you: For every one that asketh receiveth; and he that seeketh findeth; and to him that knocketh it shall be opened.' Matthew 7:7 and 8."

Knight chuckled. "Hey! That's pretty good!"

"God taught me through these verses to never give up, darling, and never to cease praying for the desires of my heart. My greatest desire concerning my family since I got saved has been that they would be saved. Oh, Knight, the Lord is so good to His children!"

"He sure is."

"And another one. 'Be careful for nothing; but in every thing by prayer and supplication with thanksgiving let your requests be made known unto God. And the peace of God, which passeth all understanding, shall keep your hearts and minds through Christ Jesus.' Philippians 4:6 and 7."

Knight beamed down at her. "Sweetheart, you have certainly come a long way in your short Christian life. I love you so very much, and all that is within my power according to God's will, I want to give you and do for you to make you happy."

"I love you so very much too, sweetheart," said Diana. "And the Lord helping me, I will always do my utmost to be the best wife to you that I possibly can."

On Saturday afternoon, January 11, 1873, the small church auditorium was comfortably full. Pastor John Steele stood on the platform while the pump organ was playing the prelude to the wedding march, and smiled at Knight, who was standing on the floor.

Martha was on the second row of pews with Derick, Deborah, Daniel, and Dennis. Just across the aisle was Annie Colburn, who sent a warm smile to Martha.

Given a prearranged signal at the back of the auditorium by the pastor's wife, the organist went into the wedding march. Martha rose to her feet and turned to look up the aisle. The rest of the crowd also rose and turned to see the bride.

Out in the vestibule, Diana was stunning in her beautiful white wedding dress. She raised her veil to plant a kiss on her father's cheek. "All right, dear father of mine. It's time to give me away to that wonderful man."

Fighting tears, Stu smiled and ushered her through the door as she gripped his arm.

When they stepped into the auditorium and moved slowly

down the aisle, Diana glanced at her watery-eyed mother, her siblings, and at Annie Colburn, then set her loving gaze on the tall, handsome groom.

Knight's face was beaming as he smiled at his beautiful bride.

Multnomah Publishers

The publisher and author would love to hear your comments about this book. *Please contact us at:*
www.allacy.com

# An Exciting New Series by Bestselling Fiction Authors

## Let Freedom Ring
#1 in The Shadow of Liberty Series

Young Russian Vladimir Petrovna is always minutes away from disaster. He is a Christian in a pagan country that exacts extreme penalties from believers. His farm is nearly destroyed by blight and he cannot pay the taxes he owes. He is a husband and father whose daughter is secretly in love with a Cossack—one of the very soldiers who persecute families like Vladimir's. Though he may lose everything he loves, Vladimir must trust God as he navigates his river of trouble. When he finally arrives in the "land of the free and the home of the brave," his destiny—and faith—are changed forever.

ISBN 1-57673-756-X

## The Secret Place
#2 in The Shadow of Liberty Series

Handsome, accomplished Dr. Erik Linden veers between heroism and accolades, failure and despair in this fascinating new historical novel. A recent medical graduate in nineteenth-century Switzerland, Erik finds himself in a crisis of faith after his former fiancée dies on his operating table. Should he give up performing surgery? Should he abandon his homeland and seek a better life in a freer place? Meanwhile, lovely young Dova, a friend in Erik's hometown, faces murderous avengers after identifying them to the authorities, even as she struggles with an affection that she must keep quiet. As the two young people cope with love's longings on opposite shores, can they find the serenity of God's covering in *The Secret Place*?

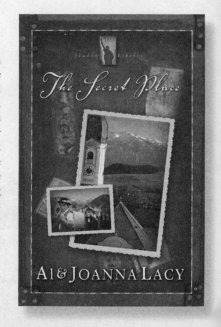

ISBN 1-57673-800-0

# Mail Order Bride Series

Desperate men who settled the West resorted to unconventional measures in their quest for companionship, advertising for and marrying women they'd never even met! Read about a unique and adventurous period in the history of romance.

# Hannah of Fort Bridger Series

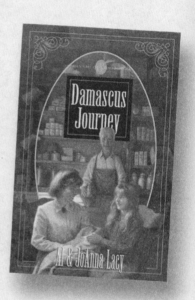

Hannah Cooper's husband dies on the dusty Oregon Trail, leaving her in charge of five children and a general store in Fort Bridger. Dependence on God fortifies her against grueling challenges and bitter tragedies.

| #1 | Under the Distant Sky | ISBN 1-57673-033-6 |
| #2 | Consider the Lilies | ISBN 1-57673-049-2 |
| #3 | No Place for Fear | ISBN 1-57673-083-2 |
| #4 | Pillow of Stone | ISBN 1-57673-234-7 |
| #5 | The Perfect Gift | ISBN 1-57673-407-2 |
| #6 | Touch of Compassion | ISBN 1-57673-422-6 |
| #7 | Beyond the Valley | ISBN 1-57673-618-0 |
| #8 | Damascus Journey | ISBN 1-57673-630-X |

# Angel of Mercy Series

Post-Civil War nurse Breanna Baylor uses her professional skill to bring healing to the body, and her faith in the Redeemer to bring comfort to thirsty souls, valiantly serving God on the dangerous frontier.

# Let's Talk fiction

A free "behind the scenes" look at your favorite fiction authors!

**Let's Talk Fiction** is a free, four-color mini-magazine created to give readers a "behind the scenes" look at Multnomah Publishers' favorite fiction authors.

**Let's Talk Fiction** allows our authors to share a bit about themselves, giving readers an inside peek into their latest releases.

**Let's Talk Fiction** is distributed in the fall, spring, and summer seasons and is filled with interactive contests, author contact information, and fun! To receive your free copy of **Let's Talk Fiction** get on-line at www.christian-fiction.com. We'd love to hear from you!

www.christian-fiction.com